SEASON OF VENGEANCE

BOOK TWO OF THE RAVEN'S WAR TRILOGY

A.J. RETTGER

A.J. RETTGER

CONTENTS

THE
Fortress of Tjarholm
City of Bhotram
CAspula
KETEN
ARTANZIA
Winterhelm
DRUSSDELL
DROssberg
City of Mailum
Valley of The Doom
City of Karlaga
THE VALERIN EMPIRE
KASPYIA
Drunah
THE SEA OF TRAGIC BEASTS
THE FORSAKEN LANDS
N

ACKNOWLEDGEMENTS

Although this book took much longer to finish than I had hoped, I am happy that it is finally here for you to enjoy. As always, this book wouldn't be here without the unsung heroes supporting me in the background. Mom and Dad, thank you for all your support over the years. I know it hasn't always been easy, but having two amazing parents who champion everything I do is a blessing and a privilege that I will never take for granted. Ryan, Tyler, and Brayden, thank you for all the wonderful memories of sitting around a table and playing Dungeons and Dragons late into the night, usually fuelled by pizza and beer. Our sessions are one of, if not the biggest, sources of inspiration for me. To all of my author friends who have stuck by me and allowed me to pick their brains, thank you from the bottom of my heart. Your expertise has helped my craft grow immensely, and I owe a lot of my success to each and every one of you. Finally, thank you dear reader. Thank you for giving my stories a chance. I sincerely hope that you can get lost in these pages and enjoy a well-earned escape from the real world.

In Loving Memory of Zeke
You were the best co-author a guy could ask for. I miss you, buddy.

ACT I

CHAPTER ONE
ROSALINE

Alex was an ugly man. The kind of ugly that stayed with you long after you'd stopped looking at him. The fact that his cheekbones had been shattered and his jaw dislocated didn't help either. Blood slowly trickled out of his mouth. His eyes stared upward, begging for mercy. But mercy wasn't something Rosaline believed in. She sat back, picking her teeth with her dagger, Boris, as she watched Alex fade in and out of consciousness.

The rest of the Brothers gathered around, watching the torture unfold with sickening amusement. Not only was Alex's punishment a spectacle, but it was also a lesson and reminder. This was what happened when you stole from the Bloody Brotherhood. The fact that this cretin had once been called a "Brother" was enough to make Rosaline's stomach churn. It was one thing to steal from people you didn't know, but from your family? From the men that shared everything they had with you? That was inexcusable, and as far as Rosaline was concerned, a much more heinous crime.

Alex let out a gasp for air, blood continuing to dribble down his chin, his almost swelled shut eyes locked onto Rosaline and his lips parted, speaking in a barely audible whisper. "Please..."

Pathetic, Rosaline thought, sneering in disgust. Growing tired of the display, she rose to her feet and approached Alex, twirling Boris in her hands effortlessly. There was no better feeling than killing a rat. She lifted Alex's chin with the tip of her dagger, exposing his throat. She could almost feel his pulse against the blade as she held it to his neck. He was weak. Too weak to be a man, too weak to be a Brother. Without hesitation, she sliced him open, spilling more blood onto the ground.

Alex fell to the ground, limp, gurgling and choking sounds escaping his lips as torrent after torrent of blood surged from the wound. The rest of the Brotherhood cheered as they watched the traitor bleed out before them. Rosaline wiped the blood off the blade onto her sleeve before stretching her aching back.

"Good riddance," a voice snarled.

Rosaline didn't bother turning to acknowledge him. She didn't need to. She had been with the Brotherhood long enough to recognize a man by the tone of his voice. It was Malek, a tall and broad man who only seemed to speak when there was something important to say.

"Winterhelm is a few days' ride from here," Rosaline announced loudly to the rest of the Brotherhood. "Once we cross the city gates, we will meet with Greaver and renegotiate the terms of our arrangement."

The Brothers nodded their heads and continued walking down the snowy road, leaving Alex's body on the roadside as carrion. It had been just over a year since Rosaline had heard from the King of Crooks. Greaver was an insufferable man, but it was necessary to do business with him. Only a fool would challenge the King of Crooks, and Rosaline was no fool. She fully understood the power that Greaver held, and she was confident that the man knew how to use it.

Malek shook his head. "I don't like the city, Roz. Too many people, too easy to get stabbed."

Rosaline's lips curled at the use of her nickname. She always hated being called Roz. It reminded her of her mother, the first person she killed, and everything she'd done to get here. She preferred not to remember the dark days before the Brotherhood, the days when she was weak, when she was like the women she now despised. Rosaline shook the sour memories out of her head. There was no room for weakness in this world, and especially not in the Bloody Brotherhood.

"Cities are the best, Malek!" a boisterous voice exclaimed, interrupting Rosaline's thoughts. "There you can drink and eat till your belly's full, and fuck till your sack's empty!"

Rosaline rolled her eyes. The voice belonged to a man named Phillip, who was nearly three hundred pounds yet deceptively quick on his feet. Phillip always had one thing, and one thing only on his mind: Finding something to fuck. At first, Rosaline found it amusing that the man could be so one-dimensional. But now, the novelty had worn off. It was like hearing the same shitty joke, day after day, until it stopped being funny and started being sad.

"We've got a job to do," Rosaline said sternly. "When we're done with Greaver, then we can think about fun, not before."

Phillip's lips turned into a frown. He knew better than to push her, but deep down she secretly hoped that he would try. Something about reminding everyone who was at the top of the food chain was intoxicating. She had fought tooth and nail to get where she was, leader of the infamous bandit group, and she wasn't going to let all this power slip through her fingertips. The Brotherhood continued down the road until they saw the signpost of an inn. The Frosted Owl. Rosaline winced, as she saw the sign; she already knew what was coming next.

"Can we stop, Roz?" Phillip asked. "My cock is dry and I need wine in my belly."

Before Rosaline could respond, Malek interjected, "Wouldn't be a bad idea to get some food before entering the city."

Letting out a sigh, Rosaline conceded. The Brothers celebrated before turning to head into the tavern. She wanted to keep her men focused on the task at hand, but letting them blow off some steam and have some fun before meeting Greaver wasn't the worst idea. If they got it all out of their system now, maybe they would actually be level-headed during the meet. Besides, now that it had been mentioned, Rosaline thirsted for some ale, and maybe a little bloodshed on the side.

The tavern smelled of roasted pheasant, fresh bread, and ale. As far as roadside inns went, it was fairly crowded when Rosaline kicked open the door, her eyes scanning the room. There were the usual looks – disgust, contempt, a little bit of fear. A satisfied smile appeared on her face. She sauntered across the room, grabbed an empty table, sat down, and whistled at the barmaid.

"What can I get you?" the barmaid said, her lip slightly quivering.

"How about a pint of ale and a good fuck!?" Phillip howled. The audible sound of the bandit's meaty hand smacking the barmaid's ass echoed throughout the tavern.

Rosaline furrowed her brow at the man. She could've stopped him, but why bother? One word from her and Phillip would sit there like a whipped dog. But the girl didn't fight back, she just stood there, shaking. Pathetic. If she wasn't willing to fight, she didn't deserve any pity. "A mug of ale for me and my Brothers," Rosaline ordered, as she undressed the woman with her eyes.

The barmaid nodded her head and hastily retreated from the table.

"Trouble's brewing, Roz," Malek said suddenly, nudging Rosaline with his elbow.

She looked around the room and found that almost everyone was glaring at her and her Brothers. A few of the men even dared to grip the hilt of their swords.

"Let them stare," Rosaline said, unbothered by the attention. "When have we ever shied away from an audience?"

Malek let out a half laugh as the barmaid came back with their mugs of ale. Phillip grabbed hold of the woman and forced her into his lap. She squirmed as she tried to fight off the fat man's vice-like grasp.

"Let her go!" a voice shouted from across the tavern.

Rosaline tore her eyes from the barmaid's frightened face to see a man clad in full plate armour storming towards them. He wore a bastard sword on his hip and his face was decorated with scars. *A knight.* Rosaline cursed silently to herself. She locked eyes with Phillip and gave a disapproving stare. Drawing the ire of a knight was not the same as a farmer. Knights were skilled and dangerous; Rosaline had to choose her next move carefully. Sensing her anger, Phillip nodded his head and let go of the barmaid at once, who quickly retreated behind the bar.

"I think it is time for you to leave," the knight commanded, his voice as hard as steel.

"No need for that, friend," Rosaline began, rising from her chair. "Just having a bit of fun. Forgive my companion. I fear the concept of chivalry escapes him."

"Leave," the knight repeated, his hand tightening around the hilt of his sword, "or else."

Rosaline tucked one hand behind her back and grabbed Boris. She had perfected this maneuver over a long and bloody career. "Listen, friend," she said as she closed the distance between herself and the knight. "We've been on the road for a mighty long time, and we're just looking to blow off some steam. I'll keep my mates in line; you have my word."

"Your word means nothing to me, scum."

Rosaline clicked her tongue. "Tssk, tssk tssk. Come now, I'm sure two civilized people like ourselves can work this out." She placed a hand on the knight's shoulder, as she had done to countless men over the years. And just like the other men, the knight's glare shifted from the bandit's eyes to her hand. A fatal mistake. Rosaline quickly pulled Boris from his sheath and slit the knight's throat before he knew what had happened. She knew it would spark chaos. That was the point. Her men were right, they needed to let off some steam, and what better time than now?

As the knight's pompous blood hit the floor, the Bloody Brotherhood sprang into action. They were like rabid dogs tearing into a days-old carcass. The patrons of the tavern screamed as they fell on the bandits' swords. Through no fault of their own, they had become the Brotherhood's playthings, finding themselves completely at the bandits' mercy.

Rosaline smiled as she looked down at the knight's confused face as he gargled on his own blood. She watched until the light in the man's eyes had faded away before walking back to her chair to watch the carnage her Brothers unleashed, all while savouring the frothy ale that slid down her throat. Once her drink was finished, Rosaline set the mug down and let out a shrill whistle. The slaughter came to a sudden pause.

"Fun's over. Best not to keep Greaver waiting."

CHAPTER TWO

RANDALL

The army of commoners looked up at their new king expectantly, eager to hear the first words that were going to be the start of a new and fair dynasty. Randall had done the impossible. He had banded criminal lowlifes and their victims against the real enemy: the nobles. The people that wielded power only to serve their own self-interest. Now that he sat on the throne, he was going to change everything. No longer would people suffer simply because they were low-born. No longer would people be viewed as expendable playthings for the ruling class. And no longer would tyranny rule over the Kingdom of Artanzia.

The former King of Crooks lifted his head and stared at the buildings that were still burning from the previous night's uprising. The smell of ash tickled his nose as he took a deep inhale, savouring the scent. He looked down at his subjects and cleared his throat.

"Brothers and sisters!" he shouted, his voice filling the city square as the remnants of the old regime smouldered in the background. "We have done what nobody thought possible. We have changed the course of history for the better!"

The crowd erupted in a thunderous cheer of triumph. Pride coloured their soot-covered faces. After allowing a moment of revelry, Randall raised a hand to silence them.

"However, our work is not yet finished." This garnered confused murmuring from the crowd. Sensing their confusion, he pointed outside the city gates. "Out there is a man who wishes to see what we've accomplished undone! The crippled king Elbert has returned from his campaign against the Islanders, and wishes to secure power for himself. The day that I hand over this kingdom, the kingdom we've devoted our blood, sweat, and tears to, is the day he'll climb up the palace steps with his own two feet." An amused chuckle escaped the crowd's lips. "I did not see the love of my life, my queen, die by the hands of these monsters only to give back what we've worked so hard for! If Elbert wants his kingdom, he'll have to pry it from our cold, dead hands!"

Once again, the mob cheered, this time so loudly that it threatened to shake the foundations of Winterhelm itself. Randall let out a breath he did not know he was holding, and looked over his shoulder to Cassius, who failed to hide a displeased frown. The king turned his attention back towards his subjects. "Everyone is to take turns watching the walls and report to me when they see Elbert's army approach. Now go back to your families and celebrate our victory, but stay vigilant."

With that, the army of peasants dispersed. Randall cracked his knuckles, trying to ease his nerves. Addressing his subjects was one thing that he dreaded. He was a man of action, not words. Words were for the nobles.

"A great speech, sire," Cassius said, his voice riddled with sarcasm.

"You disapprove?" Randall asked.

"You need to understand how a kingdom is to be run if you want to keep the crown on your head," he replied, placing a hand on the king's shoulder.

Randall furrowed his brow at the eunuch's comment. "In what way?"

"There needs to be a chain of command. You cannot have people keep watch and patrol the streets, relying simply on their honour. There need to be men, people that act as an extension of yourself, to give out orders."

"That's how the nobles used to do it, and look where it got them."

Cassius' grip tightened around Randall's shoulder. "You'd be wise to heed my counsel, Your Majesty. I'd hate to see that pretty little head get lopped off." Randall ground his teeth together and curled his hands into fists. "Do you want to be a good king?" Cassius continued.

"Yes."

"Do you want to be a wise king?"

"Yes."

"Then you will do as past wise kings have done and heed the counsel of those who know better than you."

Randall rolled his eyes, but he knew the eunuch was right. Cassius had helped him achieve his goal and had not led him astray thus far. After a moment of reflection, the king nodded his head. "Very well. Who do you suggest as people I promote?"

A pleased smile appeared on Cassius' lips. "Prominent figureheads in the neighbourhood. Men and women who have the loyalty of their constituents."

"Specifics, please, Cassius. I'm sure you already have people in mind."

"Tig and A'Chula should be your seconds-in-commands. You've known them the longest and can trust them. The others you will have to meet."

Randall let out a sigh. "Bring them to the keep. I will meet them in the throne room."

"A wise choice, Your Majesty," Cassius said as he bowed gracefully.

"Another thing," Randall began, "I want Anna's body recovered and given a proper burial."

This seemed to take Cassius by surprise. The eunuch's eyes widened and, for the briefest of moments, he was at a loss for words. "I do not think that's—"

"You said it yourself. We need her as a martyr. And every martyr needs a funeral for the people to mourn them," Randall interjected.

"Very well, Your Majesty, I will set Tig and A'Chula upon it immediately."

Without uttering another word, Randall took his leave from the eunuch. Walking through the soot-filled streets back to the keep was a cathartic experience for him. All the death, destruction, and mayhem were a means to an end. *Like a phoenix, we will rise from the ashes,* he thought as he stared at the charred remains of the buildings. As he got closer to the keep, the more bodies of mutilated nobles he came across. It would take weeks to dispose of all the corpses, but perhaps Cassius was right. Once a pecking order was established, things would go much quicker and become more orderly.

At the doors of the keep was the shredded body of Queen Vivian. The mob of peasants had literally torn her body apart, after she had been violated and beaten, of course. Randall couldn't help but smile as he pictured her last, pain-filled moments. When Cassius had suggested that he marry a noble-woman to legitimize his rule, he almost vomited on the spot. But as much as it pained him to admit it, the eunuch had a point. Unless the other kingdoms wanted their peasants to rebel against them, they would declare all-out war on Randall. However, if he married into their bloodlines, maybe, just maybe, the other kings would accept and even respect him. *A means to an end*, he told himself as he entered the keep and the blood-soaked throne room that lay inside.

The sound of his boots splashing through the lake of blood echoed throughout the cavernous room. He continued to wade through the claret liquid until he came to the foot of the throne. He allowed his body to relax on the royal seat, savouring a hard-fought victory. A few moments of respite were well deserved after weeks of scheming and plotting. And with King Elbert returning from the Isles, he would likely have to plot and scheme for the foreseeable future.

Basking in the silence of the throne room, accompanied only by his thoughts, the guilt of killing Anna came rushing back like a tsunami. It felt as if the weight of the deed was crushing his body into a small ball. When he stared at the pool of blood, he imagined how Anna's had looked, splattered across the snow at the bottom of the city walls. He shifted his gaze frantically around the room, trying to find something, anything, that would distract him from the guilt, but it was to no avail. Everywhere he looked, Anna was waiting for him. In the blank, colourless eyes of the corpses, he saw Anna's. The stone walls reminded him of the stone battlements from which she fell. His palms sweated and his heart raced wildly when the doors to the throne room creaked open, forcing him to make a conscious effort to gather his composure.

Standing in the doorway was a blood-soaked Tig. His face was stained with confusion and disappointment. He wrung his hands together as he approached the king.

"What is it?"

"It's Anna."

Randall's heart sank. He had not yet told Tig the truth. He was unsure how his friend would react. Tig loved Anna like a sister, but he was also Randall's oldest friend. Tig was the first person to accept him after Greaver. Nevertheless, he did not want to hear his friend mourn for the girl he killed. "I know. It's terrible what happened to her. But perhaps after the funeral we can—"

"That's the thing," Tig interrupted. "Her body... she's gone."

CHAPTER THREE
ANNA

Darkness filled the endless void. An unforgiving eternity of nothing. No sight, no sound, no sensations, just consciousness suspended in a featureless abyss fuelled only by hatred. The shapeless rage provided an anchor, clinging to existence for one sole purpose – vengeance. Suddenly, something grabbed the fury and pulled it from oblivion.

An all-consuming pain quickly replaced the nothingness and flashes of searing, fiery agony flared up as sensation slowly returned. Bones snapped back into place and organs painfully returned to their original forms. Her vocal cords vibrated violently and something that resembled a scream escaped her lips. The smell of burnt flesh assaulted the nose when, finally, the eyelids sprang open, only to be greeted by a dimly lit, blurry reality.

"Easy, you need to rest," a voice whispered.

Anna's mind spiraled into a full-blown panic as it dawned on her. She had died. Randall had pushed her, and she fell to her death. She remembered the pain of smacking against the frozen ground, her innards exploding in a final second of torture. Anger mixed with fear and confusion consumed her. The red-hot rage thumped through her veins. She tried to move her body, but was quickly restrained by two muscular hands.

"The magic needs time to set," the voice responded. "Try to get some rest."

The more she remembered of her past life, the angrier she got. Randall's betrayal, Cassius' manipulation, and the needless sacrifice of Maeve and Chuckles. The hair on her arms and the back of her neck stood on end. As the unfamiliar yet comforting warmth of the rage filled her body, she felt her strength return alongside it.

"She needs to be knocked out!" another voice cried out.

Before she knew what was happening, something hard cracked against her skull.

She awoke to the scent of dried blood. She peeled her eyes open. Her vision was slightly blurred, but she could make out that she was in a stone room, devoid of any light save for a lone sconce on the wall. A sudden creaking sound came from the far side of the room. Anna immediately tried to leap to her feet but could only flop to the floor. Strong, calloused hands grabbed her once again and delicately lifted her back onto the bed.

"Coming back from death is a traumatic experience," the voice said. "Your body needs time to remember what it once knew."

"Who... who are you?" Anna croaked.

"My name is Desmond. I've been tasked to watch over you until your strength returns."

Anna wanted to look at the man, but to her weakened eyes, he was just a featureless blob, a grey figure with no discerning characteristics, besides his rough hands and his soothing, baritone voice.

"Where am I? Where's Randall?" Anna asked, her voice stronger than it was before.

"All in good time, child. You need rest," Desmond replied.

"I want to know now!" Anna screamed with a surprising amount of strength. If she didn't know any better, she would've said that the walls shook.

A sigh escaped Desmond's lips and Anna saw he lowered himself into a comfortable crouch beside the bed. "You're a fighter, stronger than I thought. If you promise not to shout, I'll answer any questions to the best of my abilities."

Anna swallowed and felt a calmness spread over her. "Who are you?"

"I am but a humble servant, doing his duty."

"That doesn't answer my question."

"Doesn't it? Not only have I told you my name, but I also told you what I do. What else is there to a man?"

"What do you want with me?"

"I only want to see you return to your own two feet."

"Why..." The words got caught in her throat. They seemed so preposterous, but she swallowed her hesitation to pry further. "Why did you bring me back to life?"

This time it was Desmond who hesitated. The deafening silence filled the small room. She could hear the man's hands fidget on his pant leg as he undoubtedly searched for an answer. "I didn't," he said after a lengthy pause. "Master Mammon did."

"Who?"

"That's enough questions. Get some rest."

"The girl deserves to know the shitstorm she finds herself in," another voice interrupted from the corner. It was rough, but also youthful.

"This is not your place, Matthew!" Desmond snapped, his voice exhibiting a sudden anger that had not been present before.

"Unlike you, brother, I am not content licking that snake's boots for the rest of time," Matthew snapped back.

"Outside. Now!" Desmond shouted as he rose to his feet. Anna didn't want him to leave – she had more questions that needed to be answered – but she didn't have the strength to convince him to stay. The two men exited the room, and the door slammed shut. She expected to hear shouting or even the sound of swords clanging, but instead, she was assaulted by more uncomfortable silence.

She stared at the blurry roof as she waited for Desmond to return, only he didn't. She wasn't sure how long she waited, but it felt like days. Time moved incredibly slowly when one couldn't move. Every now and then, she would close her eyes and try to rest, but she never slept for long. Finally, after many failed attempts, she managed to fall into a deep sleep, and when she awoke, her vision had returned to normal.

Hope leapt up into her chest and she tried to move her body, only to flop onto the cold stone floor once again. Fear immediately overcame Anna, as the sensation of falling off the bed reminded her of her death. She remembered the way the air surged past her, how Randall's body shrank the closer she got to the ground, and how the sensation of her skull cracking open was the last thing she felt before she was greeted by the endless void.

"It gets easier, you know," Matthew's voice said suddenly.

She turned her head and saw the young man sitting on a small wooden stool in the corner of the room. He held a vibrant green apple half-eaten in his hand. Silently, he lifted the fruit to his mouth and bit into it. The crunch echoed throughout the room as the man stared at her with piercing brown eyes.

"Looks like I'll have to go fetch Desmond," Matthew sighed as he rose from the stool and walked towards the door.

"Wait!" Anna cried out. "Please, don't leave me."

"Desmond is tasked with looking after you, not me," he responded, with a hint of frustration in his voice.

Before Anna could plead for him to stay, he exited the room, leaving her to stare at the dimly lit walls. She wasn't sure if it was a few minutes or hours before Desmond entered the chambers. The man was older than she expected. He had a greying beard and long, silver-streaked black hair tied into a high bun.

A smile appeared on the aging man's weathered lips. "You really ought to stop moving on your own. You're not ready."

As Desmond approached, Anna tried to crawl away, only to find that her limbs didn't have the strength to push her body across the stone floor.

Concern flashed across the man's face before he lowered himself into a crouch. "Don't be afraid. Nobody here is going to hurt you."

"I've been told that before."

"The world is full of liars, but I am not one of them."

"Spoken like a true liar."

Desmond laughed. "You're smart for your age. You remind me of my daughter. But surely a smart girl like you can figure out that if I wanted to hurt you, I would've done so already."

Anna bit her lip as she mulled over the man's words. The sincerity in his voice swayed her, despite her instincts telling her not to trust him. Reluctantly, she nodded her head.

Desmond stood and picked Anna up like she was a bundle of blankets. Despite the man's age, he showed no signs of any strain. He slowly walked over to the door and kicked it open.

The sunlight burned her eyes as they ascended a stone staircase. After several moments, her eyes adjusted to the new source of light. She could see they were in the remnants of what used to be a graveyard. A small campfire had been lit in the middle between two tombstones. Matthew and an elven woman sat at the fire. There was a large tent on the far side of the ruins, directly across from where Anna had been resting.

"She's awake!" The elven woman smiled at Desmond and Anna as they approached.

"Where are we?"

"You're in Master Mammon's camp," the elf replied, her smile widening. "What is your name?"

"Anna," she replied as Desmond set her down so that a headstone propped her upright.

"My name is Evelynn; it is nice to meet you."

"Is nobody going to talk about why her eyes are fucked up?" Matthew interrupted.

"But her eyes—" Anna began, but it wasn't until he saw Desmond's harsh glare at the boy that she realized he wasn't talking about Evelynn, he was talking about her. "W-what about my eyes?" she stammered.

Suddenly, Matthew pulled a knife from his belt and tossed it at Anna's feet. "See for yourself."

Anna willed her arms towards the knife, but they failed to move. Desmond cursed under his breath and pulled the knife free from its sheath. He held the blade across from her face so that she could see her own reflection. Anna's heart sank when she saw that her once icy blue eyes had turned as red as blood.

CHAPTER FOUR
CONNIR

A strong gale blew snow into the men's eyes as they crossed through Skotheim's gates. People crowded the streets to see the return of High King Uthredd's army return from Tjørholm. Connir saw warriors reuniting with their loved ones as they broke off from the column of troops marching towards the longhouse. Bile rose in his throat at the sight. He had nobody waiting for him. Both his mother and father had died, leaving his clansmen to serve as his only remaining family.

He felt a hand on his back as a cloud of snow and ice assaulted his eyes. He turned his head, and saw the grinning face of his captain, Ragnar, looking back at him.

"You did well, boy!" he said boisterously. "Jarl Otar will be proud once he hears of your deeds."

Connir shook his head. Since his father died of sickness three years ago, he had become accustomed to Ragnar's lies. Jarl Otar was never pleased. It was why he was called Otar the Foul.

"Don't shake your head at me, boy," Ragnar growled, his smile quickly vanishing. "Everyone knows how important skalds are to the army. Without your songs, the men would not have had the courage to climb Tjørholm's walls."

While it was true that most clans held skalds in high regard, Jarl Otar's was one of the few that did not. Otar valued only one kind of man, specifically the kind that could spill another man's blood. Despite his ancestry, Connir was not that kind of man. Connir's father, Svain Whitefist, was a notorious warrior on the Isles. He was not as legendary as Grimm White-Eyes, but his name carried enough weight to make a man second-guess crossing blades with him. Unfortunately for him, Connir took after his mother. He was soft-spoken, unathletic, and avoided confrontation at all costs. On several occasions, Connir's father had proclaimed that the gods had cursed him by bestowing upon him such a "gutless son".

However, Connir begrudgingly nodded his head, not wanting to argue with Ragnar. Truth be told, he was exhausted from all the marching, fighting, and dying. The siege of Tjørholm was his first taste of actual battle, and he hoped that he would never see a battlefield ever again. The screams of his dying kin echoed through his mind. He had tried to distract himself during the march back from Tjørholm, but the monotony only made things worse.

"Hey, skald!" a voice called out. Connir turned his head and saw the face of Otar's fiercest shieldmaiden approaching him, a huge smile on her face.

"Greetings, Estrid," Connir replied. "How did you find the journey?"

"Boring, if I'm being honest. I could've used a song or two," Estrid said before giving Connir a sly wink. "Will I see you at the feast tonight?"

"Of course," Connir answered bashfully.

Estrid smiled once more before taking her leave to reunite with her loved ones. Connir's eyes lingered on her as she walked away, then he felt the sturdy hand of Ragnar slap him on the back.

"What's the matter with you?" Ragnar asked.

"What do you mean?"

"She likes you, you idiot. Estrid's a good woman, and she's unclaimed, so you won't have to kill anyone for her hand."

Connir felt his cheeks flush with colour. He had always admired Estrid, but whenever he thought about asking for her hand, his tongue got heavy and the words never seemed to come out of his mouth in the correct order; ironic for a skald. "I don't know, Ragnar..." Connir began.

"What's to know?" Ragnar exclaimed. "Does she make your cock hard?" Connir looked away awkwardly and scratched the back of his neck. "Listen, lad, a girl like Estrid doesn't come around very often; it's best to make your move before someone else does."

"If you like her so much, why don't you claim her?" Connir asked, although as soon as the words left his mouth, he regretted them. The last thing he needed was competition.

Ragnar's brow furrowed, and he suddenly came to a stop. "You're a good man, Connir, despite what Otar or anyone else says. I see that, and Estrid sees that. Now, grow some balls and ask for her hand tonight."

Connir nodded his head as he tried to stifle the tears that were forming in the corner of his eyes. Compliments were a rare occurrence in his life, so whenever he received them, they almost always brought his emotions to the surface. Just as he was about to lose his composure, Ragnar drove his meaty fist into the skald's stomach, dropping him to his knees.

"What did you do that for?" Connir wheezed.

"Can't have you cry in front of your sweetheart," Ragnar laughed as he walked away towards the longhouse.

It took several minutes for Connir to regain some air in his lungs, but once he did, he rose to his feet and broke off from the column of troops marching towards the longhouse. There was some time before the feast and there was someone he had to see.

The slobbery kisses of Bane forced a childlike laugh to escape Connir's lips. The old war hound's tail wagged fiercely from side to side as he used his weight to pin the skald to the ground. Connir ran his hands across the dog's soft fur and half-heartedly tried to push the animal aside. Finally, once he was coated in slobber, Connir tapped Bane's neck and the dog dismounted, although his tail kept wagging uncontrollably.

"How're you doing, you filthy mongrel?" Connir asked as he patted the dog's head. Bane nuzzled his muscular, rocklike head against the skald's hand.

Bane was the closest thing Connir had to a brother. The dog had served as a loyal war hound for a long time, but years of fighting had taken their toll on Bane's body. Arthritis nearly crippled the dog, and the Master of Hounds planned on putting him down. When Connir heard about this, he pleaded with the man to spare Bane's life. As a result, Bane was now Connir's responsibility. He was to feed him, look after him, and when the time finally came, bury him.

"He missed you," a gravelly voice said from outside the kennel.

"I appreciate you looking after him while I was away, Arkyn. Once Otar orders us to return home, I'll take him with me."

"Few war hounds get to experience retirement," Arkyn, the Master of Hounds, replied. "Bane is a special boy."

"That he is," Connir said as he scratched behind the dog's ear.

"Get in there, you fuckin' traitor!" a gruff voice called from down the hallway.

Connir stuck his head out of the kennel and saw a group of Uthredd's guardsmen toss a man into one of the empty kennels. "What are they doing?" he asked Arkyn.

"High King Uthredd ordered for us to keep the traitor, Grimm White-Eyes, here till they decide whose ship he is getting chained to."

Connir nodded his head. This was the *real* reason behind the feast. Every Jarl would vie for the honour to carry out White-Eyes' punishment. In situations like these, Connir knew arguments were inevitable, and when arguments and alcohol were combined, blood would be spilt.

"I'm going to go to the longhouse and join my clansmen – be sure to look after Bane while I'm gone."

"Of course," Arkyn replied.

After giving Bane one final farewell, Connir exited the kennels, but not before getting a look at the notorious Grimm White-Eyes. The man was practically a walking legend. Children on the Isles were told stories of the man's great deeds growing up. But the man in the kennel looked nothing like the man from the stories. He was dirty, bloodied, and completely defeated. A tinge of sympathy tugged at Connir's heart as he passed through the doorway.

The cacophony inside the longhouse was deafening. People were shouting over one another, the empty mugs thudding against the wooden tables, and the droning of several skalds performing their rendition of events at Tjørholm. Connir struggled to hear the songs, but from what he could hear, they weren't very good. In fact, some were downright awful. Connir's account of the siege, which he had titled "Elbert's Folly", was far superior to anything he heard at the feast.

"Think you can do better?" Ragnar asked through a mouthful of chicken.

"I know I can," Connir replied confidently.

"Let's hear it then!" Ragnar suddenly stood on the table and shouted until he got everyone's attention. "Connir Svainson wants to regale us with a song!"

Connir's face reddened at the unwanted attention. He didn't mind performing, but he hated making a spectacle of himself. He grabbed his lute from beside him and stood on top of the table.

"Put on a show for Estrid," Ragnar whispered as he took his place back at the table.

Silence filled the longhouse. Connir quickly scanned the crowd of faces and saw that only three people were smiling at him. Estrid, Ragnar, and surprisingly, Uthredd. With a gracious bow towards the High King, Connir took the lute in his hands and began plucking the horsehair strings. He cleared his throat and slowly, the melodious words escaped his lips. It wasn't long before his angelic voice and the sounds of his lute had captivated the entire longhouse. Before Connir knew it, the song had finished, and the longhouse erupted in applause. A smile appeared on his face as he basked in the adoration, his anxiety drowned out by the cheers. Giving a bow, he climbed off the table and took his seat beside Ragnar, feeling lighter than before.

"What a lovely tune," Uthredd said, his voice cutting through the applause. "Connir Svainson, you truly have a gift from the gods. Unfortunately, we cannot sit and revel in your talents all night. We have a pressing matter to discuss." Once again, the longhouse went as silent as the grave. High King Uthredd rose to his feet and pointed outside towards the kennels. "Outside sits a traitor that I have sentenced to die chained to the mast of a ship. The only question is, whose ship shall he be chained to?"

Several jarls had begun shouting and clamouring for the king's attention, when suddenly the sound of an axe splitting wood brought the noise to an end. In the far end of the longhouse sat Jarl Otar, who had just buried his greataxe into the table in front of him. "Uthredd," he began, "you know me, and you know my men. Bearn was my cousin, and that cunt rotting in the kennels gave him a dishonourable death. I demand vengeance."

The room was silent as everyone took in Otar's words. Truth be told, nobody had a more legitimate claim than Otar, but Connir was sure the other jarls would try to convince Uthredd otherwise.

"Is there any man or woman here today that believes they deserve this honour more than Jarl Otar?" Uthredd asked.

Surprisingly, nobody answered. The jarls who had been clamouring for the honour before Otar spoke had suddenly lost their voices.

"Very well," Uthredd continued. "Jarl Otar the Foul, I hereby grant you custody of the traitor Grimm White-Eyes. This brings us to our next item of business. We have been granted safe passage through the crippled king's lands to raid his neighbouring kingdom. I want us to set sail as soon as possible. Am I understood?"

The jarls grunted in agreement.

"Then let the feast continue!"

Connir raised his mug and finished his drink, eager to get some rest and relaxation.

CHAPTER FIVE
ELBERT

The fires crackled and popped as snow gently descended upon the dilapidated elven ruins. Silence filled the camp; the army's morale had plummeted since they landed their ships. Many of the soldiers had expected to be home, in the loving embrace of their families. What they had returned to, however, was their kingdom in flames. Deeming it unsafe to dock in Winterhelm's harbour, Lord Grelin instructed the fleet of ships to sail down the coastline where it would be safe to land, much to Elbert's chagrin.

The crippled king sat in his tent and stared at an old, weathered map of his city, as if the piece of parchment contained all the answers he was looking for. He wasn't sure what was agonizing him more. The fact that he had lost his kingdom, or not knowing how it happened. Finally, as his frustration came to a boil, he tore the map in half and let out a scream.

"Where are those fucking scouts!?" Elbert shouted at nobody in particular.

"They should be back around midday. We dispatched them as soon as we landed, and Winterhelm is only a day's ride from here," Lord Grelin responded, as he warily approached the fuming king.

Elbert chewed on his fingernails impatiently. He could feel everyone's eyes on him. How they judged him. *The king who couldn't keep a kingdom.* Quickly, he shook the intrusive thought out of his head and focused on Lord Grelin once again. "Inform me the minute the scouts return; I want to hear their full report firsthand."

"As you wish, Your Majesty."

Turning his chair away from the elderly lord, Elbert wheeled himself towards his tent. The snowfall in Artanzia wasn't nearly as heavy as it was on the Isles, and for that he was thankful. Despite being king, he hated being pushed around. He wanted to show that he could do the simplest tasks, like moving, by himself. Having a soldier push him around constantly would give the wrong impression.

Back within the confines of his tent, Elbert let out a strained breath. He poured himself a cup of Islander mead that he had confiscated before they departed Tjørholm and greedily gulped it down. To his dismay, the strong drink did nothing to soothe his nerves. It took everything he had not to lose his composure in front of his men. His heart felt like it was going to burst out of his chest, and tears ever threatened to pour from his eyes. He poured himself another helping of mead before wheeling over to a small metal chest in the corner of his quarters. He had told his lords that it was plunder from Tjørholm, because he knew that if they discovered the truth, they would lose what little respect they had left for him.

"What do I do, old friend?" Elbert asked, placing a hand on the metal chest. "I've done what every other ruler thought was impossible, and it cost me everything. It cost me my subjects' respect, my kingdom, and my best friend."

Taking a deep intake of breath, Elbert opened the small chest and looked at the decomposing head of Rupert Thames. He tried not to breathe in, as the stench was too much to bear, but the putrid aroma forced his eyes to water nonetheless. He had told himself that he would give Thames a proper burial when they arrived in Winterhelm, but now that his kingdom had been stolen from underneath him, Elbert couldn't bear the thought of parting with what was left of his most trusted advisor.

Unable to look at the severed head any longer, Elbert shut the chest and crawled into his bed of furs. Staring up at the roof of his tent, he wondered what happened to his beloved city. Did Keten invade, or did the populace revolt? If it was Keten, he would have to call on the eastern kingdom of Drussdell to see if they would lend him aid, but even then, there were no guarantees that they would answer the call. Of course, there was the Valerian Empire to the south, but they rarely interfered with northern affairs. Elbert hoped it was a revolt. Although peasants were formidable in numbers, they would stand no chance against a professional army. Whatever the case, he just hoped that this newfound enemy took care of Vivian for him. It was an encounter he had been preparing for the entire voyage home. Without Thames' undying loyalty, he was unsure if any of his men would carry out his orders to execute the queen, but hopefully that was irrelevant now, as the city had clearly been conquered.

Suddenly, there was a commotion from the camp and Lord Grelin burst into Elbert's tent. "Sire, riders approach!"

Elbert's heart leapt into his throat and he quickly climbed into his chair and hurried outside. The men crowded around the riders in the middle of the ruins. "Make way! Make way!" Lord Grelin shouted as he escorted his king towards the scouts. When Elbert finally caught view of the horses, his heart sank when he saw they were riderless. Both horses had a bloody burlap sack hanging off the saddle.

"Dammit!" Elbert shouted, as he slammed his fist into the armrest of his wheeled throne.

"Sire, a letter," Grelin told him as he took a sealed envelope off one of the horse's saddlebags.

Impatiently, Elbert snatched the letter from the lord's hands, cracked the wax seal, and pulled out the parchment. As his eyes scanned over the text, he could feel his blood boiling. He tightened his grip on the paper, crumpling the edges. Just as he was about to rip the letter in two, Lord Grelin spoke.

"What does it say?"

"Dear Former King Elbert. Let me begin this letter by congratulating you on a successful campaign against the bloodthirsty Islanders. Second, I wish to inform you that the people of Artanzia have seized your kingdom for our own."

Despite the rage clouding his vision, the king forced himself to read on. "Too long has the common man been stepped on and discarded as if we were scraps of rotten meat. We are no longer yours to torment. I order you to disband your army and bend the knee, provided that your legs allow you to. Sincerely, the rightful king of Artanzia, Randall the First."

A hushed silence fell over his lords. Many of the men exchanged looks with one another but none dared to utter a word. Their king was on the verge of snapping, and no one wished to draw his ire. Elbert's face was as red as a tomato, while his body vibrated with rage. His hands tightened around the letter once more as he stared blankly at the snow-covered ground.

"What are your orders, Your Majesty?" Lord Grelin asked, breaking the deafening silence.

"The rightful king!?" Elbert shouted. "Who in the blazes does this fucking lowborn think he is!? I'll be damned before I allow my kingdom to fall into that commoner's grubby little hands! Order the men to march this second! I'm going to take back my kingdom and bathe in that bastard's blood." There was a shocked stillness as the lords stared vacantly at their king. Elbert lifted his head, his brow furrowing. "Well? What are you waiting for?"

Spurred by his king's glare, Lord Grelin cleared his throat and the rest of the lords scrambled, ordering the men to prepare to march. Elbert crumpled the letter into a ball and tossed it into a nearby fire before furiously wheeling himself back to his tent.

"Sire," Lord Grelin said, as he easily caught up with the fuming king. "It would be wise to watch how you talk about the commoners around the men; many of those under our banners are commoners themselves."

"Let them listen," Elbert growled. "Let them be reminded that their place is beneath us. It seems that the people of Winterhelm have forgotten that, but they will soon be reminded."

CHAPTER SIX

ANNA

Snow blanketed the abandoned graveyard. Crowns of thick white powder appeared atop all the long-forgotten tombstones. Anna sat away from her new companions, transfixed by her reflection in the knife's blade. What stared back at her was unnerving. Her face was so familiar, yet so foreign. The unrelenting blood-red eyes made her skin crawl. She hadn't asked for this, whatever this was. Floating in the void had been serene, and ever since this Master Mammon brought her back, it was something she longed to feel again.

The crunch of snow beneath a pair of feet alerted her to someone else's presence. She wasn't sure if they had been watching her, or if they had just arrived. She did not care. She had bigger problems to worry about than being observed by strangers.

"I assume you have questions," Desmond said in his calm, fatherly voice.

"Hmph," Anna grunted. "That's an understatement."

"I checked on Master Mammon, and he is well enough to receive you. If anyone has the answers you're looking for, it'll be him."

"Is he sick?" Anna asked.

"No," Desmond began. "Bringing you back proved to be a challenging task, even for someone as gifted as Master Mammon. He needed time to recover and regain his strength."

"Is he some kind of mage?"

"Not exactly. But it is best if he answers your questions. Come with me."

Reluctantly, Anna rose to her feet, dusted the snow off her pants, and returned the knife to its sheath. She walked side by side with Desmond, staring at him. She couldn't help but notice that there was a scar behind his right ear. It looked like someone had carved a rune into the skin. The symbol had three jagged lines that plunged downwards like inverted spears. The middle spike was longer than the two on the sides, and all three spikes were connected by an inverted chevron. The longer she looked at it, the more her head pulsed with each heartbeat.

"What's that?" she asked, finally tearing her eyes away from the symbol.

"The mark of Mammon," Desmond responded. "We all have one, except you."

"We?"

"Matthew, Evelynn, and myself."

"Why?" Anna asked, her frustration growing that she wasn't getting clear answers.

"It is best if Master Mammon answers these questions."

Anna rolled her eyes but voiced no protest. She just hoped this Master Mammon would be less vague than Desmond. And that he had enough strength to answer all of her questions.

It wasn't long before Desmond led her to the entryway of a crypt. He pulled open the rusted steel gate and ushered her inside. "He's expecting you."

Anna cast a questioning glance at the man, concerned that this was a trap, but all she received was a reassuring smile and nod of the head. Against her better judgment, Anna descended into the dark crypt.

The putrid miasma of death and rotting flesh burned her nostrils. Several times she had to stop on the stone stairway to gag and regain her composure. She remembered gutting a deer that had been shot in the stomach with her father, and she thought nothing would ever stink as much as that. But the scent of this crypt made her long for that disgusting smell. When she reached the bottom of the stone staircase, she saw a dim light illuminating the main chamber. She looked around the room and saw that all the sarcophagi were open, freeing the putrid smells that had once laid dormant within them.

"Greetings," an ancient voice croaked from the corner of the room.

Anna nearly jumped out of her skin as she saw the source of the voice stir slightly. She approached the shadowy figure, clutching the handle of her knife tightly.

"No need for that knife in here, child," the voice said. "If I meant you harm, I would not have raised you from the dead."

Anna froze in place, both at the figure's words and because she was close enough to see that the man's eyes were as red as hers.

"What are you?"

Laboriously, the figure rose from his chair and slowly limped towards Anna. He clutched a staff made of bone and his facial features became illuminated in the torchlight as he drew closer. Besides his red eyes, he looked like any other man. An old man, but a man. His face was covered with wrinkles, and his teeth were yellow and rotten. He was completely bald, save for a few brambles of wispy, white hair.

"Desmond told me you had lots of questions, and I have agreed to answer them. My name is Master Mammon. And I am not from this realm."

"You mean Artanzia?" Anna asked.

"No, I mean this plane of existence. You see, it takes great strength for someone such as myself to leave my plane and come to this one. But it takes even greater strength to stay here. My kind cannot exist here without hosts, tethering me to the mortal plane. Without them, I'd fade away into nothingness, and return to my realm."

Anna's eyes widened when she heard these words. She remembered how her father made her comb through countless tomes about obscure monsters and their habits. She never thought that the study would prove to be of any use, but after hearing the man's words, she knew exactly what he was. "You're a demon."

"Clever girl," Mammon replied.

"Desmond, Evelynn, and Matthew, they're your hosts? To keep you tethered here?"

"No," Mammon corrected. "Those three are my disciples, my helpers. People that I've made deals with, but are not suitable to be a host."

Anna raised a brow. Her father's books hadn't mentioned "disciples" before. "What's the point of a demon making a deal, if it is not to get a host?" she inquired.

"You have much to learn, girl," Mammon chuckled. "Although we demons are powerful, we are not omnipotent. Sometimes we require the aid of mortals to conduct our business on this plane."

Anna eyed the ancient demon slowly. Ever since the forest, she had felt like a fish out of water, never completely understanding how to interact with others, or what was going on. But now, now she knew exactly what was happening. Silently, she thanked her father for his obsession. Knowledge of monsters was something that Anna had in abundance.

"You look weak," she said snidely. "It appears you need a new host."

"Quite right, child," Mammon mused, ignoring Anna's tone.

"Well, you can forget it," Anna replied. "I don't care that you raised me from the dead, I will never be your host nor your disciple. So you can wither and die in this crypt."

Mammon's face contorted into an annoyed frown, as if Anna had struck a nerve. He gritted his teeth and hissed, in an ancient voice that sounded like knives being dragged upon a whetstone, "Silly girl, a demon can't make another demon a host."

"What?"

"You were dead. Which means you were no longer mortal. Mortal beings cannot cheat death and still be mortal, they become something else. In order to pull you from the void, I had to imbue your body with my magic, which is something no demon has ever done. My magic, my very essence, flows through your veins."

Anna backed away from the old man. Her knees felt weak. This couldn't be happening; it was all too crazy to be real. This sort of thing only happened in fairytales. Without allowing Mammon to say another word, she sprinted out of the crypt and out of the graveyard. She ran as fast as her legs could carry her, not sure where she was going, but all she knew was that she wanted to get as far away from Mammon and his disciples as she could.

It wasn't long before Anna found herself on the outskirts of a town. Her heart leapt up into her chest, as the thought of being surrounded by normal people and the prospect of a hot meal entered her mind. She trudged into town, only to find that there were no signs of life. There was no torchlight within the houses, and most of the buildings were in disrepair. Doors were torn from their hinges, windows were shattered, and claw marks scarred their exteriors. Anna instinctively pulled her knife out of her sheath and cautiously approached one house, the snow crunching beneath her feet. Her heartbeat pounded in her head as the blood rushed to her temples.

The stairs of the front porch creaked loudly under her weight. She touched the claw marks on the wooden door. They were deep and jagged. She peered inside the house and saw that it was in complete disarray. Tables were turned over, chairs were broken, and holes punctuated the walls. Her heart stopped when she saw dried blood on the floorboards. Suddenly, it all made sense. Why the sarcophagi at the graveyard were open, and why the town was abandoned. There had been a horde of ghouls that called this place home.

Quickly, she turned on her heels to leave, but when she exited the house, she saw three ghouls staring back at her, snapping their jaws voraciously. She gripped the handle of her knife tighter and began counting the creatures as more slunk out of the other houses, their pale, blotchy flesh glistening in the sunlight. The empty sockets where their eyes should be glared at Anna, as more and more of the pack surrounded her. Her father always said ghouls were interesting creatures. They looked like if someone tried to make a dog out of human corpses. Now that she was seeing them in real life, Anna decided that was an apt description.

As one ghoul ascended the stairs of the house, she let out a breath she didn't realize she was holding in. The ghouls stopped just out of striking distance, gave a few curious sniffs, then turned around. Anna stared in bewilderment as she watched the horde return to the abandoned houses, seemingly disinterested in her.

"They won't hurt you," a feminine voice called out. Anna turned her head to the left and saw Evelynn casually sauntering into the town. "They smell Mammon on you. Ghouls know not to cross a demon."

"So, you know what he is?" Anna questioned.

"Not at first, but after a while I could put the pieces together."

Evelynn smiled as she sat down on the creaky wooden steps of the front porch and motioned for Anna to join her. Reluctantly, Anna did. She sat down and stared out into the town square, utterly peaceful and serene now that the ghouls were back hiding in the houses.

"Why did he bring me back? Does he think I'll serve him?" Anna asked.

"Demons are not complicated to understand. I've been bound to Mammon for centuries, and I've picked up a few things during that time."

"Like what?"

"Demons are attracted to emotions. That's how they choose their hosts. They sense people who are riddled with whatever emotion they crave. Some prefer guilt, others anger – there are even a few who latch on to joy. Mammon's emotion of choice is ambition. When we came across your body, Master Mammon had just been rejected by the new king of Artanzia. It was dumb luck that we came across you, but when we did, Mammon nearly drooled from the ambition radiating from your corpse."

Anna's skin crawled at the mention of Randall. Although part of her was proud that he had the foresight not to make a deal with Mammon, that part soon faded when she remembered how he pushed her from the ramparts. "I have no ambition," Anna lied.

"Come now," Evelynn scoffed, "what is the one thing you want more than anything else in this world? Just between us."

"Revenge," Anna blurted out without thinking. It was only after the word left her lips that she thought perhaps Evelynn was here to seek the truth on Mammon's behalf. She cursed herself and swore to be less forthcoming with her words.

"Against who, the person who killed you?"

Anna let out a sigh and nodded her head, as she couldn't think of a more believable lie about why a fourteen-year-old girl would want revenge on someone. Sensing a pause in the conversation, she quickly changed the subject. "You met the new king?"

"No, Master Mammon insisted on doing this deal alone, just as he had with the last king."

Anna raised a curious brow, but before she could say anything, Evelynn continued.

"How do you know the boy king?"

"What? I – I don't know—"

"Oh please – you're a terrible liar. I could hear it in your voice when you asked about him, so be honest, how did you know him?"

"I used to be his—" Anna stopped herself before she could utter the word "queen". She always hated being called that, and didn't want to tell more of the truth than she had to. "I used to be his friend," Anna lied.

"Ah," Evelynn sighed, "a lover's quarrel."

Shit, Anna thought. She must have made a face that betrayed her thoughts, as Evelynn burst into a fit of laughter.

"Like I said, you're a terrible liar," the elven woman said. "Being betrayed by a lover is never easy. I assume he's the one that killed you?"

Anna nodded her head. She didn't want to give up the truth, but it seemed Evelynn was quite clever and could piece the puzzle together quickly. "I don't understand, though," Anna continued, "that's not ambition."

"Isn't it?" Evelynn replied. "What is ambition beside a strong desire to achieve something? Do you not feel a strong desire to take your vengeance on the boy king?"

Anna thought about it for a minute. "Yes."

Evelynn shrugged her shoulders. "Sounds pretty ambitious to me."

The two sat in silence for some time before Anna's curiosity got the better of her. "Mammon told me he made deals with each of you. What deal did you make?"

Evelynn let out a sigh and looked up to the sky, watching the mist of her breath slowly drift upwards. "Like all good stories, it involves love and heartbreak." The elf paused as she brought her eyes back down to Anna. "But you'll have to wait to hear that story. It's not one I like to give away for free."

Anna scrunched up her nose in confusion. "But why would you make a deal?"

"Because I was young and in pain. I would've sold anything, including my soul, to not feel the devastation for a second longer. If that means serving a demon till the end of my days, then so be it."

"But you said you served Mammon for centuries... what do you mean till the end of your days?"

"Those are the terms of my contract, to serve Master Mammon till the end of my days. Which, evidently, is forever when you serve a demon."

"Wait, you can't die?"

"We can die, but only under special circumstances. If someone kills Mammon, we die. If someone kills us with an enchanted blade, we die. And, on the off-chance Mammon is feeling generous and releases us from his service, we die."

"So, I'm just destined to live forever, under Mammon's boot?" Anna asked hopelessly.

"It's not so bad," Evelynn consoled. "As far as demons go, he's pretty reasonable."

"You know a lot of demons?" Anna asked.

A smile appeared on the elf's lips. "Nope, but I know a lot of men who are a lot less reasonable than him."

Anna wasn't sure what it was, but Evelynn's demeanor had a calming effect on her. As ironic as it was, sitting on a run-down porch in a ghoul-infested town, this was the most at home she had felt since Randall took the throne from Greaver.

"Come on, Desmond probably has supper ready. He's not much of a cook, but he's a hell of a lot better than Matthew."

Anna took a sharp inhale of breath. This was overwhelming. Not only had she been raised from the dead, but now she was also a demon. A demon in servitude to another. Although the prospect of her future looked bleak, Evelynn's words filled her with hope. Perhaps life would not be so bad living with Mammon and his disciples. After a moment of deliberation, Anna nodded her head and agreed to stay with them, for now. She followed Evelynn back towards the graveyard.

CHAPTER SEVEN
ROSALINE

Rabbit was the worst. It wasn't so much the flavour, but the texture. The fine muscles and sinew would often get caught in the teeth, resulting in having to tediously pick one's teeth clean after eating. Rosaline would have preferred deer, but in the harsh winter months of Artanzia, you took what you could get.

It had been a few days since the tavern, and the Brotherhood would arrive at Winterhelm's gates by nightfall. Much to her Brothers' chagrin, Rosaline was setting a blistering pace. She knew that they had wanted to spend more time in the tavern, but there was pressing business to take care of.

"Where's Duncan?" Rosaline asked as she picked the last of the disgusting meat out of her teeth with Boris.

"Should be back any minute now," Malek replied as he greedily tore into the other meaty haunch of the rabbit.

"Taking his sweet time," Rosaline muttered under her breath.

"What's the rush, Roz?"

Rosaline winced before answering. "Greaver is not a man to be kept waiting."

"That old sack o' shit is past his prime!" Phillip yelled out on the other side of the camp. "He should lick our boots, not the other way around."

Rosaline put on a faux smile, but failed to say anything in response. She had seen first-hand what Greaver was capable of. Even if the man's strength diminished as he got older, his wits and cunning only grew. Truth be told, she hated working with Greaver as much as anyone, but it was undeniable that he was one of the most powerful men in the kingdom.

"I mean, the man keeps children around him!" Phillip enthusiastically continued. "I know we all like to have fun, but there are lines!"

"Didn't know you to be a man of morals, Phillip," Malek interjected, through a mouthful of meat.

This got an involuntary laugh out of Rosaline. Phillip's face became bright red and his lips quivered uncontrollably.

"Look at the big dope!" Jathan called out. "He's at a loss for words!"

Rosaline's smile grew at Jathan's comment. Not because of what he said, but because she was excited to see Phillip's retaliation. Jathan was the youngest and newest member of the Bloody Brotherhood, and was still learning the pecking order of the gang. Now and then he would vie for more power within the hierarchy, only to be quickly put in his place again.

"Keep talking, runt, and nobody, not even Roz, will be able to save you," Phillip snarled.

Rosaline raised a brow at Phillip's words. She could tell that the man was angry, but did he speak from a place of anger or arrogance? *Perhaps Phillip needs a reminder,* she thought.

"You'd have to catch me first, you fat fuck," Jathan retorted, interrupting the bandit leader's thoughts.

Just as Phillip was about to rise to his feet, the crunch of snow on the edge of camp alerted the Brotherhood to someone's presence. They all turned their heads in the direction the sound came from and saw Duncan entering the camp.

Duncan was probably the most peculiar member of the Brotherhood. Before he joined, he had been the ward of a rather wealthy lord. Some say the lord bedded his elven mother, although that was just hearsay, but the way the lord favoured Duncan in his youth certainly gave validity to those rumours. Duncan was treated as the lord's son. He received the finest education gold could buy and knew all the luxuries that life offered. But after his mother passed, Duncan ran away from the estate and lived on the streets, eventually finding his way into the Bloody Brotherhood.

That Duncan was so open about his past also made him stand out from the other Brothers. When asked about their histories, most would spew some horseshit that painted them in a favourable light. Duncan, however, told his story truthfully. He told both the good and the bad, and didn't shy away from anything ugly.

"What did your elf eyes see?" Rosaline mocked.

"You know I got my father's vision," Duncan retorted as he sat down at the fire and carved off a piece of rabbit. "There's a plume of smoke to the northeast. I know it's a bit out of our way, but might be worth checking out."

"Best not to keep Greaver waiting," Rosaline repeated.

Duncan nodded his head in understanding. "Normally I'd agree, but after seeing what lies in the elven ruins to the west, I'd like to put as much distance between us as possible."

"What did you see, Brother?" Malek asked, as he wiped the grease away from his lips.

"An army," Duncan replied. "They aren't King David's banners, so they must belong to one of his sons."

"I heard that the oldest died, and the youngest now sits on the throne. I also heard he's a cripple," Jathan stated matter-of-factly.

"Where the fuck did you hear that from, runt?" Phillip snarled, clearly still sour about the earlier exchange.

"From one of the patrons at the tavern... before things got exciting."

Rosaline turned a questioning glance towards Duncan, who shrugged his shoulders in response. "Crippled or not," she started, "Duncan's right – a royal army is bad news. We need to put as much distance between us and them as possible."

"Why are they out here?" Malek asked. "We're in the middle of nowhere, and it's not like they are returning from battle; we aren't at war with anyone."

"Did you hear an answer for that too, runt?" Phillip asked.

Jathan smiled sarcastically at the big man in response. It wouldn't be long before a fight broke out between those two, and Rosaline was eager to see if Jathan could climb up the social ladder or if Phillip would bash his skull in. But now was not the place, nor the time.

Putting her eagerness aside, Rosaline rose to her feet. "Enough," she commanded. "Let's get going, I want to see what the source of that smoke is."

It didn't take long for the Brotherhood to pack up camp, mainly because they always travelled light. They lived off the land as they travelled and really only carried their weapons with them beside the small necessities that fitted in their packs. Soon the plume of smoke could be seen in the distance, and the air grew thick with excitement. Some Brothers hungered for more debauchery, while Rosaline just hungered for something other than rabbit.

As they drew closer, Duncan grabbed Rosaline's arm and pulled her back from the group. "Might be army scouts. I should go up ahead and check it out."

"If they were army scouts, they would've seen us already," Rosaline retorted. "My guess is this is a group of merchants travelling to Winterhelm, sitting there ripe for the taking."

"You're the boss," Duncan stated with a faux bow before walking away.

Rosaline curled her lips. Duncan's passive-aggressiveness was his one trait that irritated her. He would never openly defy her, that would be suicide, but he would make a subtle comment to make sure his disagreement was known. She refused to let her irritation show, but that came with the role of being the leader. If the Brothers knew how easily they could vex her, her authority would be compromised.

Once they arrived at the grove of trees where the smoke was coming from, they crouched in the undergrowth and listened. Silence. The air was devoid of all sound save for the soft crackling of a fire.

"Something's off, Roz," Malek whispered.

"Agreed. You and Jathan go investigate."

Malek nodded his head and waved his hand for Jathan to follow. Stealthily, they crawled through the brush and were soon consumed by the vegetation. Rosaline looked around at her Brothers and saw that all their expressions were grave. Something was indeed off, and many were expecting a fight. With bated breath, she waited for Malek's signal.

"All clear!" Malek shouted after a lengthy silence.

Once she had pushed her way through the trees, she saw that the camp that was concealed behind them was more akin to a slaughterhouse. Bodies were strewn across the snow-covered ground, and wagons were tipped over and smouldering. The Brotherhood sifted through the debris and searched the bodies for any valuables, but found nothing.

"Looks like a circus," Duncan said.

"How do you know?" Malek asked.

"This many nonhumans together, has to be."

"Well, whatever they were, they had shit luck and were dirt-poor," Phillip interjected as he kicked over the corpse of a dwarven woman.

Rosaline inspected the body of an elven woman and saw that all of her teeth were missing. A chill ran down her spine. *Blacktooth.* "Let's get out of here."

"What's the matter, Roz—" Malek began.

"Well, well, well," a voice called out from behind the cover of the underbrush. "Rosaline, is that you?"

Rosaline instantly reached for Boris but stopped herself before she could grasp the handle. She knew that Blacktooth would not be alone.

Sauntering out from the foliage was a muscular man with jet-black hair and a black beard, both speckled with spots of grey. His eyes were a bright emerald green, and he smiled a disgusting smile showcasing a mouth of rotten and decayed teeth. Blacktooth got his name because of his poor dental hygiene, although there was a debate over which was more rotten – his teeth, or his heart.

"By the Gods, that is you!" Blacktooth exclaimed as he waved his hand, resulting in more bandits emerging from the trees.

"You look like shit," Rosaline snapped.

"How long has it been?" Blacktooth asked, ignoring Rosaline's barb. "I think the last time I saw you was probably around the time that you kicked me out of my gang." Blacktooth's voice was suddenly as cold as the winter wind and his eyes narrowed into slits of contempt.

"I'd let you join again, but the Brothers aren't keen on your bad breath."

Blacktooth let out a sarcastic laugh. "Always were a clever cunt." His eyes suddenly shifted to the rest of the Bloody Brotherhood, who now stood behind Rosaline. "Look at your-selves, you pussy-whipped bastards! Following around this tramp hoping she'll fuck you. You're pathetic."

"Say that to my face!" Phillip hollered as he unsheathed his blade.

"I just did," Blacktooth retorted.

Rosaline quickly counted Blacktooth's men. Unless there were more hiding in the trees, Blacktooth was outmanned, but then again, the man was never known for his strategic mind.

When Rosaline first joined the Bloody Brotherhood, Black-tooth was the only one who had been in her corner. He had seen what she could do with her hands and with Boris, and was thoroughly impressed. However, it quickly became apparent that Blacktooth was not fit to lead. The man thought only with his cock and had a habit of talking too much. On more than one occasion, Blacktooth's shortsightedness and loose lips had cost them the lives of several Brothers. It wasn't until Rosaline expressed her discontent that the rest of the Brothers backed her as their new leader.

"Can't help but notice that Alex isn't with you. What hap-pened?"

"Dumb fuck thought he could steal from his Brothers," Rosaline answered casually. "He learned otherwise."

"Poor lad was as smart as he was beautiful."

"I want him alive, kill the rest," Rosaline whispered to Duncan and Malek, who were standing on either side of her.

"Enough with the niceties, you harlot, why don't you lot just fuck off and—"

An arrow from Duncan's bow whizzed by Blacktooth's head and struck one of his men in the throat. Following their Brother's lead, the rest of Rosaline's men sprang into action. Blacktooth's gang stood in shock as the Bloody Brotherhood surrounded them and made quick work of the ragtag bandits. Rosaline watched with a smile as she saw Duncan's arrows claim victim after victim; she witnessed Jathan strangling a man with his own belt, and Phillip gouging out another's eyes with his meaty thumbs.

Rosaline charged at Blacktooth. Seeing her approach, Blacktooth grabbed one of his nearby men and shoved him forward. With a confused look on his face, the bandit swung a makeshift club at her head. She slipped past the clumsy blow, spun in close, and buried Boris' blade into his heart. A soft breath of air leapt from the man's lungs as she tore the dagger free, his body hitting the frozen ground like a sack of potatoes.

Rosaline turned her attention back to Blacktooth and cursed when she saw that he was gone. She turned her head back down to the man she had just stabbed and spat on him. *If it wasn't for you, I could've been rid of Blacktooth, once and for all.* The clearing had fallen still. Bodies littered the frozen ground, their blood staining the snow a deep shade of red. The melee was over as quickly as it began, and Rosaline and her Brothers began looting, only to find that Blacktooth's men had even fewer things of value than the circus troupe.

"Seems Blacktooth has fallen on some hard times," Duncan said as he tossed a single copper coin across the clearing in disgust.

"The man lost his job to a woman…" Phillip laughed before catching an angry glare from Rosaline. He hunched his shoulders and looked away. "Sorry, boss."

"We should go after him," Jathan suggested.

This wasn't a surprise. Rosaline had seen how Blacktooth had treated Jathan when he had joined the Brotherhood. The man tormented him relentlessly. He would berate him, beat him, and on several occasions, Rosaline suspected Blacktooth had done more. However, truthfully, Rosaline didn't care about Jathan's misery or his need for vengeance. Blacktooth was a potential problem, but not a big enough one to warrant delaying their meeting with Greaver, yet again.

"No," Rosaline said. "Let the worm crawl back to whatever hole he came from. If this was the best he could find—" Rosaline gestured to the dead bandits in the clearing "—then Blacktooth's name is worth about as much as his men. Nothing."

CHAPTER EIGHT
RANDALL

Under the hawklike supervision of Cassius, the city had soon regained some semblance of order. Many of the neighbourhood figureheads had sworn allegiance to Randall and were made into "lords", just without the arrogant title. A'Chula and Tig were treated as extensions of the king wherever they went and the city felt somewhat normal again. Something that Randall loathed.

He did not want the city to feel normal; he had intended it to feel different. His uprising was supposed to be not only a reckoning for the nobles, but a rebirth for the people. However, Cassius had guided him to make decisions that were either identical or eerily similar to the old regime. When the eunuch suggested Randall pay the neighbourhood figureheads for their loyalty, it sounded a lot like lordship. However, when Randall protested, Cassius explained that was just how the world worked and always would work.

The thing that troubled him the most was not the fact his dream was not coming to fruition exactly as he had pictured it, but that Anna's body was still missing. They had searched for her for an entire day and came up with nothing. Many offered condolences to Randall and tried to reassure him it was possible his queen survived. Randall desperately hoped that this was not the case. He didn't know what he would do if he saw Anna again. It was bad enough picturing her as a splattered corpse, but it was damn near nightmarish to imagine her alive but disfigured from the fall.

There was a knock on Randall's door. He let out a sigh before rising from his desk. Something that Greaver had never told him about ruling and being king was that you never had time to yourself. It seemed like every waking second someone wanted you for something. He opened the door and saw a dutiful Cassius standing in the doorway, hands folded behind his back.

"The council is waiting for you," the eunuch informed him.

"Already?" Randall asked.

"Yes, Tig, A'Chula, and the rest of your councillors are waiting in the former war room to discuss King Elbert's return."

Randall pinched the bridge of his nose. Ever since he became king, the only news people brought him was bad. Elbert and his army were a dark cloud hanging over his head, and he wished he could have had an evening of reprieve. Evidently, there was no rest for the wicked, or for kings. "Right, take me to them."

Cassius gave a quick bow and escorted the young king away from the royal study and down a winding staircase that led to a hallway with a pair of large oak doors at the far end. Cassius graciously opened one door for his king and Randall entered the war room.

In the summer, the room would have been breathtaking. It had an open balcony that overlooked the city and a large, scale model of the city carved into a stone table in the middle of the room. However, it was not summer, it was winter; a bitter winter at that. Every five feet a brazier burned intensely, trying to combat the cold that leaked in from the balcony. The floor had been cleared of the snow that had blown in, but either the help did not do a good job, or it had simply blown in again since they had swept.

Randall took his seat at the head of the table and looked around at his councillors. Tig and A'Chula sat on either side of him, while the figureheads took up the rest of the seats. They stared at him with expectant eyes as they blew on their hands for warmth. Not wanting to be confined in the freezing room longer than he had to, Randall got things underway.

"Right, Elbert certainly got our message by now. How are the fortifications coming?"

"The docks are secured," a dwarven man spoke up. He was barrel-chested and covered in old sailor tattoos. The tip of his grey, wispy beard touched the stone table. "My men should be deploying the sea gate as we speak."

"Thank you, Corbin." Randall smiled. Ever since the previous Master of the Docks had met his demise during the uprising, Corbin Strongarm had proven a more than capable man to assume the role. Dwarves were inventive people. The "sea gate" was a large steel cable with barbs that surrounded the outside of the harbour, preventing unwanted ships from entering the city. When Corbin proposed the idea at the last council meeting, Randall was so enthused that he immediately ordered all the forges in the city to assist the dwarf on the project.

"I still think it was a bad idea sending the scouts' heads back," Amelia Dupont muttered under her breath.

Randall turned to the buxom, middle-aged woman and scowled. She was the most successful madam in the Corridor of Pleasure. Before the uprising, her establishment served only the wealthiest people that the city had to offer, which usually included the nobles. As far as Randall was concerned, she was just as bad as those nobles, preying upon the vulnerable for her own gain. To make matters worse, he wasn't sure why she had a seat at the table. As far as he could tell, she had no real power beyond the Corridor. Cassius was adamant on giving her a council seat, however, and said that she would be vital to his success as king. He had told Randall that whorehouses, especially the ones like Madame Dupont's, were essential to ruling a kingdom. "He who controls the whorehouses controls secrets, and he who controls secrets controls the kingdom," the eunuch had said. Randall wasn't sure if he saw the former sommelier's logic, but once again, he trusted Cassius' judgement.

"A message needed to be sent," Randall replied callously. "Elbert needs to know that he is no longer welcome here, and that he should find somewhere else to spend the rest of his days."

"The man has an army, boy!" Virgil Walker interjected. "If they breach the walls, we're all as good as dead."

Randall eyed the former city guardsman. Despite his occupation, Virgil had been one of the first people to join the uprising against the nobles. Apparently, keeping order did not pay well under the old regime, a mistake that Randall was quick to fix. Truth be told, the two knew each other long before the revolt. Virgil had caught many of the Maggots stealing before, but would always look the other way if given a bribe. Now that Randall was in power, he wasn't sure how loyal Virgil actually would be, but he was the highest-ranking officer of the city guard left alive, and for now, was essential if Randall wanted to keep his crown.

"Do your job, then, and don't let them breach the walls," Randall retorted.

"Your Majesty, what I think our dear Virgil is trying to say is that Elbert has considerable might, and now we may have just angered him."

"Good. His anger will be his downfall. He will make brash, impulsive decisions that are steered by his anger. I intend to exploit that."

"Oh, is that so?" Virgil Walker scoffed. "Tell me, Your Majesty, are you a military mastermind?"

"I successfully took over an entire kingdom, so I—"

"Yes, you took over a *throne,* but the kingdom is only yours in name. I doubt half the kingdom even knows what happened. As for your revolt, you united the masses against an unsuspecting and undermanned opponent. Elbert has trained soldiers, and generals who know this city like the back of their hands. I'm afraid, unless you are withholding some brilliant tactic from us, I believe we should..."

"Should what?" Randall said, his voice rising with anger. "Surrender? And give the kingdom right back to the same vile creatures that ruined it the first time? My reign is to be a rebirth for all Artanzian people, no matter their status. If Elbert wants his throne back, he'll have to pry it out of my dead hands."

Walker rolled his eyes. "Which he will easily do, because he has a *fucking army*! This is not a game, Your Majesty, this is war. People are going to die needlessly if we don't do something soon."

"What does the rest of the council think?" Randall asked. "Who here shares the same opinion as Virgil? Who wants to give the kingdom right back to the people who walked all over us for centuries?"

"I don't," Tig said.

"Nor do I," Corbin Stronghand answered.

A'Chula shook his head. The rest of the councillors remained silent.

"Well, if that's everything—" Randall said as he rose out of his chair.

"Your Majesty, the matter is not resolved," Cassius began.

Randall snapped his head towards the eunuch and glared at him with all the fiery fury that he could muster, but to the king's surprise, Cassius did not shirk from the stare.

"How so?"

"While Virgil's suggestion was foolish, he brings up a good point about Elbert's army. We are at an obvious military disadvantage. Most of our 'troops' are better with brooms than with swords. And although the sea gate was a good idea, it now appears to be a waste of resources, as Elbert has moved his army onto dry land."

"Get to the point, Cassius," Randall huffed.

"The walls are our only advantage, and if manned properly, it will take Elbert some time to scale or breach them. Time that could be used for an ally to come to our aid."

The room went silent. The councillors looked around at one another with confused expressions, obviously lost by the eunuch's vague words.

"Who?" Randall asked, slowly lowering himself back in his chair, his frustration subsiding.

"Keten."

"What!?" Virgil Walker shouted.

"Cassius, honey, are you mad?" Madame Dupont added.

The eunuch raised a quieting hand. "Keten and Artanzia have long been rivals, true. But you represent a brand new line of kings, one that doesn't have generations of bad blood with Ketenish royalty. And, as I have previously mentioned, you need a queen to legitimize your rule. A queen of *noble* birth. This is the perfect opportunity to ally ourselves with Keten."

The mention of the word "noble" made Randall's skin crawl, but he and Cassius had argued over this for countless hours before. The other kingdoms would not accept Randall as a king simply because he lacked the proper bloodlines. But if he married into those bloodlines, as well as controlling an entire kingdom, it might be enough to stop them deposing him, or worse.

After several moments of contemplation, Randall nodded his head in agreement. "Send a message to King Kalvin. Tell him we require aid, but do so with dignity!"

"At once, Your Majesty."

"Now, if this has concluded, I—"

Suddenly the door to the war room burst open and a page stood there, panting for breath and nursing a black eye. "Your Majesty!" the page gasped. "There is someone for you in the throne room, and they won't leave without an audience. They say you know them."

"Did you summon the guards?" Randall asked rudely.

"Yes, but I'm afraid... I'm afraid this guest isn't alone."

"Cassius, you're with me. Let's see who this so-called 'guest' is."

"Who the fuck are you?" she growled.

Randall scowled at the impertinent woman. She had dark brown hair that was partially braided and wore a studded leather cuirass. Her dark blue eyes glared back at him with fiery frustration. Despite his displeasure, he felt a small flicker of interest. Steeling himself against his desires, he furrowed his brow as he leaned back into his throne. He was about to speak when he saw Cassius step forward out of the corner of his eye.

"This is the rightful king of Artanzia you're talking to, Randall the First, I suggest you address him by his proper title."

"Fuck you, Cassius," the woman barked. "Last time I saw you, you were a grovelling pile of tears and piss. I'm surprised Greaver let you live after what you did to him. Speaking of which, where is that cantankerous old bastard? I was told the King of Crooks overtook the city."

"I am the King of Crooks, *and* the rightful king of Artanzia." Randall interjected.

The woman, along with her cronies, erupted into deafening laughter. Randall's hands curled into fists. After enduring the laughter a moment too long, he slammed his fist against the armrest.

"And just who the *fuck* are you?"

The laughter came to a sudden stop. "Listen, *sire*," the woman began with faux respect, "your ass might sit in that fancy chair, but you sure as shit aren't king of anything. Tell me where I can find Greaver, and I'll be on my way."

"You can find his corpse rotting in the sewers, and if you don't mind your tongue, you'll soon join him," Cassius retorted.

"Does your cock still work without any balls or does it kind of just hang limp like a rope, or a sad worm?"

Randall curiously turned his head and saw Cassius' face flush red. He had never seen anyone get under the eunuch's skin before, but whoever this woman was, she certainly knew how.

"You still haven't told us your name," Randall said, pointing out the obvious.

"Rosaline, leader of the Bloody Brotherhood," the woman said with a flourish.

"I see you've aged like fine wine," Cassius said sarcastically.

"Unfortunately, the same can't be said for you. Time has been quite cruel to you, by the looks of things," Rosaline responded curtly.

Randall turned his head once more and saw that this remark didn't get a rise out of Cassius. Instead, the eunuch kept his calm, a slight smile plastered on his face. *Must've noticed me staring*, Randall thought.

"I think we should leave, Roz," one of the so-called Bloody Brothers whispered loudly.

"Agreed," Cassius growled.

"Tell me," Randall interjected, "what business did you have with Greaver?"

Rosaline gave the young king a questioning glance and looked at her men. "That's between us and a dead man."

Randall stood up and walked towards the woman. Surprisingly, neither she nor her men moved in response. They just stood there, eyeing him like a pack of hungry wolves would a dying stag. "For years, I was Greaver's ward," Randall began. "I've overheard a lot of his conversations and deals during my life, but I never once heard him mention you. Now, why would that be?"

"Perhaps you're not a good listener," one Brother responded, which resulted in the group of bandits chuckling amongst themselves.

Rosaline smiled and approached Randall, but he quickly backed away, making sure he was at least an arm's length away from the woman. He had no illusions about her – she was a killer, and by the look of it, a proficient one.

"I don't know what is going on here, and frankly I don't care," Rosaline started. "The Bloody Brotherhood owes allegiance to no one. Greaver and I had an arrangement, an arrangement that was benefitting him more than it was us. Something that we needed to correct. But seeing as you've done that for us already, I suppose we'll be on our way."

"What arrangement?" Randall asked.

"Like I said, that's between us and a dead man," she said, turning to leave, her men following close behind.

Randall couldn't help but admire her as she walked away for several seconds, until he felt Cassius' hot breath on his ear. "Should I have someone follow them and make sure they leave the city?"

The king shook his head. "No, we have much bigger problems than them." As if sensing his words, the bells from the top of the towers chimed relentlessly. Horns sounded from atop the walls and Tig charged into the throne room. "Randall!" he blurted out. "Elbert's army approaches!"

CHAPTER NINE

ELBERT

The walls of Winterhelm loomed in the distance. Although the smoke had long since dissipated, Elbert could still smell the fumes from the uprising. The smell of his dreams burnt to ash. He waited, with his army at his back, for the so-called king of Artanzia to accept his parlay. His fingers drummed restlessly against the armrests of his wheeled throne as his eyes refused to move from Winterhelm's closed gates. Elbert could hear his bodyguards shifting uneasily in their plate mail several paces behind him. Finally, after what seemed like ages, the gates to Winterhelm opened with a creak. Elbert let out a sigh of relief. *So it begins.*

He saw a retinue of horses ride out with a young man at the head of the formation. Although some riders were armed, Elbert remained calm. If he could survive a negotiation with a bloodthirsty Islander king, he could survive a talk with a commoner.

The column of riders came to a stop fifty paces away from the crippled king. Only two of the riders dismounted. The first was a boy, who had probably only seen sixteen winters, wearing the ceremonial crown atop his head. The second was a bald, effeminate-looking man clad in elegant, regal robes. The pair of usurpers approached Elbert but remained outside of arm's length.

"It is customary to drop to your knees when you address the king," Elbert said, breaking the silence.

"Indeed," said the young usurper. "But given your condition, I've allowed you to sit and keep a modicum of your dignity."

A rage-fuelled smile cracked Elbert's lips. If this peasant wanted to trade insults, he had no problem stooping to the boy's level. Truth be told, Elbert was probably only a handful of years older than Randall, but if there was one thing he knew about young men, it was how much they hated being reminded how young they actually were.

"Listen, *boy*," Elbert said. "What you have committed is high treason, a crime that is punishable by death. However, given that I am a merciful lord, I will pardon your co-conspirators if they denounce you as 'king' and pledge their allegiance to me, their rightful ruler."

"What about myself? Do I not deserve your mercy?" Randall responded.

"No, boy, I'm afraid you don't." Elbert raised his voice so that all of Randall's retinue could hear him clearly. "If you denounce this pile of filth that desecrates the sacred throne of Artanzia, your past crimes will be forgiven. Hand Randall over to me, and life will continue as normal."

"What if we refuse? What if we don't want things to go back to normal?" one youth on horseback interjected.

Elbert let out a small chuckle. "Look around you, son. We have greater numbers, far more experience, and better weapons than you. If you refuse my offer, I will paint the ground red with your treasonous blood."

Randall's candour instantly vanished, and a grave seriousness took over. "You and your dogs will die trying to scale our walls.

Me and my people have fought to get what is rightfully ours, and we will gladly die defending it."

"Listen, boy—" Elbert began.

"I am not a boy!" Randall shouted. "I am the king!"

"You are a thief, nothing more," Elbert retorted calmly, sensing he had the upper hand in the negotiation. "Yes, I will lose men if I storm the city, but you will lose more. I have the forces to surround the city and starve you into submission. Tell me, how long will the people's loyalty last when their stomachs gurgle from hunger? Have you started stockpiling food yet? If you were truly a king, you would look at what is best for your people, not yourself."

"And what's best for them is to reinstate you as king?" Randall answered through gritted teeth. "To restore the oppressive regime that crushed my people's hopes and dreams for generations? The same regime that is led by a cripple?"

"A cuckolded cripple, sire," the bald man added.

"I beg your pardon?" Elbert snarled, his blood pressure rising.

"I used to work in the palace as a personal servant to the late queen before the uprising. I found it quite odd the number of nightly visitors she received. On several occasions, she received several at the same time."

"You lie."

"Most of the help agreed that it was her effort to produce an heir for you. Seeing as you could not consummate the marriage given your... condition."

"Guards!" Elbert shouted. Several bodyguards stepped forward, hands on the pommels of their swords. "This talk is over. If this filth wants to die for some delusional boy's cause, then we will happily oblige."

With a swift wave of the hand, one guard grabbed Elbert's chair by the handles and wheeled him back towards the safety of their camp. He heard the young usurper call out one last insult as he was whisked away, but failed to make it out. His ears were ringing with anger. He secretly wished that he had Thames and Grimm by his side. Despite their differences in civility, the two warriors were a force to be reckoned with. If they had been here, they would've carved through Randall's retinue of guards like a knife cutting through cheese on a hot summer's day. He imagined Randall grovelling for his life as his forces died by the sword. How the boy would beg for mercy as Elbert prepared to slit his throat. He shook the idea out of his head. Now was not the time for fantasizing; now was the time for planning so that his fantasies would come true.

"We should have cut that whelp down where he stood!" Lord Penerack shouted.

"And make him a martyr? Are you mad?" Lord Grelin raged in reply.

The tent was chaos. Lords had forgotten their dignity and their civility and were screaming at one another on what the right course of action was. Many agreed with Lord Penerack and suggested they should have stormed the city and assumed control. They had almost every advantage. Others sided with Lord Grelin, who instead saw the potential fallout that could arise if King Randall was killed too hastily.

There was one in the tent who was uncharacteristically calm. Elbert sat in his wheeled throne and stared at the sealed metal box in the corner. He had brought Thames to the meeting to see if his old friend could advise him from beyond the grave one more time. His eyes fixated on the box. The grey metal looked cold and unforgiving and some rivets were beginning to rust. Elbert closed his eyes and pictured Thames' head inside the box. The darkness that it saw. He felt a stillness that he had not felt before. He saw the endless sea of black that surrounded his friend and felt the icy touch of the metal against the nape of his severed neck.

"Your Majesty?" Lord Grelin asked in a near shout. "What do you suggest we do?"

Elbert opened his eyes and nodded his head in thanks at the lockbox. "I will not sacrifice my men just to turn that boy into a martyr and become a tyrant. If I kill Randall now, I become everything that he told the people I am. I intend to prove to my subjects that I am different."

"And how do you intend to do that, sire?" Lord Penerack asked.

"Right now, Randall has the love of the people. Let's see how long the people love him when they're starving and turning on themselves."

"You want to lay siege on Winterhelm?" Lord Arlin said in disbelief.

If Elbert's legs weren't already handicapped, he was sure they would've failed him then. The former dwarven craftsman had been quiet since they returned to the continent. He spent most of his days creating schematics for things well within his capability, such as simple ploughs and horseshoes, or by tending to Sara, who had become just as sullen as he had.

"Siege is such an ugly word. Think of it more as a provisional blockade. We surround the city and wait. Once the peasants' stomachs growl, they'll turn on Randall and welcome me back with open arms. People can only be sustained on zeal and ardour for so long."

"An excellent plan, Your Majesty," Lord Grelin commented.

"Gentlemen, have your forces ready to surround Winterhelm on the morrow. I want my throne back as quickly as possible."

The lords rose from their seats, bowed politely, and exited the tent to set out about carrying out their orders.

"Not you," Elbert called out as the only nonhuman was about to leave the tent. "Sit."

"Something you need, Your Majesty?" Arlin asked hesitantly.

"I just wanted to thank you for all you've done during this endeavour. Do not be mistaken – your talents and your knowledge have allowed us to achieve the impossible."

"I appreciate the kind words, Your Majesty, but—"

"I know," Elbert interrupted. "That's why I want to tell you that your services are no longer needed. We require no siege weapons, and you have no troops to order around." Elbert grabbed a piece of parchment and an inkwell from beside him and wrote sloppily onto the paper. Once he was finished, he rolled the parchment up, poured wax on it, stamped it with his royal seal, and tossed it to Lord Arlin.

"What's this?"

"I hereby bequeath Lord Bellston's estate to you. Seeing as he is dead and my wife, his only child, also perished, the estate is vacant. Hand that scroll to the majordomo on the property and they will get you settled in."

"I... uh... I..." Arlin stammered.

"I'll send a small contingent of my royal guards to accompany you. I'll instruct them to support your claims as the property's new owner. But you must do me one small favour."

"What is it?" Arlin asked.

"Take Sara with you. This is no place for a young girl. She has seen so much death and suffering these past few weeks. She needs to get away from it all. I think growing up in the lovely Artanzian countryside will do her some good."

"As you wish, Your Majesty."

Elbert rolled his chair around the table, shook Arlin's hand, and pulled him in close for a tight embrace. He truly was thankful for the dwarf's services and he appreciated them more knowing how much Arlin hated the type of work he did. He hoped to give the former craftsman some well-deserved peace.

As the dwarf left the tent, Elbert rolled over to the small metal box, picked it up, and set it in his lap. "This will be over soon, Thames. Soon, I will have my kingdom back and you'll be given a hero's funeral and buried properly in the royal cemetery." He took a moment to wipe the tears from his eyes and repeated, "Soon this will all be over."

CHAPTER TEN
CONNIR

The aftermath of an Islander feast was like the aftermath of a battle. Bodies littered the ground, weapons were discarded, and a fair amount of blood stained the longhouse floor. Connir woke up in his chair, his beard stuck to the mead-soaked table. He wiped the crust out of his eyes and peeled his head off the sticky wood. He looked around and saw that he was one of the last to wake. Groggily, he rose to his feet and stumbled out of the longhouse. The sun's bright rays reflected off the snow and assaulted his eyes. Suddenly, the world spun, and he fell to his knees and vomited on the longhouse steps.

"Can't handle your mead?" Ragnar laughed.

Connir looked up, wiped the vomit from his beard, and gave a half-hearted smile. "What the fuck happened last night?"

"You won the game of Berserker Cup is what happened."

Connir felt like he was going to be sick again. Berserker Cup was the foulest drinking game on the Isles. It consisted of two teams. Each team would have a single "drinker", while the rest of the team would be the 'brewers'. The object of the game was to get the other team's drinker to pass out or vomit. So, the 'brewers' would mix drinks that purposefully tasted awful.

"I have to admit, Estrid looked pretty impressed with you last night."

"Really?"

"Mhmm," Ragnar replied. "Especially when you stomached that cup of goat's piss."

Before the laugh could escape Ragnar's lips, Connir heaved once again, but this time, covering his captain's boots.

"For fuck's sake, Connir, I was only joking!"

This time it was the skald's turn to laugh. Ragnar pulled him to his feet and gave him a reassuring smile. "Come on, Otar is choosing who'll be on White-Eyes' last voyage."

"Ugh, no, thanks," Connir replied. Ragnar raised a questioning brow. "I just want to go home, Ragnar, I have no interest in spending weeks on a boat watching a man starve to death."

"You owe it to the Isles to go!" Ragnar exclaimed. "You're the best damn skald the Isles has ever known! Who else has the talent to end White-Eyes' story? If you don't go, who do you think Otar will send? Linny the Loon? The man sounds like a horse's fart."

Connir smiled. "While that may be true, I'm still not going. I miss my bed, I miss my house, and I just want to relax."

"This mean you don't intend to come raiding?" Ragnar asked in disbelief.

"I've seen enough blood and death," Connir replied.

Ragnar's meaty hands grasped his shoulders. "You're an Islander! There is no such thing as too much blood and death. You're Svain Whitefist's son, for Heimer's sake!"

Connir brushed off his captain's arms and walked away without saying another word. Although he knew Ragnar's intentions were good, the man was not skilled with words. Connir hated being compared to his father. He knew he wasn't a warrior, but he hated that everyone was keen to remind him of that fact, as if he didn't feel enough shame over it already.

Trying to cheer himself up, Connir walked towards the kennel to see Bane before he prepared for the long journey home. As he entered the kennels, he stopped when he saw High King Uthredd standing in front of one cage. The king's eyes quickly shifted from inside the cage towards the skald.

"Ah, Connir Svainsson. Come to get a good look at the traitor?" Uthredd asked.

"No, uh... I'm here to see my hound," Connir stammered.

Uthredd looked at him questioningly for a few moments before a smile appeared on his face. "You know, Connir, your father helped me unite the clans."

"Yes, I am aware," Connir answered timidly, already knowing where the conversation was heading.

"I'm glad you followed in his footsteps and joined our army when we marched on Tjørholm."

"With all due respect, Your Highness," Connir started, "my father was a warrior and I'm just—"

"You've been listening to Jarl Otar too much," High King Unthread interrupted. "Despite what men like him and your father might think, skalds are essential to our way of life. Just because you did not swing a sword during the siege, doesn't make you any less of a man."

Connir nodded his head in thanks. He felt his emotions slowly bubbling to the surface and quickly changed the subject. "Can I ask what you're doing in here?"

Uthredd let out a long sigh. "Just saying goodbye to an old friend. Despite all that Grimm has done to me, I still have love for him in my heart. However, he broke the law, and nobody, not even myself, is above the law of the gods. What about you? You should be down by the beach vying for your chance to join Grimm on his last voyage."

Connir scratched his neck nervously. "I... uh..."

"Connir!" a voice called from outside the kennels.

Quickly, he turned his head and saw Estrid enter the kennels and give a quick bow of courtesy towards the king. "Where were you? Otar has selected the skald that will document Grimm's last days. You missed your chance!"

"Actually, I think I'm going to go back to Nalfdeim, start preparing things for spring."

"Oh..." Estrid started. "I was really hoping you were going to go on the ship. I would've loved to hear your rendition of White-Eyes' death."

As the shieldmaiden exited the kennels in awkward silence, Connir turned towards his king, who was smiling from ear to ear.

"Realized you've made a mistake, son?" Uthredd asked, trying to hide his laughter.

Without uttering a reply, Connir quickly sprinted out of the kennels to find Otar the Foul.

"You missed your chance, Svainsson!" Otar howled as he slammed his fist on the armrest of his chair. "The honour of documenting White-Eyes' death has been bestowed to Linny the Loon. Maybe if you weren't so busy fucking that dog of yours, you'd have been on time."

"Jarl Otar, I—" Connir began.

"I'll hear no more of this," Otar interrupted. "Head back to Nalfdeim; your services are no longer required."

Connir turned his head and locked eyes with Estrid. Her brow was furrowed and a disappointed frown stained her lips.

An unfamiliar fire suddenly lit in the skald's belly. Connir gritted his teeth and furiously glared at his Jarl. "Linny sounds like a horse's fart and you know it!" he shouted, taking everyone aback. "I'm the best damned skald on these fucking rocks and I demand to be on that ship!"

"Who are you to demand anything from me, boy?" Otar shouted as he rose to his feet. "My decision is final – now fuck off!"

Connir refused to be beaten down this easily, especially not in front of Estrid. The rage and frustration that filled his body gave birth to an ill-thought-out idea. He looked around and saw Linny the Loon laughing silently in the corner. This only made his anger grow.

"I challenge Linny the Loon to a duel! Winner gets the honour of sailing with Captain Ragnar and documenting Grimm White-Eyes' last days!"

Everyone went silent. The expression on Linny's face was one of pure shock. A smile crept along Connir's lips. In the back of his mind he wondered what expression was glued on Estrid's face, but he didn't dare look back. He continued to stare at Linny, showing his rival that there wasn't an ounce of fear in his body.

After a lengthy silence, Otar laughed maniacally. The jarl wiped a tear from his eye and sat back down in his chair. "Perhaps there's some of your father in you yet, boy," he said between laughs. "Linny, do you accept Connir's challenge?"

"I do," Linny said without hesitation.

It was in that moment that the reality of what he had just done hit Connir. His stomach sank. He was going to have to fight to the death, and he could barely hold a sword. He only hoped that Linny was a worse fighter than him, but that was very unlikely.

"Good!" Otar bellowed. "I'll give you both a day to prepare. I'll happily watch as one of you dies."

Sensing the dramatics were over, the crowd dispersed, but Connir remained frozen in place, continuing to stare at the spot where Linny the Loon once stood. He suddenly felt a hand on his shoulder. He turned his head and saw a worried Ragnar staring back at him.

"What the fuck were you thinking, Connir? You can't fight!"

"You don't understand Ragnar, I—"

"I understand. You were thinking with your cock," Ragnar interjected. There was a certain harshness in his voice that Connir had not heard before. "Estrid won't love you as a corpse."

"She won't love me as a craven either," Connir mumbled.

Ragnar let out a long sigh before shoving a sword in the skald's hands. "Come on."

"Where are we going?"

"I'm going to train you," Ragnar replied. "Otherwise I'm going to be burying you tomorrow."

"By Heimer's beard! It's a sword. You stab them with the pointy end, it's not hard to understand!" Ragnar shouted as he effortlessly knocked Connir's blade free from his grasp.

Connir let out a defeated sigh as he massaged his aching hands. He looked at the sword lying in the snow and cursed himself for ever challenging Linny to a duel. He didn't stand a chance. Every time Ragnar parried one of his strikes, the skald's sword went flying across the training yard.

Ragnar twirled his blade between his fingers. "Go grab it. I refuse to let you die today."

"What's the use?" Connir lamented. His muscles screamed in agony. Ever since he issued the challenge to Linny, all he had done was train with Ragnar. He hadn't eaten, and he had barely slept. He had hoped that he would be miraculously better overnight, but unfortunately, miracles were a rarity on the Isles. "I might as well go slit my throat in the forest and save myself the embarrassment."

Ragnar's expression softened. He dropped his sword, walked over to the young skald, and placed both hands on his shoulders. "Don't talk like that. You'll be fine. Worst-case scenario, you go to the Great Hall and dine with Heimer and your father."

Tears welled in the corners of Connir's eyes. "I don't want to die."

He had hoped that his friend would say something, anything, but all Ragnar did was pull Connir in for a tight embrace. They stood there for a while, silently holding one another. The crunch of snow alerted them that someone approached. Before Connir could turn his head and see who it was, he was forcefully shoved to the ground by Ragnar.

"Get up!" Ragnar shouted, as he walked back to grab his sword.

"How goes the training?" Estrid asked Ragnar, while Connir dusted the snow off his trousers.

He didn't hear what his captain said, but judging from the look on Estrid's face, it was the truth. Connir felt his cheeks flush with colour as he went to go pick up his sword.

"You two have been training relentlessly, you need a break," Estrid said.

"Why?" Connir snapped. "I'm not going to get any better. I fight for my life in a few hours and I can't even keep a sword in my hands."

Estrid cocked her head to the side. "Why don't you go see Bane? He always lifts your spirits. Perhaps he'll give you something worth fighting for."

I already have you, Connir thought. "You're right." As Connir left the training area he looked over his shoulder and saw Estrid and Ragnar comforting one another. He couldn't imagine what they were going through. Knowing that someone you cared about was going to die needlessly was probably the worst. Well, except maybe for knowing that you'll die needlessly yourself.

It was still early in the morning, so the streets of Skotheim were mainly devoid of people. Connir was thankful for this. He wasn't sure if he could handle the looks of pity or the whispers of gossip as he walked by. Although being alone was no delight either. His body filled with dread as he walked towards the kennels. Thoughts of what it would feel like to be stabbed or sliced in half raced through his head. His stomach churned the more he thought about it. He prayed Linny would give him a quick death, but somehow he thought he wasn't that lucky.

The smell of dried piss, stale shit, and wet dog assaulted his nose as he entered the kennels. Immediately, he thought about his death. *What will my last smell be? Is it true that you shit yourself when you die?* Connir's guts gurgled as he walked towards Bane's cage. The old war hound's tail wagged violently upon seeing his old friend, but stilled after realizing something was wrong.

Connir opened the cage and Bane instantly leapt out and began rubbing himself against the skald's legs. Connir put his back against the stone wall of the kennel and slid down it until he was sitting in the piss-soaked hay. Bane licked Connir's cheek, but when he didn't receive a playful shove or a laugh from his owner, he stopped and curled up beside Connir, resting his head in the skald's lap.

"What am I going to do, Bane?" Connir asked aloud as he scratched behind the war hound's ears. "I'm going to die because I had to impress a damned girl. What was I thinking!? I can't even hold a bloody sword – how did I think I was going to kill a man?"

Bane offered no answers. Instead, the dog let out a breath as his body relaxed beside his master's. The two of them sat there in the kennel for a while in silence. Tears silently rolled down the skald's face. He had perfected the art of crying quietly when he was a kid. Every time his father heard him crying, he would "give him something to cry about" and beat him with a leather belt, and Connir cried a lot as a child. He cried when he was happy, cried when he was sad or scared. So in order to avoid the lashings, he would swallow the sobs and allow his tears to stream down his face.

"Word of advice, boy?" a gravelly, monotone voice said, breaking the deafening silence.

Connir wiped the tears off his cheeks and took a second to regain control of his breath. "Sure." It wasn't until the word left his mouth that he realized who he was talking to. There was only one man in the kennels besides himself.

"If you've never swung a sword before, you're pissing your time away trying to learn it the day before. Sword work takes dedication, patience, and time. Three things you don't have."

"So what am I supposed to do? Beat Linny the Loon to death with my bare hands?" Connir asked.

"I don't know how big this Linny fellow is, but judging from your stature, I'd say that's out of the question," Grimm replied.

"What do you suggest, then?"

"Have you ever chopped wood?"

"Yes, but—"

"Chopping a man is no different. Ditch the sword and choose an axe."

"You really think that'll work?" Connir asked, hope filling his chest.

"I shaped a company of thieves and rapists into the most fearsome warriors the mainlanders had ever known. They all used axes."

"Are those the men that butchered our people when we went to collect the dead?"

Silence filled the kennels. As it got longer, the more Connir regretted his word choice. He didn't mean for it to sound like a barb at the legendary warrior, but it certainly had. Just when he was about to apologize to the traitor, he heard Grimm clear his throat.

"Just use an axe, boy, and you might live long enough to make that shieldmaiden yours."

Connir's eyes shifted down towards Bane, who was staring up at him expectantly. He gave the dog a pat on the head, rose to his feet, and left the kennels with renewed hope.

Ragnar was still in the training grounds when he returned. His captain's expression lit up when he saw the skald enter the arena. "Ready to master the sword?"

"No," Connir replied, "I want to duel using an axe."

Ragnar's brow furrowed. "An axe? What for?"

"I hear it's easier to use than a sword, and that splitting a man is a lot like splitting wood."

Ragnar let out a laugh. "Whoever told you that certainly isn't wrong. And judging by how well you swing a sword, you can't be any worse with an axe."

Connir let out a half-hearted smile as he grabbed a handaxe and got a feel for the weapon. It was surprisingly light. He admired the craftsmanship of the handle. It was a dark oak that had been weathered by the years, giving it a fabled look.

"Let's begin," Ragnar said as he raised his sword in the defensive position. "Attack!"

Connir swung the axe haphazardly at his captain and was astounded by how much easier it was than the sword. The weight of the axe head helped with his momentum and allowed him to recover from a missed strike more easily; the movements felt less foreign to his body, and whenever Ragnar parried a strike, the wooden handle absorbed most of the vibration, sending fewer shockwaves of pain up his arm.

For two hours, Ragnar trained him and gave him pointers. There wasn't a lot of time left to fix all the mistakes he was making, so Ragnar focused on the most critical. After the lengthy sparring session, Connir was filled with hope once again. He was not a deadly warrior, but he could now hold his own in a fight.

"Excuse me, fierce warrior!" Estrid shouted as she entered the arena. "I'm looking for a shy skald named Connir, have you seen him?"

A laugh escaped his lips as he placed the handle of his axe in the holster on his belt. His mind raced as he tried to think of something clever and witty to say, but his tongue felt like it had suddenly doubled in size and had a will of its own. "I... uh... yeah," he stammered.

"He looks like Svain Whitefist back from the dead!" Ragnar shouted, breaking the awkward silence.

"Maybe a tad more handsome," Estrid replied, giving a coy wink towards Connir.

"Is it time?" Connir asked, unsure how else to respond to the compliment.

"Mhmm," Estrid answered. "Linny is waiting for you in the centre of town. He was up all last night."

"He was nervous too?" Ragnar asked.

Estrid shook her head. "No, he was celebrating his assured victory in the longhouse with a few of his friends."

Connir's heart sank, but Ragnar slapped him hard on the back. "The gods smile on you today, Svainsson!"

"How so?"

"Your opponent is overconfident and hungover, you actually stand a chance."

Connir let out a strained breath and nodded his head in agreement. "Let's go get this over with."

It looked as if the entire city was gathered to watch the battle of the bards. Connir's stomach gurgled again as he stared at the crowd gathered before him. Jarl Otar had ordered the biggest warriors to form a circle around the two skalds to prevent them from fleeing the battle. If they tried to run, a berserker would grab them and throw them back into the fray.

"Linny the Loon and Connir Svainsson," Jarl Otar shouted, instantly silencing the crowd, "are you ready?"

Linny nodded his head. Connir did the same, although he was far from ready. He wasn't sure what was going to happen. But the way Linny was holding the side of his head and swaying from side to side meant that he had a chance.

"Choose your weapons!"

Linny stepped forward and grabbed a sword from the weapon rack. The skald tried to twirl it but the blade fell from his hand and landed in the snow. A few chuckles emerged from the crowd. Connir stepped forward and grabbed a hand axe. He wanted to use the one he had been training with, but it was dull and meant for training. The one in his hand, although far uglier than the one he had trained with, was sharpened to a razor's edge.

Jarl Otar stood in the middle of the arena, and carefully scrutinised both bards as he looked at them. Connir half expected a speech, but knew deep down there wouldn't be one. Otar was not a man for pageantry. Suddenly, Otar the Foul clapped his hands and exited the circle. The crowd erupted in cheers, excited to witness the battle of the bards.

Linny instantly rushed forward. Connir easily sidestepped away from the Loon's clumsy charge. He swung his axe, hoping to get a quick kill, but Linny parried it effortlessly with his sword. The two skalds stared at each other for a few seconds before Linny swung his sword again. Connir jumped out of the way, but this time Linny spun wildly after he missed, slicing open Connir's thigh.

A scream of pain escaped from Connir's lips as he fell to the ground, clutching his bleeding leg. The sight of the red liquid oozing out of his trousers made him feel sick. His vision blurred, and he noticed his hands were shaking.

"What were you thinking?" Linny whispered as he approached, holding his sword at his side. "You couldn't just let me have this?"

Panic filled Connir's heart, and he desperately tried to crawl away from the battle. His mind raced wildly as he thought about how he was going to get past the berserkers. The cold snow stung the wound on his leg as he dragged his body to the other side of the circle.

"Your axe! Grab your fucking axe!" a voice shouted from the crowd.

Connir looked over his shoulder and saw that he had left his axe behind when he crawled away. He tried to stand on his feet but the pain from his injured leg immediately made him collapse. As he lay there, face down in the snow, he felt a foot on his back and the tip of a blade at the base of his skull.

"Any last words?" Linny asked.

Connir tried to fight the panic that filled his body. His hands were shaking. His heart had fallen into his stomach and his bladder threatened to empty itself.

"No!" Jarl Otar shouted. A hush fell over the crowd. Both Linny and Connir looked at their Jarl in disbelief. A pang of hope filled Connir's heart. "Flip him on his back, let him see his death coming."

Just like that, all hope left Connir's body. He was about to piss himself in fear when he finally saw Estrid's face. Her expression was one of pity, sadness, and helplessness. Seeing the love of his life so disappointed in him ignited something in Connir. He would not die like this, sobbing and crying like a child. If he was going to die, he was going to die as a man.

Linny placed one of his hands on Connir's shoulders to flip him over, then Connir elbowed him in the cheek. Linny instantly dropped his sword and fell to the ground. Connir quickly crawled on top of the confused Linny and wrapped his hands around the bard's throat. Desperately, Linny clawed at Connir's face. He felt his opponent's fingernails dig deep into his cheeks. He grimaced in pain and instinctively lifted Linny's head to bash it against the frozen earth. The Loon's hands fell to his side. Connir closed his eyes as he did it again. And again. He continued to slam Linny's skull against the ground until he heard an audible *splat*. He opened his eyes and saw a red pool of blood form underneath Linny's head. Connir let go of the bard's throat and stared into the lifeless face of Linny the Loon. An expression of fear and confusion was frozen on his face.

It took Connir a few seconds to realize what had happened, but when he finally did, he puked all over the corpse of Linny the Loon.

CHAPTER ELEVEN
ROSALINE

The tavern in the Garden was surprisingly empty. Usually it would be teeming with thieves, cutthroats, conmen, and pickpockets. But ever since Randall took over the city, the Garden was left abandoned, save for a few loyalists who wanted to reminisce about the good ol' days. The innkeeper, Fletcher, was exactly how Rosaline remembered him. Strong, bald, and incredibly grumpy. In all the years she had known him, she could only recall him saying more than one syllable on three occasions.

"What do we do now?" Malek asked as he emptied his mug of ale.

Rosaline drummed her fingers against the wooden table, trying to figure out her next move. She and her Brothers had found themselves in a dangerous situation. On the one hand, being trapped in a besieged city was far from ideal. Any moment Elbert's army could breach the walls and chaos would ensue. Chaos that she couldn't control. On the other hand, sieges made people desperate, and if played correctly, they could capitalize on the people's desperation.

"At least we don't gotta deal with Greaver no more!" Phillip said, helping himself to another mug of ale.

"Then I think we should leave," Duncan interjected. "There's nothing for us here, so let's get out of here before we find ourselves out of the frying pan and in the fire."

"And walk away from the chance to be filthy rich?" Rosaline said suddenly, her fingers coming to a sudden stop on the table's surface.

"What do you mean?" Jathan asked.

Rosaline let out a frustrated sigh. "The thing about sieges is that they don't last forever. If you can survive a siege while in control of the right resources, you can walk away filthy rich when the smoke clears."

"You want us to hoard food?" Duncan asked, surprised.

Rosaline nodded her head. "We have two choices. Leave the city and continue to barely scrape by from robbing wagons; or, we can try to seize control of the food supply in Winterhelm, and walk away with the score of a lifetime."

"What's the catch?" Phillip asked as he wiped his moustache free of froth.

"The catch," Rosaline continued, "is that it's risky. The people could unite against us and take all the food back if we are too stingy with it. Or, if the walls are breached, we could die in the ensuing battle."

"Not to mention rival gangs," Malek added. "Others will probably have the same idea as us and are already planning ways to store and preserve the food so that they can extort the people out of their valuables."

"Why would people give us gold for food?" Jathan asked with a bewildered tone.

"When you're in a siege, boy," Phillip replied, "food is worth more than gold after a few days of starving. People will trade their entire family fortune for a slice of maggoty bread."

The Bloody Brotherhood looked around at each other as they realized they all had a question to ask themselves: Which was more important, their life or being filthy rich?

"We'll put it to a vote," Rosaline said, after a few moments of deliberation. "All in favour of leaving now and keeping the skin on our backs, knives in." Everyone stared at the centre of the table and saw that nobody had stabbed their knife into the weathered oak. "All in favour of risking it all and staying in the city during the siege?" Rosaline continued.

This time, every Brother stabbed their knife into the table. A smile crept along Rosaline's face. A unanimous decision, just how she liked it.

"Now that that's settled," Duncan said, pulling his knife from the table, "the next problem we have is where we are going to store all the food."

Rosaline cast a questioning glance at Fletcher, who was behind the bar, pouring himself a cup of whiskey. "How about it, Fletch? You store the food here for, oh, let's say, five percent?"

"Hmm," the innkeep answered.

That was what Rosaline liked about Fletcher. He was a man of few words, and he was not particularly greedy. He knew exactly when not to push his luck.

As a satisfied silence filled the tavern air, each of the Brothers smiling ear to ear, Phillip cleared his throat. "Can we all talk about something important to me?"

"Oh Gods," Duncan started as he put a hand over his face. "He's going to talk about fucking again."

"You're damned right I am! Did anyone else see that little twerp of a king eye-fuckin' Rosaline while we were in the throne room?"

Rosaline took a second to think back on her interaction with the new king of Artanzia. Now that Phillip mentioned it, it was hard to remember anything else besides Randall's lustful eyes. In fairness, Randall wasn't bad-looking; she had certainly bedded uglier men. But something screamed inexperience with the new King of Crooks, and she didn't feel like teaching someone how to please her. She could easily do that herself.

"He's a young man," Malek said, interrupting the silence in the room, "most of his thinking will be done with his cock. Ain't that right, Jathan?"

The young bandit's face went bright red. He opened his mouth to retort but the only thing that escaped his lips was a pathetic wheeze.

"I think we have a golden opportunity here," Phillip chimed in, taking Jathan's attention and continuing the train of thought. "Let Rosaline sleep with the boy king, get in good, and we can rob the royal palace too."

The hair on the back of Rosaline's neck stood up on end. She turned around and flashed a smile at Phillip, who had already started on his fourth drink of the hour. Slowly, she sauntered around the table, grabbed Phillip by the back of his head, and slammed his round face into the table until she heard the bones in his nose shatter. She then quickly unsheathed Boris and held the tip to Phillip's throat.

"If you think you can whore me out like some common harlot, you are sorely mistaken," Rosaline growled. "If you ever, EVER, suggest that I sleep with someone again, I'll emasculate you, shove your balls down your throat and your cock up your ass. Am I understood?"

Phillip nodded his head feverishly against the table. Rosaline lifted his head up and kneed the large man in the chin, sending him tumbling backwards out of his chair. "Get the fuck out of my sight. I don't want to see you for a few days," Rosaline ordered as she walked to the bar and grabbed a bottle of whiskey. "If anyone needs me, I'll be in the suite having a bath."

The steam from the bath slowly ascended its way to the wooden ceiling, where it formed a thick cloud of mist. The wind outside battered the shutters against the stained-glass window. This room was one of the few in the inn that kept the cold where it belonged. Outside. Sinking deeper into the hot bathwater, Rosaline twirled Boris between her fingers. She studied the effigy of the man on the handle of the dagger and found herself curious as to who it was supposed to depict. Even though she had had the dagger for many years, she could find no answers. The only person she knew who may have had some answers was the knife's previous owner, who was probably decomposed in the ditch where she left him by now. The dagger's origin and its meaning was a mild curiosity, something to ponder when she wasn't planning the Brotherhood's next score.

There was a knock on the door. Rosaline let out a frustrated sigh. A moment's peace was all that she asked for, but apparently, she was asking for too much.

"Come in."

Duncan slowly entered the room. Rosaline shot him an annoyed glare, but unsurprisingly the half-elf held his gaze. In fact, his eyes didn't leave hers, not even to take a quick glance at her naked body. This didn't surprise Rosaline – when you travelled on the road with people for as long as they had, privacy was a luxury that was quickly abandoned.

"Can I help you?" Rosaline snapped, covering herself with her arms, more out of habit than modesty.

"About what Phillip said at the table, I—"

"I swear to the Gods, if you even suggest that I sleep with that boy, I will fill this bathtub with your blood."

Duncan quickly shook his head. "No, not that, but he has the right idea. Wouldn't be the worst thing in the world to have someone poke around the palace and see what we can learn."

Rosaline relaxed the tension that was building in her shoulders. Sensing her bath was now ruined, she exited the tub, covered herself with a towel, and tied her soggy hair into a high bun before sitting down on the bed. "You want to us to rob the King of Artanzia?"

Duncan nodded his head. "He will stockpile food as well. Arguably, he will have the biggest hoard next to ours. If we are serious about exploiting the people during the siege, we can't allow him to have more food than us."

Rosaline nodded her head. "We also can't leave him with nothing. Otherwise, he will tear the city apart looking for whoever stole his food. Seeing as he used to be the King of Crooks, I'm sure the Garden will be the first place he'll look."

"It'll be a fine line. Steal just enough to hinder him, but not enough that he'll notice."

"The only problem is Cassius," Rosaline observed. "The man has his claws deep into the boy king and I'm sure he'll be taking an inventory of everything the crown gathers."

"Do you want me to kill him?"

Rosaline shook her head. "No. We shouldn't do anything rash. Find out what Randall's plans are for the siege and report back to me. Try not to get caught."

"Nobody's caught me yet," Duncan replied as he exited the room.

Once the door was closed and she was left alone with her thoughts once again, Rosaline sank deeper into the warm water, allowing her body to relax. She held Boris by the tip of his blade and stared at the effigy of the man on the handle, wondering how much blood would be on his hands in the coming days.

CHAPTER TWELVE
ANNA

A bone-chilling scream leapt from Anna's throat as she stared at the weathered tombstone sitting across from her. Her outstretched hands convulsed as she willed the slab of rock to move. Only, nothing happened. The gravestone stood still in utter defiance of Anna's will, seemingly unaffected by her screaming. Defeated, Anna dropped her hands to her sides and hung her head in shame. Several days prior, Mammon mentioned to Anna that, since his magic flowed through her, she might be able to use it. He had started to teach her how to harness and use the demonic powers – the only problem was, she had yet to show any evidence of having such powers.

"All demons have magic, it's a given, you just need time to learn how to use it," Master Mammon had assured her.

It had been a week since Anna had learned what she had become, and every waking minute had been spent training and learning what it meant to be a demon. Surprisingly, her father's knowledge had some gaps in it. Gaps that Mammon was quick to correct. She had been bombarded with so much knowledge that it felt like her brain was going to burst. One thing Anna had learned was that a connection between a demon and its host can break if the host is no longer in the ideal emotional state for the demon to exploit. Mammon had mentioned how he had made a deal with King Elbert of Artanzia, and until recently, it had been a fruitful tether to this realm. But something had changed in Elbert. Mammon was no longer connected to the king, and the demon's strength waned by the day. The demon was desperate to find a new host, and time was slowly running out. When he came across Anna's corpse, he felt her ambition radiating from her. In an act of desperation, he pulled Anna from the grave. Resurrection was no small feat, and it nearly drained him of all his remaining power. To make matters worse, Anna did not come back as human, and as a result, couldn't be used as a host.

While Mammon had grown weaker during their training, Anna had grown stronger. She felt like her old self again; even better in some aspects. She had no urge to make a deal, and didn't feel drawn to any emotion the way Mammon did. When Anna pushed the ancient demon for more information on this, she was met with silence, or the occasional vague, one-word answer.

"Any luck?" Evelynn said as she sat down beside Anna across from the tombstone.

"No," Anna mumbled. "I'm thinking that Mammon is wrong about me."

"Doubt it," Evelynn replied. "He's stayed on this plane for centuries, leaping from one host to the next. I've yet to think of a question that he doesn't have an answer to."

"Why does he change hosts so often?"

"Being tied to a demon is a draining thing. Once a demon and a mortal are tethered, the demon drains the strength out of the mortal to keep them on this plane. If the connection isn't broken, then the mortals just... expire."

Anna winced at Evelynn's answer. The more she dove into this strange world, the less it made sense. It was like pulling at a loose thread on a wicker basket. Once you started pulling, the entire basket would disappear in time. She wished her father was still here – he'd be able to explain all this to her. Several times she thought about running back to the forest to gather the books that her father had collected over the years, but she couldn't bring herself to leave. She didn't know if she had the strength to go back and see her father's decayed corpse.

The whinny of a horse broke the silence in the graveyard. Both Evelynn and Anna rose to their feet and saw that Desmond and a handsome young man had returned atop a pair of chestnut horses. Desmond and Mammon had left two days ago to go in search of a new host for the ancient demon, leaving Matthew and Evelynn to watch over Anna. It wasn't until she saw that the handsome young man had red eyes that she realized he was actually Mammon.

"You look different," Anna said as she cautiously approached the demon.

"A fresh host will do wonders," Mammon replied boisterously, stretching his back.

"Whose life did you ruin this time?" Matthew replied callously as he stoked the fire in the middle of the graveyard.

"A farmer's son," Desmond answered. "Dreamt of being the greatest bard to ever grace the world."

"How did you give him that?" Anna asked, casting a questioning glance towards the demon.

Before he answered, Mammon flicked his wrist, conjured a rocking chair out of thin air, and sat down in it, rocking back and forth. "I gave him a magical lute that enhanced his abilities."

Showoff, Anna thought sourly to herself. Out of the corner of her eye, she saw Desmond lift a large sack off one horse. "What's that for?"

"I figured we deserve a celebration!" Mammon exclaimed. "I found a new host, and now we can finally leave this shithole of a graveyard."

The idea of leaving the graveyard was a welcome one to Anna, and her stomach growled at the prospect of a feast. She had been surviving on mouldy bread for a week and was tempted to go out and hunt for some fresh meat, but Evelynn wouldn't allow it. She learned that despite Mammon having complete control of their lives, Evelynn and Desmond seemed completely loyal to the demon. Matthew, on the other hand, was the only one who openly questioned Mammon, and would often make his contempt towards the demon known. These comments never got a rise out of Mammon though – perhaps because words didn't matter when a person was bound to you forever.

"Anna, give me a hand with the food," Desmond instructed as he waved for her to follow him out of earshot from the others.

Nodding her head, Anna followed. Despite his loyalty to the demon, she liked Desmond. If Mammon was the evil parent of the group, Desmond was the good one. He had been with the demon the longest and looked out for everyone. Matthew would often argue with Desmond, but despite Matthew's callousness, Desmond rarely failed to keep a calm demeanour.

"How goes the training?" Desmond asked as he peeled a potato with a paring knife he pulled from his boot.

"Horrible," Anna sighed as she pulled a potato of her own out of the bag. "Mammon can conjure chairs and magical instruments, but I can't even get a headstone to move."

"Give it time," Desmond responded. "These things don't happen overnight."

"How would you know?"

Desmond raised a questioning glance and handed Anna the knife in his hand. "Hit this potato in the air with the knife." Before Anna could respond, he tossed the vegetable high into the winter air. Instinctively, Anna grabbed the knife by the blade and flung it at the potato. The blade skewered the hard skin of the vegetable and it landed safely back in Desmond's hand. He pulled the knife out and resumed skinning the potato. "Did you learn to do that overnight?"

"No."

"Then don't assume you can master the art of magic overnight either. It's a skill, and skills need time to develop."

Anna rolled her eyes at the paternal cliché, though she secretly missed those kinds of remarks. Desmond reminded her of her father. Although his company was comforting, it filled her with bittersweet memories. Despite his strong paternal presence, Desmond was not her father, and she was frequently reminded that her actual father was gone; that her entire family was gone.

Eager to change the subject, and hungry for more knowledge, Anna cleared her throat. "Do you know much about magic?"

Desmond shrugged his shoulders. "I know how it works in theory, but I wasn't born with the gift to channel chaos."

Anna furrowed her brow in confusion. "Chaos?"

"Chaos is what the scholars call the source of magic. An unseen element that some can channel and harness to turn into spells. But for mortals, it comes at a heavy price."

"What do you mean?"

"When mortal beings use magic, it takes a toll on them. Casting too many spells will scramble someone's mind, and often leads them into a delirium where they can't tell what's real and what's not."

"So I have to be careful?" Anna asked, a hint of fear in her voice.

"From what Master Mammon tells me," Desmond began, "demons don't have that problem. Chaos doesn't affect them like it does mortals. I've served Master Mammon a long time, and seen him do countless magical incantations for deals, and he has yet to show any signs of insanity."

"How do you know so much?" Anna asked.

"Like I said, I've been with Master Mammon a long time. After a while, small talk loses its charm and you descend deep into philosophy and how the world works."

Anna smiled. She wasn't sure if Desmond was telling her the full story, but she was determined to put the morsels of knowledge he gave her to good use. Contemplating the disciple's words, she continued to peel potatoes with a knife of her own, helping to prepare for the feast. The last time she ate food like this was when she was the Queen of Crooks. Her stomach churned at the memory. That seemed like a lifetime ago, and she wanted to leave it all behind, but then her mind pictured Randall's face and she could feel the rage burn in her heart. She had unfinished business with the new King of Artanzia, as well as his chief advisor. Once she learned how to use her new powers, she would make them pay. She would make them all pay.

After an hour, the meal was ready. Anna looked at the array of food that sat in front of her, and salivated. Fresh vegetables, roast pheasant, and somehow Mammon had even got his hands on a pumpkin pie. Anna watched the disciples greedily dig into the food, tearing apart the pheasant like ravenous wolves tore apart a stag. Gristle, juices, and grease dripped from their chins as they gorged themselves on the savoury food. Across the table,

Anna saw Mammon had very little on his plate. In fact, the only thing on it were three carrots and the smallest slice of pie imaginable.

"Not hungry?" Anna asked as she continued filling up her plate.

Mammon smiled. "Mortal food does not sustain me. In fact, it tastes like ash. I simply took a few things on my plate out of courtesy."

Anna raised a questioning brow and looked down at her plate hesitantly. It smelt absolutely divine. She scooped up a forkful of potato and pheasant and took a bite. Immediately she recoiled from the taste. It was as if she had taken a bite of sand. She spat the food out and back onto her plate, crinkling her nose up in disgust.

Mammon let out an amused snort, but failed to say anything. Anna looked down at the delicious food in dismay. Was this what her life would be now? Not being able to enjoy food any more? *No more succulent hams, no more sweet rolls...* Anna paused, her eyes widening in horror. *No more beer?* A shiver ran down her spine as tried to shake the thought from her head. As she pushed her plate away, Desmond spoke up, interrupting her thoughts.

"Where to now?"

"There's a town nearby. Eldersburg – it's not quite a city, but it'll have everything we need provision wise," Mammon replied.

"What do we need?" Evelynn asked.

"Well, I imagine we all need a hot bath and a soft bed to sleep in for a change. And now that I have my strength back, I can find more hosts."

"Fucking hell," Matthew mumbled.

"Problem?" Mammon asked.

"Nothing."

"Good."

An awkward silence took over the group, with only sounds of the occasional person chewing breaking the silence. Anna looked at Matthew and saw that his muscles were tensed, but he refused to make eye contact with Mammon. The disciple instead stared down at his food and played with a lone bean that rolled around his plate. After an excruciatingly long time, Anna broke the silence.

"When do we leave?"

"First light," Mammon replied cheerfully. "So pack your things and get some rest."

Throwing his meagre scraps of food into the fire, Mammon left and entered the crypt that he had called his quarters ever since Anna awoke.

"Why do you fight him at every turn?" Evelynn asked once Mammon was out of earshot.

"Why do you blindly follow him?" Matthew snapped back.

"There are worse fates than serving Mammon, in fact—" Desmond began.

"Tell me what fate is worse than this!" Matthew shouted, tossing his plate clear across the graveyard. "We can never die, and are bound to be in servitude to that fucking snake. But the worst part of it is that we have to help him ruin other people's lives!"

"Matthew, just calm down—"

"Fuck you, Desmond! What would your wife and daughter think of you if they could see you now? Being a mindless dog to—"

Before Matthew could finish his sentence, Desmond's fist struck the disciple in the jaw, knocking him to the ground. Quickly Desmond climbed on top of him and started strangling the boy. Anna was in shock at how quickly Desmond transformed. No longer was he the calm, collected, paternal figure that she knew. The animosity that had control over him scared her. The way his lips curled when he snarled, the way his nostrils flared... it was like he was an entirely different person.

"Stop!" Evelynn shouted. "Let him go!" When Desmond did not listen, she rose to her feet and kicked him in the throat. Both men gasped for air on the ground. Evelynn looked at Anna and rolled her eyes. "Fucking children."

Anna locked eyes with Matthew. They were bloodshot, with tears in the corners. She gave him a look of concern, which he answered with a slight nod of the head before he gently massaged his throat. Anna wasn't sure what would've happened if Evelynn hadn't intervened. They couldn't actually kill each other – would Matthew just suffocate for as long as Desmond strangled him? Anna shook the disturbing thought out of her head and rose to her feet. She gave Desmond a sour look and walked off to go to bed. The sooner this night was behind her, the better.

CHAPTER THIRTEEN
RANDALL

The cold, frost-covered railing of the war room's balcony stung the king's hands as he clenched the frozen marble. He looked out beyond the walls and saw that Elbert's army had encircled them in the night, despite his having men posted on watch. The rage inside him warmed his chest as he glared at the crippled king's army. He looked back inside the war room and saw that all of his councillors' chairs were empty. They were late. Randall continued to brood in silence for several moments before the doors swung open and the councillors shuffled into the icy room.

"You're late," the king said with an annoyed tone.

"Apologies, Your Majesty, some of us aren't used to being awake at this hour," Virgil Walker said plainly as he wiped the crust out of his eyes.

"We have been fucking surrounded!" Randall shouted, tossing a handful of ice and snow off the balcony. "And nobody sounded the alarm, nobody notified me. Elbert could've stormed the city last night, and we'd be none the wiser!"

"Whoever was in charge of the watch needs to be flogged," Tig added. There was a murmur of agreement amongst the other councillors.

"No!" Randall blurted out. "I will not treat my subjects like a tyrant. They will not meet the whip for a mistake."

"Your Majesty," Virgil Walker interjected, "they are soldiers now. And whether you like it or not, soldiers need discipline. And part of that means punishment for disobedience."

"Randall," Tig added. "He's right. We—"

"Tell me, how are we any better than that crippled bastard outside our walls if we flog our own people? Putting them to the whip will only breed resentment, and we need unity more than ever."

"Perhaps flogging is too severe," Cassius conceded. "Maybe we impose a less *extreme* punishment for the offenders. Should the people who are responsible for the watch not suffer any consequences for their incompetence?"

Silence hung in the air. Randall chewed Cassius' words as he stared at all of his councillors. As much as he hated it, they were right. If they were going to survive this siege, discipline was needed. The people were soldiers now, and they had to act like it. "Very well, have the guilty parties tossed into the dungeon for a few days. But this does not solve the problem that we are surrounded by Elbert's army."

"Not all is lost, Your Majesty," Madame Dupont said. "We still have the harbour, and trade will continue to—"

"About that," Corbin Strongarm interrupted. "It appears Elbert has sent a portion of his forces back to his ships. And those ships currently surround the harbour, blocking any supplies coming in."

"Fuck me," Randall growled under his breath.

Cassius cleared his throat. "Your Majesty, if I may, there is still a glimmer of hope in this situation."

"And what, pray tell, is that?"

The eunuch pulled a letter from his robe pocket. He elegantly unfurled the piece of parchment and set it on the table. "This is a letter from King Kalvin from Keten. He said he will talk with you about an alliance."

"You want to encircle Elbert with the Ketenish army?" Randall said, understanding where the eunuch was guiding the conversation.

"Elbert cannot fight a war on two fronts. If Keten is behind him, and we are in front of him, we have a chance to eradicate the old regime for good."

A smile crept along the king's face. "Very good, send a letter back asking for Kalvin's terms for the alliance and—"

"That's the thing, Your Majesty. King Kalvin insists on having this conversation face to face."

Randall rolled his eyes. "Does he not know that I am fucking surrounded? How in the hells am I supposed to meet him face to face?"

"Perhaps I have a solution," Madame Dupont interrupted. "There is a gentleman that visits my brothel occasionally. He is a bit of a weird fellow, but if what he says is true, he may be able to help."

"How so?" Randall asked, not sure how some rich whore-monger was going to be the answer to his problems.

"He claims to be the Royal Mage, and that he has a workshop, *below* the dungeons."

"Weird how?" Cassius asked.

"Well, he often pays for multiple women in a single session, but as far as I can tell, he doesn't touch them, but instead pays to teach them nonsense."

"Nonsense?" Walker asked.

"Mhmm," Dupont nodded. "They leave the rooms more confused than when they went in."

Randall nodded his head graciously. "Thank you, Madame Dupont. Let's go see if this mage can be of any use to us." The king rose from his chair and exited the war room, with Cassius following close behind.

"Coming to see this mage too?"

"Of course, Your Majesty."

Out of the corner of his eye, Randall could see a sly smile spreading across the eunuch's lips. "What?"

"I told you having Madame Dupont on your council would be beneficial."

Randall swallowed a smile, not wanting to give Cassius the satisfaction of knowing that he knew better than the king, once again. "That remains to be seen."

"Do you know what you are going to say to King Kalvin?"

"No. What can you tell me about him?" Randall asked, as they reached the stairwell and descended into the bowels of the castle towards the dungeons.

"If rumours are to be believed, Kalvin is a cunning man. He is opportunistic and thrives on exploiting others' weaknesses, both in battle and in trade. I fear that your proposal of marriage may not be enough to sway him. I suggest you offer him something he is scarce in to sweeten the deal."

"Like what?"

"Keten has plenty of mountains, but few woodlands. I suggest you offer him some of our abundance in lumber. But keep that in your back pocket. Perhaps he is feeling generous today."

Randall nodded his head and pushed through the door to the dungeons. As he had imagined, the dungeons stunk something foul. Somehow, the king kept the contents of his stomach inside his body as he marched past the cells. At the end of the corridor to the dungeons, there was a small wooden door that looked like it was meant for someone half Randall's height. He pulled the door open, crouched down, and entered a miniature spiral staircase that descended further into the depths of the castle. At the end of the staircase was a pale orange light. Randall followed the light until he entered a large room that was full of vials, potions, cauldrons, and books.

"Greetings!" a scratchy ancient voice called out from behind one of the wooden workbenches. Randall looked and saw a halfling appear. His white beard looked like it had been gnawed on and his spectacles, with their mismatched, coloured lenses, obscured his eyes. The halfling extended his hand. "What brings you to my workshop?"

"Are you the royal mage?" Randall asked, uneasiness colouring his voice.

"Indeed I am!" the halfling chirped, puffing his chest. "I suppose you're the new king, are you? Yes, yes, I see it now... that fancy little circlet on your head."

"It's a crown," Randall corrected.

"Crown, circlet, hat, hood, all are worn where hair has stood! Fancy metal, simple thread, still just coverings for your head!" the mage sang, clapping his hands along with the beat. "What can I help you with, Your Majesty? I assume you have business with me, as you kings never visit to ask how I am doing."

Wanting to prove that he was a different king, Randall pushed the urgency of his mission aside and collected his resolve as he prepared to indulge in small talk. "What is your name?"

"Velus Pepperfort!" the mage answered brightly. "What about you? I heard we had a new king, but I am too busy to leave my workshop." The halfling paused suddenly as his hand began to move in an uncontrollable pattern. The mage's eyes fixed on the hand, as if he was casting a trance on himself.

Finally, after several seconds, the hand came to a rest, and the mage focused his attention back on his visitors. "Hmm?"

"This is His Royal Majesty, Randall the First," Cassius answered. "I am his dutiful advisor, Cassius."

"A pleasure," Velus responded. "But come here, I must show you my latest work. It will revolutionize society!"

"What is wrong with him?" Randall asked Cassius quietly.

"It's the magic. If you cast too many spells in your life, you go insane. Or so they say," the eunuch responded.

"This was made at King David's behest," Velus said as he held up a large vial full of green liquid. "The cure for syphilis!"

Randall and Cassius gave each other a wary glance. Cassius cleared his throat. "Lord Velus, we—"

"Now, now," Velus responded, "I am no lord. I hold no lands and have no titles."

"A thousand apologies, Master Velus."

"Nor am I a master. 'Master' is used so freely nowadays; I don't want to misconstrue my skill with some hapless idiot that can brew a few potions."

"Then what should we call you?" Cassius growled.

"Hmm, a brilliant question. I suppose Genius would be an apt title. No, no, too self-important. Perhaps Grandmaster? Yes, yes! I like it. Call me Grandmaster Velus."

"Grandmaster Velus, we are on important business. We were told that you would have a way of communicating with King Kalvin of Keten. Is this possible?"

"Why, of course!" Velus exclaimed. "But I haven't used the megascope in years. Have a seat, have a seat. I'll need some time to prepare." Without waiting for his guests to find a place to sit, Velus lifted his arms straight into the air and sprinted behind the workbenches and stacks of paper, disappearing from sight.

Randall smiled, gave Cassius a shrug, and looked for a place to sit down, but every chair was covered in papers or alchemical materials. Not wanting to disturb the mage's work, he sat on the stone floor and waited.

After close to an hour, there was a sudden bang from across the room and a bright, pale blue light illuminated the mage's workshop. Randall slowly got to his feet and saw three iridescent orbs floating around a pedestal in a circle. The pedestal was made almost entirely of brass, with a small crystal placed at the top of it. Three lines of light connected the orbs to the crystal on the pedestal and a faint humming sound soon filled the air. Cautiously, Randall approached Velus.

"How does it work?"

"I have to send a preliminary signal to Keten to let them know I want to talk to them. Then if their mage is nearby, he will send a signal back and establish a secure connection."

Randall wasn't sure what Velus meant, but he figured that the basics of magic were well beyond his knowledge. Truth be told, this was the first real demonstration of magical powers he had ever witnessed. He had seen men in the street pull rabbits out of hats, or a coin out of someone's ear, but always assumed that was more sleight of hand rather than magic. This, however, was indisputable magic. There was a certain vibration in the air that made the hair on the back of his neck stand on end and his stomach churn.

Velus grabbed a nearby stool, climbed on it, and fiddled with the crystal on top of the pedestal. He turned it every which way until the orbs changed from a pale blue to a blinding shade of orange. Then he ran over to his desk, scribbled something on a parchment, and tossed it into one orb. The paper immediately turned into smoke upon touching the ball of light.

"Now what?" Cassius asked.

"We wait," Velus wheezed.

"You're bleeding," Randall said, pointing to Velus' lip.

The mage wiped a finger underneath his nose and saw that blood was dripping out of his nostrils. "Ah, I am. Apologies, casting magic is quite strenuous, and when you have done it for as long as I have, it takes a toll on your body."

They waited several moments in silence before the rotating orbs suddenly stopped and changed colour to a dull green. Right before Randall was about to ask what was happening, the orbs collided with one another, and a large window of light appeared before them. Standing on the other side of the window was a middle-aged man, wearing elegant clothes and an ostentatious crown. He had curly hair and a well-trimmed beard. A woman stood beside him. She wore dark robes and her head was shaved bald. She, too, had blood coming out of her nose.

"Introducing His Royal Majesty, King Kalvin of Keten!" the woman exclaimed, before she bowed and backed out of sight.

"Greetings, King Kalvin, we are honoured by your presence," Cassius began. "Allow me to introduce His Royal Majesty Randall the First, rightful king of Artanzia!"

Kalvin smiled politely before grabbing a cup of wine from the small end table beside him. "I trust my letter was received?" he asked in an icy voice.

"Indeed," Randall responded. "I wish to know your ter ms."Kalvin's smile widened. "My spies tell me that Elbert is knocking on your door. Soon he will either storm the city, or he will surround it. Making me your only hope."

Randall glared at the man with contempt. He knew it would be like this. Kalvin was a noble, just like Elbert. They freely spewed words like the pompous windbags that they were, but when the time came for action, they hesitated. Unless it could directly benefit them.

"Our situation is dire," Randall admitted, "but the people of Artanzia have rallied behind me as their king. I'm confident that my forces could defeat Elbert's but with you by my side, we will eliminate unnecessary bloodshed."

"You talk well, boy," Kalvin chuckled. "But why would I help you? Why should I not allow you two Artanzian dogs to fight one another, and then swoop and take out the battle-weary survivors?"

Randall chewed on his rage as he studied the king. He knew this was a bad idea. Nobles were full of tricks and deceit. They didn't give a fuck about the people they crushed. They just wanted to expand their kingdom and hoard their gold. "Because you would not have sent the letter stating that you wanted to talk about an alliance if you did not mean it."

"Have you ever considered that I just wanted to meet the boy who was able to conquer a cripple?"

Randall clenched his fists together. The knuckles in his hands cracked from the pressure. A bead of sweat slowly trickled down his back. Out of the corner of his eye, he saw Cassius take a step forward, but he quickly waved him aside. "I am young yes, but I overtook a city to become king. Tell me, what great feat did you achieve to wear that crown on your head?" Kalvin's smile disappeared in an instant. Randall struggled to keep his own behind his lips when he saw the Ketenish king's look of annoyance. "See, I have a network of spies of my own, King Kalvin, and they tell me that Drussdell, your neighbour, is preparing for war," Randall lied. "You and I both know that they would be fools to march south against The Valerian

Empire, so that means they will march north, into Keten. You cannot afford to fight a war on two fronts. If you wait for Elbert and I to kill each other, and send men into my kingdom, you will leave your own kingdom defenceless. If you come to my aid and we defeat Elbert before the Drussdellian invasion, then you will not only receive a powerful ally, but you will also receive support against Drussdell."

A silence sat between the two kings as they studied one another carefully. Finally, Kalvin's smile reappeared, and he clapped his hands. "You're smarter than you look, boy."

"In exchange for your support against Elbert, not only do I swear to come to your aid when Drussdell invades, but I am also prepared to give you a percentage of our lumber yield, a commodity that you sorely need."

"Hmm," Kalvin responded as he took a sip from his wineglass. "Your letter said that you were also asking for my daughter's hand in marriage. Is that off the table now?"

Randall shot Cassius a furious glance, but held his tongue from scolding the eunuch in front of the foreign ruler. That would come later. "Many of my court believe that I need a wife to legitimize my rule. But a king needs a kingdom, not a queen."

A chuckle escaped Kalvin's lips. "Forgive me for being blunt, but you have no kingdom, you have a city. A city that is likely to be besieged any day now."

Randall took a sharp inhale of breath and held it before for a few seconds before slowly releasing it. His heart was beating wildly, both out of anger, and fear. He could feel his body weight shift to the balls of his feet as he waited in anticipation for Kalvin's next words.

"But, perhaps, with my help, you can secure the rest of Artanzia."

Randall felt his shoulders sink out of relief. "So, we have an accord?"

"Indeed," Kalvin responded. "Keten will come to your aid, and together we will kill that cripple and extinguish that cursed bloodline once and for all."

Randall nodded his head, and in an instant the window of light disappeared and the workshop was once again illuminated by torchlight. Turning his head to the halfling mage, Randall smiled. "Thank you, Grandmaster Velus. I would like to offer you a position on my council of advisors. Your services would be appreciated."

"Thank you, Your Majesty. I will gladly lend you my knowledge when required."

With a polite bow, Randall and Cassius left the mage's workshop and began the long ascent back to the throne room. Their walk was filled with an awkward silence. He knew Cassius was choosing his words carefully, and he wanted to let the eunuch stew in the silence for as long as was bearable.

"You spoke well in there," Cassius began.

"Thank you," Randall replied.

"How did you know about Drussdell's plans to invade?"

"I didn't; it was just an educated guess. Why else would he agree to speak? If he truly did see our weakness as an opportunity, he would've dispatched his forces without a response."

"A wise conclusion, Your Majesty."

"I am confused, though," Randall said, trying to mask the anger that filled his body. "On why my chief advisor would send out a marriage proposal without my knowledge."

Cassius stopped. The two of them locked eyes with one another. Surprisingly, Cassius' face did not have an expression of fear or submissiveness on it, but instead frustration. "We have been over this, Randall," the eunuch began. "You need a wife. Not only to legitimize your rule, but to produce an heir and secure your legacy. It is what kings do."

"Need I remind you that I am your king!?" Randall shouted. "I will marry who I please! Now that we have Kalvin's support, I no longer need to whore myself out to those fucking nobles!" The king took several seconds to calm himself. He wanted his next words to not be misunderstood in any way. "Never go behind my back like that again. Am I understood?"

"Yes, Your Majesty," Cassius said through gritted teeth.

"Good, now leave me be. I have a siege to plan."

CHAPTER FOURTEEN
CONNIR

Vomit surged out of his mouth. He could feel the acrid bile tear up his throat with each heave. The events immediately following the battle of the bards was one big blur for Connir. From what he could remember, both Ragnar and Estrid hugged him, and Jarl Otar had declared him the winner. But other than that, he could remember nothing. He was lost in a haze of guilt, shame, and disgust.

Although he could walk away with his life, he wasn't sure if he was better for it. He had just killed a man, and not only that, but a man he had known since he was a boy. To make things worse, it was not a clean death. In fact, having your skull bashed in while being strangled had to be one of the most excruciating ways to go, in Connir's eyes. The thing that made Connir feel the worst was right after he realized he had killed Linny the Loon. The surge of adrenaline, the relief, that feeling of achievement, it felt good. That's what made Connir sick to his stomach. Not only had he snuffed out a human life, but for a split second, he had also enjoyed it.

"Connir!" Ragnar called out. "I've been looking everywhere for you!"

Connir lifted his head and wiped the puke from his lips. "Needed some air."

Ragnar placed a hand on the skald's shoulder. "You did well today, your father would be proud of you."

Connir's stomach churned at the comment. His father's approval and acceptance were all that he ever wanted in his life. The irony that his dad would be proud of him now, when he was most disgusted in himself, was not lost on Connir.

"I think I'm going to see Bane," Connir mumbled before shrugging Ragnar's hand off his shoulder.

"I've a favour to ask," Ragnar began. "I want you to join me when I meet with Arnvald tomorrow."

"The shipwright?"

"Yes, he says he has something to show me before we embark on the voyage and I want you to see it with me."

Connir nodded his head and walked towards the kennels without another word. He wasn't sure how he was going to overcome the mountain of grief that was sitting in his stomach and forgive himself. As he walked, he felt heavier, as if he was carrying Linny's corpse on his shoulders. He hoped that a visit to his oldest friend would make him feel better, but he had his doubts.

Once inside the kennels, Connir collapsed. The weight of his guilt forced him to his knees. Tears formed in his eyes, and he looked at his murderous hands. They shook uncontrollably. He wanted to grab an axe and chop them off at the wrist, but he wasn't sure if he would ever have the stomach to pick up a weapon again.

"I see you survived," a voice called out from a cell.

Connir lifted his head and saw Grimm White-Eyes' face pressed against the bars. A flicker of petulant anger ran through him, and before he could think better of it, he spoke his mind. "The axe was no use."

"Helps if you hold on to it," Grimm replied. Connir raised a questioning brow, but Grimm replied with a shrug of the shoulders, "I hear things."

Connir swallowed his misplaced anger and hoped that the legendary warrior would have more guidance for him. "How do you do it? How do you live with yourself after you've killed someone?"

There was a long pause before Grimm answered. The traitor stroked his wild beard and picked some fleas out of his mangy head of hair. Finally, after a sufficient time to think about the question, Grimm answered, "The first ones are always the hardest. You remember every detail, see their faces when you close your eyes at night, and hear their screams in your head. But each kill gets easier. Once you've killed five or so men, they all start to fade and blend together."

A shiver ran up Connir's spine. The way Grimm spoke about death with such familiarity unnerved him. The traitor's blunt honesty only made the pit in his stomach only grow. This was not the answer that Connir wanted. Slumping against the stone wall across from Grimm's cell, Connir slid down it until his backside touched the hay, which was frozen to the cobblestones. "Do you still remember your first?"

Grimm nodded his head. "Mhmm," he said. "When Uthredd and myself were just boys, we were playing together when an older boy pushed the future High King. Infuriated, I grabbed a piece of lumber from beside me and cracked the boy across the head with it. Until that point, I always thought death would be loud, like there would be a noise associated with it. But the only thing I heard was the air rushing out of his lungs. He was dead before he hit the ground."

"I'm sorry," Connir said after a brief pause. He wasn't sure what else to say. Killing another man was bad enough, but when you were a boy... he could only imagine. "You know you saved my father's life once?"

"Who?"

"Svain Whitefist."

"Ha!" Grimm chuckled. "You're that whoreson's boy? If I had known that, I'd've let you die."

"Why's that?" Connir asked angrily.

"Your father was a horrible soldier. Sure, he could kill, but he couldn't follow orders. The only reason that I saved him on that battlefield was because it was on my way to kill the other clan's jarl."

Connir was at a loss for words. His father had told him the story of the mighty Grimm White-Eyes saving his life countless times. In the story, Grimm was granted with the same reverence as the gods. Svain always said he never had the chance to repay his debt, but was eternally grateful for what the barbarian had done that day.

"Tell me, where's your father now?" Grimm asked.

"Dead," Connir answered.

"Hmm. Tell me, are you as good a skald as they say you are?"

"Who's they?"

"Uthredd told me a few things that night you interrupted our talk. He said that you were a gifted skald, whose voice was a gift from the gods."

"I like to think I'm the best," Connir said, trying to hide his pride as best he could.

"Good," Grimm said as he backed away from the cell door. "I want the story of my last voyage to be a good one."

Sensing that the conversation had ended, Connir rose to his feet and went deeper into the kennels till he saw Bane, whose tail was wagging wildly as his master approached. Connir unlocked the door and entered the kennel with his faithful war hound. He laid himself down, allowing Bane to snuggle up next to him, and fell asleep while stroking the dog's head.

"Wake up, you layabout!" Ragnar shouted as he kicked Connir in the foot to stir him from his deep sleep.

The skald groggily rubbed the crust out of his eyes, stretched his back, and pushed Bane off his lap as he rose to his feet. Sleeping in the kennels had been a poor decision, as his body was now sore and screamed in pain as he willed his muscles to move. "What time is it?"

"Just after sunrise," Ragnar responded. "We still have to meet Arnvald and embark today."

"Today?" Connir gasped, suddenly feeling awake. "But the rivers are still frozen – how are we supposed to get to the sea?"

"Word has it Uthredd ordered Arnvald to build a sled to carry our ship, pulled by a team of oxen until we reach the coast."

Connir let out a sigh and patted Bane on the head. "Time is of the essence, then?"

"Mhmm," Ragnar grunted. "Now, let's get moving, I want to see what this madman has planned for us."

As they left the kennels and headed towards the shipwright's workshop, Connir couldn't help but wonder what he was about to see. He had never met Arnvald, but he was quite famous on the Isles. He was said to be as inventive as a dwarf, but as mad as a mage. And if what Ragnar said was true, that he had constructed a sled to pull an Islander longship across the frozen rivers, then it appeared the stories were more than just stories.

Just on the outskirts of Skotheim, along the now frozen riverbank, sat Arnvald's house. It was nothing glamorous, just a simple hut with a thatched roof, but the man's workshop was another matter entirely. A wooden structure that appeared to be erected by giants stood on the riverbank, it had a tall, helmed roof that was constructed entirely of wood. The workshop was long enough to house two longships and had plenty of space to store felled trees out of the elements. As the two men approached the workshop, they noticed bits of metal along the ground.

"Is he a blacksmith now as well?" Connir asked, picking up a sizeable chunk of discarded steel.

"Heimer's craftsmanship flows through Arnvald's veins; it would not surprise me if the madman knew how to work metal as well."

"Ragnar!" Arnvald shouted from atop a longship that was on a large wooden sled already on the river. "You came!"

"Of course I did, Arnvald. Now, what is it you have to show me?"

Climbing down from the sleigh, Arnvald pointed to the ship with immeasurable pride. "This just might be my finest ship. Fit for the Gods themselves!"

"Is that metal on the keel?" Connir asked.

"Why, yes, it is, Connir Svainsson!" Arnvald shouted.

"You know me?"

"Of course! Word has already spread about the battle of the bards, and who won the honour to compose the ballad of Grimm White-Eyes' last voyage."

Connir's stomach churned at the mention of the brawl. He could still feel the surge of adrenaline that forced him to bash Linny's brains in. It took all of his willpower to not lose the contents of his stomach again. Thankfully, Ragnar changed the subject before Arnvald could get another word in about the battle.

"Won't the metal weigh us down? We'll sink!"

"Not this metal," Arnvald answered cheerfully. "This is dwarven metal, looted last raiding season. Very difficult to work with, but once you learn its secrets, a whole new world of possibilities opens up!"

"How so?"

"The metal is as light as a feather, yet when I attack it with an axe or sword, it doesn't make a dent."

Ragnar let out a sigh. "It's like pulling teeth," he whispered to Connir. "Why do we need a metal-plated keel on our ship?"

Arnvald climbed up on the sled and pricked his finger against the pointed edge of the metal keel. He held up his finger to show a small drop of blood forming on the tip. "As sharp as your sword! Usually, we raid once the rivers thaw, but it is still the dead of winter. With this metal, you should be able to slice through the mainland's frozen river with ease."

Ragnar let out a laugh. "I'll never understand how these thoughts come into your head, Arnvald. You truly are blessed by Heimer himself."

"That is why I carved him on the prow. So he can see your deeds and join you on this remarkable voyage!"

"Thank you," Ragnar bowed. "Do you need a hand hooking up the oxen?"

"No, no!" Arnvald shouted. "It shan't take me long. Once I get to Skotheim, the priests will bless the ship, and you will be on your way!"

"We'll see you at the ceremony," Ragnar replied as he grabbed Connir's elbow and led him away from the shipwright's workshop.

On the journey back to Skotheim, Connir realized he hadn't asked who else was joining them on the voyage. He hoped Estrid would be one of the warriors going. Some time alone with her on a ship might be just what he needed to strengthen their bond.

"Ragnar," Connir started, his heart about to leap into his chest, "who did Jarl Otar select to accompany us on the voyage?"

A slight smile appeared on the captain's lips. "He kept it within clan, with only a few outsiders."

"Outsiders?"

"Mhmm. There are a few from Bearn's clan, that seek to avenge their jarl's death. Then there is a shieldmaiden from Clan Geirsson. The last outsider is a berserker from the Beastfolk of the northern reaches of the Isles."

"A Beastfolk berserker?" Connir asked in disbelief. He had met no one from the aptly named Beastfolk clan, but they were legendary on the Isles. Claiming to have descended directly from the gods themselves, they stayed in the far reaches of the Isles, feasting on wild berries and mushrooms that were said to turn you into an animal when ingested in battle. He was never sure how Uthredd had brought the Beastfolk under his banner, as they had always valued their independence, and during past conflicts, had chosen the path of neutrality. "Have you met him?"

Ragnar shook his head. "I saw him in the longhouse, but I've yet to speak with him. I must admit, I'm excited to see him use the mushrooms on the raid."

Connir nodded his head. He secretly hoped that he would have the chance to try some of the magical food while on the voyage. Growing up, the fantastical tales of the Beastfolk always astounded him, and now, not only to meet one, but to be raiding together? It was almost too good to be true. "What about Estrid?"

Ragnar's smile quickly disappeared, and, after a slight pause, he shook his head. "Jarl Otar chose one of Bearn's men over her. Said that 'she was essential for protecting the clan back on the Isles'."

Connir's heart sank. It seemed that every chance he had to grow close with Estrid was dashed away by forces beyond his control. He cast his eyes down to his feet and let out a sigh, unable to hide his disappointment. Suddenly, he felt a hand on his shoulder.

"She'll wait for you, Connir," Ragnar said in a comforting voice. "Good things come to those who are patient."

"How do you know?"

"I've been around a few winters, Connir Svainsson. Despite what you may think of me, I do in fact know a few things."

Connir involuntarily smiled. "Thanks, Ragnar."

"Now, come on, let's get ready for our voyage!"

The entirety of Skotheim had gathered on the frozen river to see the group of warriors set off on their unprecedented journey. The priests were aboard the ship and had just finished sacrificing a goat, to appease the gods and give Ragnar and his crew safe passage to the mainland. Then came High King Uthredd's personal housecarls, who were escorting a chained Grimm White-Eyes to the ship. Jeers erupted from the crowd of onlookers, and a few even dared to throw rocks at the traitor as he struggled to board the ship. Once aboard, the housecarls chained him to the mast and took their leave. Standing atop the sled, High King Uthredd raised a silencing hand, preparing to address his subjects.

"For the first time in history," he began, "we set forth to raid new lands. Lands that have previously been inaccessible. But with the newfound alliance with King Elbert of Artanzia, we will bring back riches to the Isles!" The crowd cheered wildly before Uthredd raised another silencing hand. "The priests have assured me that the Gods give their blessing to this voyage." The king waved his hand, and Ragnar and his crew boarded the ship. "Captain Ragnar, I wish you luck on your journey. May Heimer watch over you." After receiving a curt bow from Ragnar, High King Uthredd took his leave.

Connir was readying his things and tying his shield to the side of the ship when he felt a soft hand touch his. He looked up from what he was doing and saw Estrid staring back at him.

"It saddens me to not be going with you," Estrid admitted. "but I cannot wait to hear of your deeds when you return. Plus, you'll have a new ballad for me, right?" She winked at Connir as she let go of his hands.

"It'll be the greatest song you've ever heard," Connir replied, smiling ear to ear. With that, the two took their leave from each other. After the rest of the crew said their farewells, Ragnar cracked the whip and a team of slaves helped the oxen pull the sled down the frozen river.

The cheers of the crowd faded as they journeyed further. Connir stood on the prow and basked in their adoration until he could no longer hear their voices. Once it was silent, he turned his head forward and closed his eyes, as he felt a gentle breeze blow through his hair.

Ragnar stood at the head of the ship and faced his crew. "Let us go kill some mainlanders!" The crew erupted in cheers, as they were all eager to carve their names into legend.

CHAPTER FIFTEEN
ELBERT

The fifth day of the siege began exactly the same as the first four. The sun rose in the east, its lights reflecting off the snow-covered hills. The wind was mild, the sun was shining, and the temperatures were surprisingly warm for an Artanzian winter. The weather had been on their side since they surrounded the city.

Elbert let out a sigh and lay in his bed for a few more minutes trying to recapture the sweet sensation of sleep. Just as he felt his eyes rolling into the back of his head, he heard the unmistakable clank of plate armour outside his tent. There was a long pause before a voice spoke through the thick canvas.

"Your Majesty?"

"Yes," Elbert groaned, refusing to open his eyes.

"The lords have convened for the morning briefing."

Annoyed, Elbert slammed his fists into the bedding. He wasn't sure why they had to have morning briefings when nothing happened. Truth be told, a siege was rather boring when you weren't the one trapped inside a city's walls. After a moment's delay, the king reluctantly instructed the guardsman to enter.

Callum was probably only a few years younger than the king himself. He had wavy blond hair and a clean-shaven face with a strong jawline. Elbert had learned to tolerate the young guard ever since he took over caring for the crippled king after

Thames' death. Although Elbert preferred the soft hands of servant girls dressing and bathing him, he had learned to endure the rough hands of guardsmen during his time in Tjørholm. Despite being tasked with less than glamorous jobs, Callum was always eager to serve his king.

"Are you ready for the meeting, Your Majesty?" Callum asked as he stood at attention at the entryway of the king's tent.

"Best get on with it," Elbert sighed as he stretched his upper back.

Dutifully, Callum readied the crippled king for his day. Truthfully, Elbert had found this experience much more enjoyable when it was done by Thames. He had known Rupert ever since he was a boy and had considered him a close friend; having a friend help you was much less awkward than having a stranger see you completely exposed. Especially because a king should never be seen as vulnerable. As the guardsman combed his hair, Elbert's eyes remained locked on the steel chest that Thames' head was confined to. Knowing that his friend was nearby helped stem the anxiety he endured every morning.

"How's morale in the camp?" Elbert asked, hoping to break the awkward silence that had become a morning routine.

There was a slight hesitation before Callum answered. "The men are eager to serve you, Your Majesty."

"So, they're bored," Elbert snorted.

"I... uh..." Callum stammered.

"No need to make excuses for them, Callum. Like them, I grow tired of sitting here and twiddling my thumbs, waiting for something to happen, but this is a siege of attrition. If I can retake my city without spilling a single drop of loyal Artanzian blood, then I will do so."

"A wise and gracious decision, Your Majesty."

Elbert rolled his eyes. He missed the loyal but honest words of Rupert. This boy would say and agree with anything that might get him promoted, whereas Thames would tell the king the way things were. He was not afraid to give Elbert bad news, even in the direst of times.

Once the king looked dignified, he lazily wheeled himself out of his tent and into the encampment. A retinue of royal guardsmen stood at attention and silently followed him as he continued to roll past the tents of soldiers. As he traversed through the camp, Elbert noticed just how much boredom had sunk its claws into the Artanzian ranks. Men were half dressed or unarmed, posts were abandoned, and on several occasions, he saw soldiers unconscious outside their tents. The king furrowed his brow as he rolled by. *Maybe there was something to address in the morning meeting.*

At the outskirts of the encampment sat a large tent, inside which was a table holding a map of the city. All of Elbert's lords had gathered around the table and were standing at attention once he passed through the canvas threshold.

"Good morning, Your Majesty," Lord Grelin greeted him. "I trust you slept well?"

"I did, Lord Grelin," Elbert replied. "However, my mood was quickly soured when I saw my army is in complete and utter disarray. Men are not at their posts and some are not wearing armour or carrying weapons with them. What if the enemy attacked?"

"Sire," Lord Penerack began, "it is highly unlikely that the usurper would launch an assault on us and—"

"This is supposed to be an army!" Elbert shouted. "This is not a ragtag band of peasant militia. I expect my men to act like soldiers! If that is too much for them to handle, then flog them. A few days of rest does not justify a total breakdown of decorum. Am I clear?"

"Yes, Your Majesty," the lords said in unison.

"Very well, what news do you have for me?"

"There have been murmurs within the camp, Your Majesty," Lord Penerack began.

"What kind of murmurs?"

"The kind that soldiers have after not being paid," Lord Grelin interrupted.

Elbert let out a sigh. "How are we supposed to pay them any more? All of our gold is inside the fucking city! We only brought enough for our expedition."

"If the soldiers are not being paid, mass desertion could be a real possibility," Lord Penerack explained.

"Or mutiny," Lord Grelin whispered.

Elbert massaged his temples. He could feel a pounding in his forehead. "What are our options, then?"

"We can requisition some gold from nearby towns and villages. But it won't go over well," Lord Penerack suggested.

"Instruct the commoners that if they donate their gold now, they will be repaid triple that amount through a monthly stipend once we retake the city. Have we sent a requisition force for food and other supplies already?"

Lord Grelin cleared his throat. "We sent a small contingency of our forces to gather food from the nearby villages, as you instructed, but the locals..."

"The locals?"

"The locals claim that they have no food to give. They say they already paid their dues after the harvest, and if you take what little they have now, they'll not make it to spring."

Elbert winced at the words. He gripped the arms of his chair. Even though Randall had only captured a city, it seemed like his whole kingdom was turning against him. "The food we brought from the Isles dwindles by the day. *We* are not supposed to be the ones starving in this siege," Elbert growled, locking eyes with his lords.

"Your Majesty, if I may," Lord Penerack cut in. "Why don't we take the food by force? We are well within our rights to requisition the grain from them. Make an example out of these people to the other villages. If they will not abide by the law, then they must be prepared to meet the swift strike of justice."

Elbert shook his head. "No. I will not order my men to bully my subjects into submission."

"I'm afraid it's our only option," Lord Penerack replied.

"If I send a group of soldiers to steal from my subjects, I am exactly what that boy says I am. A monster. That may be the easiest option, Lord Penerack, but I refuse to sully my name as king for convenience's sake."

"Then what do you suggest we do?" Lord Grelin asked.

Elbert thought about it for a moment. He had made impossible deals in the past; he remembered how easily he and High King Uthredd came to an agreement back on the Isles. Perhaps he could do it again? Pull off the impossible? "I will go with a small escort of guards to the town and speak to them man to man."

A stunned silence fell over the group of lords. "Your Majesty, you can't be serious?" Lord Penerack blurted out.

"And why can't I?"

"Because you just complained about men abandoning their posts," Lord Grelin interjected. "Now you suggest you do the same?"

Elbert felt the bile rush up his throat at Lord Grelin's words. His fingers curled around the metal armrests of his throne and the burning sensation of rage filled his chest. "I am not abandoning my post," the king growled through gritted teeth. "I am going on a kingly mission to make sure that we do not starve as we wait for our enemy to submit. If you accuse me of abandoning my duties again, Lord Grelin, I will cut out your tongue and feed it to the dogs, am I understood?"

Lord Grelin nodded his head.

"What if you send one of us instead?" Lord Penerack suggested. "The men will surely lose morale when they see their king leave. I believe an envoy is the best solution if you insist on reasoning with the commoners."

Once again, Elbert dismissed the idea with a shake of the head. "No, it has to be me. They will be more understanding when they hear the words come from my mouth. As for the men's morale, do not worry. I shan't be gone long. Until my return, you have command of the army, Lord Penerack."

The lords bowed their heads in understanding, and Elbert rolled out of the tent. He would've felt more comfortable leaving the army under Lord Grelin's control, but after his blatant disrespect, Elbert would sooner die than reward that kind of open defiance. Outside the tent, Callum was waiting.

"What are your orders, Your Majesty?"

"Gather five of the finest swordsmen you can find. We are going on a little adventure."

"We?" Callum asked in disbelief.

"Of course, I need someone to tend me while I am away."

In a few hours, a crowd of soldiers had gathered around the wagon, as they heard rumours of their king's sudden departure. Sensing his men's confusion, Elbert spun his chair around to face his men, his chin lifted high in the air.

"Gentlemen," Elbert began. "It has come to my attention that our food supplies are dwindling. But fear not, for my guardsmen and I are going to the local villages to requisition their food. In three days' time, we will be back with enough food to sustain us for the winter!"

There was a small chorus of cheering but Elbert assumed it was born out of courtesy rather than vigour. After the smattering of applause died down, he continued, "Lord Penerack will act as commander in my stead until I return. Upon my arrival, I expect this encampment to look like the dignified and disciplined army I know it is."

With that, Elbert and his guardsmen were ready for their expedition. Four royal guardsmen mounted their horses while Callum was ordered to drive the wagon that would carry the king and his chair. Truth be told, Elbert was less than thrilled at the idea of travelling in anything less than a royal carriage, but he knew there was no other way. Begrudgingly, he sacrificed his pride and cozied himself in the back of the cart. With no further delays, the convoy of guardsmen rode towards the first settlement.

By the time midday came around, boredom had fully gripped Elbert. Unlike his guardsmen, he had no surroundings to look at, only the picturesque blue sky, whose novelty wore off in the first hour of the journey. He craned his neck to see the back of Callum's head in the front of the wagon. Before he could speak, he heard a guardsman warn, "Keep your wits about you, men, bandits frequent these roads."

Elbert gulped nervously. He suddenly doubted himself. Was five men enough? Surely royal guardsmen were better fighters than some lowly bandits? "Should we be worried?" Elbert asked, struggling to remember the guardsman's name.

"No," the guardsman replied. "But it never hurts to err on the side of caution, Your Majesty."

A wave of guilt surged through Elbert as he realized he did not recognize the man nor know his name. To make matters worse, the guard was quite old, which would imply he had been a member of the royal guard for a long time. "What do you know of this town?" Elbert asked, eager to change the subject.

"Eldersburg is a fairly large town, a borderline city, if you will," Callum responded. "I feel like they would give the most out of all the other nearby settlements."

"The ealdorman's a right cunt," the ancient guardsman observed.

"What makes you say that?" the king asked, as he tried to figure out a way to discern the man's name.

"My brother used to live there until a few winters ago," the guardsman replied. "He would write to me every month and tell me about the happenings in the town. Almost every letter he sent he was bitching about that ealdorman, and how he would line his pockets with extra taxes that he wouldn't report to the crown. Needless to say, my brother and the ealdorman didn't get along."

"Why wasn't this brought to our attention?" Elbert asked in disbelief.

"They were just accusations and rumours, Your Majesty, nothing substantiated. Plus, King David wasn't in the best state to launch a full-scale investigation, Gods rest his soul."

Elbert nodded his head in understanding. Near the end of his reign, his father's delirium was a curse on the kingdom. The man was so out of touch with reality that he refused to listen to reason and even the simplest requests were met with outright hostility.

Elbert pulled his blanket up higher and rubbed his hands together for warmth. He was glad that today was a mild day, but he would have much preferred that the siege took place in the summer.

As the sun set, the convoy came to a sudden halt. Elbert was jolted awake, not realizing that he must have dozed off. "What's going on?" he slurred.

"There's another cart in the middle of the road," Callum answered. "We think it could be an ambush, bett—"

A warm sticky fluid splattered across Elbert's face. He looked up and saw Callum's panic-stricken expression staring down at him. An arrow was jutting out of his neck, and a steady stream of blood was leaking out of his mouth. Screams of enraged men soon filled the air and was soon followed by the clanging of steel swords. Elbert quickly covered himself in blankets and took off his crown, hoping that the bandits would spare a poor cripple.

It wasn't long before the sounds of battle died down. Elbert was frozen in fear. He dared not move an inch. He was afraid even taking a breath too soon would alert the bandits to his presence. He could hear laboured breathing, and then a sharp and sudden stabbing sound ended it. The king winced. From what he heard underneath the safety of his blankets, five guards had not been enough for a bandit attack.

"Check the cart!" a gruff voice called out.

Elbert's heart stopped. His ears rang and his breathing became shallow. Even when the blankets were removed from him, he did not react. He wanted to run, to bargain even, but fear had paralyzed his mind. All he could do was sit frozen in place until he was discovered.

"Oi! There's a cripple back 'ere!"

Elbert heard the footsteps of a man come over. He felt the cold, calloused hand turn his cheek until they made eye contact with one another. The man had a crooked nose and a face full of scars that only a mother could love. The bandit smiled, revealing a mouth of yellow teeth. "You're coming with us."

Slung over the back of a horse with an empty sack over his head, Elbert felt utterly defeated. His royal guards had been eviscerated, and evidently it was rather easy to kidnap a cripple. He didn't know where the bandits were taking him, but he knew it couldn't be any place good. He heard his lords' words from that morning ring in his head as he bounced with every step the horse took. Silently, he cursed himself for being so foolish. He should've sent one of them instead. Now the bandits would undoubtedly ransom him for half the kingdom. He only hoped that they did not have more sinister desires. Painful memories from Tjørholm that he had repressed came rushing back into the forefront of his mind. He could hear the Islander's voice and could even smell his breath. He hyperventilated. Right when he felt he was going to suffocate, the bag was removed from his head and the man with the scarred face greeted him with a toothy smile.

"We're here," he said as he lifted Elbert off the horse and onto his shoulders.

The king thought about flailing, about fighting, but what good would it do? He was a cripple. He couldn't defeat a gang of outlaws singlehandedly, even if he had a weapon. Elbert looked around and saw that they had stopped in front of a secluded cave deep in the woods. Torchlight illuminated the interior, and a small plume of smoke exited the mouth of the cave.

The bandit grunted slightly as he walked into the opening. Once inside, it was clear this was where the bandits had been camping. There was a crude table, some makeshift cots, a cauldron, and some cages tucked away in the back of the cave. Sitting by the campfire was a large man with dark skin. He wore exotic robes that were decorated with gold and turquoise silks. His head was free of all hair, save for his neatly trimmed beard.

With a sense of care, the scarred bandit dropped Elbert by the fire and then warmed his hands. The large man frowned and shot a dirty look at the scarred bandit.

"What the fuck do I want with a cripple?" he asked in a heavily accented voice.

"He's worth money," the scarred bandit replied bluntly.

"We are slavers, Gavin, how am I supposed to sell a cripple? I'd be lucky to get a single fucking mark for him!"

"He's royalty," Gavin replied.

Elbert suddenly panicked. "I'm not royalty! I'm just a simple merchant, I trade glassware and—"

Gavin let out a hearty laugh. "You must be a mighty rich merchant to hire royal guards to escort you!"

Elbert's heart sank. Travelling with discretion was not something he had considered. "Please, just let me go. I'll pardon all your past crimes and I'll—"

"Pardon our crimes?" the dark-skinned man guffawed. "He must be someone very important. You know, I heard a rumour that Artanzia had a crippled king. You don't think…"

The two slavers exchanged looks with one another, before their eyes lit up like stars in the endless night sky.

"By the Gods, we've got a fucking king!" Gavin exclaimed.

"Leave us, Gavin, I wish to speak to our honoured guest alone."

Without uttering another word, the bandit with the crooked nose left. Rising to his feet, the large man walked over to the table and picked up a wooden bowl. He then filled the bowl with whatever was in the cauldron and handed it to Elbert.

"Rabbit stew," he said. "I admit there's not much flavour, but it'll keep you warm."

Elbert hesitantly grabbed the bowl and gave it a quick sniff. It didn't smell sour or tainted, but then again, he didn't really know what poison smelled like. Begrudgingly, he took a sip from the bowl.

"My name is Xerxes," the man stated. "And you are Elbert of Artanzia, son of the late King David."

"Seeing as you know who I am," Elbert started, his voice becoming as cold as ice. "Then you know what I am capable of. If you do not release me immediately, my army will—"

"Will what?" Xerxes asked. "My men cut down your guards with ease. As far as your army knows, the king is dead."

The sickening realisation made Elbert's stomach churn. His lords would fear the worst when he didn't return and would likely send out a search party for him. But that would take several days at least. He just had to make sure these slavers stayed here till then. "Are you from the Forsaken Lands?"

Elbert asked, already knowing the answer. But the only way he could think of prolonging their stay was through conversation.

"As you on the continent call it, yes," Xerxes answered. "But in my tongue, we call it Kovar."

"I've never been, but when I was young, we received royal dignitaries from there. If I recall correctly, they were all women."

"Yes!" Xerxes smiled. "In Kovar, women have all the power. Men are only viewed as a necessary evil needed to bring in future generations. I happen to be from a very wealthy family, and as such, am one of the few men born in Kovar that are free."

"And with your freedom, you decide to imprison others?" Elbert asked scornfully.

Xerxes shrugged. "A man has to make a living. And there is no greater commodity than slaves in Kovar."

"You're taking us back there?" Elbert asked, his heart suddenly racing.

"You, I am not sure about," Xerxes replied. "The women of Kovar expect me to provide the greatest quality of breeding stock, and I am afraid that a cripple does not meet their standards."

Elbert's eyes looked in the back of the cave and saw that the cages were full of boys who had just barely hit puberty. "Children are high-quality breeding stock?"

Once again, Xerxes' charismatic smile appeared on his face. "Kovari women are very strong-willed. But you men from the continent are even more stubborn than they are! Boys are much more impressionable."

"If you can't sell me, what do you want from me? You're holding me ransom? I am in the middle of a war! Name your price, and I'll see to it that you and your men live the rest of their days as rich men once I retake my city."

"Retake your city?" Xerxes gasped. "You've been usurped?"

Elbert winced at the words. Not only did he curse himself for giving too much away, but the idea that he had "lost" his kingdom, especially to a commoner, was too painful to bear.

"This changes everything!" Xerxes exclaimed. "Perhaps this usurper would pay me for your head, hmmm?"

"I assure you that would be quite impossible."

"What do you mean? You do not think I could cut off your head? I am a strong man, Elbert, son of David. I am capable of many things."

"No, I mean, my army has surrounded the city. You'd have to go through my men to deliver my head to Randall."

"There is an expression in Kovar. Cut the head off a snake, and the body will die. You understand what I am saying, yes?"

Elbert felt sick. His skin went visibly pale and his hands shook uncontrollably. Was this how his reign was going to end? After becoming the first king to wage war against the Islanders, he was going to die in some cave at the hands of some unimportant slavers?

"There are several ways to enter a city unnoticed." Suddenly, Xerxes whistled sharply and Gavin entered the cave once again. "Gavin, I want you to don the armour of one of the guards that you killed. Go to Winterhelm and tell the new king that we have Elbert in our possession. We will happily gift him to His Majesty – for a price. If he is interested, he can meet us at Eldersburg."

Gavin nodded his head and left the cave. Xerxes stood up and gave Elbert a toothy smile. "Try to enjoy your head while you still have it."

CHAPTER SIXTEEN
ANNA

Eldersburg differed from Winterhelm in many aspects; the main difference, however, was the smell. In the capital, there was a sewer that kept most streets free of bodily fluids. In Eldersburg, such luxuries could not be afforded. People emptied their chamberpots onto the street, not caring if someone was splashed as they walked by. Despite this, there was no shouting nor arguments – it was as if getting splashed by shit and piss was a normal experience.

Anna heard the wooden shutters of an overhead window slam open and quickly leapt out of the way as the refuse from the chamberpot hit the street. Thankfully, she managed to stay clean, Matthew, however, was not so lucky as his pants were now a deeper shade of brown.

"Oh, for fuck's sake!" he shouted as he shook his now wet pant leg.

Mammon took a deep breath through his nose. "Smell that?" he said, with a slight lilting tone to his voice. "That's the smell of civilization."

"Smells like shit," Matthew muttered under his breath.

"Beats the smell of rotting corpses," Evelynn replied, punching Matthew playfully in the shoulder.

They continued to walk through the streets until they saw a large open square that was crowded with people. Vendors had erected their stands and were peddling their wares on the streets. Most sold food, but after a cursory glance, Anna saw that some sold trinkets and oddities as well. Out of habit, she stretched her fingers and prepared herself to steal whatever she could. Before she could leap into action, Mammon's firm hand gripped her shoulder. "There," he said, pointing to the end of the square, where a large wooden building stood. It had two large oak doors at the front with a wyvern's skull hanging above them. "That's where we'll be staying for the next few days. The Horned Wyvern."

"All wyverns have horns," Anna grumbled under her breath as she followed Mammon through the sea of bodies.

"Wyvern, my ass," Evelynn said as they approached the inn. "That has to be the skull of a dragon, it's massive!"

Anna looked at the skull above the doors and let out a laugh. From what she read in her father's books, the skull was probably from a young wyvern; it probably hadn't even reached sexual maturity yet. Dragons could reportedly be as large as some cities – hanging the skull of one off a tavern wall would be impossible. She was about to correct Evelynn, but decided against it. Nobody liked a know-it-all.

Mammon threw open the doors of the tavern and sauntered up to the bar. The place was teeming with people from all walks of life. There appeared to be farmers, craftsmen, artists, guards, and of course, a few people of questionable morality. Anna and the disciples followed the demon until they were all at the bar. A strong, burly man exited the kitchen and greeted them, but when he saw Anna, his face contorted into an ugly sneer.

"What's wrong with 'er eyes?" the innkeeper growled. "She sick?"

"No, she just has—" Mammon began.

"I'll 'ave no lepers in 'ere. Filthy mongrels, spreading disease and whatnot."

"I assure you she is not sick. Just a gift from the Gods," Mammon lied.

"Alright, then. 'Ow can I 'elp ya?"

"Two rooms. One for myself, and these four can share the other. Both must have a tub; I refuse to travel another day stinking like a rutting buck."

"Aye, I can do that."

"How's your laundry service?"

"Me wife Madlyn can remove any stain, guaranteed."

"Excellent, have her wash our clothes at once!"

"That'll be—"

Before the barkeep could finish, Mammon dropped a large pouch of gold onto the counter. The audible clank of that many coins quieted the tavern for a short while, before the patrons resumed their conversations.

"My companions and I will pay for our drinks ahead of time. I assume this will suffice?"

"Indeed, it will, me lord!" the innkeeper exclaimed.

Mammon nodded his head in thanks. A small girl, close to Anna's age, emerged from behind the counter and escorted them upstairs to their rooms. Mammon's room was much more lavish than the one that the disciples were forced to share, but there were three large beds, a couple of luxurious chairs, and an ostentatious porcelain tub in the room's corner.

"I'll bring you some hot water, and a privacy screen for your baths," the small girl said before quickly taking her leave.

Evelynn quickly flopped on the one bed and wrapped herself in the blankets. Matthew immediately removed his soiled clothes and climbed into the empty tub. Desmond eased himself down into one of the leather chairs and allowed his body to relax. Anna exited the room. She had no interest in bathing in front of the others. She was walking towards the stairs when she saw Mammon exit his room as well.

"Going for a walk?" Mammon asked curiously.

"I want to see what the merchants are selling in the square."

Mammon furrowed his brow. "Don't get caught. I have no interest in bailing you out of jail."

Before she could respond, the demon descended the stairs and exited the inn. Anna shook her head petulantly and did the same. Outside the tavern was a wall of noise. People were bartering, shouting, and engaged in meaningless conversation. Like a wolf eying its prey, she watched each of the merchants, looking for the easiest one to steal from. On the far side of the square was a dark-skinned merchant peddling exotic food. He was an enthusiastic salesman, but clearly did not have his wits about him. Several times, he would leave his booth and chase down potential customers trying to change their minds. An unattended stall, ripe for the taking.

After taking a moment to stretch, she sprang into action. Seamlessly weaving her way through the sea of bodies towards the merchant's stand, a devious smile appeared on her face. This was what she needed. Something to make her feel like herself again. Ever since she had been resurrected by Mammon, life had felt like a strange dream. But this, this was so familiar that it made her feel like her old self. Before she could reach the stand, the merchant returned, after failing to persuade an uninterested customer. She sharply turned and feigned interest in a neighbouring merchant's wares. The stand was filled with dusty tomes, and was by far the least popular in the square. The saleswoman, who was middle-aged and had a streak of silver in her otherwise ebony hair, approached Anna.

"A word of advice, dear?" she said in a matronly voice.

"Mhmm," Anna replied politely, although her eyes were still watching the exotic food stand.

"Stealing from Moses would be a poor decision."

Anna's eyes went wide and her head spun around to see the woman smile at her. "Why's that?"

"His stall is magically enchanted. Nothing leaves that stand unless he wants it to. I'd hate for a pretty young thing like you to end up in jail."

Anna clenched her teeth in frustration. Her eyes darted between the woman and the foreign man's stall. After a few moments of contemplation, she gave up on the idea of stealing food. If this woman knew her goal, then there was a good chance that others had noticed her as well. She had gotten rusty. "Thank you for the advice." As she turned away from the stand, the middle-aged woman tapped her gently on the shoulder. Anna turned her head.

"If you would like a better life, might I suggest picking up a book? I find knowledge is the greatest catalyst in changing one's life. I'd even part with one of my books for free."

Begrudgingly, Anna nodded her head. She didn't know why she agreed; perhaps it was to appease the woman. She feigned interest over several tomes until she came across a black leather-bound book titled *A Beginner's Guide to Demonology*, by a Professor Hanubis Moretz. "Can I take this one?" she asked, trying to hide the excitement in her voice.

The woman gave her a curious glance, but ultimately shrugged her shoulders. "Perhaps you'll be a professor one day," she said encouragingly as she handed Anna the book.

Anna thanked the woman and hurried back to the tavern. She was eager to learn more about her situation and whether she had any powers, like Mammon thought. Her hand rubbed the cold leather face of the book as she read the title over and over again. *Alright, Professor Moretz, let's see what you can teach me.*

After scrubbing the layers of filth off her skin, Anna had the tub refilled with clean water. She allowed her body to soak as she dove deeper into Professor Moretz's book. She couldn't believe the wealth of knowledge that the book held within the confines of its pages. She learned that demons almost always had a telltale sign they were not human. Some had certain sounds that would accompany them, others had scents, while some could even change the way the air tasted. It seemed like everything about demons was in this battered old book – except for learning how to control and use their magic. The closest Professor Moretz came to this topic was hypothesizing that since demons feed on emotion, their power must also come from emotions.

Anna tossed the book on the bed as she dried herself off. Even though the tome did not have the answers she was looking for, she still found it interesting. The nostalgia of reading a book about the supernatural had helped relax her body. When she focused hard on the words in Moretz's tome, she forgot where she was and, for a moment, felt like she was back in the woods in the safety of her father's hut.

As she donned her freshly washed linens, there was a knock on the door. Evelynn opened it a little and peeked her head through the crack. "Are you coming down? Mammon gave us an open tab!"

Drinking was the last thing on Anna's mind, but truth be told, her eyes were tired from reading so much and she could use a break. She nodded her head and descended the stairs, seeing that the tavern was filled to the brim with patrons. There was hardly enough room for the barmaids to serve the tables without spilling the mugs of ale. On the far side of the inn was a bard on a stage whose singing was unlike anything Anna had ever heard. His fingers danced along the strings of his lute and his angelic voice filled the entire tavern.

Evelynn grabbed her by the hand and whisked her away to a small table near the entrance of the inn. Matthew and Desmond were sitting together, smiling and laughing. Anna raised a brow as she watched the two slam their mugs together and embrace one another. *Seems they've gotten over their little spat.*

"Anna!" Desmond shouted. "Glad you could join us!"

"Where's Mammon?" Anna asked.

"Probably at the local whorehouse," Matthew slurred.

"Do demons have sex?"

"Whores are good hosts for him," Evelynn answered. "There's not a whore in the world that doesn't long for something more. He feeds off that ambition and desperation."

Anna nodded her head, but her mind was racing with questions. She wanted to know more, and she also wanted to know why she didn't feel drawn to anyone's emotions. What she wouldn't give for a conversation with Professor Moretz.

"I see your leg is still brown," Evelynn said as she nudged Matthew's arm.

"Take any stain out, my ass," Matthew grumbled as he slurped from his mug. "I think I can even still smell the shit."

The three disciples laughed as the barmaid brought Anna an ale. Hesitantly, she grabbed the mug and took a sip. As soon as the frothy booze hit her lips, the memories of her and the Maggots celebrating in the Garden came rushing back. Chuckles' endless jokes, Tig's pigheadedness, Maeve's sisterly nature, and Randall's... As soon as the King of Crooks entered her head, rage surged through her body. Her lips stained her face in an ugly grimace, and she squeezed the mug till it cracked.

"What's the matter?" Desmond asked, gently touching Anna's arm.

Before she could answer, there was a shout from across the inn. "Oi, freak! What're you looking at!"

Anna must've been staring at the drunk as he and his three equally drunk friends staggered over to their table. The man who shouted at Anna slammed his fist on the table. He was breathing heavily and his breath stank of vodka. He could barely stand straight, his body swaying from side to side as he glared at the four of them through his bloodshot eyes.

"I said, what're you looking at... freak!"

"Maybe she wants to fuck you!" his friend replied.

"That it? You want some of this? Perhaps you and your friend would care to join me upstairs? I've never fucked a red-eyed girl before."

"That doesn't surprise me," Anna snapped back. "The only thing you've probably fucked is your neighbour's sheep."

"What did you say?" the man growled.

As he leaned forward to grab Anna, Matthew shot up out of his chair and slammed the drunk's face into the table. One of the man's friends caught Matthew in the jaw with a wild haymaker. Anna jumped onto the table and kicked the man in the teeth, sending him sprawling to the ground.

Within a matter of seconds, the entire tavern erupted into an all-out brawl. Chairs flew through the air, mugs were smashed on people's heads, and bodies were thrown through walls. The floor soon became slick with blood, booze, and vomit. Anna was pummelling the drunken man's face when someone tripped over her and knocked her to the ground. Before she could get back up to her feet, several bodies piled on top of her, pinning her to the tavern floor. She wriggled and writhed, trying to get free of the pile of bodies, but there was too much weight. She was stuck.

She wheezed for air as her eyes darted around the tavern until she spotted Matthew, pinned helplessly to the floor by the drunk's friends. Each man was taking a turn punching and kicking the disciple. Blood slowly trickled out of his mouth as he locked eyes with Anna. He winced in pain with every blow and tears were streaming from his eyes.

"Stop..." Anna wheezed, as she got one of her arms free from the pile. She reached out towards Matthew with her outstretched hand, closed her eyes, and shouted with all the air in her lungs, "Stop!"

Everything happened within a few seconds, but it seemed to drag out for an eternity. All the weight on top of her suddenly disappeared. Anna opened her eyes and her jaw dropped – the world around her was disappearing and turning to ash. Several patrons screamed in pain as they disintegrated into a small powder, while others stared at their bodies in confusion as they faded away. She saw a young couple in the corner, hiding from the fight, crumble away, their bodies joining into a singular mound of ash.

She closed her eyes and plugged her ears, but the screams of terror still found their way through. She felt the soot and the ash of bodies stick to her face. Her body tingled violently. It was as if the vibrations from the people's screams travelled and resonated through her body. And then suddenly, it stopped.

Anna opened her eyes once more and saw that the only thing around her, besides the three disciples, was a mountain of ash. She rose to her feet and looked around. The entire town had disappeared. Anna's skin went visibly pale when she realized what this meant. She did indeed have powers, and she had just used them to wipe an entire town out of existence.

"What have you done!?" a voice called out. Anna turned her head and saw a rapidly aging Mammon wading his way through the lake of ashes. "What the fuck have you done!?"

CHAPTER SEVENTEEN
ROSALINE

It had been a week since Elbert's army surrounded the city. While everyone else was panicking, Rosaline and the Bloody Brotherhood sprang into action. They would kick down doors in the middle of the night, steal food, and beat anyone who resisted to a pulp. In three days, they had stolen enough food to have an iron-like chokehold on the city. The Brotherhood then stayed dormant for the next three days. They forced the people to stew in their starvation, making sure they realized that famine was an actual possibility. Then, on the seventh day, Rosaline and her Brothers spread word across the city that the people could buy back their food. The commoners' desperation clouded their need for vengeance, and they soon lined up, valuables in hand, to buy back what was taken from them.

As the sun set on the seventh day of the siege, Rosaline laughed, rubbing two gold coins together. Even after one day of selling they had become filthy rich, and their profits would only grow. She looked around the empty tavern and saw her Brothers revelling in their newfound wealth. Even Fletcher, the typically stoic innkeeper, was grinning from ear to ear. The only one not indulging themselves in the mountain of coin was Duncan. Ever since he was tasked with finding Randall's stockpile, he hadn't been himself. Every day he would sneak into the castle and scour it for any signs of the king's hoard, but his efforts thus far had all been for naught. He would walk into the tavern every evening with his head hung low. Rosaline knew not to press him, Duncan was more than capable of doing the job, but time was of the essence.

Wearing a friendly smile, she walked over to the sulking bandit and brought him a mug of ale. "How goes the search?" she asked, already knowing the answer.

"I don't understand," Duncan said as he took a sip from the mug Rosaline brought. "How the hell can that boy hide all that food?"

"He's not just a boy," Rosaline corrected. "Remember, this is the kid that usurped not only Greaver, but the actual King of Artanzia as well. He's cunning, smart, and resourceful. It would make sense that his stockpile is well hidden."

"Personally, I think the eunuch is behind this," Duncan replied. "I suspect Cassius predicted what we would do and is trying to undercut us."

Rosaline nodded her head. Cassius was a resourceful and intelligent man. He always thought three steps ahead of everyone, but that would be his downfall. His ego wouldn't allow him to believe that someone had outsmarted him. It bit him once in the ass, and Rosaline was going to make sure it would happen again.

"Leave the eunuch to me," she said as she rose from the table. "Just try to enjoy the coin tonight."

As she made her way to the exit, she saw out of the corner of her eye that Malek was staring at her. Knowing that this meant he wanted to talk, she walked over to him and sat down at the table.

"What's eating Duncan?" Malek began.

"You know how he is," Rosaline answered. "He's a perfectionist, so he's kicking himself for not finding Randall's hoard yet."

"He needs to hurry, Roz," Malek warned. "Randall could undermine us, especially if he finds out what we're doing. He has a genuine love for the people, and I doubt that he'll take it kindly when he learns we're robbing them blind."

"Give Duncan time. Randall's a smart boy, he would have hidden the food well when preparing for the siege."

Malek looked like he had more to say, but he voiced no more concerns. Taking that as a sign that their conversation had ended, Rosaline exited the tavern.

The winter air was still but cold. It was eerily quiet, and the faint sounds of the surrounding army carried over the walls and into the city. Rosaline was walking toward the Corridor of Pleasure, eager to indulge her carnal desires, when she heard a pair of effeminate voices talking. Her curiosity piqued, she stealthily approached the source of the voices. Peeking out from behind the cover of an empty merchant's stall, she saw one voice belonged to Cassius. He was talking to a woman, who was cloaked in a long black hood and a dark dress. It was clear the woman was irate, as her hands moved frantically as she talked. They were walking away from the palace and towards the Corridor of Pleasure. Seeing as it was on her way anyway, Rosaline followed, hoping to glean some information on the king's missing hoard.

Despite the late hour, it was hard to make out what the two were talking about while remaining hidden. There were a few words that Rosaline was confident she heard, though: 'Randall', 'people', 'Kalvin', and 'food'. Although she didn't know what any of that signified, she continued to follow, hoping to catch more tidbits of their conversation. On the edge of the Corridor of Pleasure, the two stopped, and Rosaline quickly ducked behind a building, hoping not to be seen. Peeking her head around the corner, she saw the two embrace before the woman walked away, towards the brothels. Cassius, on the other hand, continued walking, and to Rosaline's surprise, did not head back to the palace, but instead made his way towards the docks.

Eager to learn more, Rosaline followed at a distance. Cassius must have been in a hurry, as he was almost in a full-out jog. Struggling to keep up while also being stealthy, she lost sight of him. Figuring that he had walked into one of the warehouses that filled the dock district, she cut her losses and went to grab a drink. Thankfully, there was a half-decent tavern not far away, frequented mainly by sailors. She continued to walk for a few more minutes until she came to a barrel outside an old, musty building that reeked of grog. The barrel had the words *The Lusty Leopard* painted on it. Smiling, she entered the establishment, hoping to get a half-decent drink.

With Elbert's blockade in place, the sailors were landlocked, and as a result, the tavern was full. As she walked up to the bar to order a drink, she noticed everyone was looking at her. She knew it was probably for two reasons. The first was that nobody came to The Lusty Leopard unless they were a sailor, and she was clearly not a seadog. The second reason was that women didn't visit establishments where the patrons were seamen. Sailors were hard, short-tempered men, and would often bring trouble. Thankfully for Rosaline, she was equally short-tempered and knew how to take care of herself.

"What'll it be, love?" the innkeeper asked. Both of his eyes were bruised and purple, and his nose was bent in an unnatural angle. "Just so you know, food is scarce right now, some bastards broke in at night and ransacked the place. I tried to stop them, but they busted my nose."

Rosaline feigned concern as she assured the innkeeper that grog was just fine. She made a mental note to herself to ask the boys if they had robbed this place. While the tavern owner looked worse for wear, suffering only a broken nose was quite generous by Bloody Brotherhood standards.

As she paid for her drink, she was turning to find a table when she felt a calloused hand plant firmly on her ass. She turned her head and saw the ugliest man she had ever laid eyes on smiling back at her. She didn't think it was possible, but she was pretty sure that the man had barnacles stuck to his skin.

"Care to join me for a drink, lassie?" the man said in a salty, gravelly voice.

Smiling politely, Rosaline set her mug of grog down and instinctively reached for Boris, but stopped herself and looked at her surroundings. The ugly man's friends were watching with disgusting smiles on their faces, as well as several other patrons too. She knew that if a fight broke out, she would be screwed. Feigning interest, she removed the man's hand from her ass before placing the mug of grog she had just purchased in his hand.

"What ship do you sail?"

"The *Intrepid*," the ugly man replied proudly. "I'm the captain."

Rosaline rolled her eyes. The man was clearly captain of nothing, but she played along. "Why don't I grab a bottle and you and your friends can tell me what it's like to sail the open seas?" she said, purposely making her voice higher than normal and batting her eyes.

The sailor, seemingly in disbelief that his charms had worked, stared at her dumbfounded for a few seconds before nodding his head and returning to the table. Rosaline turned to the innkeep and said, "Give me a bottle of your strongest spirit."

The innkeeper gave a sly grin and handed her a bottle of clear liquid. "Planning a fun evening?"

"Oh, you have no idea," Rosaline replied with a wink.

She saw out of the corner of her eye the ugly man regaling his friends in a tale, their attention solely on him. Taking advantage of their distraction, Rosaline snuck out of the bar with the bottle of spirits in her hand. She made her way towards the harbour and began scanning the ships that were docked until she saw one with the word *Intrepid* painted on the side. With a venomous smile, she tore off a piece of her shirt, stuffed it in the bottle and lit the fabric on a nearby torch. Holding the bottle in her hands, she took a moment admiring the flames as they crawled along the piece of cloth and towards the alcohol. With a casual shrug of the shoulders, she heaved the bottle onto the deck of *Intrepid* and heard an audible smash. She watched with glee as the ship and its sails were quickly consumed by the fire. Satisfied with her work, she walked out of the docks, and waited till she saw the sailors from The Lusty Leopard clamour out of the tavern in panic.

"Causing trouble?" a familiar voice said from behind her.

Startled, Rosaline spun around and saw the eunuch smiling coyly back at her. Trying to hide her surprise, Rosaline shrugged her shoulders before turning to admire the burning ship once more.

"You know, Rosaline, I've been having a terrible day," Cassius lamented.

"Is that so?" Rosaline replied, voice riddled with insincerity. "Need a shoulder to cry on?"

Ignoring the jab, Cassius continued, "See, as the chief advisor for the king, I hear everything that troubles his young mind, and it is up to me to find a solution."

"What is Randall worried about?" Rosaline asked, hoping that Cassius would make his point soon.

"There have been reports that a gang of outlaws are going around the city and stealing people's food. No doubt trying to extort the people out of their hard-earned gold during this difficult time."

"Tssk. Tssk." Rosaline clicked her tongue. "The nerve of some people."

"Since Randall took the throne, crime has increased, but that happens when you have an outlaw for a king and no city guards to maintain order. The boy's outlandish idea that the entire city will band together as one big commune is outrageous. That being said, there isn't a thief in this city that would dare to cross Randall. Not after all that he's accomplished."

"I see where this is going," Rosaline chuckled. "But if you're accusing the Bloody Brotherhood of stealing from the king, you better have some proof to support your accusation."

"I don't have proof yet, but perhaps I should check out Fletcher's tavern tomorrow morning? See what he has stored?"

It was difficult for Rosaline to maintain her façade of disinterest, but she kept her reaction to Cassius' statement to a minimum. "While you're checking Fletcher's, I might go have a word with the king."

"Turning yourself in?"

"No, perhaps he and I will go visit the brothels and I can show him where it all happened."

"Where what happened?"

"Where you lost your balls. I'm sure he'd love to hear how much of a snake you truly are."

Cassius' face went white and his smirk disappeared in an instant. Rosaline grinned venomously. She approached the eunuch, grabbed the collar of his flamboyant shirt, and pulled him close.

"You're not as smart as you think you are, Cassius. You've been outsmarting a boy; not really an intellectual challenge. If you want to take down me and my Brothers, I'll gladly drag you to the gallows with us."

After a few brief seconds of terror, Cassius shook himself free of Rosaline's grasp and straightened his collar. "Always a pleasure, Rosaline," he said in a cold voice.

Rosaline watched as the eunuch walked away with a smile on her face. Today was a good day. Not only had she put that arrogant prick of a eunuch in his place, she also taught some sailors a valuable lesson in respect. *This is a day to remember.*

CHAPTER EIGHTEEN
CONNIR

The wooden runners of the sled scratched against the ice of the frozen river. The oxen grunted with every laboured step, and the crack of Ragnar's whip was the only motivation they received. The other Islanders tried to help as much as they could by pushing the sled occasionally, but, truth be told, the oxen were doing all the work. It was snowing lightly, and as the sun set behind the tall mountains in the west, they prepared to make camp for the night.

Connir was to fill up buckets of snow so that they could melt it and give the oxen water, while the others were preparing the fire or settling in for the night. It had been three days since they left Skotheim, and they had been fortunate that the weather had been as accommodating as it had. If Connir had the choice, he would've taken peaceful weather at sea rather than on land. Ragnar's confidence never wavered, however, as he continuously stated that Heimer was watching out for them and that their voyage was blessed by the gods.

"Hurry up, boy, the oxen are parched!" one of Bearn's men shouted.

Connir rolled his eyes. Out of all of his newfound travelling companions, Bearn's men were the worst. He would have given anything to have Estrid here with him instead of them. In an act of defiance, the skald sauntered over to the fire with two buckets of snow and tossed them at the barbarian's feet.

"The fuck is your problem?" the man growled. "Just because you killed Linny you think you're the next Grimm White-Eyes. I'd break your spine and use it as a toothpick."

"Watch your tongue, Axel," Ragnar said, without looking up from sharpening his blade. "Connir is one of us, and if you talk to him like that again, I'll cut out your tongue."

The barbarian scoffed. "He's the one with the fucking problem."

Not wanting to get into an altercation with the man, Connir walked away, grabbed his share of the stew that had been prepared, and sat down across from the angry berserker.

"Are you trying to piss them off?" a voice said from behind Connir. The skald turned his head and saw that Knut, the Beastfolk berserker, had sat down beside him. He was a tall, burly man whose face was covered in runic tattoos. He had a single braid of hair that ran down from the top of his head to the small of his back, and a big bushy beard. His hands were swollen and calloused. He carried a large axe with him, and, on his belt, he had a small leather pouch where his mystical mushrooms were kept.

"They started it," Connir grumbled quietly.

"How?"

"Long story."

"Fine." Knut shrugged. "Keep your secrets."

Connir wasn't sure why he was in a sour mood; perhaps it was because Estrid had been forced to stay behind, or perhaps it was because the soles of his feet throbbed painfully with every heartbeat. He hated marching. He had come to this revelation during his march to Tjørholm, and the march back to Skotheim nearly killed him. When they had first returned from the siege,

Connir was sure he would never have to march again, but here he was, three days into another agonizing journey.

"I'm bored," Skaði, the Clan Geirsson shieldmaiden, muttered as she tossed another log onto the fire.

"Me too," muttered one of Jarl Bearn's men. "Hey, skald, how about doing your job and playing us a song?"

Connir's brow furrowed, but he caught Ragnar's glare out of the corner of his eye and relaxed his body. "What do you want to hear?" he sighed as he set down his bowl of stew.

"Let's hear 'The Ballad of Ulf Sand-Beard'!" Bearn's other man shouted. "The first Islander to sail to the Forsaken Lands!"

"Pah!" Knut spat. "I'd rather hear about a warrior, like Bloody Barik, the first Beastfolk berserker!"

Connir grabbed a stale bun and walked back to the ship to grab his lute. Although he knew he had a long journey with these people ahead of him, he could not bring himself to find them all that endearing. The only person who made the trip remotely tolerable was Ragnar. He took a deep breath in and forced himself to calm down. *Think about Estrid. Think about the ballad you'll have for her when you return*, he told himself as he climbed aboard.

As he rummaged around the ship, trying to find his lute, he heard a dry cough that startled him. He turned his head and saw Grimm moving slightly. The legendary warrior had been so quiet during the past three days that Connir had assumed that the man had already passed.

"You going to eat that?" Grimm asked in a raspy voice, nodding towards the stale bun that the skald held in his hand.

"I planned on it," Connir answered.

Grimm didn't reply. Instead, he looked up to the sky and stuck out his tongue to catch a few of the falling snowflakes, savouring the moisture they left behind as they melted on his tongue. Instantly, a pang of remorse surged through Connir's body. This was the man that had saved his father's life. Without Grimm, Connir would not be here. Whether he liked it or not, he was beholden to Grimm. He looked at the warrior's body and saw how he had withered away since his capture. His eyes were sunken and his cheeks were hollow; his once muscular arms had nearly halved in size. Unable to shake the sense of debt that was spreading though him, he tossed him the stale bun.

The chains rattled as Grimm caught the bread roll mid-air. A heavy silence hung between the two Islanders for a while. Connir stared at the warrior's milky white eyes and realized that it was hard to see what he was thinking. Grimm's face was stoic and unwavering. Finally, after the lengthy pause had run its course, Grimm ravenously devoured the bun in his hands. Connir turned his head and couldn't help but smile. A wave of pride washed over him as he continued to look for his lute. After several seconds of searching, he pulled the lute out of his bag, disembarked the ship, and walked back to the fire.

Retaking his spot beside Knut, he tuned the instrument. "Did we decide on a song?" he asked as his fingers nimbly turned the knobs at the top of the lute's neck.

"We did," Ragnar replied. "How about 'March to the Mainland'?"

"A classic," Connir replied as he readied his lute. He stretched his fingers before he plucked the horsehair strings, and waited a full measure before filling the evening air with his angelic voice.

Heimer whispered to me,
"Raid the towns overseas.
We'll butcher their men and bleed them dry,

Burn their houses and rape their wives!"
Heimer shouted at me,
"Go and claim glory.
Kill our enemies by the score
And settle down with a right plump whore."

It was a quick song, but it never failed to get a group of Islanders riled up. The entire camp was clapping their hands along to the beat as Connir sang both verses. As the last note of the song approached, Connir performed a flourish and plucked the strings, allowing the sound to fade softly into the distance.

Everyone was silent for a moment after the performance, but soon they all erupted in raucous applause. Connir graciously took a bow, picked up his bowl of stew, and resumed his meal.

"You've a gift, boy!" Skaði exclaimed as she clapped her hands. "Give us another!"

"Let the skald eat his meal, for Heimer's sake!" Knut shouted, slapping Connir on the back.

"How long till we reach the coast?" Skaði asked.

"Probably another day, if everything goes well," Ragnar replied. "Once we hit the coast, we'll be on the mainland's soil in no time."

"Who's doing what while we sail?" one of Bearn's men asked.

"I'll operate the rudder. Connir and Skaði will handle the rigging. Knut, Gunnar, and Axel will handle the oars. Questions?"

There was no reply. Connir grabbed another bowl of stew and went to head back to the ship.

"Where are you going?" Knut asked. "We want more songs!"

"Something didn't sound right," Connir lied. "My strings need to be changed. I'm going to finish my meal while I find what's going on with my lute."

"It sounded fine!" Skaði shouted, but Ragnar raised a silencing hand.

"Connir has a better ear than all of us. If he says something's wrong, it is. Plus, think of how much better it'll sound once he fixes it!"

Nodding his head in thanks, Connir walked back to the ship. He carefully climbed aboard, balancing the bowl of stew in his hand as he did so. Once aboard, he walked straight over to Grimm and set the bowl in his lap. The warrior looked up at him, in what Connir could only assume was an awestruck stare.

"Can't have you die this early on the journey. You need to see the sea one more time," he said, trying to mask how he truly felt from the traitor.

"If the others find out—" Grimm began.

"They won't, unless you're going to tell them."

A smile flickered on the traitor's lips, before quickly vanishing. "Thanks."

"Is it true?" Connir asked, feeling compelled to make conversation with the man who saved his father's life.

"Is what?"

"That you raped High King Uthredd's sister-in-law?"

"Why do you care?"

"If I'm going to write the ballad about your last voyage, I'd like to know the truth of how you got here. Not just the rumours," Connir lied.

Grimm finished eating his bowl of stew and let out a sigh. "I didn't rape her, but I bedded her." Connir raised a questioning brow. "I loved my wife, Freja, and as long as I draw breath, I will always love her. But Aslög and I had that unspeakable bond. Have you ever locked eyes with someone and just instantly known that you wanted each other?"

Connir instinctively shook his head. Had he ever experienced that? What if Estrid felt as strongly about him as he did about her, but he was too oblivious to pick up on the signs? "No," he said after a moment of deliberation.

"When I met her at Eirik's wedding, I knew she would be trouble. This had been during Uthredd's unification campaign, and I hadn't seen my family in a long time. I tried to fight off my impulses, but I soon succumbed to her charms."

"I assume Prince Eirik found out?" Connir asked.

Grimm nodded his head. "We were able to keep it secret from both our spouses for a few months, but we weren't careful enough. I can only assume that when Eirik confronted Aslög, she lied through her teeth and told the prince whatever she had to in order to keep her head."

"That's when Eirik murdered your family," Connir said, able to fill in the gaps.

"Mhmm," Grimm grunted. "I was away with Uthredd when it happened, but when word reached me, I hunted Eirik down and butchered him like the dog he was."

"Why did you run? Why didn't you just tell Uthredd? You two grew up together, surely he'd believe you?"

Grimm's brow furrowed and his lips twisted into a disgusted frown. "If you saw what Eirik did to my family, you'd understand. I didn't want justice; I wanted vengeance."

After taking in the weight of Grimm's words for several moments, Connir decided he had heard all that he needed to for the night. He rose to his feet, grabbed his lute and the empty stew bowl, and walked back to the fire.

"Get everything sorted out?" Ragnar asked as Connir rejoined the group of raiders.

"Mhmm. What do we want to hear next?"

For the rest of the evening, Connir performed for his new companions. They spent the evening singing, laughing, and occasionally dancing to Connir's songs. Once the sun had set and everyone had fallen asleep, Connir turned his attention back towards the ship and softly plucked the strings of his lute, trying to find the melody for the song that would tell the tale of Grimm White-Eyes' last voyage.

CHAPTER NINETEEN
RANDALL

When Randall first set foot in the Royal Library, his body filled with rage. How dare the nobles hoard all of this knowledge away from the people? He made a silent promise to himself that, once the siege was over, he would share all the books, scrolls, and tomes with any citizen who wanted them. However, after spending several hours there, his rage subsided as he discovered that the majority of the books were useless drivel that wouldn't interest anyone, which explained why most of them were covered in a thick layer of dust. Royal lineages, dynastic family trees, and chronicles of great deeds by nobles that were no doubt embellished seemed to fill every page in the cavernous room. Despite the small forest of slaughtered trees that must have been in the room, not a single book gave him any idea on how to get around Elbert's blockade and bring food into the city.

After what felt like his three-hundredth book failed to provide any useful information, Randall stood up and threw the tome across the room in a fit of frustration. He slowly sank back into his chair and sipped wine from his goblet. His eyes were sore and his head throbbed. He had been in there all evening, and judging by how many of the books he had yet to read, he would be in there until the siege ended.

The most infuriating part of the library was not the fact that there was a lack of useful information, but the fact that there seemed to be no rhyme nor reason to the organization of the books. They were not categorized by subject matter, author's name, or date of publication. It was almost as if someone bought a hoard of books and threw them into this room with no intention to ever read them.

"How goes the search?" a soft voice said from behind the king.

He didn't know how long Cassius had been standing there, so he decided to not mince words. "Fucking horrible." He took another sip of wine to ease his frustration. "All these fucking nobles care about is themselves, and it appears that their heads were so far up their own arses that they didn't even think to write anything useful down! All they care about is who fell out with who and where that put him on the social hierarchy."

"Perhaps you should retire for the night? A fresh set of eyes may be helpful."

"We're running out of time, Cassius." Randall sighed. "Elbert has surrounded our city, King Kalvin's army is Gods know how many days away, and our city is starving. I need to find a way to get food in."

"A noble endeavour, Your Majesty, but we cannot get through Elbert's army. And with the harbour blocked by his ships—"

Randall's eyes widened with an idea. "Fetch me Grandmaster Velus!"

The former sommelier raised a questioning brow. "May I enquire why?"

The young king's face contorted into an ugly sneer. Cassius rarely questioned him, but Randall was noticing that the eunuch was rebuffing his orders more and more frequently.

"I wish to speak with him. Is that not a good enough reason?" Randall snapped.

Cassius bowed eloquently. "A thousand apologies, Your Majesty, I will fetch him right away."

Randall scowled behind his advisor's back as he exited the library. He wasn't sure what had gotten into Cassius, but he was not the same man that helped him usurp the throne. Something had changed, and Randall was not sure if it was for the better.

After a longer than expected break, Cassius returned to the library with the wizard in tow.

"You wished to speak with me, Your Majesty?" Velus said as he tried to stifle a yawn.

"How familiar are you with alchemy and other chemical reactions?"

Velus shook his head in surprise. "I am fairly well-versed, Your Majesty, but spells are more my area of exp—"

"Do you know of a compound that would allow me to burn wood, even if it is exposed to water?"

The mage sat down on the floor and scratched his head with his foot, as if he were a dog. After a few glances exchanged between the king and Cassius, Velus rose to his feet as if unaware of his behaviour a few seconds prior. "There is a compound called phoenix fire, but it is highly volatile and quite dangerous if mishandled—"

"Do you have the elements necessary to make it?" Randall pressed.

"Yes, but—"

"How long until you have enough to burn a small fleet of ships?"

Cassius' brow once again raised in curiosity.

"A few hours, Your Majesty, it doesn't take much, but as your advisor I urge you to heed the risks!"

Randall rose from his chair, towering over the ancient halfling. Velus instantly shrank back in fear. Randall softened his eyes, dropped to his knees, and placed a hand on the mage's shoulder. "People are starving, Velus," he said in a soft voice. "If we don't do something, this city will be filled with nothing but corpses. Destroying Elbert's ships is the only way we can feed our people."

Velus straightened his posture and lifted his chin high. "You can count on me, Your Majesty."

Once Velus had left the room, Randall waited in the heavy silence between him and Cassius. He could tell that his advisor had something on his mind.

"Something to be said when a madman warns you about how dangerous something is."

"Despite Velus' quirks, I still believe his sanity is very much there."

Cassius chuckled softly. "Did you miss the part where he thought he was a dog? I was half-surprised when he didn't bark and lick himself!"

Randall had to suppress a smile. He liked Velus, and he did not think it was appropriate for a king to mock his advisors behind their back. "If it helps us get food into the city, I wouldn't care if he jumped on the furniture and meowed like a cat."

Cassius smiled politely. "Curious why you didn't just ask him to destroy the ships with his magic? I assume that would be the fastest course of action."

"Somehow, I don't think Velus is the type of person who would knowingly kill dozens of men. Besides, if what you say is true, I need him to keep his wits about him in case I need to reach out to King Kalvin again. If he completely loses his mind before the siege is over, I'm afraid that we'll be isolated from the outside world once again."

"A wise conclusion," Cassius responded. "Permission to speak candidly?" Randall nodded his head. "When you first told me you wanted to overthrow Elbert and reclaim his kingdom in the name of the people of Artanzia, I thought you were unrealistic. But now, after some time on the throne, I'm seeing that you are made for this. So many usurpers throughout history fail to claim the throne, and even fewer prove themselves as capable rulers. I'm happy to say that you are the exception."

Randall smiled, although he didn't want to. He was sure Cassius meant to compliment him, perhaps sensing the rift growing between them and hoping to repair it, but all Randall gleaned from the eunuch's flowery words was that he had doubted him in the beginning. Everyone doubted him, except Anna. His stomach churned as the memory of pushing her off the ramparts played once again in his head. The look of disbelief on her face as she fell, the way her body shrank the further she dropped, and the pang of instant regret he felt as soon as her feet left the ramparts. He had been so busy with the siege that he could push his grief for Anna to the back of his mind, but now all the repressed emotions came forward. It was like someone had opened the doors to a dam inside his head. But instead of a torrent of water, it was a torrent of painful memories.

"I'm going to get some rest," Randall said, trying to hold back his tears. "When Grandmaster Velus is done with the phoenix fire, assemble the council. I want to go over the plan."

"As you wish, Your Majesty."

Randall left the room while he still had his dignity. He could feel his stomach gurgle with regret and the guilt stuck in his throat. Once he was alone in his chambers, he knew he was going to be a mess. He just hoped that he didn't run into anyone on the way there. He kept his eyes downward as he walked through the palace's halls. He heard the servants shuffle about silently, but he refused to acknowledge them. He didn't want anyone to see him as weak. A weak king can't keep a kingdom.

He opened the door to his chambers and quickly shut it behind him. He walked over to the bed, which was clad with the finest linens and the softest silks. Exhausted, he collapsed into it, letting the goose-feather mattress slowly absorb him as his guilt consumed him. He let out a pained scream into the mattress, hoping that the bedding would muffle the sound from escaping the room. Tears flowed from his eyes freely and his temples throbbed painfully with each heartbeat.

After the first wave of sobbing had finally subsided, he rose to his feet and opened the frost-covered window, hoping that the cold winter air would kill his senses. However, opening the window only gave Randall's grief more vigor, because the first thing he saw when he opened the window was the rampart that he had pushed Anna from after he had claimed the city.

His stomach contorted into a series of nasty knots, and he collapsed to the ground, sobbing. He clenched his teeth tightly, doing everything he could to stop the crying. His mind couldn't help but replay all the memories he had with Anna. He remembered how he rescued her from the pickpocket when she first arrived in the city; he remembered their first kiss and the first time they lay with one another. But the memory that replayed the most was his last memory with her. The one where he pushed her to her death.

The second wave of crying was long and gruelling, but after what seemed like an eternity, the tears stopped. He slowly got to his feet and walked over to the washbasin in the corner of his bedchamber. He splashed the water on his face and tried to hide the redness in his eyes. He had never experienced grief like this, not even when his sister had died. After her death, he pulled himself together rather quickly – perhaps it was his anger at the nobles that allowed him to keep himself under control. But Anna was a different story. There was nobody to blame but himself. Sure, Cassius had told him that she needed to die, but he was the one who actually killed her. He raised his eyes and stared at himself in the mirror above the basin. His lips contorted into an ugly sneer. He hated himself. The sight of his own face repulsed him in this instant. He wanted to smash the mirror into a thousand pieces but knew that it wouldn't ease his pain.

In a moment of brief clarity, as he stared at his own pathetic visage, he made a vow. No more innocent people would die by his hands. The only blood that would stain his hands would be that of Elbert's men, and any other who was foolish enough to stand against him. But he promised himself that nobody else would die that didn't deserve it. Anna's blood was a permanent stain on his soul, and he'd be damned if he added more innocent blood to it.

Drained from the emotional onslaught he had just endured, Randall walked over to the bed and collapsed into it once more, falling into a deep and dreamless sleep.

A sudden knock at the door stirred Randall from his slumber. He lifted his head from the satin pillows and saw Cassius standing in the doorway.

"The council has been gathered and is waiting for you," he said, before bowing politely and exiting the room.

Randall rose to his feet, blinked away the last remnants of sleep, and stretched his back. He walked over to the still open window and closed it, but not before noticing the moon hanging high in the night sky.

He exited his chambers and walked towards the war room. He wasn't sure if it was the nap, or if it was his new vow, but something felt different. He felt lighter, as if a weight had been lifted off his heart. He knew he'd never truly forgive himself for murdering Anna, that was a given, but he was determined to take that lesson with him going forward, and prevent any more wanton death.

Upon his entering the war room, the councillors rose out of their chairs and bowed graciously. Randall waved a dismissive hand and took his seat at the head of the table. The councillors retook their seats, and the meeting began.

"What's this all about?" Virgil Walker growled as he pulled his cloak tighter around his body. "It's the middle of the damned night!"

"Grandmaster Velus has devised a way to stop Elbert's naval embargo on the city," Randall answered before motioning for Velus to hold up a jar of the phoenix fire.

"What the blazes is that?" Tig asked.

"Something that will burn Elbert's ships to the bottom of the sea."

"Hmph," Virgil Walker scoffed.

"Tig, A'Chula, and myself will take the phoenix fire out to Elbert's ship tonight in rowboats. Stealth is of the utmost importance. If Elbert's men catch wind of us, this will end terribly."

"Your Majesty," Cassius interjected. "I cannot, with good conscience, let you go on such a perilous mission. Send someone else in your stead."

"No," Randall answered bluntly. "I will not order my subjects to do something that I won't do myself. These are *my* people, Cassius, and *I* intend to protect them."

"Your Majesty," Cassius replied, his voice firmer than before, "I really must protest this idea; I think you need to—"

"Throughout my people's lives, they have been ruled by cowardly people who refuse to get their hands dirty. They viewed us as disposable, as tools to be used and discarded at their whims. I will not be that kind of king. The people of Artanzia deserve a better king. They deserve a king who will fight for them just as much they fight for him."

There was an awkward moment of silence around the table before Tig broke it. "Not sure if you thought of this, Randall, but how are we supposed to burn the ships? They're on water, and the flames will be quickly snuffed out."

Smiling, Randall gestured for Grandmaster Velus to take the floor. The halfling nervously cleared his throat and stood on his chair. "Phoenix fire reacts violently when exposed to water. It will ignite in flames that will burn anything – even steel will melt under its fire."

"Sounds dangerous," Corbin Strongarm interjected.

"My, yes!" Velus exclaimed. "When exposed to a large body of water like the sea, I'm afraid of what will happen to the fire. I'm afraid that we'll create a great inferno that will destroy anything and everything touching the water."

Randall's heart sank. This must've been the risk that Velus was trying to tell him about earlier. He silently cursed himself; he should've listened to the wizard before he brought this before the council. Recklessness was not a good look for a new king.

"What can we do to contain the spread of the fire?" Cassius asked, taking attention away from the king.

"To protect the city, I could cast a protective barrier around the harbour, shielding us from the flames. Phoenix fire burns out rather quickly; however, when it is on a large body of water, I do not know how long it'll burn for."

"Is there no way to extinguish the flames?" Amelia Dupont asked.

Velus shook his head.

"What about with your magic?" Tig asked.

Randall shifted uncomfortably in his seat. He wanted to use the phoenix fire because he didn't want Velus to tap into his magical reserves, but now that seemed inevitable. The fire would be too uncontrollable to contain through non-magical means.

"There is a spell I know that *might* work, but it is very time-consuming and awfully draining."

"Can't you just blow up the ships?" Amelia Dupont asked. "You're a wizard, for Gods' sakes."

"There are many schools of magic," Velus replied nervously. "Evocation was one that I never gave much credence to. I prefer the schools of divination and abjuration. I'd rather protect than hurt."

"You're in a war, halfling," Virgil Walker growled. "We need you to kill."

"No," Randall chimed in with an authoritative voice. "I will not order *any* of my subjects to do what they are not willing to. Grandmaster Velus, this other spell you talked of, is it safe for you to perform?"

"Safety is not the issue," Velus replied, his confidence slowly returning to him. "It requires a lot of preparation, and I'd have to be close to the ships for it to work. Meaning, I'd have to come with you."

All eyes at the table shifted towards Randall. He could feel their anticipation for his next words. Swallowing some of the anxiety that was bubbling up inside of him, Randall walked around the table and knelt beside mage's chair. "Velus, I need you to do this for us. Your city, your fellow Artanzians are counting on you. I promise that, as your king, I will protect you from harm. Nothing bad will happen to you, I swear it."

Velus looked deep into Randall's eyes. The king could see the fear in them, but he also saw the glimmer of something more – bravery, perhaps? Taking a deep breath in, Velus nodded his head. "Okay, but it'll take me an hour or so to prepare. Come find me at the docks, when you three are ready."

Randall embraced the halfling tightly. "Thank you, Grandmaster Velus, your deeds will not go unknown. The scribes will write about this day and your bravery." Randall rose to his feet. "The rest of you are to keep an eye on the city while we are away. I doubt Elbert will launch an assault tonight, but you never know: vigilance never hurts."

The councillors nodded their heads in understanding, and, with everything concluded, Randall took his leave. He had lots to think about, and even more to prepare for. Tonight was going to be an eventful night.

The black gambeson was tight around his chest and made him feel unnecessarily bulky. Randall had never worn armour before, and now he understood why; it was incredibly uncomfortable. He supposed that the cloth armour was better than plate, especially when stealth was of the utmost importance. However, he still didn't believe that wearing padded armour was going to be much help against arrows or swords.

"Looking like a true king," Cassius commented from the corner of the room.

Randall looked in the mirror and he felt his ego swell when he saw his reflection. The black armour, the sword on his hip, and a modest circlet on his head made him look like the warrior kings of yore. Trying to hide the smile on his face, he turned to the eunuch. "I'm nervous about this." Cassius raised a single, questioning brow in response. "What if it goes wrong? What if we can't contain the phoenix fire? Am I being too hasty?" Randall confessed. As much as he resented Cassius for going behind his back on matters of state, the former sommelier had never steered him into danger.

"Yes, but not in the way you think," Cassius said after a moment's hesitation. "I'm confident in Grandmaster Velus' ability to contain the phoenix fire. However, risking your own life, when others can easily take your place, is being hasty."

"I told you; I will not ask my subjects to do something that I myself am not willing to do."

"Yes, Your Majesty, but you have to realize which roles are more important for the realm. It is easier to find someone to go along with Tig and A'Chula and sabotage Elbert's ships than it is to find someone to be king should you fall."

Randall opened his mouth to respond, but before the words could leave his mouth, he realized the eunuch was right. If he fell, even if the mission was successful, what would happen to the city? What would happen to the kingdom? "What do you suggest?" the king asked, sensing that Cassius had already devised a solution.

"I'd advise you against going on this foolhardy endeavour. But I understand why you think you must. We are in a siege, and morale is running low amongst the people. If they see their king take action, it will raise their spirits and only strengthen their loyalty to you. However, if something goes wrong, you need a contingency plan so that everything you fought for doesn't disappear overnight. Name a successor, even if it is temporary."

"Who do you have in mind?"

"I would happily take up the burden of being sovereign should you perish, or until you find a suitable wife that will govern by your side. None of the other councillors have any knowledge in governance. I cannot see another option."

Impulsively, Randall clenched his jaw. As much as he didn't want to admit it, the eunuch was right once again. If he appointed anyone else, order would collapse under the new successor's incompetence, and if he didn't appoint anyone, the city would still collapse. Cassius was the only option. However, a smile crept along the king's lips. A few weeks ago, he would've blindly appointed Cassius as his successor if the worst should happen. Now, however, things had changed. Cassius was trying to organize deals behind his back. On top of that, Randall wasn't entirely sure that the eunuch was sharing all the information he knew with his king.

"I know that you just want to prepare for the worst, but don't worry, I will not die tonight. That's what the armour is for," Randall said with a wink before leaving the room, making his way to the harbour with his companions.

The cold air was eerily still, which meant sound would carry across the water easily, making stealth even more important. Randall stared out at the sea and watched the breath leave his mouth and turn into mist. He always wondered why the ocean never froze in winter, even on still nights such as this. Perhaps it was simply too big to freeze? Or maybe the fact that it was always moving stopped the ice from forming.

"The vases are loaded up, Randall," Tig said, interrupting the king's thoughts.

"Good, let's get to work."

The four men rowed silently out of the harbour. Corbin had arranged for the sea gate to be lowered so that their boat could enter the open sea. In the distance, the soft glow of lantern light illuminated the ships that blocked the harbour. From what Randall could see, there were four ships. Tig and A'Chula paddled slowly, while Velus clutched the volatile vases close to his chest.

The plan was simple. Douse an arrow in the phoenix fire, and launch it at the ships. Even if they missed, if the chemical brew worked like Grandmaster Velus said it would, an inferno would start as soon as it hit the water and would consume all of Elbert's ships. The trick would be to shoot the arrow closer to the ships than their boat, so that they didn't burn in the ensuing flames before the ships did.

Once in range, they sat back and listened. By the sound of things, most of the ships' crews were asleep, as there was little noise coming from the decks. A'Chula grabbed the bow that they had brought with them and dunked an arrow into the vase of phoenix fire. Taking aim, he drew the bowstring back and loosed the arrow at the first ship. There was an audible splash, but the night remained black as coal.

"What happened?" Tig asked quietly. "I thought you said if it touched water, it'd burn?"

"It should be burning!" Velus hissed. "I followed the instructions perfectly."

Randall was about to chastise the mage when he felt a tap on his shoulder. He turned around and saw A'Chula pointing to a space in between the two ships. A pale, orange glow was emanating from below the water's surface, getting brighter by the second.

"Holy shit," Randall whispered.

A'Chula grabbed another arrow and plunged it into the vase. Once again, he drew the bowstring back and loosed it at the other ships. By the time the fourth arrow left his bow, an enormous wall of flames had erupted between the first two ships. Bells were ringing and some sails had already caught fire. After a few minutes of panicking, Randall saw silhouettes of men jumping off their ships as the vessels were engulfed in flames. Randall smiled when he heard the screams of the burning men as they realized they had jumped off a burning ship and into a wild inferno.

The fire lit up the entire sky in a bright orange. All four of Elbert's ships had been consumed by the phoenix fire in less than five minutes. Their charred remnants sank to the bottom of the burning sea, along with their crews. Randall watched proudly as the fourth and final ship sank beneath the water's surface. He could feel the heat of the fire on his face, and it wasn't until then that he realized that it was closing in on their boat.

"Alright, wizard," Tig said, looking at Velus. "Now's the time!"

Velus laid his notes on the floor of the boat, and carefully read through them before standing on one of the benches, closing his eyes, and extending his arms upward. The halfling muttered his incantations silently, and Randall felt the hair on the back of his neck stand up. It seemed like the air vibrated, and he noticed that Velus' skin got sickly pale. A small stream of blood trickled from his eyes and nose as he continued to mutter his incantations. Tig reached out to touch the mage, but A'Chula slapped his hand away and shook his head.

Velus' eyes suddenly opened, and they glowed as bright as the inferno before them. His voice was loud and thunderous, almost deafening to Randall. Velus' hands shook violently and glowed an iridescent orange. Randall turned his attention to the fire and realized that it was dying down. Velus was absorbing the flames.

After several minutes of chanting, the fire had disappeared completely. Velus collapsed limp in the boat, glowing as bright as a torch. Randall quickly grabbed an oar and began rowing back to the city. Once they were across the sea gate and safely back in the harbour, Randall saw the docks were crowded with people, undoubtedly amazed by the spectacle they had just witnessed. Corbin Strongarm met them at the end of one of the docks and secured the boat.

"We need a healer!" Randall called out as he lifted the glowing Velus out of the boat. Truth be told, he wasn't sure if a healer could do anything for the mage, but he figured it was worth a try. A few burly sailors sprinted down the dock with a stretcher in hand. Carefully, Randall placed Velus on the stretcher and ordered Tig and A'Chula to accompany the mage to the healers.

Turning his attention to the plumes of smoke in the middle of the sea, Randall felt a calloused hand grab him by the wrist. "You did well, Your Majesty, you saved the city," Corbin Strongarm said.

"No," Randall corrected, "Velus saved the city."

CHAPTER TWENTY
CONNIR

The waves smacked against the hull of the ship. A strong, salty gale had caught the sails, and they were making good time towards the mainland. Life at sea was harsh, especially during the winter months. The boat was cramped, both with people and supplies, which made comfort and privacy impossible. Quickly, the Islanders became familiar with one another's musk, the smell of rancid body odour burning their nostrils in the tight, confined space.

It had been three days since they had reached the shoreline. Connir remembered how happy he was to see the ocean. He couldn't bear the idea of walking another step, but now that he had been trapped in the ship for three days, he would've given anything to have some more space from his companions. It didn't take them long to unload the ship; the sled was designed for the ship to slide down into the water once the braces were removed, and they were fortunate: they were able to catch the tide before it went out.

The wind had been at their backs almost the entire time during their voyage, which Ragnar claimed was a sign from the Gods of their favour. He was confident that they would reach the mainland that night, and Connir couldn't be happier. The sooner he was back on dry land, the better.

The monotony of sailing was excruciating. The only way Connir could pass the time was by continuing to talk with

Grimm, albeit in hushed whispers. Some of the other crew members questioned him when they saw the two of them talking, but Connir assured them he was only collecting background knowledge so that his ballad was historically accurate. This explanation seemed to be acceptable to the others, as nobody openly protested, but a few dirty looks were given. Connir was just thankful that nobody had noticed him giving Grimm scraps of food during their voyage. That would've been a lot harder to explain.

He wasn't sure what it was, but he was completely enthralled by the legendary warrior. Any story that Grimm could share, Connir eagerly ate up. His life had been incredible, one fantastic deed after another. He could hardly believe he was talking to such a man. Of course, Connir heard about the rumours of Grimm being blessed by Heimer himself, but Grimm denied these rumours, claimed that he was lucky more often than not. A part of Connir felt sorry for the old warrior, though. To have such an amazing life end by being chained to the mast of a ship, to die of starvation or exposure, was unfitting. Men like Grimm deserved to go to the Great Hall to dine with Heimer. Connir understood why Uthredd denied Grimm entry to the Great Hall – it was a fair punishment for his crimes – but it almost seemed like a waste, to have such a legendary life end this way. How was he supposed to compose a master ballad with such an anticlimactic end?

"I can't take it anymore!" Knut shouted as he shot to his feet. "Every day we just stare out at the fucking water, nothing to see, nothing to do. Just sit and wait. It's driving me insane!" "Patience, Knut," Ragnar replied from the stern. "The wind at our back is strong. We should reach the mainland as the sun sets."

"Not soon enough," Knut grumbled under his breath.

"Can't wait to rape and pillage, eh?" Skaði teased.

"These fucking mainlanders won't know what hit them!" Knut roared.

"Remember, High King Uthredd has a treaty with King Elbert, we aren't to raid until we get to Keten," Ragnar reminded him.

"Come on, Ragnar," Axel chimed in. "Allow us to have a little fun. Nobody will know the difference if we raid a village or two. We need to stretch our legs!"

"No," Ragnar answered firmly. "We are to follow High King Uthredd's orders. I will not be the one responsible for jeopardizing the new treaty 'tween the Isles and Artanzia."

"How is that fucker not dead yet?" Gunnar said, pointing at Grimm. "We've been gone for almost a week. Should be dead by now."

"He's got a strong spirit," Ragnar replied. "It'll take more than a few days of starving to kill the mighty Grimm White-Eyes."

"I say we toss him overboard now, get that craven out of my sight," Axel replied.

"We will do no such thing. High King Uthredd sentenced him to a painfully long death, and I will not be the one to ease his suffering by cutting his sentence short," Ragnar snapped.

"Come on, Ragnar," Gunnar replied, rising to his feet. "Dead is dead. Besides, he murdered Jarl Bearn in cold blood. Let's just kill him now so that we have more legroom." There was a murmur of approval from the others.

Connir cautiously looked at Grimm. Even if he wasn't chained up, he wouldn't stand a chance. His muscles had atrophied, and he had lost considerable weight since they captured him at Tjørholm. The skald then turned his attention to Ragnar, who now had a hand on the pommel of his sword.

"If you openly defy me again, Gunnar, I'll reunite you with your jarl."

"The fuck did you say, you bootlick?" Gunnar snarled, grabbing his hand axe by the haft.

Ragnar let go of the rudder and unsheathed his blade. The hiss of the steel echoed over the silent ocean. Connir watched nervously. He knew that conflict was inevitable; he only hoped that Ragnar would come out victorious. If Gunnar killed their captain, he wasn't sure how long it'd be before the others turned on him. He knew that Gunnar and Axel were not fond of him. As for Knut and Skaði, he didn't know how they felt. Connir didn't think they'd openly attack him, but he didn't think they'd rush to his aid either.

The two Islanders swung at each other violently, the longship rocking with every attack. Connir desperately grabbed the side of the boat, trying not to lose the contents of his stomach. He leaned over the side and stared into the blue water. He blinked a few times and swallowed his spit, hoping that would dissuade his breakfast from coming up. He looked over his shoulder and saw Gunnar swing wildly at Ragnar's head. Ragnar expertly ducked the attack and thrust his blade into the warrior's belly. Silence descended on the boat. Gunnar dropped his axe as he stared down at the river of blood that was streaming from his stomach. With a sharp twist, Ragnar pulled his blade free, pushed Gunnar's dying body over the side of the ship, and returned to the stern.

"There's your fucking legroom."

Despite being relatively young, Ragnar had a knowledge of sailing and the seas that would rival even the most seasoned sailor. Just as he had predicted, the continent was in sight just as the sun was setting over the western horizon. Connir stretched his aching muscles. He couldn't wait to disembark the ship and go back on dry land, He also wouldn't mind being further away from the pool of Gunnar's blood which had collected at the bottom of the ship. Most of the crew were fortunate enough to only have their boots soaked in their former comrade's blood. Grimm wasn't so lucky, as he was still chained to the mast, forced to sit in the crimson puddle.

As they approached the mouth of the river that would lead them to Keten, Connir watched Axel nervously. He had been eerily quiet since his clansman died at the end of their captain's sword. An ugly grimace had stained the warrior's face and Connir figured that retaliation would come soon and that Axel was just biding his time.

"Oars!" Ragnar called out as he turned the rudder to guide the ship into the mouth of the river. "The wind won't be strong enough to fight the current."

Nodding their heads, Knut, Axel, and Skaði stuck their oars over the side and began to row. Connir wasn't thrilled about the situation he found himself in. With Gunnar dead, Skaði had to take over his role as a rower, which left Connir all alone in dealing with the rigging. He wasn't exactly green when it came to sailing, but Connir definitely felt less anxious when he had someone else helping him. As he clambered around the deck of the ship, trying to take the sail down, he felt the eyes of the other Islanders on him. He felt his stomach churn with discomfort and his fingers became heavy. They fumbled around uselessly as he tried to tie his knots, which always came undone. After several minutes of struggling, Skaði stood up, quickly tied the knots properly, and resumed rowing. An air of awkwardness descended upon the ship. Connir felt completely and utterly emasculated. He was going to go sit down by his lute when Ragnar interrupted his sulking.

"Grab an oar, Connir!" The bard nodded his head and did as his captain ordered. "Come on, Arnvald," Ragnar muttered under his breath as he waited for the first sheet of ice to appear.

"It's warm," Knut mentioned. "Warmer than the Isles."

Skaði nodded her head. "Ice should be thin. We'll bust through it no problem."

They continued to row upriver, Connir's back aching every time he moved. They followed the beat of Ragnar's stomping foot, and their captain was setting a blistering pace. It had been years since he had worked this hard. He felt blisters starting to form on his hands. It felt like he was holding a rod of fire. Unwilling to be seen as a further burden on his crewmates, Connir dug deep and pushed on. His muscles burned and pleaded for him to stop, but he just gritted his teeth in response. After what felt like hours of rowing, there was a sudden lurch and the ship's momentum slowed.

"It's the ice!" Ragnar called out. "We need to keep going."

"It'll be dark soon," Grimm said suddenly, surprising everyone. "If you don't stop now, you won't see what's coming up the river."

"Shut up, traitor!" Axel snapped.

"I've been on more raids than all of you combined. I know sailing upriver at night is especially dangerous. If you actually want to see the new lands that Uthredd promised you, I'd stop for the night."

Silence. Connir looked around at his crewmates and saw that they were all expectantly looking at Ragnar. Connir turned his attention to his captain and saw that he was considering the traitor's words. "Fine," Ragnar said after a lengthy pause. "We'll beach it."

Connir, along with Knut, jumped off the ship and helped guide it so that it was parallel to the shoreline. They then grabbed ropes and tied it securely to some nearby trees. Once their ship was safely anchored, they were able to savour being on solid ground once again. It was Connir's first time on the mainland, and he was astonished by how different it was from the Isles. Instead of being miserably cold with more rocks than trees, the mainland was an oasis of trees with warm weather that rivalled most summers on the Isles. If this was what the mainlanders called "winter", he wasn't sure how Elbert and his men survived when they invaded. He was also confused about why anyone would want to leave this place. Everything one could ever want was here.

"I want an early start in the morning, so let's get some sleep," Ragnar ordered. "Connir, you're on first watch."

The skald nodded his head. He didn't mind being on watch. It would give him more alone time with Grimm, and he could hopefully glean more nuggets of history that he could add to his ballad. He had thought about releasing his chronicle of White-Eyes' life as a trilogy. The first would detail the warrior's rise to fame. The second would tell the tale of how he became Shield of the Isles and fought alongside High King Uthredd during the unification wars. And the third, starting with his murder of the High King's brother, would chronicle Grimm's fall from grace and inevitable death.

Once everyone was fast asleep, Connir snuck back onto the ship to talk to Grimm. The legendary warrior appeared to be waiting for someone. He sat upright and stared at the side of the ship through his milky white eyes. But when he saw it was Connir, he let out a sigh and rested his head against the mast of the ship.

"It's you," Grimm whispered.

"Who else would it be?" Connir replied.

"I was hoping it was one of the others so that I could finally get some peace."

"Why would you want that?"

"Look at me, boy," Grimm said. "I'm already a corpse. Let me die with some dignity."

"But I need to know more about—"

"I've got no more stories to share. You know everything. Now do me a favour and end this."

"You... you want me to kill you?" Connir asked in disbelief, struggling to keep his voice low.

"Just let me die with honour. Put a dagger in my hand, then stab me here." He pointed to his chest, right where the heart would be. "You've killed one man, skald; you can do it again."

"But Uthredd said—"

"Uthredd isn't here," Grimm snarled. "Once I'm dead, you can take the dagger back and nobody has to know you let me die with honour."

"Grimm, I don't know if I—"

"For Heimer's sake, boy, you owe me!" Grimm said, lunging forward till his chains were taut.

"How do you figure?" Connir asked incredulously.

"I told you everything about my life, you're the only person who knows the truth, and the only bastard who's going to get filthy rich off that truth. The least you can do is ease my pain and let me die with dignity."

Connir looked deep into Grimm's eyes. He felt a lump in his chest. He knew it was wrong, but he did owe Grimm. Not only for telling Connir his life story, but for saving his father's life, which inadvertently saved his own. Against his better judgement, Connir nodded his head and left the ship. He already had one dagger, but needed another, if he was going to do this right. He slowly crept up to Ragnar's sleeping body, and, as quietly as he could, pulled the dagger from his captain's belt.

As the blade slowly left the scabbard, a long and high-pitched hiss filled the night air. Connir looked around the camp, but nobody else seemed to hear it. He continued to pull the dagger free until it almost leapt into his hand. He clutched the small blade to his chest and watched as Ragnar stirred in his sleep, but thankfully, he didn't wake.

Letting out a breath, Connir snuck back onto the ship. He handed Grimm the dagger and sat back, watching the old warrior. He felt as if this moment deserved some sort of reverence. He wasn't sure what he should say. How do you console someone you're about to kill? Stomaching his anxiety, he asked, "Any last words?"

"Don't miss," Grimm said matter-of-factly.

Connir wasn't sure what he expected, but that certainly wasn't it. In fact, Grimm's last words only made him more nervous.

"Need me to show you again?" Grimm asked.

Connir nodded his head. Grimm grabbed his wrist and pulled the skald in tight. He guided Connir's hand so that the tip of the dagger was right above his heart. Connir had closed his eyes to gather his courage, when he felt something ice-cold pierce his chin. At first he thought it was the wind. When he opened his eyes, he realized how stupid he had been. Grimm had stabbed his dagger into Connir's mouth.

His heart raced wildly as he felt warm blood trickle down his chest. He thought about calling for help, but when he opened his mouth Grimm drove the blade further into his skull. A soft moan escaped his lips and his body fell limp to the floor of the ship. He lay there, motionless, in a pool of his and Gunnar's blood, staring at the man that murdered him.

Grimm tore the dagger free from Connir's head, causing the skald's body to twitch, and began picking the lock of his shackles with the tip of the dagger. As the edges of the world faded to black, the last thing Connir heard was Grimm's solemn voice.

"At least you died with honour."

INTERLUDE
UTHREDD

It was a particularly vicious night. Frost covered all the windows and the unrelenting cold seeped into the houses, threatening to freeze everyone and anyone inside. All the hearths in Skotheim were set ablaze, desperately trying to heat the homes, and High King Uthredd's longhouse was no exception. Braziers were lit every few feet, and in the king's private chambers a large fire burned in the fireplace. The wood snapped and popped as the fire slowly consumed it, embers slowly drifting up the chimney and out into the freezing night.

Sitting in front of the fire was High King Uthredd. He had slept little since he returned from Tjørholm, and tonight was no different. When he closed his eyes at night, his mind seemed to run wild, unable to calm itself down. He would stay up all night until the exhaustion finally consumed him for a few peaceful hours of sleep. Guilt was slowly eating away at him.

Lost in the fire that was burning in his hearth, Uthredd's mind began replaying bittersweet memories. He remembered how growing up, he and Grimm would always get into trouble. One particular memory, the night they accidentally burnt down a brothel, brought a pained smile to the king's lips. He remembered how his father welcomed Grimm into their home and raised him as his own son. He also remembered how when he confessed his dream to unify the Isles, Grimm immediately supported him, even when his own brother did not.

There was a stirring behind him. He turned his head and saw his wife, Ingrid, moving in the bed. Once she had stilled, Uthredd turned his attention back to the fire and thought of his brother. He remembered sparring with Eirik and looking after him on their first raid together. Then there was the time when he and Grimm got Uthredd so drunk that they convinced him to try juggling swords to impress one of the village girls. Luckily, the only thing the future king lost that night was a little pride. He missed his brother; he wished he could have had the chance to talk to him before he acted. Before everything went to shit.

He continued to watch the flames dance on top of the logs, his mind so preoccupied replaying painful memories that he did not hear his wife leave the bed.

She placed a gentle hand on his shoulder. "What troubles you, husband?"

Uthredd tore his eyes from the fire and stared into his wife's steely grey eyes. "Nothing, Ingrid. Go back to sleep."

Ingrid slowly let go of Uthredd's shoulder and walked around to stand in front of the fire, arms crossed.

"It's nothing," Uthredd repeated. "Truly."

Ingrid's hand was a blur as she slapped her husband across his face. The resounding crack echoed throughout the room.

"Do not lie to me. You have barely slept since you returned from Tjørholm. I'm your wife – if you can't tell me, who can you tell?"

He stared at her for several seconds, contemplating her actions. Ingrid was a mild-mannered, soft-spoken woman, so the slap caught him off guard. But he also knew that she wouldn't resort to such methods if she wasn't desperate to reach him. Begrudgingly, he let out a sigh. "Am I a good king, Ingrid?"

"What makes you think you aren't?" Ingrid asked in a concerned voice. "You did what others thought impossible – you united all the Islander clans under one banner. No other king could ever do such a thing. Of course you are a good king!"

"Then why do I feel like a fraud?" Uthredd whispered, rising from his chair. "I am the only Islander ruler to have his lands invaded, and instead of slaughtering the foreigners, I brokered a deal with them, like some kind of coward."

Ingrid tilted her head slightly and placed a hand on her husband's cheek. "You stopped needless bloodshed. Just like you did when you unified the clans. The mainlander king was willing to see reason. You saved hundreds, if not thousands of lives. That is the mark of a good king."

Uthredd shook his head. "If I'm such a good king, why couldn't I protect my brother?" he snarled in a shaky voice, pushing her hand away from his face. "And when I finally caught his murderer, I didn't have the stomach to take his head right then and there! I'm a failure as a king."

Ingrid stepped forward and pulled Uthredd in for a tight embrace, despite his efforts to push her away. She slowly stroked the back of his head and shushed him the way a mother might do to an unruly child. "You did the right thing with Grimm," she whispered. "I know he was like a brother to you, and he helped you unite the clans, but a clean death was too good for him. He deserves to rot on that ship."

Uthredd slowly backed out of the hug, shaking his head. "That's just it," he whispered.

"What is?"

"You don't know Grimm like I do, Ingrid. The man is blessed by Heimer himself. When he was only days old, his father abandoned him in the woods for the wolves to feed on and—"

"And three days later, he showed up at his parents' front door covered in blood. I've heard the story before. What is your point?"

Uthredd sighed. "I've known Grimm my whole life. He has cheated death more times than any man should be able to. Even if there is the slimmest chance of survival, he will find it."

Ingrid backed up slowly. "Uthredd, what are you saying?"

"When I sentenced Grimm to starve, chained to the mast of a ship, I knew damn well that he was going to find a way to cheat death once again. I couldn't kill him..."

Ingrid's mouth dropped open. She shook her head in disbelief, before uttering out a single question. "Why?"

"I owe everything to Grimm! When I told him I wanted to unify the clans, I didn't even have to ask him to pick up his sword. He did it without hesitation. Eirik didn't join till I had almost all the clans under my banner already. Grimm was there from the start. The kingdom we have, the crown that sits atop my head is because of the blood that man spilt for me. I cannot kill a man I owe so much to. I cannot condemn my best friend, a man I love like a brother, to death. But in doing so I've failed my people. I've failed my blood."

Ingrid's body softened and she gave a reassuring smile. "No one will ever know. If he is half as smart as you think he is, Grimm White-Eyes will never set foot on the Isles again. He knows he's a dead man here. We can tell the people that the ship was lost in a storm. You don't have to carry this secret alone anymore. I'm your wife, and I will be at your side till the day we enter the Great Hall."

Uthredd wiped the tears from his eyes and once again welcomed his wife's embrace. The two of them stood there and held one another, listening to the soft cracking of the fire deep into the night.

ACT II

CHAPTER TWENTY-ONE
GRIMM

The soft, orange rays of the sun stirred Grimm from his slumber. He opened his heavy eyes and saw the thin layers of snow sparkling. A fresh layer of ice had formed around the ship during the night. Groggily, he painfully rose to his feet and stared at the corpses of his Islander captors. It was not the first time he had slept next to rotting bodies, but he hoped it would be the last.

Grimm had spent the entire voyage plotting his escape, and although he knew it wouldn't be easy, he never expected it to be as difficult as it was. Killing Connir was easy, although it brought him no joy to do so – the boy was too eager to learn the legendary warrior's story and soon dropped his guard when he was alone with Grimm. The next part was just as easy, picking the lock of his shackles with the dagger Connir had given him. It took longer than Grimm expected, but he eventually escaped from the chains. The hardest part of his escape was killing the others while they slept. Thankfully, the captain had killed one of Bearn's men during the voyage, so that was one less person to worry about.

The actual killing of his captors was easy, just sneaking up on them while they slept and either plunging the dagger through the base of their skulls, or slitting their throats, depending on how they slept. The hard part was the amount of effort moving required. He hadn't moved in days. His muscles were weak, and he had lost considerable weight. Every kill took more and more energy out of him, and by the time he had slit Ragnar's throat, he was forced to fall into a deep sleep.

He took a step towards the ship and immediately collapsed to his knees. His legs were wobbly and could no longer support him. He didn't realize how much the adrenaline carried him last night. He looked down at his atrophied legs and a sarcastic grin spread across his face. *Now I know how Legless feels.* As the image of the crippled king entered his head, the smile on his face slowly dissipated. After his betrayal, whenever Grimm thought about Elbert, rage consumed him, a fiery rage that would send bile up his throat, as he remembered how the cripple sacrificed Grimm and his men in order to save Uthredd's pride. It was dishonourable and disgusting, and it made Grimm's stomach churn.

However, something had happened during his time in captivity. His rage had calmed, and he no longer felt animosity towards Elbert. Being alone with his thoughts for days on end gave Grimm time to reflect, plus, Connir forcing him to relive his most "legendary" feats didn't help matters, either. Grimm had come to the realization that he had spilt enough blood in his lifetime. He wanted to come to the mainland for his freedom, and now, after spilling more blood, he finally had it.

The idea of having complete and utter freedom was both exciting and terrifying to Grimm. He didn't know what he was going to do. Perhaps he'd travel the continent, or become a merchant, or learn a trade. At that moment, his stomach growled in hunger. He realized that if he didn't eat, and force his body to move, his newfound freedom would be over before it started. Forcing himself back to his feet, he arduously walked back on board the ship, collapsing several times as he did so.

He stepped around Connir's corpse, and out of the corner of his eye, saw the frozen look of shock and horror on the skald's lifeless face. The sight caused a pang of something in Grimm's stomach, but he pressed on and helped himself to the provisions left on the ship.

He had heard tales of men starving at sea and then eating so much that they vomited once they returned to the Isles. Grimm did his best to eat as much as he could to feel full, but not so much that he would lose all the nutrition of the food. The last of the provisions were mainly salted fish, stale bread, and a few pickled beans. Savouring every bite and washing it down with snow, Grimm felt like he was in the court of a king. The temptation to eat everything in sight was almost too much to ignore, it had been so long since he ate anything besides the measly morsels Connir gave him. The only thought that kept this temptation at bay was that if he ate and vomited everything back up, he would have to hunt, which he was in no condition to do.

The rest of the day Grimm spent trying to regain some of his dignity and strength. He forced his muscles to move a little at a time; he shed his soiled clothes and bathed himself in the river; and stole clothes that fitted from the corpses. Truth be told, he didn't find winter on the mainland to be that cold. He was quite content being naked in the elements, as the weather was closer to the summer seasons on the Isles rather than the winter months. But he figured it was probably because he was acclimatized to the harsh winter of the Isles and that his body was playing tricks on him. Hypothermia was the last thing he needed to worry about, so he clothed himself, just to be safe.

During one of his many moments of respite throughout the day, he rummaged through the dead Islanders' pockets. He found a few gold coins, a couple of silver rings that could be sold for food if he ever made it back to civilized society, and a bag of mysterious mushrooms that was taken from the dead Beastfolk berserker. Grimm had heard tales of these mushrooms before; they were said to transform anyone who took them into their spirit animal while in battle. Although he had never seen it happen with his own eyes, he suspected the rumours were true, since members of the Beastfolk clan were incredibly secretive about the magical mushrooms and berries they gathered.

As the sun set on his first day of freedom, Grimm climbed aboard the ship and wrapped himself in the sails for warmth. He wished he had the strength to build a fire, but given how difficult it was to simply move, that was out of the question. He also knew that it would not be safe to sleep outside the ship. The corpses of his captors would soon attract predators, and he knew he was in no condition to fend them off.

The second and third day of Grimm's newfound freedom was much like his first. He slowly tested the limits of his body, while trying to ration the remaining food. When the sun rose on the fourth morning, Grimm awoke to the sounds of flesh being torn apart and bones breaking. He peered over the side of the ship and saw a pack of wolves devouring the corpses on the shore. Although he was safe inside the ship, he knew the beasts would hinder his efforts to regain his strength. He paced up and down the ship's body several times, trying to get the blood flowing in his legs. The wolves saw him pacing but paid him no mind, as they continued to feast on the Islanders' corpses.

As the sun set on the fourth day, Grimm pushed his body further. He grabbed Connir's ankles and dragged him to the side of the ship. Every inch was a battle, and the skald's lifeless body certainly did not make things any easier. Once the corpse's feet hung over the ship's side, Grimm grabbed his shoulders and lifted as much as he could using his tired legs. He heard the growling of the wolves waiting for a fresh meal at the edge of the ship. His knees shook and wobbled as he continued to lift the body higher into the air. Just as he was about to toss Connir overboard, Grimm's knees buckled and he collapsed face first onto the ship's deck. He heard the sickening crunch of his nose breaking against the hard wooden planks.

Letting out a scream of pain and frustration, he rolled over onto his back and placed two meaty fingers on his disfigured nose. He took a few seconds to gather his breath, and, with a sharp inhale, pushed it back into alignment. He was pathetic, a shadow of his former self. He looked up at the orange sky and wondered what his wife would think of him now if she could see him. A smile appeared on his lips as a humorous thought entered his mind. Freja would probably laugh and mock him. He could almost hear her melodic voice chastising him. *This is what you get for fucking that harlot behind my back. You're a damned whoreson, Grimm White-Eyes!* His smile faded slightly as he continued to look at the sky. He would've given anything to have his wife here with him. Even if she would only scream and curse him, he would happily pay any price set before him to allow that to happen.

He stared into the sky until the orange hue of the setting sun was slowly consumed by the unrelenting black void of night. He turned his head to look at Connir's face, and let out a long breath. "One more story." He took a few moments to find the right words and cleared his throat. "After I killed Eirik, I knew my life was over. My wife and son were gone. I had just murdered my best friend's brother, and I would have the entire

Isles searching for me, eager to take my head. I was truly and utterly alone."

He paused for a moment, noting the small waver in his voice. "I was prepared to live a lonely, bloody life. A life of selling my sword to the highest bidder. But after Tjørholm..." There was a lump in his throat. Taking a deep breath, he swallowed, forcing it back down into his stomach. "I spilt a lake of blood for that legless prick. A lake of Islander blood..." Grimm looked at his hands for a brief moment before turning back to Connir's lifeless face. "I've been a warrior, a killer since before I can remember. It's the only thing I've ever been good at. But, I don't know if I can anymore. I don't know if I want to."

Grimm turned his attention back to the sky. He wasn't sure if the dead could hear prayers in the Great Hall, but he figured it was worth a shot. "Freja. I know I've wronged you, but I promise with this second chance in life I will try to be the man you always wanted me to be. I will abandon the sword, and shall not spill another man's blood, unless it is in self-defence. I promise this. I only hope that you and Einarr will forgive me when I finally enter the Great Hall."

The deafening silence of the night was the only response he received. Even the wolves were eerily quiet. Deciding to save his strength for the morrow, he closed his eyes and fell asleep.

Around midday, he tried to throw Connir's body overboard again. But this time, he stopped himself before even attempting it. It felt wrong; he felt guilty. Connir deserved better than to be ripped apart by a pack of wolves. He walked over and pulled the sail over Connir's body, hoping that keeping the corpse from sight would make things better. *It was them or me*, he told himself, hoping his guilt would magically disappear.

On the sixth day, the wolf pack left. He was surprised that they did not try harder to enter the boat, but perhaps they had had their fill of human meat after eating four entire corpses. Once he was sure that the wolves would not return, he exited the ship and resumed his training regimen. He started by venturing into the woods and gathering small twigs and grass, something that he could start a fire with, in case the wolves returned during the night. He placed the grass on a rock so that it could dry out in the sun. He had just finished building a pyramid out of the sticks when he heard the distinct sound of a twig snapping in the undergrowth. He quickly pulled the dagger from his belt and eyed the tree line. If it was one wolf, he might be lucky and be able to kill it. If it was a pack, he knew this would be his end, but he was determined to take a few of the beasts with him.

A man emerged from the brush, bow and arrow in hand, and upon seeing Grimm, immediately ducked back behind cover. "Easy there!" he called out. "Don't want no trouble, just tracking a pack of wolves."

"They left," Grimm replied, his knees starting to shake.

The man poked his head out once again and saw the eviscerated remains of the Islander crew on the ground. "Wolves get them?"

"Mhmm."

The stranger emerged from the underbrush and threw the bow over his shoulder. Despite putting his weapon away, the man approached cautiously, his eyes constantly darting back towards Grimm to make sure the Islander hadn't moved.

"They've been sniffing around our camp lately. I'm s'posed to drive them away."

Grimm's legs screamed from exhaustion, and despite trying to blink the pain away, they buckled underneath him. He hit the ground with a hard thud and he felt the dagger slip through his fingers. A pained groan escaped his lips and he heard the quickened footsteps of the stranger approach. He kicked Grimm's dagger out of reach and looked down at him, still cautious. After several seconds of scrutiny, the man took a waterskin from his hip and poured it into Grimm's mouth.

"Drink," he instructed.

Despite his instincts saying not to, Grimm took a cautious swig. When the refreshing water touched his tongue, he greedily took a few more pulls from the canteen.

"You look like shit," the man said, pulling the waterskin away from the Islander's lips and attaching it to his hip. "How did you survive the wolves?"

"Slept on the ship," Grimm replied. The man took a look at the longship and Grimm immediately hoped that he didn't go investigate. Connir's rotting corpse was still on board, and if discovered, Grimm would need to think of a new lie about how he died.

"You Islanders?" the man asked, rising from Grimm's side and backing up several paces.

"Mhmm."

"You here for raidin'?"

"They were."

"What about you?"

Grimm hesitated before answering. He narrowed his eyes before ultimately deciding that honesty was the best option. "I want a fresh start."

The man raised a brow before helping Grimm to his feet. "Come on," he said. "We'll get you looked after at the colony."

Grimm did not want to go with the man, but he didn't really have a choice. He was in no condition to fight back, and given the circumstances, figured that this man and his people were his best chance at survival.

"I'm Gareth," the man said.

"Grimm."

The two men walked slowly through the forest, frequently taking breaks to rest Grimm's weary body. The man kept his distance, but offered the Islander water during the breaks. The further they walked into the forest, the more it became apparent that Gareth was not leading Grimm towards civilization. There were no roads, no signposts, nothing. Just a quiet secluded forest, in the middle of nowhere.

"Where are we going?" Grimm asked, his suspicion rising.

"The settlement," Gareth replied.

"Does this town have a name?"

Gareth shook his head. "No. Our story is a lot like yours. We all wanted a fresh start, a place where we could leave the evil of the world behind and begin anew."

Grimm nodded his head, although he wasn't sure what the man exactly meant. In any case, this settlement still sounded like his best path forward.

"We're small yet, but we hope to be self-sufficient soon. This year we are going to be clearing part of the forest to plant a field for some crops. We have to go into town often and get supplies," Gareth continued, helping Grimm to his feet once more.

"Sounds... peaceful," Grimm replied.

"We try our best. You got a family?"

"I did."

"Ah," Gareth said, scratching the back of his neck. "Sorry to hear that. I lost my first son to a fever. I thought dwarves were supposed to be immune to that kind of stuff, but it appears he inherited my constitution."

"Dwarves?"

"My wife, she is a dwarf. So technically Malcolm was a half-dwarf, but he looked more like his mother than he did me. He died two winters back."

"I'm sorry," Grimm said. His mind instantly thought of Sara. Part of him wanted to track her down and reunite with her, but he knew if he did that, he would have to spill a lot of blood. He told himself that Elbert would take better care of her than he ever could. She would live a nice, pampered life as a page or cupbearer until some fat lord married her. She would have a good life, and he lied to himself that he could live with that.

After a painfully long journey, Gareth led Grimm into a clearing, where several small wooden buildings with thatched roofs formed something that resembled a town. Children played in the clearing while the adults of the colony prepared for spring. It was a quaint settlement, and Grimm felt a smile crawling across his face.

The people of the colony stopped and looked as Gareth and Grimm came into view. Several mothers ushered their children inside and a few of the men clutched whatever tools they had in their hands more tightly. Then, a stocky, muscular man with dark skin and a shaved head walked into view and smiled brightly at the two men. His presence seemed to put the others at ease.

"Gareth! You've returned, and not with meat, but with another mouth."

Although the words seemed sarcastic, Grimm did not sense any coming from the man. He couldn't help but stare at him. He had never seen anyone with skin as dark as his. He tried to think back to all the times he raided the mainland, to see if he recalled seeing anyone with skin like his, but at the moment, he was drawing a blank.

"I figured he could use our help, Uriel," Gareth said, his head turning down slightly. "The wolves killed his crew."

"Crew? Are you a merchant?"

"It was an Islander longship, said the others came for raiding, while he wanted to get a fresh start."

Grimm side-eyed Gareth. Although the man was just relaying information, Grimm wished that he would've had the chance to speak for himself. However, judging by his way with words, perhaps it was best that Gareth spoke for him.

Uriel eyed Grimm curiously, as if appraising a work of art, before smiling and pointing Gareth to the smithy. "Set our new friend there and get him some food. I'll talk to him after he gets some rest."

Grimm tried to hide his surprise. Just like that? Either these people were fools, or they were saints. He knew, more often than not, that saints and fools were the same thing. But, not willing to look a gift horse in the mouth, Grimm nodded his head in thanks and, with the help of Gareth, worked his way towards the smithy.

The blacksmith's forge was secluded away from the rest of the colony, and Grimm didn't mind that. He was away from prying eyes and it allowed him to eat and rest at his own pace.

They had offered him some fresh bread and some jerky, which Grimm was more than thankful for. Anything was better than the morsels of salted fish that Connir had been sneaking him. He spent an hour or two relaxing and building up his strength once again. He hated to admit it, but the walk through the brush with Gareth took a lot out of him, even with the number of breaks they took. There was a pain of disgust in his chest. He hated being reminded that he was a shadow of himself.

Suddenly, Uriel appeared and pulled up a stool across from Grimm. His welcoming aura had vanished. "Gareth showed me what happened to your crew. The wolves didn't leave much for the birds." Grimm nodded his head, sensing the man had more to say. "Seems these wolves are smarter than your average pack though – we found the body of a man stabbed on the deck of the ship."

Shit, Grimm thought. Of course it wouldn't be that easy. He shifted slightly, trying to get his body in a position where he could either run, or fight, although both options would most likely lead to the same outcome.

"Who are you, really?" Uriel asked, brow furrowed.

Grimm took a few seconds to choose his words carefully. Sensing no other option, he figured that it was best to come clean, especially since they had seemingly discovered everything already. "I was their prisoner. I was sentenced to die chained to the ship."

"That explains the shackles we found. What did you do?"

"It's a long story."

Uriel took a deep breath, staring at Grimm with a great intensity. Much to the Islander's surprise, the man did not have an ounce of anger in his face. He seemed more curious; cautious, but curious about finding out the truth. After a lengthy pause, Uriel spoke. "How do we know you aren't going to kill us in our sleep as well?"

Grimm's eyes widened with shock. His mouth moved as he tried to think of a response, but before any words could leave his lips, Uriel gave him a knowing smile.

"Don't look so surprised. You're practically a skeleton. How else would you kill them? I know you Islanders are not fond of poison. Something about 'dying honourably'?"

Grimm nodded his head.

"If you want to stay with us, there are some rules here," Uriel started. "First, nobody eats for free, everyone must pull their weight around here. Second, you may not brandish weapons of any kind in our settlement. We follow the teachings of the Golden Sun, who teaches us that every man, woman, and child are worthy and deserve love and compassion, and that violence is not only a thing to abhor, but to avoid at all costs."

Grimm let out an amused snort. "So, you're pacifists?"

Uriel's face contorted into a disappointed frown. "We do not kill, if that is what you are asking. Nor do we permit violence of any kind in our colony."

Grimm let out an exasperated sigh and handed over his dagger. "Very well, consider me a pacifist." *Mainlanders,* he thought. *Leave it to weak people to worship even weaker gods.* Despite this thought, however, Grimm was willing to follow their rules so long as they provided food and shelter for him and allowed him to get his body back to full strength. Plus, he remembered the promise he had made to his wife a few days earlier – perhaps it was fitting that he had found his way into a pacifist commune. What better way to start a new peaceful life?

"Not so fast," Uriel said, a smile spreading across his lips. "Like I said, everyone has to pull their weight around here." The man rose from his stool and grabbed a large sack of bricks from outside the smithy. He dropped the heavy sack in front of Grimm with a grunt. "If you can bring these to the far side of camp, then we'll happily welcome you into our community." Uriel turned to leave, before stopping in the doorway. "See if you're worth feeding."

Grimm's face contorted into a frown. He resented being treated like this. Not only did he have to prove himself useful, but it was clear that these people didn't see him as a threat, and he was not sure what pissed him off more. All in all, though, moving a bag of bricks was not too difficult a task, and he counted himself lucky. Gathering his strength, he rose to his feet and tried to pick up the bag, only to realize that he couldn't move it an inch. *Shit.*

Coated in a thick sheen of sweat, Grimm dropped the final brick on the pile with a pained breath. Wheezing, he stood over the heap and glared at it with contempt. He had had to carry each brick individually, and he never wanted to see them again. His hands throbbed, and his legs burned in excruciating pain, but he had done it. He looked up and noticed that the moon was high in the sky. Turning around, he saw a proud Uriel smiling at him.

"You did well, although it took you longer than I thought."

"Hmm," Grimm grunted, too tired to speak.

Uriel tossed the Islander a flask of water and turned back to camp. "Welcome to your fresh start."

CHAPTER TWENTY-TWO
ROSALINE

It took four days for the smoke from the burning ships in the harbour to dissipate. Once the suffocating haze finally left, the city became livelier. People exited their homes and several celebrated Randall's victory openly. The removal of Elbert's blockade provided a glimmer of hope over the starving city. Sailors left the harbour to resume their trade, and the prospect of more food and supplies coming into the city was enough to sate the citizens' rumbling bellies, at least for the time being.

The only people not excited by the news of Randall's victory were Rosaline and the Bloody Brotherhood. Having trade resumed was the worst thing that could've happened to their enterprise. With more food coming in, people would be less inclined to pay them for their stolen food, and might even alert the guards to the location of the stolen goods. As a result, the last four days consisted of sleepless nights for Rosaline, as she tried to figure out how to navigate these treacherous waters. There were several nights she spent scheming and plotting how her and her Brothers could get out of this without having their necks wrung by a noose.

There was a knock on her door. Rosaline lifted her weary eyes from the dozens of papers in front of her and shouted at whoever was on the other side of the door to come in. Duncan opened the door, a scroll of paper in each hand. Rosaline raised a questioning brow.

"Come to bring me more reading material?"

"Kind of," Duncan said as he pulled up a chair across the table from his leader. He tossed one of the scrolls to her. Rosaline begrudgingly unravelled the parchment and looked at the symbol scrawled onto the paper in black ink. It depicted an arrowhead with a skull in the middle. Two daggers were crossed behind the arrowhead and a handprint was on the forehead of the skull.

"Am I supposed to know what this is?" she asked.

"I saw it on some men carrying a bunch of food around the city. Seems we have competition."

Shit, Rosaline silently cursed. This was the last thing they needed. "And the other scroll?"

Duncan unrolled the second scroll and placed it in front of her. It appeared to be an advertisement for an enchanter. *Marvellous Micah's Magnificent Magical Items.* "The man sure loves the letter 'M'. But besides the wonderful alliteration, why do I care?"

Duncan smiled coyly. "We need an out if the guards come to our door. And what better way to profess our innocence than having no food here for the guards to find?"

Rosaline smiled in understanding. "You want to hire this Micah to hide our stash?"

"Mhmm," Duncan replied. "Although he might not want to work for a gang of dirty degenerates like us."

Rosaline smiled. "Then we ask a second time, only more... *assertively.*" Leaning back in her chair, Rosaline's smile widened. Duncan was proving his worth yet again. Her faith in the half-elf had been wavering. He had failed in finding Randall's stash, and just when she was about to give the job to someone else, he brought her this – a solution to a problem that she desperately needed to resolve.

"Right, I'll send Malek and Jathan to check out our rivals, while Phillip and I will pay this mage a visit."

"What about me?"

"You *need* to find that stash, Duncan." As soon as the words left Rosaline's mouth, the air in the room changed. The half-elf's shoulders slouched, and a frown appeared on his face. "It is important that we at least find where they are hiding it. If we know where it is, then we can strategize how we are going to secure it."

"Does it even matter anymore?" Duncan asked. "The harbour is open and trade has resumed. In a week, the people will have food and our risk of getting caught increases. We should cut our losses and get as much as we can in the next few days, then flee the city."

"I will not tuck tail and run simply because the guards might come knocking on our door. Besides, what if Elbert gets more ships and reinstates the blockade? I'm not going to leave gold on the table that's ripe for the taking. Now, find that stash or I'll get someone who can." Despite her appreciation for his finding the mage, Rosaline couldn't afford to be soft on Duncan. The boot had to be pressed down further on the man's throat. She needed results.

Duncan nodded his head, and silently, with an air of contempt, left the room. Rosaline let out a frustrated sigh as she rose from the table and readied herself for a talk with Marvellous Micah. She was no stranger to manipulating people; in fact, she was quite good at it. She knew a multitude of ways of getting people to do what she wanted. She could bat her eyes and flirt with the man, but the thought made her stomach churn. The surest and most enjoyable way was to let Boris handle the negotiations, until Micah was a snivelling puddle of piss-soaked fear. She grabbed Boris by the hilt and stabbed the enchanter's flyer into the table.

"Let's go pay Micah a visit."

Finding Micah's shop proved more challenging than Rosaline expected. The location of the mage's store was less than ideal. It was in a narrow alley that was filled with refuse from the neighbouring buildings. Since the alley was so cramped, the smell of the waste hung stagnantly in the air, threatening to choke all potential customers with the putrid miasma. Rosaline took a deep breath, entered the alley, and opened the door to the store. The plan was simple: she would go in the front and distract Micah, while Phillip snuck in through a back entrance in case the negotiations needed to go into a more *physical* direction.

Once Rosaline crossed the threshold of the store, she wasn't sure which was worse, the alley or the actual shop. The shop smelled like dusty tomes, which was downright heavenly compared to the smell of the alley, but there was no room to walk. The entire floor space of the shop was covered in junk. Some objects didn't even look like potential wares that Micah could sell to customers, it was towers of garbage, discarded objects piled on top of each other. Empty soup bowls, broken spoons, a table that looked like it was ready to snap under its own weight at any second. If dragons collected useless filth, she imagined that this was what their lairs would look like.

"Is someone there?" a feeble voice called out through the piles of trash.

"Umm, yes," Rosaline replied, trying her best to speak like the type of person she despised the most, a helpless damsel. "I'm looking for Marvellous Micah?"

"That'd be me!" the voice answered. There was the sound of movement, before a loud crash sent one of the pillars of garbage plummeting to the shop floor. Debris went everywhere, although it didn't change the level of the shop's cleanliness.

Emerging from the pile of junk was an elderly halfling. He had thin strands of grey, wispy hair protruding from an otherwise bald head and wore a homely-looking tunic accompanied by a pair of dust-covered spectacles. Micah took the glasses off his face and wiped the lenses on the bottom of his shirt. "Now, what can I help you with, dearie?" he asked as he returned the spectacles to his face.

"I'm looking for something magical," she replied, as she pretended to peruse the mage's "wares".

"Well, you've come to the right place!" Micah exclaimed. "What sort of enchantment are you looking for? But be warned, I don't make love potions, although I assume a beautiful lady like yourself has no trouble in that department."

Rosaline forced a polite smile. "I'm looking to hide some valuables. With all the stories of robberies lately, you can't be too careful."

"Hmmm," Micah said as he scratched his chin in thought. "I could put an arcane lock on a safe if you have one. That way, it will only open if a certain phrase is uttered."

Out of the corner of Rosaline's eye, she saw a large person shuffle quietly behind one of the towers of garbage that littered the shop. *Surprising how a man like that can move so quietly*

."Unfortunately, my valuables are quite large, and won't fit in a standard safe."

"Well, what about something I call the boundless bag?" Micah suggested.

"What is that?" Rosaline asked, realizing the man seemed obsessed with alliteration.

Micah smiled widely and held out an outstretched hand in front of him. Rosaline wasn't sure if he was planning on leading her somewhere deeper inside the store. She was about to take his hand when he whistled sharply, and a leather pouch flew across the room and landed gently in his hand.

"This little bag," Micah began, "holds an entire, bottomless universe inside it. No matter how much you put in, it will never grow in size, never get heavier, and, of course, never get full."

Rosaline eyed the bag curiously. "And I can put anything inside it?"

"If it can fit in the bag, yes. Although, I wouldn't recommend putting anything living in there. There's no air, so I'm afraid it would suffocate."

Rosaline's eyes darted to the side, where she saw Phillip waiting to pounce in a low crouch. She turned her attention back to the oblivious shopkeeper. "And how much is this little trinket going to set me back?"

"Well, a lot of work goes into making one of these," Micah admitted. "I could give it to you for, let's say, a thousand gold pieces?"

"You're kidding."

"And that's with the pretty young girl discount!" Micah added.

Phillip raised a questioning eyebrow. Rosaline ever so slightly shook her head. There was no way that he could reach the mage without knocking some of the clutter over. Besides, mages were dangerous to get into a fight with. One false move, and he'd turn them both into frogs, and they'd call the cluttered shop their home for eternity. Rosaline turned her head back to the mage and noticed that his brow was furrowed into a deep frown.

"Expecting someone?" Micah asked, slowly tucking the bag into his cloak.

Rosaline forced a smile and slowly inched her one hand toward Boris. "No, not at all, just seeing what other fantastic items you have in your shop."

Micah nodded his head, his eyes fixed on Rosaline's. "What did you say you were keeping in the bag again?"

"My food and valuables," Rosaline responded, her fingers a hair's breadth away from the tip of Boris' hilt. "I need to protect me and my family from all these break-ins."

Micah scratched his beard with one hand. "Yes, can never be too careful these days..." The mage's eyes were as cold as ice as he started to twist and move his free hand.

Rosaline's eyes widened as she realized he was about to cast a spell. She tore Boris free from his sheath and flung the blade at the halfling's chest. Micah leapt out of the way and started running to the side, weaving and bobbing between the towers of junk. Rosaline followed the sound of the mage's footsteps until it stopped suddenly, and an audible crackling sound emerged from behind one of the stacks of garbage. She quickly dove out of the way towards Boris, as a beam of energy tore through the debris in the shop.

"You'll find that I am harder to rob than your usual victims!" Micah shouted from behind cover.

Rosaline was crawling towards Boris, hoping to stay as quiet as possible, when she heard the sound of muffled screaming, followed by the distinct sound of vertebrae snapping. Retrieving her dagger, Rosaline rose to her feet and saw Phillip standing over the halfling with a look of disgust.

"You alright, Roz?" Phillip asked, not taking his eyes off the mage.

"Mhmm," Rosaline replied, approaching the two men and seeing that Micah was still very much alive, but unable to move.

"Thought he was going to turn you into a frog or something," Phillip said, bending down and pulling the bag from the mage's cloak. "Pleasure doing business with you, sir," the bandit said, before pulling his dagger free from its sheath.

Rosaline's hand shot out like an arrow and grabbed Phillip's arm forcefully. He looked up at her, confused, almost offended that she would stop his kill. "Don't tell me you're going soft."

Rosaline shook her head. "No. It's better to let the bastard rot away with the rest of his junk."

"But he's seen our faces. What if someone comes by the shop and helps him?"

Rosaline let go of Phillip's hand and smiled. "Hard to rat us out without a tongue."

"What the hells is that!?" Jathan recoiled as the wet, bloody object bounced across the wooden table.

"It's a mage's tongue!" Phillip roared. "Go on, rub it for good luck!"

Malek, Phillip, and Rosaline laughed at Jathan's expense, then slammed their mugs of ale together and greedily slurped them down. As the laughter died down, Rosaline leaned back in her chair, swirling the ale around her mug absently, her eyes locked onto the disembodied tongue that sat in the middle of them as a macabre centerpiece.

Jathan leaned forward and looked at the tongue with wide eyes. "Gods, how did you even cut it out in one piece?"

Phillip smiled, beaming with pride. "First, you gotta dislocate the jaw so you have space to work. Then you have to twist it so you can cut it out at the base. Then you just pull."

Malek raised his mug. "To Micah."

"To Micah!" they echoed, clinking mugs.

After a well-deserved drink, Malek and Jathan were about to recall their own day when the doors to the tavern burst open. Standing in the doorway was Duncan, covered in sweat and panting heavily. Rosaline turned around on her stool and gave him a once-over. Judging by how drenched in sweat he was, he must have sprinted all the way to the Garden from the palace. "Did you find the stash?" she asked.

"No, but you're not going to fucking believe this."

CHAPTER TWENTY-THREE
RANDALL

When the haze from Elbert's smouldering ships cleared after four days, the entire city rejoiced. People flooded the streets and greedily inhaled the fresh air. Sailors hugged one another openly as they readied their ships to sail. The hungry bellies of the people seemed to stop grumbling, knowing that trade would resume and that food would no longer be scarce. However, the celebrations were bittersweet for Randall. While he was happy that his people would no longer be starving, he missed the greyish-black haze. Whenever he left the palace or inhaled the suffocating smoke, a sense of pride washed over him. It was a constant reminder that he had dealt a powerful blow to Elbert, and by doing so, kept his city and his people free from the tyrant's grasp a while longer. Although the threat of hunger had momentarily been avoided, there were other problems that Randall had to quickly solve, the first being that they were still surrounded by Elbert's army and essentially under siege. To make matters worse, there were reports that Elbert and his men were trying to find more ships to resume the blockade. The crippled king only had the ships that he had taken to the Isles at his disposal, and with those at the bottom of the sea, it seemed Elbert was trying to find ships for hire that would replace them.

The second issue that Randall faced was a problem inside the city walls. There were reports that a group of people were robbing the citizens of their stored food and then selling it back to them at an inflated price. The king wanted to investigate these claims, but Cassius had assured him he would handle it personally.

The third and perhaps the most troubling problem that plagued the king was Velus. Ever since he absorbed the fire from Elbert's ships, he had been unresponsive. For four days he had been in the infirmary, and Randall visited him every day. The healers assured the king that they would let him know if there was any change in the mage's condition, but that didn't stop him from visiting the halfling. He owed Velus a debt, one that he likely could never repay. The least he could do was spend a handful of minutes of each day at the man's bedside.

The king's daily routine had become rather monotonous since the burning of the ships. First, he would leave his bed, pour a modest glass of wine, walk onto the balcony, and stare out over the city. He loved listening to the sounds of people going about their daily lives; the wall of noise that stemmed from the city was soothing to him. Even though it still got well below freezing at night, Randall slept with the balcony window open, just so he could fall asleep to the city's unique soundscape, just like he had when he slept on the streets.

The second thing he would do to start his day would be open his door and debrief with his page, Arthur. The boy was a few years younger than Randall, but seemed full of zeal to serve his new king. The page was waiting outside the king's door every morning with a scroll of the agenda in hand. Arthur was appointed by Cassius to help organize the king's schedule. Randall knew the eunuch had become very busy since he had seized the crown, so the fact that more menial tasks, such as reading the daily itinerary to the king, was delegated to a dutiful servant was not surprising.

After the reading of the daily schedule, Randall would take a moment of reprieve from his kingly responsibilities for as long as he could and visit Velus in the infirmary. It was a brief moment of respite from the ceaseless crises that were constantly brought to his attention throughout the day, but it was a needed one. In fact, the only moments that Randall could truly be himself were with Velus and when he walked out onto the balcony first thing in the morning. One thing that Randall had not anticipated about being king was the need for putting on a façade for everyone else. But when Elbert surrounded the city, he quickly realized that the people looked towards their king for stability and security. As a result, he took it upon himself that he would never show the people how stressed, scared, and overworked he was. This was his city, and he would sooner work himself into the ground before handing it back over to the nobles.

Once Randall ensured that his kingly attire looked presentable enough, he opened the doors to the hallway from the bedchamber, and, unsurprisingly, Arthur was standing there eagerly awaiting his king.

"Are you ready to hear today's schedule, Your Majesty?" Arthur asked emphatically. He had shaggy red hair that almost covered his green eyes. Freckles dotted his cheeks and his two front teeth were chipped. The king turned his attention to the boy's hands and noticed that his knuckles were bruised.

"Did you win?" Randall asked, gesturing at the hands.

"Yes, Your Majesty," the boy replied, his cheeks flushing with colour.

"Good. Now, what does the day have in store for me?"

The page unfurled the scroll and began reading off the items that the eunuch had written down. "First is an appointment with a woman named Abigail Morris. Says she has a pressing matter that is to be heard by the king's ears only."

Randall raised a brow. The name sounded familiar, but he had been bombarded with so many people's names since he took the crown that he could be imagining the familiarity. Then, his heart sank. *An assassin?* Elbert had surely heard about his ships burning by now – perhaps he had sent in an assassin to finish the siege once and for all. *I will have Tig and A'Chula by my side when I meet her.*

"The second item on today's itinerary," the boy continued, "is the council meeting later this morning."

"Is that all?" Randall asked.

"Yes, Your Majesty."

"Very well, might as well get things started. Fetch me Tig and A'Chula, and we shall meet Abigail Morris after I check on Grandmaster Velus."

The page bowed. "As you wish, Your Majesty."

The infirmary stunk like death. It had been used to treat the dying members of the former city guard, and the stench of their demise still lingered in the room, no matter how many times Randall ordered it cleaned. Because of the rot that hung in the air, rats would often sneak their way into the building and feed on the dead or dying men when the healers weren't looking. Randall had also ordered for the vermin to be controlled, but either the healers were so busy tending to the dying that they didn't have time to catch rats, or there was a never-ending horde of rats inhabiting the city.

As with every visit to the infirmary, Randall asked the healers how Velus was faring. To nobody's surprise, his condition had not changed. The mage was stable but unresponsive. The king then pulled up a chair and examined Velus' flesh, to ensure that the rats had not been feasting on the helpless halfling. Velus' skin was as white as alabaster, but bore no teeth or claw marks. Randall breathed a sigh of relief as he pulled up a chair beside the mage's bed, then let out a long, exasperated sigh and whispered so that the healers and other patients could not hear him,

"The haze is finally gone. People can breathe once again, and the ships can leave the harbour. Soon our city will be teeming with food again and it is all thanks to you." Randall looked at Velus' expressionless face. He had hoped the good news about the city would stir the halfling awake, but his hopes were quickly dashed by Velus' lifeless body. If the healers had not told him that the mage was alive, Randall would've been sure he was sitting next to a corpse.

"I owe you a debt that I can never repay, Velus," Randall continued. "Not only as a king, but as a citizen of the new Artanzia. If you ever wake up, I promise I will give you anything you want. You want an estate in the countryside? Done. You want a harem of wives to keep you company? Done. You want an endless supply of gold to fund your magical experiments? Done. Whatever you want, I'll give to you. Just, please, wake up."

Just as Randall touched Velus' arm, there was a commotion across the infirmary. Randall lifted his head and saw the man in the bed across the room seizing uncontrollably. The healers quickly tried to restrain him, one whispering an incantation while touching the man's forehead. After a handful of seconds, the man stopped moving, but, judging from the healers' faces, it was not because of their magic.

A pit formed in Randall's heart. He looked at Velus and squeezed the mage's arm tightly with his right hand. "I don't know what to do. Every minute of every day another crisis pops up. It feels like I'm in a lake, and there's a heavy stone tied to my foot. No matter how hard I fight, the weight is dragging me down and I can barely keep my head above the surface." Randall paused for a moment as a thought ran through his head. A tear formed in the corner of his eye. "Anna would know what to do," he said, sadness colouring his voice. "Her death helped me unite the city and secure the throne. But now I'm starting to think that it was too heavy a price to pay. If I hadn't listened to Cassius, she would still be here and perhaps you wouldn't be lying in this bed. I—" Randall stopped himself mid-sentence. This was the first time he had ever openly spoken of his betrayal to Anna. His eyes quickly darted around the room to see if anyone had heard him. Thankfully, the healers were too busy dealing with the dead man across the room to worry about the king's whispers, and Velus, as always, showed no signs of hearing Randall's words.

Not wanting to risk another slip of the tongue, Randall patted Velus on the arm and walked out of the infirmary, where Tig and A'Chula were waiting.

"You called?" Tig asked.

"I'll explain on the way."

Abigail Morris was a slender, petite woman with sunken cheekbones and hollow eyes. Dark, matted hair hung over half of her face. Her skin was dirty and her clothes ragged. A malodorous stench exuded from her that threatened to fill the entire throne room. She was nervously wringing her hands together while she waited for the chance to voice her concerns to her king. Under the right circumstances, she would have been a very beautiful woman, but the siege had obviously taken its toll on her.

Upon seeing her, Randall felt ridiculous for having Tig and A'Chula tag along. This woman was clearly no assassin, just one of his loyal subjects who had been hit hard by the series of events that had befallen the city. Taking his throne, he waved her forward and greeted her with a warm smile.

"I'm told you have a pressing matter to broach with me?" Randall said in a soft voice.

She nodded her head as her eyes darted between Tig and A'Chula before finally settling on Randall on the throne.

"Don't worry," the king said, "they're only here as witnesses to your statement."

Taking a deep breath, Abigail cleared the hair out of her eyes as best she could. "We're dying, Your Majesty," she said in a hoarse voice, before succumbing to a coughing fit. Tig took a step forward but was quickly waved away by the woman.

"Who's dying?" Randall asked, leaning forward in his throne.

"Your subjects!" Abigail shouted in between the coughs. "Our city is surrounded, we are being beaten and killed over our food, and for the last four days we choked on the smoke from the burning ships whenever we left our homes. But from what we can see, nothing is being done about it!"

Randall was taken aback by the woman's boldness. It was clear why she was nervous before meeting him; she was going to berate a king, something clearly born out of utter desperation.

"You will not talk to His Majesty with such—" Tig began, but Randall held up a silencing hand.

"Ms. Morris, I hear your concerns, but the end is nearly here. Without the naval blockade, trade can be resumed. We have allies coming to our aid to remove the surrounding army at our walls, and I have my top advisor looking into the extortion of food."

"Pah!" Abigail spat. "My husband and I took up arms for you because we thought you would lead us to a better life. You *told* us you would give us a better life. Now, I'm trapped in this cursed city with three young mouths to feed and a dead husband to bury."

"I'm sorry to hear about your husband, I truly am. I'd be happy to help in any way I can with the funeral arrangements. As for the food—"

"I don't want your help organizing the fucking funeral!" Abigail shouted. "I want you to stop the bastards that did this to me and have done this to countless other people in your city. And, yes, the ships have left the harbour, but by the time the captain and crew go to their destination, barter and haggle over the price, load up the goods, and sail back it'll be weeks before any of us see so much as a loaf of bread. Please, Your Majesty, help us, or else you won't have anyone to rule over."

Randall felt his stomach churn. There was a lump in his throat and he found it hard to meet the eyes of the starving woman. How could he be so stupid? He felt foolish not considering the travel time, and the logistics of trade before he started celebrating his victory. The woman was right – it would be weeks, maybe even a month, before the merchants could bring fresh food and supplies into the city. After a moment of silence, he nodded his head, rose from his throne, and, as uncomfortable as it made him to do so, locked eyes with her. "You have my word, Ms. Morris, I will look into these matters personally. The crown is here to protect its subjects, not only from opposing armies, but from all other plights as well."

The two stared at each other for several seconds in an excruciating silence. She raised one of her brows before ultimately nodding her head and thanking Randall, then turned and shuffled out of the throne room.

Once the giant oaken doors of the throne room closed, Randall shouted for Arthur. The discomfort of being in front of such a desperate person had disappeared under the rage that was slowly filling his body. This was unacceptable, and he'd be damned if he let his people continue to waste away under his watch. That was something the nobles would have allowed, and he would not turn into the thing that he hated more than anything in this world.

"Yes, Your Majesty?" Arthur asked, bowing low as protocol dictated.

"I want to start the council meeting right away. Go fetch the others."

Sensing the king's anger and the urgency of the situation, Arthur nodded before breaking out into a sprint to fetch the others. Randall rose from his throne, his face beet-red and breathing heavily.

"What're you going to do, Randall?" Tig asked, a sense of fear staining his voice.

"I'm going to remind everyone of who is actually king."

The war room was especially cold that day, Randall having made a point of not lighting the braziers and sconces in the room. As he waited for the others to arrive, he stared at the thin veil of fog that left his mouth with each furious breath. For too long, he had let these people, these so-called councillors, lead him astray from building the kingdom that he actually wanted to build. It was time for a reckoning, and he was going to put everyone in their place, even Cassius. Before he could stew in his anger for any longer, the doors to the room opened with a bang. The six councillors shuffled into the room, instantly pulling their cloaks tighter to try to stop the heat leaving their bodies. Everyone sat in their assigned seats and eyed Randall as he glowered at the head of the table. Tig, A'Chula, and Corbin Strongarm all had a mix of fear and trepidation in their eyes, while Amelia Dupont and Virgil Walker had annoyed expressions plastered onto their faces. The only person who seemed unbothered by the early summoning and the unusually chilly room was Cassius. He stared at his king with a look of complete indifference.

"What is the ploughing problem?" Virgil Walker snarled, breaking the lengthy silence that hung in the air. "It's bad enough you pulled me from my duties early, but now you have it colder than the damned Mjältön Isles themselves!"

Leaning forward in his chair, Randall glared at the former guardsman, trying to contain his rage as best he could. "I had an interesting conversation with one of our citizens today. She—"

"Your Majesty," Amelia Dupont interrupted through chattering teeth, "could we please light the braziers in here? I'm absolutely frozen solid. I'm afraid I won't be able to give sound advice under such conditions."

"These conditions are exactly why I brought you all in here to begin with," Randall said, his voice shaking with anger. "These are the conditions that our people face every day. Perhaps you have been afforded too many luxuries as my councillors and have become completely blind to the bleak, daily reality that this city and these people face."

"Your Majesty," Madame Dupont replied, "the winter is hard for everyone, but don't forget, we have won a mighty victory. Elbert's blockade is no more, and it is thanks to you and Grandmaster Velus. It won't be long before the other kingdoms send food and aid—"

"Do you know how long the voyage is to Caspula or the Valerian Empire from Winterhelm, Madame Dupont?" Randall waited for the woman's response, but she quickly averted her gaze and shrank into her seat. "By the time that the merchants reach a port, barter and haggle over the price, load up the goods, and sail back it'll be weeks before these people get the food that they need." Randall shot up out of his chair and pointed out of the balcony towards the city proper. "Need I remind you that these people *died* for us to be here! They believed I would be a different type of ruler, and that we would usher in a new age that would make their lives easier. And so far, we have failed them."

"Your Majesty," Corbin Strongarm interjected, "I think it is safe to say that we all want the people of this city and this kingdom to thrive. But let's not kid ourselves, they're *peasants.* They will always find something to complain about. You must not let them sway you. You have to be a strong-willed king, otherwise they'll sense your weakness and take advantage of you every chance they get."

Randall's head snapped towards the dwarf's direction. He glared at him with a furrowed brow and an ugly sneer. Suddenly, he began marching towards the Master of Dock's chair with intent.

"Your Majesty!" Cassius shouted as he shot to his feet. The eunuch's voice stopped the king in his tracks, but also put him on the receiving end of Randall's ire. "The food crisis will be solved soon; you have my word. I am close to uncovering the culprits for all the raids. When I find those responsible, I swear you'll be the first to know."

Before the king could speak, Virgil Walker let out a hearty laugh. "Pah!" he spat. "You couldn't find your own cock with both hands, how the hells will you find these thieves? Your Majesty, leave it to me. My men and I will sniff out these bandits and have them hanging from the city wall in two days' time, mark my words."

"No!" Cassius shouted. "Please, Your Majesty, the last thing we want is Councillor Walker's men knocking down doors and inciting panic. This job requires a more delicate touch. Please, give me more time."

Randall stared at the eunuch for several seconds in silent rage before he shook his head and gave a definitive answer. "No, Cassius, I will not have my people starve while you try to find the criminals responsible. I think a more forceful hand is needed here. In the meantime, I want the crown's food stocks to be divvied up and distributed to the people. Each neighbourhood gets the same amount, including ourselves."

The councillors gasped and groaned in astonishment. In unison, they pleaded with the king not to do something so rash, but it fell on deaf ears. Randall had made up his mind – if the councillors were perhaps cold and hungry then maybe they would work as hard as he did to make this city and kingdom one for the people to be proud of. "I have spoken!" Randall shouted. "Virgil, I expect you to root out these cancers quickly. And if I hear one more complaint of people going hungry, I'll have someone's head." Without waiting to hear any more objections, Randall stormed out of the war room.

Tig and A'Chula flanked the king on either side. Sensing that his friends had something to tell him, Randall stopped and let out a hot breath of anger. "Yes?"

However, he was surprised to see Tig and A'Chula smiling at him. Tig placed a hand on the king's shoulder and let out a small laugh. "I've never seen you so mad before."

"Listen Tig, I don't want—" Randall started, before A'Chula also placed a hand on the king's other shoulder.

"You're right." Tig interrupted. "All those people care about are themselves. It should not be problematic for a king to say 'feed the people' when they are starving. If they can't see that, maybe it's time to let them go..."

There was a pain in Randall's chest as he considered Tig's words. Cassius and his councillors seemed to fight and rebuke Randall at every turn, but then again, the idea of letting them go felt wrong. Cassius had helped him so much – not only did the eunuch help Randall depose Greaver, but also helped him organize the rebellion and was the most politically astute member of the council. Without him, Randall wasn't sure if he would still be king.

Just as Randall was about to respond, he saw Cassius hurry out of the war room, approaching him. Randall leaned over to Tig and A'Chula and dropped his voice to a whisper, "I want you to spread the food to the people, tonight, and to hells what the councillors think."

Tig and A'Chula nodded their heads in approval as Cassius arrived, slightly out of breath. "Randall," he gasped, "think this through, it is not wise to—"

"Not wise!?" Randall shouted. "It is not wise to what – listen to my people's concerns? I wanted to make this a kingdom for the common man, and so far, I have not done that. Instead, I have been listening to people who only care about themselves... well, no more! It is about time that I became the king that I want to be."

"Randall, listen to me. You're making a mistake. I—"

"My only mistake was listening to you! You told me to kill Anna, you wanted me to marry nobility, and you insisted I structure a regime that is almost identical to Elbert's! How am I supposed to be any different if I do the same fucking thing! I—"

"Listen to me!" Cassius yelled, a vein protruding in his bald forehead. The sudden display of anger was enough to take the king aback. The eunuch quickly swallowed and lowered his voice back to his usual quiet tone. "You cannot reshape the world overnight. People do not like change. If you want to build the kingdom that you say you do, then you have to trust me. It must be implemented gradually, and we certainly can't make sudden changes when we are in the middle of a siege. We must take care of the wolves at our door before we start redecorating the house."

Randall considered the eunuch's words and clenched his fists. Every part of him wanted to shove Cassius away – but his warning hung in the air like a noose. Cassius was right. If Randall kept burning bridges, there'd be no kingdom left to stand on. As much as his anger begged him not to concede, the king relented, submitting to Cassius' reason. "Still, that is no excuse for my people to—"

"Yes, I understand," Cassius said, putting a hand on Randall's shoulder. "I have failed you; I will admit that. Suggesting that you marry into Keten's nobility was certainly misguided. As for Anna, I wish she was here with us now, trust me, I do, but I believe that her sacrifice has helped the people relate to you. We all experienced loss – that's why the people love you. You're relatable and you're one of them. Their health and safety should be your top priority behind dealing with Elbert." The eunuch's brow became furrowed and his grip tightened on the king's shoulder. "But you cannot treat your councillors like that. I thought you were going to kill Corbin. We are not the nobles. We are your loyal advisors, who are trying our best to guide you during this difficult time. If you turn hostile to them, your support will vanish. We need to keep our emotions in check."

Again, the former sommelier's words soothed the king's anger. He hated to admit it but Cassius was right – that display in the throne room had not been kingly, more like a petulant child not getting his way. "You're right, Cassius. I'm sorry, should I—"

"Your Majesty!" Arthur shouted. Randall turned his head and saw the page sprinting towards him with a desperate look on his face.

"What is it?"

"There's... a man... in the throne room," Arthur wheezed, gasping for air between breaths. "You're going to want to hear what he has to say."

Randall and Cassius exchanged looks with one another before setting off for the throne room. Judging by Arthur's state, it was a very important message. Randall just hoped that it wasn't more bad news.

The man in the throne room had his hair tied up in a neat bun, which exposed the nasty scar that covered half of his face, and he was wearing the bloodstained armour of Elbert's royal guard. Seemingly unbothered by Randall's presence, the man simply chewed on his dirty fingernails as the king approached.

"Interesting attire you have," Randall said as he assumed the throne. "I remember when I cut down several men wearing the same armour as I took the city."

"And good riddance to them, Your Majesty," the man said as he executed a clumsy bow. "But I am no royal guardsman, I just had to wear this while I slipped through Elbert's encampment."

Randall raised a brow. Not only did this man breach the city walls without alerting anyone, but did so by donning an enemy uniform. "So, if you're not a guardsman, how did you get that armour?"

The man let out a toothy smile. "Well, you see, Your Majesty, my employer is a merchant from Kovar. Due to the nature of our trade, I have to go out and procure product for us to take back."

Randall scrunched his face in confusion. He looked over at Cassius. The eunuch slowly leaned over and whispered, "Slavers."

"Exactly," the man said. "While I was out finding product for us to secure, we came across a certain caravan. One that was transporting a certain cripple..."

Randall's heart skipped a beat, and he nearly leapt out of the throne. "You have Elbert?"

The slaver's toothy smile widened. "He can be yours... for the right price."

CHAPTER TWENTY-FOUR
ELBERT

Condensation from the stalactites dripped onto the cave floor, the echo of the splashing sound filling the cavern. The cool spring air had an almost icy chill to it inside the cave walls. The only source of light was the still smouldering embers of the slavers' fire from the night before. Elbert wasn't sure how long it had been since he had been captured. Several days for sure, perhaps a week. All he knew was that the days had blended together. As Xerxes and his men prepared to transport their cargo to Eldersburg, Elbert was left alone with his thoughts in the darkness.

During his isolation, Elbert had gone through three main phases. The first stage was to desperately try to secure the means of his escape. His first idea was to sharpen loose bits of shale from the cave floor on other rocks to use as makeshift knives. After several failed attempts, however, it was clear he lacked the skill and finesse to actually carry the idea to fruition. In fact, the only rewards for his labours were several cuts in the palms of his hands when the pieces of shale broke as he was sharpening them. His second idea was to convince the other captives to unite and rebel against the Kovari slavers. This also proved ineffective, as the boys in the cages refused to acknowledge the king's existence. His third and final attempt was to bribe some of Xerxes' men when he was not around. He promised gold, wine, and beautiful women, but his promises fell on deaf ears.

Either Xerxes' men were extremely loyal, or they saw through the king's desperate pleas.

The second stage of Elbert's isolation was one of quiet contemplation. Alone with his thoughts all day, the people around him refusing to acknowledge his existence, there was little to do but think about his current circumstances. The first thing Elbert thought about was how curious it was that, despite the nature of Xerxes' trade, he and his men were not cruel to their captives. They made sure all the slaves ate well, and when a fight occasionally broke out amongst the boys, they were quick to settle the disputes. It struck Elbert as odd that slavers would show care and attentiveness to the people they planned on selling into servitude, but after a while, he concluded that such devotion was purely from a business standpoint. Slaves would fetch a higher price if they were well cared for and not abused.

However, that realization led Elbert down another line of thinking. If the boys were well-fed and not abused, why didn't they rebel against their captors? Why didn't they band together and fight back? Sure, some of them would die, but certainly fighting and dying for your freedom must be better than to live out the rest of your days in servitude to someone else. Another question was: why did they refuse to respond to Elbert? At first, he thought they didn't want to make escape plans with a cripple, seeing as he would be next to useless in the actual revolt, but then he thought perhaps they had heard what Xerxes had said the night Elbert was first captured. He was being sold, simply to be executed. There would be no benefit dealing with a soon-to-be dead man, even if that man was technically a king.

The last phase of Elbert's isolation was a quiet acceptance of his fate. There would be no chance of escape, and soon his head would be mounted on top of Winterhelm's walls for all of his army to see. Starved for human interaction, he had tried to talk to Thames as if he was there, but he quickly stopped, as it felt ridiculous. His best friend's severed head was back in his tent outside the city – there was no way that Thames could hear his questions or give advice anymore. He was completely, utterly alone.

"Good morning, Your Majesty!" Xerxes exclaimed as he entered the cave and sat beside the crippled king. "Are you ready to depart for Eldersburg? Soon I will be a rich man, and you will return to your city."

"Just long enough for Randall to take my head," Elbert sighed, defeated. Although he had longed for human interaction, Xerxes' choice of topic left much to be desired. Curious, he looked the slaver in the eyes, and noticed that there was no joy but also no remorse or grief. As far as he could tell, Xerxes would lose no sleep over selling Elbert to be executed.

Suddenly, another man walked into the cave. He was tall and had curly black hair that was tied into a messy, frizzy bun at the top of his head. His complexion was like Xerxes', so he must have been from Kovar as well. The man spoke to Xerxes in a throaty language that Elbert assumed to be their native tongue, which struck him as odd since the slavers had never spoken it before, at least not in his presence. The tall man nodded his head, spun on his heels, and left after a crisp salute.

"What's going on?"

Xerxes turned his head and smiled. "It seems my men have found me a new horse. A beautiful mare. Fitting for a man like me, yes?" Unsure what the slaver meant by that, Elbert nodded his head. "My men will load you up on the caravan, and we will be on our way."

Elbert watched as Xerxes' men entered in and out of the cave at a hurried pace. The slavers dragged the young boys out of their cages in the cave and into the cages that were placed on their carts. Once all the slaves were loaded up, the same tall man that spoke to Xerxes earlier entered the cave and effortlessly threw Elbert over his shoulder. Elbert thought he would be thrown in one of the cages with the other slaves, but upon exiting the cave, he quickly realized that they were already full. Before he could ask where he would ride, the tall man tossed Elbert onto the back of his horse as if he was a dead stag. The man then tied the king to his saddle so that escape was impossible and mounted the horse.

This is humiliating, Elbert thought. *They should just kill me now and save me the embarrassment. At least it'll only be a handful of boys and these slavers that would really know how pathetic my last few days were.*

Xerxes suddenly appeared on an unruly, black warhorse. The mare kicked and whinnied uncontrollably as the slaver desperately tried to control it. After several failed attempts to get the beast to fall in line, Xerxes dismounted, cursed in his native tongue, and spat on the ground. The horse, which was inexplicably calm now, stared at the slaver with complete indifference. A couple of the boys in the cages chuckled at the spectacle, but when Xerxes shot a fiery glare in their direction, they quickly fell silent.

"You think that this is funny, huh?" Xerxes snarled as he approached the cage. "You know, back in my homeland, it is rude to laugh at another's misfortune." He pulled his dagger from his belt and held it close to the cage for all the boys to see. "Perhaps if I cut out your tongues, you'll learn some manners." There was an eerie stillness in the air. Elbert looked around and saw that none of Xerxes' men showed any signs of discomfort; a few even had smiles on their faces. "Get me the keys!" Xerxes shouted.

Elbert's heart sank as he saw the boys in the cage back up as far as they could from the steel door where Xerxes was standing. It was then that a stupid idea came to him. He took a deep breath, but he knew that if he was going to have any hope of escaping these men, he had to endear himself to his fellow captives. Swallowing his fear, he cleared his throat and shouted, "Why punish the boys because you aren't man enough to ride the horse?"

Xerxes spun on his heels and directed all his ire at Elbert. "What did you say?"

Elbert doubled down, hoping that his resolve would hold. "I mean, I could ride that damned thing and I don't even have any working legs."

A few of the other slavers whispered amongst themselves as they watched on. Xerxes' brow furrowed, but then his body relaxed and a venomous smile appeared on his face. "Very well, Your Majesty. Please, why don't you show me how it's done, hmm?" he said, tucking his dagger back into his belt.

"Wait, what?" Elbert asked.

Two of the slavers undid Elbert's restraints and carried him over to the warhorse. Xerxes held the mare, who was already anxiously stamping her feet, by the reins, and grinned from ear to ear. The men placed Elbert on top of the horse and began fastening his legs to the stirrups.

"What are you doing?" Elbert asked, fear plainly colouring his voice.

"Giving you a bit of help," Xerxes hissed. Once the king was secured, the slaver let go of the reins, slapped the horse on the rump, and stepped back.

Unsurprisingly, the horse began spinning and kicking wildly. Elbert's upper body flailed like a rag doll atop the mare and his vision blurred as the horse spun faster and faster. Bile leapt out of his mouth and onto himself and the horse as he struggled to grip the reins in his hands. The slavers laughed in unison at the sight of the helpless king. Elbert tried to pull back on the reins, but as soon as he did, the horse bucked. Before he knew it, his head hit the ground and everything went black.

The jolting of a horse walking on the frozen dirt shook Elbert awake. He blinked his eyes, trying to get the world around him to come into focus. He craned his neck to see his surroundings and instantly winced in pain. A soft hiss escaped his lips as he tried to gauge the severity of his injuries. The tall man riding the horse scoffed quietly. Out of the corner of his eye, Elbert could see the man did not turn around and check on him. Instead, his eyes remained fixed on Xerxes, who was riding a dark chestnut instead of the unruly black mare that had knocked Elbert unconscious. Even though it pained him, Elbert smiled ear to ear at knowing that the slaver had been bested by a simple horse.

"You got a lot of balls, Your Majesty," the tall man whispered.

Elbert raised a brow. This was the first time any of Xerxes' men had talked to him without giving him an order. Desperate for conversation, the king responded,

"I don't know what you mean."

"Hmm," the man grunted. "Pissing off your captors to save some would-be slaves is quite brave. Stupid, but brave."

Elbert let out a laboured laugh. "How bad is it?"

"I didn't think you could get any uglier, but you proved me wrong."

"What's your name?"

"Ada."

"What happened to the mare? Xerxes give up?" Elbert said, trying to hide the mirth in his voice.

"Hard to ride a horse that doesn't have a head," Ada replied bluntly.

Elbert's heart sank. "He killed it?"

"Mhmm," Ada replied. "No point having a horse you can't ride."

Just as Elbert was to express his further disgust, Ada's horse came to a sudden stop. "What is it?" Elbert asked, grimacing through the pain in his neck.

"There's a man ahead."

Shit, Elbert thought. *They are either going to butcher this man or enslave him. Hopefully, they give him a quick death.* Ada kicked the horse into a slow trot and he rode up beside Xerxes. Despite the pain, Elbert turned his head to see the stranger. The man wore a battered, black leather gambeson with silver studs in the shape of swords. He had thick grey hair and a grey, unkempt beard. The knuckles on his gauntlets were covered in dried blood and he carried a sword on his back. The stranger locked eyes with Elbert, and he felt a shiver run down his spine. The man clutched his sternum as if in pain, but quickly let go to turn his attention to Xerxes and the other slavers.

"Greetings," Xerxes said cheerfully. "A fine day, isn't it?"

"Any chance you've seen a black mare?" the man said in a gravelly voice. "She ran off a few days ago after being spooked by some wolves."

Elbert raised a brow. Although this man looked terrifying, it was clear that he had spent more time fighting than mastering the art of lying.

"I'm sorry, we haven't come across any horses like that. We've been too busy gathering merchandise to notice errant horses," Xerxes replied convincingly.

The stranger pointed to the carts carrying the cages of boys. "Slaves?"

Xerxes' smile quickly disappeared. "Is that a problem?"

"Not at all. Life as a pleasure slave in Kovar is probably better than any life they'd have here as free men."

Xerxes' smile returned as he clapped his hands. "You look like you know your way around a sword – how would you like to join our little company? We always need good men, and there's good coin to be earned."

"Already have a job," the man said plainly. "But I'd buy that cripple off you," he added, pointing to Elbert on the back of the horse. "Can't be that expensive, can he?"

The slaver sucked in the air through his teeth. "I'm sorry, good sir, that one already has a buyer. You're welcome to peruse my other merchandise, though!"

The stranger shook his head. "No, I want that one." He unsheathed the sword from his back and revealed a blade that was as black as death. The air suddenly got cold, and Elbert could see his breath. The slavers' horses pranced in place and a few whinnied uncontrollably.

One slaver, a man with a light complexion and dusty blond hair, rode up beside Xerxes and whispered in his ear. Elbert tilted his head trying to listen to the conversation, but only caught a few words.

"Order... swords... monster hunter."

The king nearly pissed himself in excitement. A member of the famed monster-hunting guild was standing in front of him. When they were children, his older brother, Talbot, used to keep him up all night telling him stories of the most famous monster hunters. To see one in the flesh was a rarity, as the reality of risking your life fighting deadly beasts was about as enticing as it sounded. The members of this guild were esteemed swordsmen, and cutting through a bunch of slavers would be mere child's play, especially for a grizzled veteran like the one that stood before him.

"Like I said," Xerxes spoke, his voice firm, "he is not for sale."

The man's eyes darted to each of the slavers. After what seemed like a lifetime, he sheathed his blade once more. "Very well. Let me see the others."

Xerxes dismounted his horse and led the man towards the cart of boys. The two men walked so close to Elbert that the king could smell the death and decay that lingered on the monster hunter's clothes. He watched the man's hands as he approached. The stranger made a quick, but almost imperceptible flick of his wrist and Elbert felt a sudden weight in his shirt pocket. Were his hands not bound, he would've reached in and grabbed it. By his judgement, it had the same size and weight as a coin.

The monster hunter stared at the boys in the caged cart for several minutes, before ultimately shaking his head. Xerxes, ever the salesman, offered the man several boys for the price of one but the swordsman seemed uninterested in the Kovari slaver's stock. As Xerxes walked back to his horse, clearly disappointed by the lack of a sale, the monster hunter called out to him,

"Where are you heading?"

"Eldersburg! Always a good place to gather more supplies," Xerxes replied with a wink.

The stranger shook his head. "You won't find any stock there."

"And why is that?"

"I just came from Eldersburg, or what is left of it. Nothing there but a pile of ash."

"Bandits?" Elbert blurted out. He locked eyes with the swordsman and his skin turned to gooseflesh, before Ada's firm hand struck the king in the ear, forcing him to break eye contact with the stranger. Silence hung in the air, the slavers clearly thinking the same thing as the former king.

Once again, the man shook his head. "It wasn't burnt to the ground or razed. There's literally nothing left. No bodies, no buildings, nothing. It's as if the entire town was wiped off the earth overnight."

Xerxes bid the man farewell and thanked him for the news about Eldersburg. He talked in his foreign tongue to a few of his men and they slowly turned the convoy to the east. With a ringing ear, Elbert watched the mysterious monster hunter walk away, seemingly indifferent to the king's suffering. He wanted to call out for help, beg the man to rescue him and take him back to Winterhelm, but he was also scared that another backhanded slap from Ada would make him completely deaf on one side of his head.

The slavers travelled till sunset and made camp in a small grove. A few of the men started a fire and cooked a large pot of stew. Xerxes, Ada, and a few of the other native Kovari talked amongst themselves in their throaty mother tongue, with a map laid out in front of them. Elbert's bonds were cut, and he massaged his face ever so gently while he watched the slavers, making sure that no one was paying close attention to him.

When he was sure that nobody was watching, he reached into his pocket and pulled out whatever the mysterious stranger put there. It was a small coin. But it was not made of gold, or any other precious metal he had seen. In fact, it didn't look like currency at all. It was made of a dark grey metal that was unbelievably cold to the touch. On one side of the coin, there was a weird-looking sigil or seal imprinted, a series of lines inside of a circle surrounded by strange runes. On the other, there was a depiction of a skull with an open mouth. It was similar to a human skull except it had three protruding horns at the top of its head and razor-sharp fangs instead of teeth.

Elbert ran his thumb across the faces of the coin. When he ran it over the skull's mouth, he felt an incredible heat radiating from within. He brought the coin closer to his face so he could get a better look through his bruised eyes, and saw that there was a small, almost imperceptible opening between the jaws. Just big enough to stick a fingernail into. The king looked up again and saw that nobody was watching. Despite his better judgement, he pressed his thumbnail into the skull's gaping maw. The skull's eyes instantly turned red as its jaws slammed shut on Elbert's thumb.

The king screamed in pain, feeling like he was surrounded by flames. He tried to pull his thumb free of the coin, but the effigy of the skull refused to let go. The stench of burnt flesh and burning hair filled Elbert's nostrils as he watched in horror as the flames ate away his skin. The pain was agonizing. He felt himself being burnt alive, and the more he screamed, the hotter the fire burned. Soon, he was unable to scream or make any sound other than a faint wheezing as the flames filled his lungs. After what seemed like a lifetime, the charred husk of Elbert collapsed lifelessly to the ground.

CHAPTER TWENTY-FIVE
ANNA

Several days had passed since the destruction of Eldersburg, and barely a word had been spoken. Master Mammon was irate and refused to speak. To make matters worse, his body was deteriorating rapidly after losing yet another host. Desmond, Matthew, and Evelynn said little either. The only time they acknowledged Anna's presence was when they would cast a concerned or wary look her way. She could tell that they were scared of her.

This isolation gave Anna time to think. Now that she knew she had powers, she felt a fierce determination to understand and control them. Every night she would reread Professor Moretz's book, hoping to catch a tidbit of knowledge that she might have missed on previous reads. On nights when sleep eluded her, she hesitantly tried to gain mastery over her powers. Most nights were fruitless, but one night, when the guilt was haunting her, she was able to conjure a small blue flame on the tip of her finger. She held it there, for several seconds amazed at the tiny flame. She watched it dance atop her fingertip, and was surprised that it was not hot. In fact, it had no sensation at all. If she closed her eyes, she had no idea whether the flame still existed or not. Mesmerized by it, she watched the flame peacefully for several minutes before eventually snuffing it out with a flick of her wrist. It was oddly comforting to know that her powers could be used for something else other than total annihilation.

One particular morning, the sloshing of footsteps crossing wet grass woke her from her sleep. She saw Desmond approaching her, and her heart leapt up in her chest as she rose to her feet. Desmond gave her a half smile and greeted her meekly. "Good morning, Anna."

"Morning, Desmond."

"Master Mammon would like a word with you."

Before she could ask a question, Desmond turned on his heels and walked back to the main camp. Anna let out a frustrated sigh and followed. She had taken up the habit of sleeping away from the others for two reasons. First, it was easier to practice her magic in solitude. Second, she was sick of their worried stares. The less she was reminded that she was a freak, the better.

As she entered the main camp, she smiled at both Evelynn and Matthew warmly, but both disciples returned her greeting only with half-hearted smiles of their own. When she flipped open the flap to Master Mammon's tent, she was surprised to see that the decrepit man she had met in the crypt was once again sitting in front of her. Mammon's ancient, wrinkled face scowled at her as she entered his dwelling.

"Look who it is," the demon said with a hint of contempt in his voice.

"Desmond said that you wanted a word with me."

Mammon's lips curled further into an ugly sneer. "Yes, I need you to find me a new host. Preferably one young and full of life."

"Why not send one of the others? I don't—"

"Because the others didn't kill my last one!" Mammon shouted. "You fucked this up, and you're going to fix it!"

Anna's brow furrowed. "And what if I say no?"

"Then we will all return to the hells. Desmond, Evelynn, and Matthew's souls will be eternally tormented while you and I will be trapped in that plane of existence. Despite the pleasant name, I have no intention of returning there.""But you already escaped the hells once, right? Couldn't we do it again?"

"Pah!" Mammon spat at Anna's feet. "Do you have any idea what I sacrificed to get here? It takes centuries, millennia even, to travel across planes of existence. It is not as simple as just 'doing it again'."

"I don't even know where to look. Where is the nearest—"

Mammon held up a silencing hand. "Take Matthew with you; I'm tired of staring at his constant frown. As for where we are, we've been travelling east, and I suspect we are close to the Artanzian-Ketenish border. Which means a sizeable city called Oxworth will be nearby. Where it is exactly, I am not sure. Find the main road, and there should be signs to point you in the right direction."

"And what do we do when we find someone?"

Mammon sighed. "Matthew knows what to do. Do not fuck this up." The demon shooed her out of his tent with a flick of his wrist. Anna gave him an icy glare before ultimately taking her leave.

Outside the tent, Matthew had already packed up their belongings and handed a bag to Anna. "Ready to get going?"

A deafening silence hung in the air. They had been travelling along the main road for several hours now and neither had said a word. Anna had tried to start a conversation with Matthew, but the words kept dying in her throat just as they were about to leave her lips. She could tell he feared her, and who wouldn't? She was no different than the creatures her father would obsess over; she was a monster. Thankfully, the silence was the only unbearable part of the travels. Spring was rapidly approaching and with it came milder weather. The shining sun warmed their bodies and melted away the snow and frost that had covered the land the night before. In several places, the grass had reappeared and was already changing colour back to its normal, vibrant green.

Finally, after what seemed like a lifetime, they came across a signpost that read *Oxworth,* with the number two beside it. Anna's stomach churned uncomfortably. Soon, she would be condemning a soul to keep Master Mammon in this world, and the idea didn't sit well with her, but the thought of returning to the hells with Mammon didn't seem appealing either. She took a deep breath and vowed only to swindle a person who deserved to lose their soul. Some common lowlife or thug whose ambitions were more than they could stomach. As she was silently vowing to only curse someone deserving, Matthew cleared his throat, the first noise he had made since leaving their camp. Anna turned her head and raised a brow.

"Two miles to Oxworth."

Anna waited for him to continue, but he didn't say anything more. Anna's mouth fell agape. Hours of travelling together in silence and his first words were a painfully obvious comment. Unable to bear it any longer, she let out a scream of frustration and grabbed Matthew by the collar of his shirt.

"Do you hate me? Eldersburg wasn't my fault! I couldn't control it! I never asked for any of this, I never—"

"Who said I hated you?"

"I see how you all look at me, how you refuse to talk to me... you think I am a monster! I didn't mean to hurt those people, I—"

Matthew pulled Anna in for a tight embrace, suffocating her rambling against his chest. After a few moments, he let go and looked her in the eye, grinning from ear to ear. "We don't hate you, Anna, nor are we scared of you. We were all just taken aback. You did something that nobody, not even Master Mammon, could do. Yes, your powers are a bit... uncontrollable right now, but when I saw what you did, I wasn't scared, I was excited."

"Excited?"

A small laugh escaped Matthew's lips. "Yes! For the first time in centuries, I can finally escape Mammon's grasp. You are the key to that, Anna. You are stronger than him, you just need to work on control."

"Is that why you've all been avoiding me?"

The disciple nodded his head. "This isn't an easy thing to talk about. If Mammon ever found out, he..." Matthew trailed off, his eyes losing focus before returning to Anna's. "But with you, everything's changed. We just need to bide our time until you have enough control to kill him. Please set us free, Anna."

"Wait – wouldn't killing Mammon also kill all of you?"

"I'd rather be dead than serve him any longer. We've hurt enough people as his thralls. It is time to end this, it is time for us to be free, even if it can only happen through death."

Anna was at a loss for words. In an instant, all of her feelings over the last several days were invalidated. The disciples didn't hate her; they were planning a coup against a demon and obviously had to exercise a great degree of caution. After several moments of contemplation, she nodded her head. "Alright, I'll help you if I can. But we need to find Mammon a host first, otherwise we'll all be banished to the hells alongside him."

"Let's see if we can find someone in Oxworth." Matthew turned on his heels and began following the road towards the city, only to pause and cast a playful smile at Anna. "Try to leave it in one piece this time, will you?"

Oxworth was much like Winterhelm, only on a much smaller scale. The buildings were smaller, the streets were smaller, even the people looked shorter than the ones who lived in Artanzia's capital. The only thing that was the exact same was the smell, the indistinguishable odour of over a thousand people living near one another. Anna took a deep inhale in and savoured the scent. Although she preferred to be free of a city's walls, there was a small part of her that loved urban life. The people, the opportunities, the food, the small luxuries that life offered when you weren't constantly fighting for survival like in the wilderness.

"Let's start here," Matthew said, gesturing towards an ornate alehouse.

"No," Anna said, digging her heels into the ground suddenly. "That place looks too fancy."

"Exactly," Matthew replied in a confused tone. "We need to find ambitious people, and nobody is more ambitious than the second or third sons of wealthy lords. This is where they'll be."

Anna shook her head. "No. If we are going to keep Mammon around until I get my powers under control, I am not hurting innocent people. We need to find someone who's ambitious but deserves to lose their soul."

Matthew rolled his eyes. "Rich people are just as guilty as the poor." Anna winced at the disciple's comments, not because they were wrong, but because they reminded her of Randall. She gritted her teeth and clenched her fists, before Matthew sensed the tension. "Fine, I promise to not pick anyone who isn't a real bastard. Let's split up – you try to find an establishment of ill repute, and I'll see if I can find some rich slaver or something. We'll meet back here in an hour."

Anna nodded her head and took off. As she weaved her way through the sea of people, she carefully scrutinized them, just as she would a mark when she and Randall planned to rob them. It surprised her how effortlessly her instincts took over, and soon she knew she would find herself in Oxworth's underbelly.

Suddenly, she bumped into someone and was knocked to the ground with a hard thud. Immediately, she checked her pockets to see if anything had been lifted off her, then she realized she had nothing of value anymore. She also saw the person who had sent her sprawling to the ground. He was a young man with wavy, golden-blond hair and a pair of bifocals on his face. He wore a simple green jerkin paired with brown trousers. He was picking up a bunch of loose papers on the ground and stuffing them back into his sack. It wasn't until he stood back up that Anna realized just how large he was. He towered over everyone and was built like a golem. Giant muscles bulged from underneath his clothes, threatening to rip the fabric apart at the seams.

"Shit! I'm so sorry... Here, let me help you up." The boy extended a large, calloused hand to her. Graciously, Anna grabbed it and the giant youth effortlessly pulled her to her feet.

"I'm Mason. I'm sorry, I really should be more careful. Sometimes I feel like a bull in a rose garden, especially when I'm late for class."

"Class?"

"Yeah, I was on my way to the lecture hall right now! Are you a student of the college as well?" Anna shook her head, not sure what he was talking about. "Oh, well, you should definitely come," Mason continued enthusiastically. "There's a symposium this week and a bunch of professors from colleges all across the continent have showed up. Today is Professor Maternus. He is from the Valerian Empire, he's the professor of astronomy in Kaspyia, the capital."

"What's that?" Anna asked.

"Apparently it's the study of the stars," Mason said, pointing to the sky. "I've read his first book, and while most is a little lost on me, I remember him saying that even though we can't see the stars during the day, they are still up there."

Anna stared at the sky in amazement. Who in their right mind would want to study a bunch of little dots? It seemed like a useless endeavour and an effective means of wasting one's life. She was also surprised that someone of Mason's build would be interested in such a stupid thing.

"I hope his lecture will answer a few of my questions, and help me understand it better. Tomorrow is Professor Moretz, a demonology professor from Drussdell, and then the day after is Professor Hawk, who—"

"Wait, did you say Professor Moretz? As in Hanubis Moretz?""Yes! Are you a fan of his work?" Mason asked excitedly.

Anna nodded her head. "And he's here tomorrow?"

"Mhmm. We could go together, if you want? I'd love to hear your thoughts on his work."

"You've read his book?"

"*Books,*" Mason corrected. "I started with *A Beginner's Guide to Demonology,* then I read *Sigils and Seals: How to Trap a Demon,* then just last week I finished his latest book *How to Change Your Life: A Summoner's Guide.* I'll admit, I didn't fully understand the last book as I was rushing to have it done before he got here, so I'll have to read it again."

"Can I—"

"I'm sorry, but the lecture is going to start soon and I don't want to be late and have to sit in the back. I really must be going."

"I'll come with you!" Anna shouted. "I love stars – they fascinate me, I'd love to know more about them," she lied, hoping that it was convincing.

Mason's mouth grew into a goofy, boyish smile. "Perfect, follow me!"

The air in the lecture hall was stale, like a crypt's. Rays of sun beamed in from the large windows on the side of the room, illuminating the tiny dust particles that hung in the air. With each breath, Anna could see the particles move in the airflow, only for dozens more to take their place seconds later. Professor Maternus droned on in a monotonous voice as he drew pictures on a chalkboard. Anna had tried to ask Mason more about Professor Moretz, and what he had learned from the other books, but she was quickly shushed by some of the other students.

Unable to ask questions about what she was really interested in, her mind wandered. At first, she tried to pay attention to the lecture – after all, if she had to sit there the whole time, she might as well learn something. However, it was when the Valerian professor suggested the stars did not move and it was actually the earth moving that she stopped listening. Anna had heard tall tales before, although they usually involved magic beans, or a goose that could lay golden eggs. But this professor's theories seemed to be rooted in the same delusional world that those stories took place in. Everyone knew that the world was flat, and if it spun, like this so-called "expert" suggested, everything would fly off the edges. Trying to find something else to occupy her time other than the ramblings of a madman, she noticed the other people in the hall. Some sat there and listened to Professor Maternus' insanity, while others, like Mason, hastily scribbled down every word he said on a piece of paper.

Anna then turned her attention back to the professor, staring at him with deaf ears. She had never seen anyone from the Valerian Empire before. He had tanned, dark skin, although considerably lighter than A'Chula's. He wore a round hat of red velvet with a large feather sticking out the side. His tunic was black with gold stitching and his pants were the same colour as his hat. A large, but trimmed, dark moustache hung above his lips. He was a rather large man who had clearly enjoyed a life of decadence. Anna could hear the slight wheeze the man made every time he inhaled, and several times during the lecture he choked on his own spittle.

This was not how she thought an intellectual would look. Admittedly, she hadn't known how they would look, but this was certainly the last thing she expected. The evidence of living a pampered life somehow took away the professor's credibility. Anna wondered if Professor Moretz was anything like Professor Maternus, and shuddered at the thought. She reminded herself of the tales she had heard about the Valerian Empire over the years, how the cities were paved with gold and how the empire always paid better than the northern kingdoms.

After a painful three hours, Professor Maternus had finished talking. Ready to be free of the stuffy classroom, Anna stood up, only for a few students to raise their hands and ask questions about the lecture. Anna slumped back down into her seat and prepared to suffer a little while longer. Another hour passed as the students relentlessly asked question after question, Mason included. After a lengthy pause after the final question, Professor Maternus bowed and the lecture hall emptied. Anna quickly shot to her feet and darted towards the door, eager to be free of this place.

Outside the lecture hall, Mason grabbed her by the shoulder. "Wow, wasn't that something!? I never would have thought of the earth being round before today. What did you think of Professor Maternus' lecture?"

"I think the man is off his fucking rocker," she replied under her breath.

"I'm sorry?"

"Never mind," Anna answered. "Truthfully, I found it hard to focus, I was too busy thinking about Professor Moretz's lecture tomorrow."

A smile appeared on Mason's face. "Yes, I hear he is a very charismatic professor, and if he speaks the way he writes, I know I won't be able to take my attention away from him. You know, I'm done with class for the day. Would you want to grab a drink with me? We could talk about Moretz's work, if you want?"

Anna nodded enthusiastically. "Lead the way."

The tavern was dingy and covered in a thin layer of dust. The windows were covered in years' worth of grime, blocking most of the natural light coming in. The air was heavy with the stench of stale beer, blood, and piss. Anna looked around the tavern and raised a questioning brow at Mason, who sat across from her as they awaited their drinks.

"It's the cheapest place to get a drink," Mason confessed. "You don't have a lot of money being a student."

Anna smiled and nodded as if she understood what he meant. The barmaid arrived and dropped their two mugs of ale onto the table with little regard for her patrons or the drinks. The brown swill splashed onto the table and onto the floor, but judging by the stains that surrounded them, this wasn't the first time. Anna raised the mug to her lips, took a hearty swig, and almost immediately gagged. She hadn't discovered what could kill a demon yet, but she wagered that this drink wasn't too far off the mark. She let out a throaty cough as she watched Mason down his drink without batting an eye.

"It's an acquired taste," he said sheepishly.

"So, Professor Moretz..." Anna started, still tasting the putrid ale on her tongue.

"Yes! When I read his first book, I found it very interesting how he theorized that a demon's power is derived from the same emotion that they feed on. Pride, envy, happiness, guilt, everything and anything that makes us human, is a source of food for them."

Anna nodded in agreement. "What do his other books say about demons?"

Mason smiled as he scratched his head, appearing to be deep in thought, but Anna suspected that the youth already knew the answer to her question. "His second book focuses on the idea of sigils and seals, and their relationships with demons."

"What are they?"

"Professor Moretz theorized that each demon has a sigil, or seal, that can essentially trap them in place. They are very archaic in design and lots of the runes are in Infernal, the language of the hells."

Anna leaned forward on to both of her hands. "Fascinating," she enthused. "Does it show any of the sigils in the book?"

Much to her disappointment, Mason shook his head. "Unfortunately, no. Professor Moretz claimed that printing the sigils in his books would only endanger the public. The foreword of the book states: 'Demons are powerful creatures, and should not be harassed unless by a trained professional with years of experience'."

Anna did her best to hide her disappointment, but, judging by Mason's reaction, she failed to do so. Suddenly, a familiar voice called out from across the bar and the hair on the back of her neck raised up. She turned around and saw Matthew approaching the table.

"Anna! You didn't tell me you found a friend!" he said in a boisterous and insincere voice.

"A friend of yours?" Mason asked, as he watched Matthew approach.

"I'm her big brother," Matthew lied as he pulled up a chair to their table. "Tell me, what are your intentions with my little sister?"

Mason's face quickly turned red, and he tugged at the collar of his shirt. "Nothing, we were just talking academics, that's all! We were at Professor Maternus' lecture earlier today."

Matthew leaned back in his chair; a grin that made Anna's stomach churn appearing on his lips. "A scholar, eh? Judging by the size of you, I'd suspect you to be a dockhand or a lumberjack."

Mason laughed bashfully. "I get that a lot. My father was a miner-turned-blacksmith, and my mother always said I am the spitting image of him."

"Was?" Matthew asked.

Anna's heart suddenly sank when she realized what Matthew was doing – he was probing into Mason's life to see if he'd be a suitable host for Mammon. She wanted to speak up in protest, but the words got caught in her throat. She was disgusted that Matthew would even consider someone like Mason, especially because they had agreed to find someone deserving. But then she realized that Matthew was wincing, ever so slightly. Every once in a while, the disciple would touch the mark, and she realized that he wasn't in control. This was Mammon's doing.

"Mhmm," Mason responded, interrupting Anna's thoughts. "He had his leg crushed by some ore that he was trying to offload into the smithy, so he can't do it anymore."

"Why didn't you take over the smithy? I mean, you certainly have the size for it," Matthew said through stiff breath.

"I told him I didn't want to spend the rest of my days hammering metal on an anvil; I wanted something more for myself in life. I want to learn everything I can about the world, and how we all fit inside it."

"An ambitious fellow, I see why my sister has taken a liking to you."

Anna curled her lips into a frown, and her hands into fists. Even though it was Matthew's voice, she could tell they were Mammon's words.

Mason locked eyes with her, and, sensing her discomfort, rose from his chair and bid both of them farewell. "Wait!" Matthew called out. "If your father isn't working, how is your family getting by?"

"Oh, my mom washes some of the nobles' linens once a week."

"That's it?" Mason nodded his head. "Tell you what, my sister and I work for a wealthy lord, and I'm sure if you explain your situation to him, he'd be more than happy to help you and your family out, for the right price. Call it a favour for a favour."

"Really?" Mason said, his eyes lighting up with excitement. "Absolutely – when can I meet him?"

Matthew's smile widened further. "He'll be here by midday tomorrow."

"I can't wait! Thank you, thank you so much!"

Anna watched in horror as Mason practically ran out of the tavern. She turned to Matthew, hoping to see some sign of regret. But instead, he just looked exhausted. He was slouched like a marionette that had just been let go, and his eyes were glassy with fatigue. He rubbed the back of his neck, fingers twitching over the red, angry mark behind his ear.

"Fuck, that was agonizing..." he whispered.

"What the hells, Matthew!?" Anna shouted, finally regaining control over her voice.

The disciple jumped slightly and gave her a confused look. "What?"

"We agreed to go after someone who deserved it!"

"Wasn't my choice," Matthew explained. "Mammon is getting impatient."

"You don't even get a say?" Anna asked in disbelief, realizing just how helpless Matthew and the other disciples truly were.

Matthew looked down at his lap and refused to say anything.

"We can't trick Mason, though; he doesn't deserve it!"

"I can't help you," Matthew sighed. "That boy is perfect for Mammon, and he's the demon's ticket to staying here a little longer."

"We just need more time. Maybe... maybe—"

"Unless you already know how to rid us of Mammon for good, time is a luxury we don't have. I'm sorry, Anna, it has to be this way."

An unnerving silence descended between the two of them as the sickening realization that Matthew and the other disciples were truly powerless against Mammon dawned on Anna. If she wanted to get rid of Mammon, she was going to have to do it herself. Completely and utterly alone.

CHAPTER TWENTY-SIX
ROSALINE

Kenton, Lord of Owls, was a legend in Winterhelm. Not only was he well-versed in the school of divination, but he also had the uncanny ability to see through the eyes of his owls. He was probably the most well-informed man in the city. The only problem was that the man was certifiably off his rocker. Apparently, surrounding yourself with nothing but owls for company rapidly deteriorates a person's sanity.

Rosaline sat in the small living room of the house. She had tried to find a place that wasn't covered in owl pellets and droppings, but when she discovered that no such place existed, she acquiesced and sat in the chair closest to the exit. She didn't want to be here, but she had to see if Duncan was right. If a group of slavers had captured King Elbert, then this siege was going to end within a fortnight. The problem was, however, that they were surrounded and she couldn't risk any of the Brothers to go out and confirm the story. Thus, she was sitting in owl shit, waiting for an old man to likely confirm the truth. She couldn't wrap her head around how the man in the royal guard uniform could enter the city. Granted, she had little experience in the slave trade, nor reliable connections, but Rosaline thought she knew every secret entrance into the city. All of which were surrounded by Elbert's army.

The floorboards creaked as Kenton made his way into the room and sat down across from the bandit leader. Even though the man was blind from old age, it seemed as if he stared right through her, as if he could see her very soul. A sharp wheezing sound filled the owlery as the old man took a deep breath inward.

"So, when does the owl tell you what it saw?" Rosaline asked, as she shifted her body from side to side in the chair.

"Owls do not talk."

Rosaline waited for more of an explanation, but it seemed that Kenton thought that was enough. Letting out a sigh of frustration, she continued to fidget. "If I'm going to wait here all day, could you at least offer me some tea?"

"Owls have no need for tea," Kenton replied.

"You do know that I am not an owl, right?"

"Yes, owls do not talk."

Rosaline's fingers instinctively twitched as she craved to rip Boris from his sheath. It was bad enough that she had to sit in this shit-covered house all day waiting for a bloody owl to return, but the fact that the Lord of Owls couldn't put more than a simple sentence together made it that much worse. *Perhaps I should've sent Phillip here. At least then Kenton would have an intellectual equal to talk to.*

"Hoo!" an owl screeched as it landed in the room, flapping its wings as it landed on the coatrack.

"Finally."

"That is not the owl," Kenton replied stoically.

"It looks like the same owl to me," Rosaline countered. "Maybe you should take another look."

Instead of responding to the bandit leader's jab, Kenton began clicking his tongue against his teeth. The owl's head pivoted and stared at him, its beady eyes locking on to its master before flying into the next room and returning moments later with a dead mouse in its talons. The owl landed on the end table beside Kenton's chair and ripped the mouse to shreds, before carrying the tiny morsels of eviscerated mouse to Kenton's open mouth and dropping them in.

Rosaline clamped her lips shut as bile from her stomach rushed up into her mouth. It took every ounce of willpower to swallow the vomit back down her throat, although she wasn't sure it would matter. Vomit would probably pair nicely with the current owl pellet décor.

"Food?" Kenton asked, as he chewed another piece of shredded mouse.

"No, thanks, I had a big rat on my way over here. If I eat now, I'll spoil my dinner."

Either Rosaline's sarcasm was lost on the Lord of Owls, or he chose not to be bothered by it. Several hours passed. Dozens of owls flew in and out of the house during that time, none of which were the "right" owl, although they all looked the same to Rosaline. Right when Rosaline was about to deem it a lost cause, another owl flew into the house. A smile appeared on Kenton's lips as he cooed the bird over to him. He scratched the back of the owl's neck and fed it several chunks of mouse before gripping it with both hands and snapping its neck.

The sudden crack of vertebrae jolted Rosaline's body into full focus. The mundane waiting had lulled her into a state of passive boredom, but the minute the owl died, her instincts took over again. Kenton set the owl corpse down on the table and pulled out a small knife. He carved open the bird's body and removed the internal organs with great skill. Several other owls watched from the corner of the room, either undisturbed by the murder of their kin or glowering in silent contempt, Rosaline couldn't decide which.

After all the organs were removed, Kenton broke the ribs apart from the spine. He gripped the hollow bones in his hands and shook them before throwing them onto the table beside the corpse.

"Hmmm," Kenton groaned as he stared at the bones through his blind eyes.

"See something?" Rosaline asked snidely.

"The king is ash."

Rosaline raised a brow. "What does that mean? Is he dead, burned to death?"

"I also see the viper losing its hold on the raven."

Rosaline shook her head. What the hell did that mean, besides the fact that it didn't answer her question? Frustrated by the nonsensical answer, Rosaline decided to press further. "Who are the viper and raven?"

"The owl shows me no more."

"Great," Rosaline said, exasperated, before tossing the blind man a purse of coin. "Thanks for the fucking insight." Before Kenton could reply, she slammed the door of the owlery and stormed off back to the Garden.

The fresh spring air did wonders for her as she pondered her next move. If Elbert was taken, or dead, then one of two things would happen. The lords of Artanzia would choose a new king from amongst themselves, although she doubted they would ever agree in a timely manner. The other option was that Elbert's army would stand down, and the lords of the kingdom would recognize Randall as their new king. Neither option excited her. If the lords chose a new king, they would still be surrounded and the siege would continue, which would allow the Brotherhood to make more money through extorting the citizens of Winterhelm, but that also meant increasing the chance of getting caught. Conversely, if the lords recognized Randall as their new king, the Bloody Brotherhood could leave the city uncontested and continue ransacking the countryside, but they would lose out on thousands more in gold.

Then there was the second riddle: *The viper losing its hold on the raven.* Rosaline scoffed aloud. The city was crawling with vipers – schemers, backstabbers, and cutthroats. That could be anyone. As for the raven... who the hells knew? She didn't even know what a raven *was* supposed to represent.

"Excuse me, darlin'?" a rugged, gravelly voice called out. Rosaline turned her head and saw a man sitting in the street in soiled rags. Every inch of skin was covered in grime and he had jagged, claw-like fingernails. The strong scent of cabbage assaulted her nose as he spoke. "Buy an old veteran somethin' warm to eat?"

Rosaline smiled and crouched down so that she and the beggar were eye level with one another. "You're a horrible liar. I can smell the cabbage you had for lunch on your breath halfway across the street. If you want easy marks, I suggest you try the Upper City."

As she turned to walk away, the beggar's voice called out to her once again. "If you can't buy me food, the least you can do is give me a moment of your time. The Bloody Brotherhood doesn't need us as enemies."

Rosaline froze on the spot. She turned her head and glared at the beggar, who was smiling from ear to ear, obviously proud of his wits. She wanted to gut him right then and there, but she knew that if the man was supposed to set up a meeting between criminal bosses, he would likely not be alone.

"And who is 'us'?" Rosaline asked impatiently.

"We call ourselves the Harbingers. A few of your Brothers stopped by the other day, roughed up a few of our men. Me boss wants to know how you plan to rectify the situation."

"Tell me where I can meet your boss, and I'll be sure he gets an apology letter and a lovely gift basket."

"Nah, ain't gonna work like that, love. You're going to have to come with us."

Before she could react, Rosaline had two burly men standing on either side of her as the beggar rose to his feet. Her eyes darted between each of the men, carefully calculating if she could kill them before being overpowered. Unfortunately, she knew she could only kill one for sure – anything more than that was a game of luck rather than skill. Besides, the two men flanking her looked like they had been fed bricks their entire life, and knew that they were much stronger than she was. Not sensing much of a choice, Rosaline conceded. "Lead the way."

The men had escorted her down several dark alleys before coming to what appeared to be an abandoned warehouse. Once inside, she saw the Harbingers were using it as their base of operations. She quickly scanned the warehouse and saw several workers filling barrels with presumably stolen valuables and loot. The three men then led Rosaline into a small side room and sat her down at a bloodstained table before leaving her alone. A few candles illuminated the room ominously.

As much as she hated to admit it, she was scared. She had been cornered before in life, but never this badly. While she was alone, she took a moment to allow the mask of indifference to fall before she met with the Harbingers' leader. *If they're going to kill you,* she whispered to herself, *then you're at least going to gut some of the fuckers on your way out.*

Suddenly, a door on the other side of the room creaked open, and a halfling with long curly hair and a sizeable moustache entered the room. He walked into the room with a slight limp in his gait and propped himself across the table from Rosaline.

"I appreciate you taking the time to meet with me, Rosaline," the halfling said with faux sincerity.

"Of course!" Rosaline replied. "I love being invited for tea at knifepoint. I love the décor – really sells the bloodthirsty bandit mystique you got going on."

"Glad you like it! All the bloodstains are authentic, you know. My men suggested using red paint, but I'm a stickler for authenticity. People can just tell when you go that extra mile."

Rosaline's fake smile vanished, as her anxiety and annoyance grew. "What do you want?"

"Tssk, tssk. And here I thought the foreplay would last a little longer. Aren't you even going to ask who I am?"

"No," Rosaline replied coldly. "I know who you are. You're some little weasel that thinks he can squeeze the Bloody Brotherhood for coin. I've been in these conversations before and they're always the same, so if you don't mind, let's skip the pissing contest and get to the matter at hand." The halfling raised a brow, but after a momentary pause, gestured for Rosaline to continue. "Over the years, the Bloody Brotherhood has built a reputation, one aptly built with a lot of blood. We've dealt with petulant young upstarts like you before, so trust me when I say..." Rosaline leaned in closer and stared at the halfling's eyes with an icy glare "...we will burn this warehouse and your shit-eating organization to the fucking ground, and I'll hang your flayed body in the streets to serve as a reminder for everyone not to fuck with the Brotherhood."

Silence hung in the air for several seconds before the halfling's smile widened. "Very scary. How long did you work on that little speech? I'm impressed. But you aren't going to do anything except for what I tell you to, and do you want to know why?"

"Enlighten me."

"Because you're in my kingdom. You don't leave this warehouse without my say-so, and you are not leaving this room alive until you concede to my demands. Simple."

"Which are?"

"The Bloody Brotherhood will become underlings for the Harbingers. All the gold and valuables you have extorted and will continue to extort will come to us. As a reward for your loyalty and diligent service, you and your 'Brothers' will receive a compensatory ten percent of the profits."

"Is that all?"

"No, there is still the matter of your men beating some of mine quite literally to death. No amount of gold can repay me for that loss, for, you see, one of the men who died was my brother. For that, I demand a pound of flesh, an eye for an eye, a Brother for a brother. Do I make myself clear?"

"Crystal."

"Good. Now, unless you object to any of these terms, I think our business is concluded here."

Rosaline tried to voice a protest but fear gripped her throat shut. She didn't want to agree to these terms, but if the halfling was going to let her walk out of the warehouse unscathed, then she was willing to say anything to get out of there.

"Deal."

"Excellent!" The halfling clapped his hands and stood up from his chair. The two burly men from before entered the room, and one placed his meaty hands on Rosaline's shoulders, pinning her to the chair. Just as the Harbingers' boss was about to exit the room, he paused in the doorway and turned around. "I don't know about you, but I feel like this room could use a little bit more red. Gentlemen, start decorating."

"Hells, Roz, what happened to you?" Malek asked as Rosaline limped her way into the tavern, leaving a trail of blood on the floor behind her. She sat herself down at the bar, grabbed a bottle of strong spirits, and took three hearty gulps. After the burning in her throat subsided, she glared at Malek with contempt through her swollen eyes.

"You not doing your job fucking happened!" She hurled the bottle at Malek's head, losing her balance and falling to her knees as she did so. Jathan quickly ran over and picked up his leader, who drove a sharp knee directly into his guts. Grabbing the bar for support, Rosaline slowly lifted herself to her feet. "When I ask you to take care of our rivals, I mean fucking take care of it! Make yourselves useful and find me a healer, unless you want to find a way to cock that up as well."

Malek nodded sheepishly as Jathan slowly rose to his feet, groaning and clutching his stomach as he did so. She snapped her fingers and Fletcher brought her another bottle. Slowly and painfully, she limped upstairs to her room, where she intended to drink till the pain subsided and she could pass out in her bed, hoping to forget the events of the day.

CHAPTER TWENTY-SEVEN
RANDALL

The mood in the war room was tense. All the councillors talked amongst themselves about the news the slaver had brought. Elbert had been captured, and, for the right price, would be sold to them. Excitement filled the king's body as he pictured removing the cripple's head and staking it to the front of the city walls for all to see. Soon, the siege would be over and his reign of peace and prosperity would begin. It was so close he could almost taste it.

"Has nobody considered this being a bloody trap? I mean, the man was wearing a royal guardsman's uniform!" Virgil Walker shouted, slamming his fist onto the table. "Clearly Elbert takes us for fools and wants to lure us out from behind our walls."

"Gods, I can't consider anything on this empty of a stomach," Corbin Strongarm said passive-aggressively.

Randall glared at the dwarf. Although their rations had been cut back, the people were much better off for it. Going behind his council's back added a lot of tension to the room, but the king knew it was the right move, even if he got an earful from Cassius and the others.

"Please, Virgil," Madame Dupont interrupted, her voice heavy with derision, "I doubt a cripple can conjure a scheme like that."

"Heh," Virgil scoffed. "Elbert is many things – temperamental, petulant, insecure – but he is not an idiot." The former guardsman turned his head to Randall. "Your Majesty, think about the timing. This man shows up, out of nowhere, telling you he has the enemy king in his hands, only after we've dealt Elbert a devastating blow by destroying his blockade. Doesn't that strike you as suspicious?"

Randall reluctantly nodded his head. "I'll admit that the timing is a coincidence. However, if this was a plot by the crippled king, why not send assassins instead of a messenger? Clearly his men know how to enter the city – why try to lure me out when he can breach the walls? No, the slaver is telling the truth. I will not let that vile cripple escape the headman's axe, and I will personally see to it that his tyrannous bloodline ends with him. The people of Artanzia will finally know peace under a ruler who is just like them, and genuinely cares for their wellbeing."

"How did he get into the city?" Tig asked, voicing a concern that everyone had. "Seems unlikely that he slipped through Elbert's camp and used one of the gates without either side noticing him."

"Slavers are a secretive bunch," Madame Dupont began. "They have secret passageways known only to them, that can only be opened using their own language, known as Slaver's Tongue."

"And how do you know this?" Randall asked.

Madame Dupont smiled at the king, the way you would smile at a child for asking a rather obvious question. "I run a brothel, Your Majesty. After a good fuck, men love to run their mouths."

"It makes sense," Cassius interrupted. He had been uncharacteristically quiet until that point in the meeting. "Slavery is outlawed in the north, so transporting people from here to other parts of the world, like the Forsaken Lands or the Valerian Empire, would require a large degree of secrecy."

"How much gold are the slavers asking in exchange for Elbert?" Corbin Strongarm asked, furiously jotting notes down on a piece of parchment as the meeting carried on.

"Seventy-five thousand crowns," Cassius responded.

"Hells, that's a lot of coin," Virgil Walker growled.

"But surprisingly reasonable for the price of a king," Corbin countered.

"A former king," Randall corrected.

"Can the kingdom financially afford this?" Madame Dupont asked.

"King David, before his passing, hoarded money like a dragon. While, I admit, seventy-five thousand crowns will put a sizeable dent in the treasury, I believe after several years of higher taxes we will recoup our losses," Cassius replied.

Randall let out a frustrated breath. He did not want to unfairly tax his subjects, but he also could not pass up the opportunity to solidify his rule. "Fine, let's do it."

There was a hush in the war room. All the councillors looked at the king in disbelief. After a moment's pause, Cassius cleared his throat. "I believe they also want a selection of our prisoners every year to bring back to the Forsaken Lands as slaves."

"Tell the slaver I agree to his terms."

"Randall," Tig blurted out, "are you seriously going to sell people into slavery?"

The king looked at his old friend and smiled. "I'm going to tell that slaver whatever he wants to hear until I have Elbert in my grasp. After that, his head can rest on the pike next to the cripple's, for all I care. Tell Gavin we set off for Eldersburg at nightfall."

"We?" Cassius asked.

"Of course. I'm going to parade the tyrant through the streets myself. I am the hero who is going to save Artanzia, and I am the man who will bring the last of the nobles to justice."

"Absolutely not!" Virgil shouted. "Have you gone mad, boy?"

Before Randall could scold the grizzled veteran, Cassius interjected. "Virgil is right, Your Majesty. You travelling with the slavers is unwise. If it is indeed a trap set by Elbert, we'll be doing exactly what he wants. We cannot hand you over to him; we cannot jeopardize the future of the kingdom."

"I will not send just anyone on this journey, Cassius. It has to be me."

Suddenly, A'Chula rose to his feet. The mute walked over to the king's side, dropped to one knee, and placed a hand over his chest. "Mmm," he grunted.

Randall's eyes widened in disbelief. A'Chula had escaped slavery once, and it cost him his tongue. That he was willing to enter that world again in Randall's name was touching. "Are you sure?" the king asked softly.

A'Chula nodded his head. Randall looked around the council and everyone seemed satisfied with sending the former slave to recover Elbert, with the exception of Tig, whose mouth was open in shock.

"Then it's settled. A'Chula and a small retinue of volunteers will accompany Gavin to Eldersburg and recover Elbert. Any questions?" The room was silent. "Good. Meeting adjourned."

The sun was high in the afternoon sky, illuminating the entire city and melting what little snow remained from the particularly brutal winter. Wanting to celebrate his stroke of good luck, Randall sat on the balcony connected to his room with a carafe of wine and look out over his city. He poured himself a glass and spun the drink around several times before taking a deep inhale. The decadent, earthy aroma of the wine made his head spin slightly as he allowed the drink to breathe before taking a sip. Since taking the throne, he had grown fond of drinking fine wine. Cassius had taught him how to properly prepare the drink, and how to describe the taste of it without "sounding like a boor". At first, Randall didn't see the point of talking about wine, but Cassius was adamant on its importance, since nobles typically loved to have wine tastings. They were a necessary event when negotiating trade agreements, alliances, and marriage proposals with vassals and even other rulers. If Randall wanted to be taken seriously as a king, Cassius insisted he learn to be a wine connoisseur. After a few minutes, Randall helped himself to a sip from his glass. The strong fruity flavour of the wine excited his tongue as he swished it around his mouth for several seconds before swallowing it. It was a rich yet complex bouquet of fruit with notes of raspberries, black-currants, and pomegranates. Each fruit was expertly balanced, with no one flavour overpowering the others. "The nobles sure do know their wine," he said to himself as he poured himself another glass.

"So, you're one of them now, eh?" a voice said from behind him.

Surprised, Randall hopped out of his chair and saw Tig standing in the middle of the room, and judging by the look on his face, he was not too pleased with his king.

"What exactly is that supposed to mean?" Randall asked.

"You've changed, Randall," Tig stated bluntly. "Right when I think you're becoming your old self again, you pull this shit. The Randall I knew, the one who I would've braved the hells for, would have never sent A'Chula with slavers."

Randall scoffed. "A'Chula is his own man; he didn't have to volunteer if he didn't want to."

Tig's brow furrowed. "What do you think will happen when the slavers see a former runaway slave? Do you think that they'll let him walk away free? He'll end up in chains again, and Gods know what piece of his body they'll cut off this time."

"Gods, Tig, you're worrying like a woman. Cassius keeps saying I need a queen, but judging by how you're nagging me, I already have one."

"Fuck you! Ever since you let that eunuch into your life, the world's gone to shit. The Maggots are gone. You hardly have time to see A'Chula and me anymore, not to mention that Maeve, Chuckles, and Anna died needlessly for your deluded dream. When will it be enough, Randall?"

Randall stormed across the room and stood nose to nose with his oldest friend. "The world was always shit; I'm the only one trying to fix it! Do you not remember starving in the streets, eating rats until we scrounged enough coin to finally buy a hot bowl of gruel? You want to go back to that life, be my guest! I need people by my side who believe in me, and believe in what I want to achieve."

"So that's it, huh? Who cares about the mountain of bodies and rivers of blood that you leave in your wake, as long as you get your crown? You say you hate the nobles because they didn't care about us, but you're just like them, wearing your fancy clothes and drinking your wine. Cassius and the others are turning you into the monster that you always hated, you're just too dumb to see it. The only difference between you and Elbert now is that you can walk."

Before Randall could respond, his fist impulsively struck Tig across the chin. Surprised by the blow, Tig staggered back a few steps before regaining his balance and glaring at Randall. He shook his head and spat a bloody tooth on the floor. "What would Anna say if she could see you right now?"

Tig's comment was like a knife to the heart. The hair on the back of Randall's neck stood up on end and his heart sank as he realized what had just transpired. He wanted to apologize, but his body was frozen in place. Instead, he watched Tig exit the room, slamming the door shut as he left. The king was left alone in his room, staring at the closed door while his fist throbbed from punching his best friend in the face.

CHAPTER TWENTY-EIGHT
GRIMM

Spring had nearly arrived. Leaves were blossoming on the trees, grass had emerged from beneath the snow, and the world was beginning to thaw. Despite the early hour, Grimm was atop a ladder, rake in hand, knocking the snow off the thatched roofs so that it didn't melt into the houses. It had been almost two weeks since Gareth first brought Grimm to the commune, and in that time, almost all of his strength had returned. As long as he kept helping, the followers of the Golden Sun were more than happy to give him all the nutritious food he could eat. He had lost several pounds of muscle, but it was slowly returning as he spent most of his days chopping wood, or trying to learn how to work the blacksmith's forge.

"Grimm!" Uriel called out. "Come down for breakfast."

Grimm turned his head and nodded politely before descending the ladder. Aprat from Uriel and Gareth, most of the people of the commune gave him a wide berth, which he didn't mind. Occasionally, they would smile and wave, and he would do the same, but he spent most of his days focusing on getting his strength back.

"Saved you some," Uriel said as he extended a wooden bowl of grey gruel towards the Islander. Grimm nodded in thanks and followed Uriel to a secluded place where the two of them could eat in peace. This wasn't unusual – every day the two of them would sit alone and talk. Uriel said it was because he wanted Grimm's wits to recover as much as his muscles, but Grimm knew better. The man was trying to get a read on him, and whether his people were safe with him around.

"You're looking strong," Uriel said as he sat down on a fallen log. "I dare say you could chop a tree in two with a single swing of the axe."

A half smile crept onto Grimm's lips. He appreciated the compliment, although he had never been able to chop a tree in half with one blow. A man, on the other hand…

"How are you finding it here? Have you given any more thought to joining us for service?"

Grimm let out a snort as he slurped a spoonful of the gruel down his throat. "I already have a god."

"And look where he led you. Starved, betrayed, and basically a corpse in a foreign land. I can't help but think that the Golden Sun wanted you to find your way to our community."

"Isn't it too early to argue about religion?"

Uriel let out a laugh. "Fair enough. But how are things? Judging from what you've told me, your past life was chaotic and full of violence. How does it feel to finally have peace?"

"Good," Grimm lied, although it pained him to do so. Peace was all that he had wanted for as long as he could remember, but between raiding as a young man, helping Uthredd unite the Isles, killing the High King's brother, and serving a foreign king in a war against his own people, he had never truly been at peace. But now that he had it, it left a sour taste in his mouth. Peace was just so… *boring.* There were several nights where he prayed some bandits or wild animals would attack, so he would have something to do. Every day was painfully mundane. Wake up, work, eat, work, eat, sleep, and repeat. If this was what the rest of his life was going to look like, he almost regretted not dying on the voyage over. But he had made a promise to his wife that this was a new beginning, and he was going to see it through.

"It's hard to let go of our past," Uriel said suddenly after a lengthy pause. "When we escape all that we've ever known, it feels like we are being dishonest with ourselves. But nobody is violent by nature – it's taught and indoctrinated in us at a young age."

Grimm rolled his eyes. When Uriel wasn't trying to sway him to his god, he was trying to convert him to the pacifist lifestyle. It was endearing that the priest could see how much Grimm struggled with transitioning to a peaceful life, but he felt that Uriel's ideology was inherently wrong. He had seen the worst in people; he had seen greed, jealousy, cruelty, depravity, and wanton death. Violence was just how the world worked, and that would never change.

"Don't shake your head at me, you know I'm right. The only true defence against violence is education. If we teach compassion, violence will no longer exist. Show the world that there is another way, a more peaceful way."

Grimm groaned with a bit more attitude than he intended and shook his head. "No. The only defence against evil, violent people are good people who are better at violence."

"How are you any better than them, then?"

Grimm smiled as he helped himself to another spoonful of gruel before replying, "'Cause I'm the cunt still standing."

Uriel, nodded, defeated, stood up, and went to make his way back to camp. Before he left, he stopped and touched Grimm softly on the shoulder. "Be careful, Grimm. A man who fights evil should take care that he himself does not become evil. It's easy to become what you hate."

Grimm nodded, masking his indifference to the priest's words. He had had enough philosophy for one day. He finished his bowl of gruel in quiet solitude. After he was finished, he returned to the settlement and resumed his daily chore of monotonously chopping wood. Although it was a far cry from wielding an axe in battle, it was the closest he could get in his newly found peaceful life. The rhythmic swinging of the axe, along with the satisfying sound of splitting a log, allowed Grimm to escape reality for several hours. His mind brought up treasured memories of his past. His first raid, his courtship of Freja, the time Uthredd and him nearly burned down a brothel in their youth, among other memories.

"Grimm," a voice called out, pulling the Islander out of his memories. He looked down and saw a mountain of split logs and blood slowly trickling out across his palms. He let go of the axe and saw that his hands had blistered while chopping wood. Turning around, he saw Gareth standing behind him.

"I think that is enough firewood," Gareth said with a half smile. "It's time for supper."

Wiping his bloodied hands on his pants, Grimm made his way back to the middle of the settlement where supper was being served. With the cold, miserable winter behind them, the commune had decided to celebrate the spring solstice with a feast. The left-over winter rations were taken out of storage for all to enjoy, along with freshly baked bread and roasted salmon. Thankful for such a bountiful feast, Grimm had filled his plate with as much food as it could hold. As he left camp, ready to go eat in solitude, he heard Uriel call over to him.

"Grimm! Come join us!"

Grimm shrugged his shoulders and walked over to the table where Uriel, Gareth, his wife, and a few others were sitting.

Taking a seat at the end of the table, he ate while the others prayed in thanks to their god. Once the prayer was finished, idle smalltalk broke out. Grimm sat at the table in silence, taking in everyone's stories. After everyone had their fill of food, Uriel surprised everyone with a few bottles of wine he had stashed away, while the children of the settlement played nearby, uninterested in the alcohol.

Begrudgingly, Grimm helped himself to a single glass of wine, although he was never a fan of the stuff. He sniffed the glass and curled his lips in disgust at the smell.

"Not a fan of wine, Grimm?" Gareth asked.

Before he could answer, a woman snorted at the other end of the table. She was short and petite, with pale skin that contrasted with her ebony black hair and yellow eyes. Grimm remembered her name was Isobel, and that she and her husband were among the first people to join Uriel in establishing the commune. Unfortunately, her husband had passed away from illness several winters ago and now it was just her and her son, Seamus, left.

"Do they even have wine on the Isles?" she asked, taking a sip from her cup.

Although her voice was condescending and slightly derisive, Grimm couldn't help but notice a playful look in her eyes, as if challenging him, though to what, he wasn't sure.

"It's too cold on the Isles to make wine, but we manage to take a few bottles back with us every raid," Grimm told her as he took a sip.

"So don't you like it?" Gareth pried. "I saw how you curled your nose up at it."

"It's too fruity and sweet, which makes the hangovers from it the worse. I remember getting drunk on wine the night before a big battle with Uthredd, and the next day was excruciating."

"What happened?" another person asked. She was a stocky, ginger woman with a nearly shaved head. Despite her large and muscular frame, Grimm had never seen her do a day of manual labour. In fact, she did most of the cooking for the settlement, while also teaching the kids the tenets of the Golden Sun.

"Yes, tell us," Isobel urged.

Grimm helped himself to another sip of wine before he started the story. "Well, Uthredd, who is like a brother to me, woke me up in the middle of the night saying that he had stolen a case of wine from his father, the jarl. We were probably twelve or thirteen, so we didn't know any better, we thought it would be just like ale. Uthredd and I polished off probably two bottles each before passing out. In the morning, his father found us covered in wine and beat us like rented mules. Then, for added punishment, he put us in the vanguard of his army."

Grimm paused for dramatic effect. "All I remember feeling as I looked at the other jarl's army approach was nausea. I was sweating uncontrollably, my armour felt like it weighed a thousand pounds, and my head was pounding as if Heimer was using it as his personal forge."

"What did you do?" Gareth asked.

"I lasted about five minutes into the battle before I vomited all over myself. I remember stripping down naked in the middle of the battlefield to cool off and not feel so encumbered by my armour. Next—"

"Wait, you fought naked?" Uriel asked in disbelief.

"Mhmm," Grimm grunted. "Next is a blur of blood, severed limbs, and the screams of dead men. After the battle, Uthredd's father was so amused by me fighting naked that he gave me the first choice in loot, even before himself."

"What did you choose?" the ginger woman asked, leaning further onto the table.

"I chose what any young man would choose. A sword."

The table nodded and murmured, as if that was a good choice. He was looking over at Isobel, whose face had contorted into an ugly frown, when there was a shrill scream from across the camp. Everyone, including Grimm, rose to their feet and raced over.

In the middle of a clearing just outside the main settlement was Seamus, with a pool of blood forming around his head. Isobel instantly fell into hysterics while the rest of the parents questioned the other children.

"We were just playing!" one child blurted out.

"Yeah! It's not my fault that Seamus can't walk on his own two feet," another added.

Snarling like a lioness, Isobel left her son's side and lunged at the boy before being restrained by several other adults. During the commotion, Grimm walked over to Seamus and inspected the wound. He had seen men die many times in a variety of gruesome ways. He had seen men trip on twigs and impale themselves on branches; he had seen men slip and crack their skull open on rocks; but he had also seen his fair share of attacks to the head with a blunt weapon. This was definitely the latter. The injury was on the side of Seamus' head, just above the temple. Cuts and bruises along the boy's arms and hands suggested a fight had taken place. He also noted there were no rocks large enough in the clearing to crack someone's head open the way Seamus' was split apart.

"It's not our fault!" the second boy cried out as his parents shielded him from the others.

"Everyone, just take a deep breath," Uriel said in a calm voice. "We can't let our tempers get the better of us. It is only by keeping level heads that we will find out the truth." Uriel walked over to the parents shielding their boy from Isobel's fury and gently ushered them aside. He bent down to one knee so that they were eye level with one another. "Godfrey, tell me what really happened."

Grimm gritted his teeth, telling himself not to get involved. He owed nothing to either Isobel and her son or Godfrey and his parents. But he hated liars – they were dishonourable, and if children were not punished for lying early on, it would become a constant problem. Letting out a defeated sigh, he rose to his feet.

"I can tell you what happened, they attacked Seamus with a club."

"We didn't!" Godfrey exclaimed. "He just tripped and fell!"

"Liar," Grimm snarled. "Where's the club?"

"Don't call my son a liar, you heathen!" Godfrey's father said, stepping forward so that he was inches away from Grimm's nose.

The Islander tried to suppress a smile. He could feel the anger and adrenaline coursing through his veins, welcoming the intoxicating, familiar sensation. It was the first time he had felt alive, truly alive, since arriving at the commune.

"There are no rocks on the ground in this clearing that could give the boy a wound of that size. The wound is also on the side of his head instead of the back or front. Finally, there are cuts and bruises along Seamus' arms, which meant he tried to defend himself. So, yes, your boy's a liar." Grimm took a step forward towards Godfrey's father. "Perhaps if you had done your job as a father and a man, you wouldn't have raised a lying, snivelling, coward," he goaded.

As he expected, Godfrey's father took the bait and swung a wild haymaker at the Islander. Grimm parried it with ease, his old instincts taking over, and he quickly countered with a hard right hand to the nose, knocking the man to the ground.

Godfrey and his mother rushed to the man's side and Uriel quickly got between them and Grimm. "Go back to the settlement, Grimm, we'll talk there." His voice was angry and commanding.

Grimm nodded his head and walked back to the settlement but not before whispering to Uriel, "The only defence against violence..."

As the newest addition to the commune, Grimm did not have the most luxurious accommodation. In fact, it was little better than an outhouse, but he couldn't complain – it blocked the wind and had a small fireplace for heat. He sat on his bedding for several hours, waiting for the impending judgement. He was sure the community of pacifists would banish him. Despite his previous boredom and frustration, the thought of being exiled from the community tore him apart. These people took him in when he had nothing, nursed him back from the dead, and accepted him. Like it or not, they were the closest thing he had to a family. On the other hand, getting the blood pumping and punching Godfrey's father filled him with such vigour that he couldn't help but smile or even laugh. He was feeling like his old self again, and nothing made him happier. Suddenly, there was a knock on the door. He opened it, but instead of finding a furious Uriel, he saw Isobel, with a small wicker basket in her hands.

"I brought you these, as a way of saying thank you," she said meekly.

Grimm nodded his head, taken aback by the act of kindness, and brought the basket inside.

"It's just—" Isobel continued "—Seamus isn't the biggest of boys, and that little shit Godfrey and the others torment him. If you hadn't intervened, I just know they would've gotten away with it."

Grimm sat back down on the bed. "Your boy, how is he?"

"He's with Nettie. She thinks he will make a full recovery. I had to leave; I can't stand to see my little boy like that—"

Grimm sat silently as Isobel wept uncontrollably. He was never the best at comforting people. He eyed the doorway, thinking he should leave Isobel alone with her tears, but there wouldn't be enough room to squeeze by her. Unable to make an escape, he awkwardly put a hand on her shoulder and gave a slight squeeze, hoping it was the right thing to do.

"Ever since Seamus' father died," she said, fighting to get her words out through the tears, "Seamus has struggled to fit in. I know he's hurting, and I don't know how to help. Plus, he's getting to the age where his father should be teaching him how to be a man. I worry he's too soft..." Her voice trailed off as she looked Grimm in the eyes. "Can you teach him? Can you teach him how to defend himself and how to be an honourable man?"

Grimm impulsively raised a brow. It was an interesting proposition, especially because he was confident that the Islander definition of 'honourable' differed from the mainlander one. He eyed the exit once more, but escape was still unlikely. Desperate not to feel like a fish out of water, and be free of this conversation, he agreed. "Sure, I'll teach your son. If he recovers." As soon as the last sentence left his mouth, he knew it was a mistake. He clenched his jaw in frustration. Isobel's face had nearly gone as white as snow at the comment when Uriel walked into the doorway, seemingly to the rescue.

"He'll make a full and swift recovery, Isobel. The Golden Sun shines brightly on him." Isobel smiled half-heartedly and hugged Uriel as she left the shack, leaving the two men alone.

Grimm saw Uriel was calm and collected instead of angry, like he expected him. As crazy as it sounded, he would've much preferred anger. Grimm waited for Uriel to speak, anticipating the word 'banished' to exit the man's lips.

"I haven't been honest with you, Grimm." Uriel sighed as he sat down on the bed beside the Islander. "I left the Church of the Golden Sun a number of years ago. As far as the Church is concerned, I'm a heretic and a blasphemer."

"What do you mean?"

"My parents left Kovar before I was born and settled in the southern reaches of the Valerian Empire. There, as a young boy, I grew up and was indoctrinated into the Church of the Golden Sun. Everything I preach to the community – forgiveness, peacefulness, and love for fellow man – were the tenets I was taught." Uriel's voice wavered at the last few words before pausing. After several moments, he continued, "However, several decades ago things changed. The Church's leadership shifted and, as a result, its dogma shifted as well. Instead of preaching togetherness and pursuing a life of peace, they advocated the persecution and the execution of nonhumans. They blamed elves, dwarves, and halflings for humanity's problems, believing that they were a disease that needed to be purged."

"Why are you telling me this?" Grimm asked.

"I came to the Northern Kingdoms to try to establish a community under the Golden Sun's original teachings. But it seems I've failed. People are inherently violent, and if there is no consequence of violence, will act on their base desires."

Grimm's heart sank a little. To see a man so shaken in his faith was upsetting. He thought about what to say for several seconds, cursing his inability to form the right words. After an uncomfortable silence, Grimm decided to tell a story.

"Do you know who High King Uthredd is?" he asked.

"Only from the little you told me," Uriel replied.

"He is the first Islander to unite all the clans under one banner. Nobody in the history of the world had ever even tried it, let alone done it. When we were boys, he would talk about uniting all the clans into the world's most fearsome army. Everyone, including myself and his brother, called him insane. We told him he dreamed too big, that Heimer would punish him for such ambitions. But he did it, the mad bastard pulled it off. It took years of war and bloodshed, but Uthredd achieved his dream."

"What's your point?"

"No matter how insane your dream is, don't lose faith."

Uriel nodded his head thoughtfully for several moments before speaking. "You're right. Just like Uthredd and his war, I too must persevere. Thank you, Grimm." With that, Uriel stood up and started to leave, before stopping in the doorway. "You have been sentenced to a week of hard labour for using an act of violence to solve a dispute. Do not let it happen again."

Grimm nodded his head as the priest left his shack. He sat there, a sense of relief washing over him as he realized he was being allowed to stay in the community. He thought about Uriel's dream of a peaceful and loving world and laughed silently to himself. The world was far too cruel for that kind of insane dream... but then again, he had been wrong before.

CHAPTER TWENTY-NINE
ELBERT

Pain. That was all that he felt. Excruciating, intolerable pain. He felt the flames burn him alive and turn his body to ash, and now, he felt the fire burn him once again, but this time giving shape to his body instead of destroying it. He felt how his body was rebuilt from ash, how the fire singed his nerve endings and burnt the skin back on to his body. Every second was agonizing. Once his voice had returned, he screamed with every ounce of strength he had. He curled his body into a ball and gripped his hair so tight with his fists that he thought he was going to rip it out. Then suddenly, it was over.

Elbert stayed in the foetal position for a few seconds, whimpering quietly and shaking uncontrollably. The cool evening air gently kissed his naked body. After a few deep breaths, he uncurled, and looked around to see where he was. What he saw nearly stole the air from his lungs yet again. Sitting close by was the monster hunter who gave him that damned coin.

"Not a pleasant experience I take it?" the man said in his gravelly voice as he offered Elbert a canteen of water.

Hesitantly, Elbert reached out for the canteen. He pulled the cork and sniffed the contents. It smelt like water, but then again, the coin had looked like a coin. Casting the stranger a wary glance, Elbert took the smallest sip. When the cool drink hit his lips, he instantly began guzzling the water down. He could still feel the residual heat of the fire in his chest.

Before he could drink his fill, the stranger snatched the canteen away from Elbert's grasp and corked it before tossing him a few tattered clothes and looking at him with a determined glare. "I'm going to ask you a few questions now. You will answer them plainly and directly. Do you understand?"

"Hold on," Elbert exclaimed after licking a few remaining water droplets from his lips. "Who in the hells are you? Why did you give me that coin, and why—"

The monster hunter held up a silencing hand. "Do you understand?" he repeated.

Elbert furrowed his brow in frustration; he deserved an answer. But as he studied the monster hunter's face, it was clear the man was in no mood to give answers. Begrudgingly, the king nodded his head.

"How long has it been since you made your deal with the demon?"

"What?" The man sighed before approaching Elbert with a balled fist. The king held up his hands. "Please! I don't know what you mean! I know nothing about any demon."

The stranger paused for a moment before removing his shirt. Elbert gasped when he saw the monster hunter had a large metal disc in the middle of his sternum, identical to the coin that Elbert had had. "This allows me to track demons," the man said, pointing to the plate of metal. "It burns when I come close to one, or someone they've been in contact with. So, please, for the sake of time, when did you make your deal with the demon?"

Elbert shook his head. "I didn't make a deal with a demon! The only person I've made a deal with was some swindling magus who stole my legs!"

The stranger backed up and sat back down. "What did this magus look like?"

"I don't know… old. Decrepit, like he was on the verge of death."

"What did he promise you?"

Elbert thought back to the magus' exact words. "He promised to transform me into the greatest ruler Artanzia has ever known."

The stranger let out a small laugh as he donned his shirt again. "So, the bastard feeds on ambition," he said absently to himself.

"Can you please explain to me what is going on? My name is Elbert, I'm the King of Artanzia. Please, I need to get back to Winterhelm, my army and my people need me."

After a lengthy, silent deliberation, the man nodded his head. "Very well, I s'pose you're owed a few answers. My name is Mikkel. I am a member of the Order of Swords, the monster-hunting guild. Unlike my other brothers, who take contracts on a variety of monsters, I only pursue demons."

"Demons?"

"Mhmm. Hellspawn, infernal creatures that can only live on this plane of existence by using someone as a host and feeding off their emotions."

"What does this have to do with me?"

"The magus that saw you, the man who 'took away' your legs, was actually a demon who tricked you into an infernal contract. He needed to use you as a host, feeding off your ambition, to stay in this plane of existence. Based on how you described him, I would say that he didn't have much time left before he returned to the hells, but your deal with him gave him more time here among us."

Elbert's head was swirling. Demons were real and not just a bedtime story concocted by the priests to scare young children into doing good deeds? This couldn't be happening; it was all too weird.

"I've been tracking this demon for quite some time. His trail led me to Eldersburg, which I found in ash, which then led me to you. Although, judging by how much it stung when I saw you, I'll say that you're an old host. That he has discarded you, or that the terms of your deal were fulfilled."

"You're mistaken," Elbert said. "He said he would make me the greatest king Artanzia has ever known. But look at me, I'm a cripple. What's so great about this?"

Mikkel smiled. "Greatness is a relative term. Everyone has their own definition of it. Tell me, what have you done since the deal?"

Elbert let out a frustrated breath before regaling Mikkel with the tale of his reign thus far. How he snuffed out disloyal lords, how he became the only king to launch a war on the barbaric northern Islanders, how he defeated those Islanders and secured a peace treaty with them, only to have his city taken away by some peasant upstart when he returned.

"You sound great to me," Mikkel laughed. "You've done impossible things, things no other king has ever done. And you did it all without being able to walk or wipe your own ass. I think it's safe to say that the people of Artanzia are going to remember King Elbert the Cripple."

"Fantastic... I feel so lucky."

"You should. This demon doesn't leave too many hosts alive; in fact, you're the first one I've come across. Now, exactly how long ago did you last see him?"

Elbert opened his mouth to answer, but paused. He didn't rightfully know. So much had happened that the days and weeks blurred together. Had it been a month? Two months? He couldn't know for sure. "I'm not too sure," he admitted. "It was right after my coronation that he saw me, in the middle of winter."

"Shit," Mikkel grunted. "Very well, thank you for all your help, King Elbert, and I wish you the best of luck." With that, the monster hunter rose to his feet and walked away.

"Wait!" Elbert cried out. "You can't leave me here! Please, I'll pay you your weight in gold to take me back to Winterhelm! I'll make you a duke! I'll die out here!"

Mikkel paused as he was tightening his gambeson. "You want me to stop hunting this demon, and put countless people in danger, to drag your ass back to Winterhelm?"

"When said like that it sounds bad, but there are countless people in danger in Winterhelm who need their king!"

"From what you've told me, it sounds like they have a king already."

The words struck Elbert like a hammer. All the air leaked out of his lungs and he tried to mouth a response, only for a pathetic wheezing sound to escape his lips. Desperately, he tried to find his voice as Mikkel began walking away. "You're supposed to protect people!" Elbert shouted, surprising himself by how forceful his voice was. "Members of the Order of Swords are supposed to protect people. Not just leave them to die."

Mikkel slowly turned around and looked the crippled king in the eyes. "We are supposed to protect people from *monsters.*" He gestured to the empty woods surrounding them. "And I don't see any monsters."

Elbert watched in horror as the monster hunter left him alone, naked, and in the middle of nowhere.

The sun had just finished its descent for the day when Elbert finally managed to clothe himself. The shirt was the easy part, but trying to put pants on his useless legs proved to be a challenging task. He first tried to put them on like he had always done, before he was king. However, his legs had different ideas and refused to go into the proper places. When that didn't work, he tried to hook the waistband around his toes and shimmy into the legs, which also proved fruitless. It took several hours of him rolling, cursing, and screaming, but by some miracle, the pants were now on his legs, although they were a few sizes too large. Panting, trying to catch his breath, he thought, *How the hells did Thames make that look so easy?* It wasn't until he had a moment to think that he realized how dark the woods were. He heard creatures moving in the underbrush and the ominous rustling of leaves in the wind. The king's mouth suddenly went dry as he realized how vulnerable he was. He couldn't even put on pants, how in the blazes would he protect himself from animals?

There was a sudden snap of a branch to his left, and Elbert darted his head. He thought he saw a shadow dart through the brush, but couldn't make it out what it was. *A wolf? A boar? Oh Gods, is it a bear?* Elbert shook his head. *No. Get a hold of yourself. You are not going to die in this Gods-forsaken forest. That is not how your story ends.* The distant howl of a wolf sent a chill down his spine and filled his heart with fear. *Fuck me.* He desperately tried to search the forest floor for anything he could use to defend himself, but all he found was a small, blunt stick.

There was another crack of a twig in the underbrush. This time, Elbert saw a pair of eyes staring at him. He swallowed whatever spit he had in his mouth and gripped the small branch with both of his trembling hands. The beast slowly crawled out of the bush, chittering and chattering as it revealed itself. Illuminated by the moonlight, Elbert could see it was a small homunculus. Its skin was red, and it had a small, somewhat feeble pair of wings on its back. Three spiked horns protruded from its bulbous head. The creature walked on two feet, dragging its knuckles along the ground towards Elbert, clicking its tongue in rhythmic fashion.

"Get back!" Elbert shouted as he swung the branch at the beast. "I'm warning you!"

The small humanoid creature cocked its head to one side, as if confused. After a few seconds of the two staring at one another, the creature resumed its approach. Elbert's heart felt like it was going to burst through his chest. His guts gurgled and popped; sweat formed on his brow. Despite his fear, he slowly slunk backwards, till his back was against a sturdy tree trunk, his eyes never leaving the creature.

There was another sound in the underbrush, and both the creature and Elbert looked toward it. Emerging from the trees was Mikkel, a small knife in his hand. Elbert breathed a sigh of relief. He turned to look at the monster and saw that the creature felt no such relief. Its brow furrowed, and its eyes locked on to Elbert once again.

"Don't even think about it," Mikkel warned.

The creature hissed and lunged toward Elbert. The king closed his eyes and heard steel sinking into flesh. He opened his eyes and saw Mikkel's knife sticking out of the creature's head.

"I... I knew you'd come back."

"Mhmm," Mikkel said as he tore his knife free from the monster's skull.

"What was that thing?"

"An imp."

"Why did it come after me?"

"You have the stink of the hells on you. Your deal with the magus has left a mark on you, a mark that anything infernal can follow."

"So, I'll be hunted down by those things till I die?"

"I wouldn't worry, imps aren't particularly clever, and they only strike when someone is alone. You'll be fine."

"Is there no way to stop them?"

"They'll stop once I kill the demon that took your legs."

"What made you come back for me?"

"I never left."

Elbert furrowed his brow in confusion until it dawned on him. "You used me as bait, you bastard!"

"I needed an imp."

"You fucking whoreson! I can't believe that you—"

"Save your breath, you can scream at me all the way to Oxworth."

Elbert shook his head. "Oxworth? That's by the border, the complete opposite direction! I need to go to Winterhelm!"

Mikkel gave him a scolding glare. "I said we are going to Oxworth."

"You can't make me!" Elbert said defiantly as he crossed both his arms.

Paying him no mind, Mikkel carved open the imp and ripped out the creature's innards. Using the demonic creature's blood, he painted a sigil on the ground and placed certain organs along the intersecting lines. Once satisfied with his gruesome art, he lit a torch and threw it in the middle of the sigil. The flames danced along the lines of blood, engulfing the organs in a blazing inferno. Once the whole macabre scene was ablaze, a dissonant, spectral whinny filled the air. Suddenly, jumping out of the flames, was a large black warhorse. Elbert's jaw dropped when he realized it was the same horse that Xerxes had forced him to ride. The same horse that had been decapitated by the slavers.

"How... how did you—"

Throwing Elbert over his shoulder and securing him to the horse's back, Mikkel mounted the great mare and kicked it into a gallop, leaving the still smouldering sigil and the desecrated corpse of the imp behind.

The two men rode for hours. On several occasions, Elbert tried to strike up a conversation with the monster hunter, but he never answered. Instead, Mikkel seemed intent on running his new mount back into the ground, but to Elbert's disbelief the mare never tired. Its thunderous hooves shook the earth, galloping at breakneck speed throughout the night. Elbert was amazed by how obedient the horse was. When he had first encountered the beast, it was so obstinate that Xerxes resorted to removing its head. But now that Mikkel had taken the reins, all the creature's previous unruliness had disappeared completely.

The constant bouncing and jostling pained the king's chest as his limp body slammed against the mare's rump. If they did not stop riding soon, Elbert was afraid that all of his ribs would be broken. Then, as if answering his silent prayers, the horse slowed down to a casual trot and then finally, stopped completely.

Elbert lifted his head and saw that they had come to a serene clearing that was illuminated by the pale moon, hanging high in the night sky. A collective of birch, poplar, and oak trees protected the clearing from the wind, and a small, lapping creek ran through the middle of it. The king was in complete awe. It was as if the Gods had created this place for the sole purpose of relaxation and finding inner peace.

"We'll make camp here," Mikkel said as he climbed down from the mighty warhorse. Before Elbert could answer, the monster hunter had already thrown the stricken king over his shoulder as if he were a beast that he had slain. Setting him down, Mikkel pulled out a small pouch from his belt and emptied a number of strange-looking items from it. There was a large, black stone, a clump of metal that looked like wool, and what appeared to be dead grass. After making a small pile with the grass and metal wool, he placed the black stone on top, whispered an incantation, and a small fire formed at the base of the pile.

"I don't mean to be rude," Elbert asked, "but how do you know how to do all of this?"

"They taught us," Mikkel answered dryly.

Elbert raised his brow questioningly. He had been raised in a castle where everyone kissed his ass as prince and later king, so he had lots of practice spotting clumsy lies.

"Why are you not telling me the truth?" Elbert prodded. "It's not like I'm in any position to leave. I'm stuck with you."

Mikkel did not reply.

"I mean, that sword, that thing in your chest..." Elbert continued. "Sacrificing imps for a horse... the Order cannot just give away this knowledge freely."

Mikkel raised his head and glared at the king. "Who said this was for free?" he snarled. "I paid for this in blood, sweat, and loss. Do you know how the Order gets most of its members? Orphans. We were children dying on the street when some swine came and offered us a 'better life'. Sometimes I wish I had just starved on those streets instead of joining."

There was an uncomfortable pause between the two men. The only sounds to fill the air of the clearing were the lapping of the creek and the black mare cropping the grass.

"So why did you join?"

Mikkel let out a half-laugh. "When you are nothing but skin and bones and a man tells you he will clothe, feed, and teach you to take care of yourself, you take the deal. When you're desperate, even a snake looks like a helping hand."

"So, you made a deal with a proverbial devil yourself."

"You're more right than you know."

Elbert gave Mikkel a questioning glance, but the monster hunter refused to say another word. Sensing that was all the conversation he was going to get for the night, Elbert rolled on to his back, massaged his bruised chest and drifted off to sleep.

CHAPTER THIRTY
ANNA

The raucous chittering outside the window signalled, much to Anna's dismay, that the morning had inevitably come after a sleepless night. No matter how badly she wanted to fall asleep, the idea of using Mason as a host for Mammon filled her with so much anxiety, she wanted to jump out of her own skin. Letting out a frustrated sigh, she decided that there was no point lying in bed any longer. Perhaps if she started her day, she would find someone else and Mason would be spared the cruel fate Matthew had promised him.

Once dressed, Anna opened the door to leave her room and noticed that there was a book with a note attached sitting in front of it. She scanned the hallway to see who left it, but it was still too early for anyone to be awake, let alone to be leaving books in front of a strange person's door. Picking it up, she read the note.

Anna,
Can't wait to hear your thoughts.
- Mason

Upon removing the parchment from the book's cover, Anna let out an audible gasp when she saw that it was a copy of *Sigils and Seals: How to Trap a Demon,* by Professor Hanubis Moretz. She looked back and forth between her room and the stairs that led downstairs to the tavern's main floor. She could go and look for someone to save Mason from a deal with a demon, or she could stay in her room and read as much of the book as she could, in hopes of it having an answer on how she could free herself and the others from Master Mammon. Anna had taken a step towards the stairs when a thought popped into her head. *The sun has barely risen, it'll be hard to find someone at such an early hour. What harm can come from reading a few chapters?*

Trying to hide her childlike excitement from herself, she went back into her room, closed the door, and cracked open the tome. The first thing Anna noticed was the foreword that Mason had mentioned the day before. There was a slight tremble in her hands as she turned the pages to the first chapter.

Demons do not belong in this realm, and as a result must be expelled by a trained professional whenever their existence is discovered... From the first sentence, Anna was hooked. Her eyes devoured the words on the page ravenously as if they were starving beasts and the small letters printed in ink were their only form of sustenance. Her fingers crinkled the soft vellum as she flipped hastily from one page to the next, eagerly consuming all the knowledge the book held. It wasn't until there was a sudden knock on her door that she took her eyes off Professor Moretz's words. Setting the book down on the oaken nightstand, she got up and opened the door to see Matthew standing impatiently on the other side.

"Gods, I thought you were going to sleep the entire day away!"

Anna looked out of the window in horror, noticing that the sun was nearly at its peak. She had wasted the entire morning reading the book. Suddenly, her stomach sank. "The lecture!" she screamed as she pushed past Matthew and darted down the stairs before sprinting towards the lecture hall.

The doors to the auditorium boomed like thunder as Anna barreled through them. All the students, and even Professor Moretz, stared at her disapprovingly following her interruption. In a panic, she scanned the hall trying to find Mason, which wasn't hard given the boy's large frame. Sheepishly, she walked up the stairs and quietly sat beside him.

"Did I miss anything?" Anna whispered.

"Not much, he was just introducing his work and his credentials. Speaking of, did you get my book?" Mason whispered back.

"Yes! That's why I was late."

"*Excuse* me, madam," Professor Moretz said in a slow, theatrical drawl, his voice dripping with mock sincerity. "Not only do you grace my lecture with your *tardy* arrival, but you now have the *audacity* to whisper sweet nothings in your paramour's ear, while I *endeavour* to *educate* your fellow students."

Anna impulsively slunk down in her seat, her eyes darting nervously towards Mason, whose face was as red as a tomato. After several long, silent seconds of avoiding eye contact with Professor Moretz, the renowned demon expert resumed his lecture once again, his voice as thick as molasses and delivering his words in a theatrical rhythm, emphasizing certain words and syllables as he talked. "Now then, a demon is a *curious* creature. They are *supremely* powerful and their abilities know almost no —"

Anna's hand shot up in the air. "Have you ever heard of a demon destroying an entire town?"

There were a few snickers in the lecture hall. An amused smile appeared on Professor Moretz's lips before he quickly regained his composure. "Well, madam, I'd be *lying* if I said I'd heard of any demon possessing said ability; I dare say that it is *not* impossible though." The professor paused, allowing a dramatic silence to fill the auditorium. "We know such *precious* little about these beings that no one, not *even me*, can say for certain what type of havoc they can *unleash* upon us."

Anna nodded her head. Although the news was disappointing, she was thankful for it nonetheless.

"As I was saying," Professor Moretz resumed, "we don't rightly know what demons are capable of. They are beings of *immense* power, but that power comes from us. Demons *need* us, whether we be an elf, dwarf, halfling, or a human, they cannot reside on our plane of existence without using us as hosts. Much like a leech must feed off your blood to stay alive, a demon must *feed* on your emotions to live amongst us. But—"

Anna's hand shot up once again. This time, she raised it so fast that she felt a slight pinch in her shoulder. "Excuse me, have you ever heard of a demon not needing a human host?"

Another smile from Professor Moretz. "In my first book, *A Beginner's Guide to Demonology,* I theorized that there are hundreds, if not thousands of demons trapped in the hells. *Those* demons do not need a human host. As I said, demons only need us once they have already escaped the confines of the hells."

Anna furrowed her brow. She already knew that; she had wanted to know if there had ever been a demon like her before. She was about to ask a follow-up when the professor's deep, charismatic voice filled the room again.

"Now, you might be thinking, 'Professor Moretz, how in the blazes are we to fight these creatures, these *abominations,* that feed off our very emotions, the *very thing* that makes us people?' You're right for wondering that, but fret not, my friends, all is not lost. We do know *some* things about these creatures that can help us *combat* their wickedness. Demons *must* strike an accord with you. That means you *cannot* become a host for them against your will. Secondly, as I mentioned in my second book, *Sigils and Seals: How to Trap a Demon,* you can trap a demon if they step into the proper seal. A seal is that demon's name, *written* in their own infernal script."

Anna gasped at this news. This would be her way out, how she could trap and defeat Master Mammon. The only problem was, she didn't know the infernal language.

"That means, that every demon has their own seal or sigil. And—" Professor Moretz stopped and sighed as he saw Anna's hand in the air once again. "Now, madam, I love answering questions more than *anyone* else. But if we are to get through this lecture, I must insist that you hold your questions till the *very* end."

Slowly lowering her hand back down to her side, Anna nodded her head in agreement. Without her interruptions, Professor Moretz could dive into the contents of his books, as well as some unpublished, and unconfirmed, theories about demons. Anna hung on every word. Although Professor Moretz talked with a strange cadence, emphasizing words that were not critical to the sentence, it seemed to compliment his deep, drawling voice. The way he talked was as if he was more minstrel than scholar. He charismatically moved around the front of the class, using fluid and energetic hand movements to help convey his message. Anna could've sat there and listened to Professor

Moretz till the end of her days. As the end of the lecture neared, she couldn't help but wonder what her father would think about this. *Had he ever had the chance to attend a lecture, or was all his knowledge strictly from those musty old books?*

With a gentlemanly bow, Professor Moretz bid the students farewell and thanked them for their time. As they shuffled out of the lecture hall, Anna made a deliberate point of staying till the end. Once it was just she and Professor Moretz left in the lecture hall, she cleared her throat.

"Excuse me, Professor Moretz? If you have time, I'd love to ask you some more questions."

An appreciative smile appeared on the professor's face. "Ah, yes, the troublemaker. Before you *pluck* more nuggets of knowledge from me, I must admit that I found your questions to be *quite* curious. *Tell* me, have you been studying demonology for long?"

"Not for very long," Anna admitted. "But once I read your first book, I became a little obsessed."

A small laugh escaped Professor Moretz's lips. "I can see that. Now, what questions do you have of me? I don't promise I'll have *any* answers, though, but 'tween us two smart people, I'm sure we can figure *something* out."

"Do you know how to write the name 'Mammon' in infernal script?"

Suddenly, the professor's cheery demeanour vanished, and a frown stained his face. He leaned forward and whispered, "What makes you ask such a question?"

"Just genuine curiosity."

"Tssk, tssk." Moretz clicked his tongue. "I'll give you one *more* chance. If you *insist* on feeding me malarky, then I'm *afraid* I must do the same."

Anna studied the professor's face for several seconds, trying to figure out how much of the truth, if any, she could reveal to the demonologist. What would the repercussions be? Would he hunt down Mammon along with Desmond, Matthew, and Evelynn? What would he do if he found out that she had been resurrected by a demon? The swarm of questions stormed in her head like a tempest while she continued to examine the professor's face, which was as stoic as a statue.

"My father, he made a deal with the demon, and I want to set him free," Anna confessed, deciding to only reveal the necessary truths to Professor Moretz.

After a lengthy pause, the demonologist nodded his head. "Very well, I will see if I can be of *assistance.* Do you know the *terms* of your father's pact?" Anna shook her head. "*Drats!*" Professor Moretz exclaimed as he scratched the edge of his chin. "The *easiest* way to free someone from a demon's clutches would be to *nullify* the terms of their deal."

"If it helps, I'm pretty sure Mammon feeds on ambition."

Professor Moretz's face lit up for a fraction of a second, before the disapproving frown appeared again. "What makes you think that?"

Anna gulped. "My father is an ambitious man. We have very little, and although he never admitted it to me, I could see the way he looked at the nobles. He wanted to be like them, not just another gutter rat scrounging for coffers," Anna lied, trying to create a persona of her fictitious father from thin air and hoping that it was believable.

"The grass always *seems* greener on the other side of the fence, but the grass is *really* greener where you water it." Professor Moretz allowed his words to hang in the air for several seconds before continuing. "As for your question, I cannot help you. The infernal *lexicon* is lost to me. I understand it no more than a *cow* understands the common tongue. *But,* there might be a man who can help you."

Anna's eyes lit up.

"His *name* was Mikkel. He *came* to me after my first book, and *taught* me some things. Things that no *ordinary* person ought to know."

"Do you know where I can find him?"

Professor Moretz shook his head. "Unfortunately, no. He *seemed* to be more of the *travelling* type. He had a *feathery* grey head of hair and an *equally* grey, shaggy beard. He also wore *curious* studded leather armour. *Unfortunately,* that's all I know."

Anna let out a sigh. It wasn't much to go on, but it was something. "Thank you, professor."

Suddenly, there was a loud chime from the bell tower outside the university. Anna's heart sank when she realized that it was midday. Mason would be meeting with Mammon at any second. Hurriedly, she exited the lecture hall, only to be frozen in place by Professor Moretz's voice.

"Here!" he said as he forced a piece of paper into her hand. "This is my *address* in Drossberg. If you find him, or learn anything regarding *demons,* please write me. I'd be *more* than happy to compensate you."

Anna smiled and nodded before sprinting out of the class-room, without bidding Professor Moretz farewell. She ran through the campus grounds, weaving through the crowds of students, and when a few wouldn't move, she pushed. The dingy tavern was not far, but she feared she was too late. As her lungs and legs burned from exertion, she continued to hurry, praying, hoping, that she'd be able to save Mason in time.

She cursed herself for losing track of time, for allowing herself to be enveloped by Professor Moretz's words, no matter how interesting they were.

Seeing the tavern's rundown, dirty door come into view, Anna breathed a sigh of relief. She barrelled through the door and almost tumbled into a table of drinks. She scanned the room frantically until she saw Mason sitting at a secluded table in the corner with Master Mammon and his disciples. She froze in place, an icy shiver running down her spine, as she saw Mammon extend his hand towards Mason's. "Mason, don't!"

Mammon, Mason, the disciples, and a few of the more sober patrons of the tavern stared at her as she hurried over to the table.

"Anna? What are you doing?"

"Don't do it, Mason!" she pleaded, gasping for air, as she tried to keep her voice down to not to cause a commotion.

"Anna..." Mammon growled in an ancient voice.

"He's..." She paused and looked around to ensure that nobody was eavesdropping. Once she was sure the coast was clear, she whispered in a harsh voice, "He's a demon!"

"Really?" Mason asked.

"Anna!" Mammon hissed.

"Yes!" Anna said, ignoring the daggers that Mammon was shooting at her with his eyes.

"You have a deal!" Mason said enthusiastically, grabbing Mammon's hand.

"What!?" Anna and Mammon uttered in unison.

"Look, my father's forge is about to shut down, and my mother is working herself ragged trying to keep us off the streets. I'll be damned if I stand by and let my family fall into ruin. I won't let my parents down, and if I need a demon's help to do it, then so be it."

Mammon grinned ear to ear. "Nice to meet a man of logic. Now that our business has concluded, I must bid you farewell." The demon and his disciples exited the tavern while Anna stared at Mason, dumbfounded. She couldn't believe that the boy just threw his life away without a second thought. After a long, awkward silence, Mason cleared his throat.

"I'm sorry, Anna. I don't expect you to understand, but I have to do what's best for my family."

"Mason, didn't you—"

"No," he said firmly. "This isn't up for debate. It's my life, not yours. Now, please, go back to your master and leave me alone."

The words struck Anna like a twelve-pound hammer. Her face went beet red and tears welled up in her eyes. She wanted to reach out and slap the ignorant boy across his face, but couldn't. Instead, she just stood there, shaking, before finally walking out of the tavern, too disgusted to say another word.

Outside the tavern, Matthew was standing by the door. "Anna, I'm—"

"Fuck you," she cut him off in a cracking voice. She bumped him with her shoulder as she stormed past him and deeper into Oxworth, in search of a dark corner to cry in.

CHAPTER THIRTY-ONE
RANDALL

The room was a scene of utter chaos. Books and parchment were strewn about the floor, loose pages floating around like ghosts in the gentle spring breeze that blew in through the balcony window. Shards of the crystal carafe of wine were scattered across the marble floor like little knives waiting to stab an unsuspecting foot, a red puddle forming in the middle of the room. The wooden bed frame had been destroyed in a fit of rage and the silken bedding tossed out the window to the city below.

The king sat there, chest heaving, as he stared at the destruction he had unleashed on his room. When Cassius had told him that Tig had left shortly after A'Chula and the slaver departed, Randall descended into a frenzy. His closest and oldest friend had betrayed him, a man that he considered a brother had abandoned him. A single tear rolled down his face as he tore apart one of the goose-feather pillows, one of the few things left intact in the room.

There was a soft knock on the door and it slowly creaked open. Cassius slowly peeked his head in and his eyes widened with shock as he took in the absolute ruin in the room. Without betraying his thoughts, the eunuch slowly entered and knelt beside the king, putting a hand on his shoulder.

"Your Majesty," he said in a soft voice, "I regret that my news this morning unsettled you. That was not my intention.

I merely wished to keep you informed of the developments in your court." Randall braced himself; he knew Cassius well enough to expect a "but" whenever the eunuch adopted this tone. "But," Cassius continued, "this is no way for a king to behave when bad news reaches his ear." He gestured to the disaster around him.

"Tig was my best friend!" Randall seethed. "How could he do this to me? How could he just leave after everything?"

"Randall, friendships change as we grow. You're not the same boy who led a gang of street urchins; you're a king now. Tig couldn't see that. He wanted things to stay as they were, clinging to the past while you moved forward."

Randall's eyes widened, and a touch of redness appeared on his cheeks. "You heard?"

"Half the castle heard your little spat," Cassius replied, standing and dusting off his clothes. "It's for the best that Tig left. We can't have people tied to the past holding us back. We have a world to change, remember?" He extended his hand to Randall, who sighed and took it, allowing Cassius to help him up. "Now, how about some good news? I hear Grandmaster Velus has awakened."

"Lead me to him."

As Cassius escorted the king through the winding hallways of the castle, Randall battled the maelstrom of emotions inside him. The residual anger and betrayal at Tig's sudden departure lingered in his chest, while a torrent of embarrassment sank in as he imagined one of the servants having to clean up the mess in his room. But the strongest emotion he felt was a combination of excitement and anxiety. Velus had been comatose for a long time, and although Randall visited the halfling every day, he was excited to finally speak to the wizard.

Outside the infirmary, a group of healers waited in front of closed doors. Cassius, with his head high in the air, commanded them to open the door. The healers looked sheepishly at one another before a portly dwarven man stepped forward, polishing his spectacles on his white shirt.

"Your Majesty, I don't believe Grandmaster Velus is ready for visitors."

"I don't understand, is he not awake?"

"He is, but..." The dwarf scratched his beard. "He is not the halfling, you remember. I suspect taking out Elbert's ships muddled his mind."

"As if it weren't already muddled to begin with," Cassius whispered under his breath.

"I want to see him," Randall commanded in a thick, authoritative voice.

"Of course, Your Majesty... just prepare yourself." Without explaining further, the healers opened up the doors to the infirmary, where a restrained Velus lay in his bed. The halfling's eyes were hollow and stared at the king void of emotion as he approached. The room was dimly lit, the soft murmurs of other patients creating a somber atmosphere.

"Velus?" Randall said in a soothing voice. "It's me, Randall."

"No... no, you're not real, you died in the fire. They're tricking me again!"

Randall bent down to one knee, so he was eye level with the wizard. "Velus, it's me, I swear." The king smiled, hoping to reassure the halfling.

Velus' breathing quickened. "The blockade... did we stop them? Are they... are they still here?" He craned his neck towards the window, as if expecting to see enemy ships looming in the harbour.

"They're gone. The blockade is gone, and it's all thanks to you."

For a brief moment, clarity returned to the halfling's eyes. "I... I remember. But then... fire. So much fire." His voice trembled, and his breathing became shallow and rapid once again. "They're in my mind. Whispering, always whispering."

"Velus—" Randall whispered as he extended a hand towards the wizard.

"Get away from me!" Velus screamed. "You're not real, none of this is real! Fire! Fire! Fire!" The halfling writhed uncontrollably in his restraints, his eyes wide in terror.

The healers quickly surrounded him, one of them pinning the halfling down, while the other doused a cloth with liquid from a small bottle and held it over the mage's mouth and nose. After a few breaths, Velus' movements slowed, and his breathing became shallow as he fell back into a deep sleep.

Randall backed away, watching in horror at what had become of his wizard and advisor. His court was dwindling by the minute. He felt Cassius place a hand on his shoulder, but quickly shrugged it off. "I need to be alone." Before Cassius could open his mouth in protest, Randall walked away.

He wasn't sure where he was going; all he knew was that he wanted to get away from everything. Cassius, the disaster of his court, the crown, all of it. He needed a break. It felt like the walls were closing in and his grip was slipping on the throne that he had fought so hard for. The fact that Elbert's army continued to lurk outside the city walls certainly didn't help matters.

Trying to think positively, he hoped that the slaver was telling the truth – that his band had in fact captured Elbert and that A'Chula hadn't been sent out for nothing. He silently wished for the mute's return, not only because if he brought back Elbert the siege would be over, but because A'Chula was the last remnant of his former life.

Then the thought of Anna popped into his mind, specifically how he killed her. He winced in disgust as the memory replayed in his head. How could he betray the girl who loved him unconditionally? How did he ever justify her death? Looking back, it sickened him how he had killed her simply so he could have a martyr for people to rally around. A sickening knot formed in his stomach as he wondered what Anna's last thoughts were before she smashed against the frozen earth. Did she feel rage? Was she mad at him just like he was mad at Tig? Or was she confused, unable to comprehend how the love of her life could kill her so easily?

These tormenting questions swirled in his mind, like ravens circling a carcass, pecking at his thoughts until they were raw and unraveling.

It wasn't until he hit a solid stone wall that Randall was able to escape the unrelenting torture of his own mind. He looked up and a quiet laugh escaped his lips. *Of course,* he thought. *The Garden.* He hadn't meant to come here, but his body remembered. While his thoughts spiralled, something deep down inside him had led him home. He was ashamed to admit it, but ever since he took over the city, he had forgotten about the old sanctuary. He ran his hand across the worn stone until he found the loose brick the doorman used. A click echoed softly as the hidden door shifted, and the stone split open to reveal the last place Randall truly felt at home.

Although the Garden was never in pristine condition, it certainly had appeared that the old criminal sanctuary had fallen into disarray upon him seizing the crown. Vines and shrubs had grown unchecked, and some buildings had crumbled under the weight of the vegetation. Most of the fences had likely moved out of the courtyard ever since the King of Crooks became the King of Artanzia.

"Why, Your Majesty," a voice loudly called out, "I wasn't expecting such a delightful visit today."

Randall turned his head and saw one of the Bloody Brothers staring at him with a shit-eating grin on his face. He was a fat man with a large gut hanging over his belt. Dried vomit stained his scruffy beard, and his bloodshot eyes implied one hell of a hangover. "I see you've taken over Fletcher's tavern."

"Taken over?" the bandit gasped, hand clutching his heart in mock offense. "We would never! We are simply renting it out. Private function, you see?"

Randall raised a questioning brow. "In that case, mind if I take a look?"

"Like I said, *private* function. Besides, wouldn't ya rather drink outside on such a lovely day?"

"Come now," Randall said as he slowly sauntered toward the tavern. "Surely you can spare an invitation for a king?" Before the bandit could reply, the door to the tavern opened, a bruised and battered Rosaline leaning in the doorway. "You look like shit."

Rosaline smiled, although it looked as if it pained her to do so. "You sure know how to talk to a lady, Your Majesty."

"I thought you and your Brothers left the city?"

Rosaline's smile faded in an instant. "What do you want?"

"Nothing. I came here to reminisce. As much as I love fine wine and silken sheets, they don't hold a candle to the mite-ridden blankets Fletcher used to give us, or that swill he called ale."

"Something troubling you, my king?"

Randall shook his head. Despite Rosaline's caring tone, he knew that this woman was anything but a confidante. Anything he told her would be wielded as a weapon. "No, just needed to get out of the castle. Be seeing you."

"Did Cassius ever tell you why Greaver kicked him out?"

The dangling question made Randall stop in his tracks. On several occasions, he had asked Cassius that very question, but the eunuch had always dodged it. "You know the story?"

Rosaline gestured with her head for the king to follow, and with a heavy limp in her gait led him to the old throne room from where Greaver ruled the criminal underworld. He paused for a brief moment and examined the throne. It was odd – when he was younger, he thought that Greaver's throne was the ultimate symbol of power, but now that he had sat upon an actual throne, he saw it for what it really was, little more than a sad slab of driftwood. Rosaline led Randall into the dining room and sat at the head of the table, exactly where the king had slit Greaver's throat months ago. She gestured for Randall to take a seat, and hesitantly, he obliged.

"You're probably wondering why there was never a Queen of Crooks," Rosaline began. Randall opened his mouth to reply, but the bandit leader raised a silencing hand before he could utter a word. "You're going to want to hear this, Your Majesty, this is a very important story." She paused, her dagger-like eyes locking on to Randall's, emphasizing her last sentence. "And like any good story, this one is about love. There used to be a whore named Catalonia, and I'm told the things she could do would send a shiver down your spine. You men are simple creatures, you think with your cocks. And with one good fuck you lot fall ass over tits for some girl, and with Catalonia's skill set... well, she had more than her fair share of suitors, Greaver among them. Unfortunately for Greaver, and everyone else, Catalonia's heart belonged to someone else. A handsome young man named Cassius."

"But he's a eunuch," Randall blurted out.

Rosaline frowned for a moment, before continuing her story. "Cassius had told everyone he was a eunuch, in order to spy on the clientele of the brothel. During the king's frequent visits to see Catalonia, Greaver and Cassius became acquainted, and eventually Greaver offered the would-be eunuch a job – spy on the other clients of the brothel and report back to the King of Crooks. Thus began a beautiful partnership, until a certain snitch squealed to Greaver that Cassius actually had a cock and balls, and was using said cock and balls to fuck Catalonia's brains out."

Randall gulped audibly; he knew exactly where this was going.

"So, Greaver called Cassius into the throne room. He had his men rip Cassius' trousers off, exposing his fully functioning genitalia for all to see. Cassius dropped to his knees, pleaded for the King of Crooks to spare him. He swore how he meant nothing by it and how Catalonia meant nothing to him, how she was nothing more than a cheap fuck. Well, that pissed Greaver off no end, so he grabbed the dullest blade he could find and castrated Cassius right then and there, for all to see. Leaving no doubt in anyone's mind that he was now *actually* a eunuch."

Randall's brow furrowed as he tried to process the new information. "Why are you telling me all of this?"

"Because, for some unexplainable reason, the people believe in you. You have an army at the gates, food is running scarce, and yet they still champion the boy king who took the throne of Artanzia in the name of the people." Rosaline paused for a moment and leaned forward on the table, her predatory eyes never leaving Randall's. "I heard about what you did, divvying out food from the royal stash to the starving subjects. It's about time they had a king who gave a shit about them. And if you truly want peace and prosperity for your subjects, you should know the people you surround yourself with. Make no mistake, Your Majesty, Cassius is a viper. Don't give him the opportunity to strike."

Randall nodded his head but chose to say nothing. He could tell that the bandit leader chose words carefully. She was mirroring her beliefs and ideals, although it wasn't born from a place of concern, but one of manipulation. Yet, despite her motivations, her message hit home.

Both rose from their chairs and slowly meandered their way out of the dining room, through the decrepit throne room, and into the main courtyard of the Garden. As the king approached the door to the hidden alcove, he paused, and gave one last glance towards Rosaline and her men.

"What happened to Catalonia?"

Rosaline smiled. "She was beside herself, and upon hearing of her lover's fate, slit her own throat."

CHAPTER THIRTY-TWO
ROSALINE

"What the fuck was all that about, Roz?" Malek asked as Rosaline and the rest of the Bloody Brotherhood watched the king leave the Garden.

"I decided to plant some seeds," she replied, still looking at the door, "and possibly take care of a problem for us."

"The fuck does that mean?"

Rosaline sighed and slowly turned on her heels. "If that naïve little pup thinks we actually give a fuck about the people in this kingdom, then when shit goes sideways, he won't come sniffing around here. Plus, maybe now he'll be too busy looking at that worm by his side to even worry about what we're getting up to."

Malek grunted in approval as he walked back into the tavern. Once she was finally alone, Rosaline let out a pained breath that she had been holding in since the king's arrival. She felt her knees buckle and a slight tremble in her lips.

It wasn't like her to let someone interfere without consequence. Randall's little act of generosity, handing out the royal food stores, had thrown a wrench into her operation. Annoying, but nothing her Brothers couldn't fix. They were already back to raiding homes and shops, bolstering their own stockpile with whatever they could pry from clenched fists. The real problem was the Harbingers. The halfling and his men still had a debt to pay. For what they did to the Bloody

Brotherhood, and for what they did to her. She intended to make good on her promise to them... no matter the cost.

Entering the tavern, she limped by all of her Brothers, and slowly and arduously worked her way up the stairs to her room, where Stitch, the former resident healer in the Garden, was waiting for her. Kicking open the door to her room, she limped in and plopped down onto the bloody chair where Stitch had been working on her before Randall's unexpected arrival.

Stitch grabbed the half-empty bottle of rye from the table and took three hefty swigs before passing it to Rosaline, who smiled in thanks before taking a few generous gulps herself and removing her blouse. She looked down at her ribs and saw a disgusting, purple bruise with small splotches of yellow covering almost her entire midsection. Although she had been fixed up by Stitch more times than she could count, she knew that this was likely beyond the man's capabilities. She needed a mage, not a healer. After several moments examining the contusion, the old drunkard turned and lifted the lid off a wicker basket, pulling out a large, wriggly black leech pinched between his fingers.

"If you think you're going to put that worm on me, I'll kick whatever teeth you have left down your throat," Rosaline snarled.

"Ha!" Stitch laughed in his gravelly, coarse voice. "Save your fangs, lass, you're in no condition to kick anyone's teeth in. It's a miracle you can bloody move."

Stitch placed the leech on Rosaline's abdomen, and she immediately winced in pain. She watched as the little creature squirmed on top of her skin, before finally sinking its teeth into her flesh.

"How the fuck does losing more blood help, anyway?" Rosaline asked through gritted teeth.

"Your humours are all outta whack. There's too much blood in your body, so the leeches are removing the excess. Once your humours are balanced again, you'll be as right as rain."

Rosaline rolled her eyes. Admittedly, she knew little about the body or how it healed, but Stitch sounded like a madman. If he hadn't fixed her up so often in her days before the Brotherhood, she would've kicked his ass out of her room. But, much to her chagrin, the old drunkard deserved the benefit of the doubt. Again, she winced in pain as Stitch placed another leech onto her body.

"Something for the pain?" Stitch asked, pulling a vial full of white powder from his pocket.

A wicked smile appeared on Rosaline's lips as she snatched the small vial from Stitch's hand. She removed the cork, poured out a small line on her hand, and snorted the powder. Immediately, she felt the effects of the drug; all the pain in her body dissipated save for the slight burning sensation in her nostrils, but after a few seconds the feeling faded. Letting out a relaxed sigh, she slumped in her chair, handing the vial back to Stitch.

"Still snorting aerion? Don't you know it's bad for you?"

"Pfft," Stitch scoffed as he too helped himself to a short line of the powder as well. "Says who? The clergy? Like they know anything about healing. A small dose takes away the aches in my bones and steadies my hand. And when I can't sleep at night, a larger dose knocks me out."

"Who's selling that stuff nowadays?"

"No one you know. Some young little shit named Ravix that charges bloody five crowns for a vial."

"What happened to what's-her-name?" Rosaline asked as she tried to snap her fingers together, as if that would bring back the name to her head. "The redhead with the violet eyes. She used to have the entire aerion market cornered in the city."

"You're not gonna believe me, but she got out."

"Out?"

Stitch nodded his head. "According to the rumours, the lass used to sell to some little shitling of a noble. Of course, the parents were too preoccupied to notice that sort of thing, so the pup's older brother tracked her down to raise hell."

"Then what?"

"The two got one look at each other and fell in love. She quit the game and married into the Artanzian nobility."

Rosaline curled her nose in disgust before letting out an amused laugh. She looked down. She hadn't noticed that Stitch had placed five more leeches on her midsection.

"Ironic, isn't it?" The healer chuckled as he put the lid back on the wicker basket.

"What is?"

"Well, I imagine that girl died like the rest of the nobles in the city when Randall took the throne. Slaughtered by her own people." Stitch rose to his feet, chuckling at his own grim remark as he packed up his things. "I'll be back in fifteen minutes. Let the leeches do their job."

Rosaline nodded, leaned back in her chair further, and closed her eyes, allowing the rays of the sun to shine on her through the dusty window in the corner of the room. She thought about what Stitch had told her, about the fate of the former aerion dealer. It was a sad story, that much was true, as she always liked the girl, but that was how the world was. You endured hardship, pain, and suffering, and then you died, violently, either by the hand of someone else or some beast. Very few people she knew died of old age, save for Marvellous Micah. The hair on the back of her neck stood up on end as the image of Micah dying helplessly on the floor of his shop soaked in his own piss ran through her mind. She tried to blink the memory out of her head, but it was all she could see. It was as if someone had branded that image into her brain with a hot iron.

Suddenly, she felt woozy, and the room spun. She gripped the arms of her chair tightly and clenched her jaw as she tried to fight off the nausea and uneasiness, but the more she fought, the stronger the feeling became, before she ultimately passed out.

"Elar Durin," a feminine voice whispered as Rosaline regained consciousness. She felt a soothing, cool sensation spread over her aching body, and when the sensation dissipated, all the pain left with it. She lay there motionless for a few moments, savouring how good it felt to finally be pain-free once again. As she opened her eyes, she saw a familiar, disgusted face staring back at her, and Rosaline's heart sank. *Why did it have to be her?*

"All appears to be in order, Duncan," the woman cooed, her voice riddled with condescension. "Although, I don't think my magic is strong enough to cure that rotten core of a heart."

"I'd say it's a pleasure to see you again, Clarice, but..." Rosaline said, her voice trailing off as she thought of the perfect insult. "To be quite honest, I—"

Clarice held up a hand. "Save me that remarkable wit, Rosaline." Her voice was painted heavy with sarcasm and disdain. "I'm only here for the gold, not the company."

Rosaline glared at Duncan from the bed. The fact that even a single coin was going to Clarice made the bandit leader want to vomit. She'd sooner toss her entire fortune into the ocean than let this bitch get her paws on any of it.

A vulpine smile appeared on Clarice's lips as she followed Rosaline's eyes. "Don't be too hard on the pup, Roz. He was worried about you. I mean, what would he do without his fearless leader?"

"Enough," Duncan said, his voice low and deep with authority. He tossed a large coin purse at Clarice and gestured to the door with his head. "Off with you."

Clarice grabbed her chest with mock offence. "My, such manners! I can tell you taught him well, Roz. Be seeing you."

"I fucking hope not," Rosaline muttered under her breath as she watched the mage leave the room. Once the two bandits were alone in the room, Rosaline let out an angry, exhausted sigh. "Of all the fucking mages in the city, you had to pick her!?"

"She was the only one willing to come."

"Should've let me fucking die."

Duncan smiled. "I should've – that mage just cost us five hundred crowns."

Rosaline sat straight up. "You gave that cunt five hundred of our fucking crowns!?"

The half-elf's smile disappeared instantly and a nasty frown appeared on his face. "What was I supposed to do, Rosaline? Let that drug-addled, demented fuck continue to put leeches on you? Stitch's mind left him decades ago. You needed help, real help, and I got it. You're *welcome.*"

"Pfft," Rosaline scoffed.

"That's it?"

Rosaline opened her mouth to reply, but thought better of it. It was hard to argue with someone who had literally just saved your life, although she'd never admit it aloud. "Couldn't you have held a mage at knifepoint or something? Why Clarice?"

"Because she needs gold to get out of the city. Apparently, with the blockade down, some people are choosing to leave the city with merchants, they just need to buy their way on to a ship."

"The people don't trust the boy king?"

Duncan shook his head. "Rumours are swirling. People say Elbert is going to find more ships to reestablish the blockade, while others say he is going to scale the walls. Nobody knows what's going on, and they don't want to be caught in someone else's war."

The door to the room suddenly opened and Phillip poked his head in, grinning from ear to ear. "Need to talk to the boss." Nodding his head, Duncan silently left the room, shutting the door behind him. Phillip stood at the foot of Rosaline's bed, smiling like a small child staring at presents under the tree on the eve of the solstice.

"So... I saw Clarice come down from here..."

"Shut up."

Phillip's smile widened. "I knew all you needed was a good fuck!"

Rosaline let out a long breath. "I'm not in the mood. It's bad enough I had to see her today, let alone pay her five hundred fucking crowns."

"You know there are cheaper whores in the city, right?"

Rosaline leapt to her feet, grabbed Boris from the end table beside the bed, and had nearly pulled him free of his sheath before Phillip backed away with his hands in the air.

"Alright! Alright! I know something that'll cheer you up, though."

Rosaline narrowed her eyes.

"There's someone waiting for you in a nearby warehouse. Malek figured you'd want to have a talk with him."

Rosaline raised a brow. "Who?"

"A certain Harbinger," Phillip replied, his smile widening.

"It'd be rude to keep our guest waiting, then," Rosaline said, as she gathered her things.

"Before we go," Phillip said, "what's it like to fuck a mage?"

The door to the warehouse opened with an ominous creak. What Rosaline saw inside made her heart skip a beat with glee. An ocean of freshly spilled blood, and the corpses of Harbingers soaking in the crimson pool. She took a deep breath and stepped inside the building, savouring the sloshing sound her footsteps made as she walked across her enemies' blood. The barrels in the warehouse where the halfling's men had stored their goods had been smashed open, undoubtedly by Malek and the others, and were left empty on the floor, much like the corpses of their former owners.

"He's in the back room Roz," Malek began. "Figure you'd want to have him all to yourself. We'll head back to the Garden, but Jathan will stay here to keep watch."

Rosaline nodded in thanks and entered the room where she had first met the Harbinger leader. The room was exactly as she remembered it, albeit with a few more bloodstains on the floor and table. Chained to a chair in the middle of the room was the curly-haired halfling, with singe marks on his upper lip where his moustache used to be. When he saw Rosaline enter the room, she saw the flicker of hope die in the his eyes. That alone would have been enough to satisfy her need for vengeance, but she knew she had a job to do. The Harbingers would become a shining example of what happened when someone crossed the Bloody Brotherhood.

"The room looks so much bigger on this side of the table," Rosaline said as she sauntered toward the halfling. "I couldn't help but notice that my men helped you decorate the rest of the warehouse. It looks *very* authentic now."

"Cut the shite," the halfling growled. "Just kill me and get it over with."

Rosaline let out a deep guttural laugh. "I don't know if you're naïve or stupid, but there is not a hope in all the seven hells that you are going to die quickly." She squatted down till she was eye level with the halfling and allowed a wicked smile to appear on her lips. "I told you what I was going to do to you, and I'm going to take my sweet time doing it."

Rosaline watched from among the crowd of onlookers as the Harbingers' warehouse was consumed by the fire of a smashed lantern, the flayed body of a halfling nailed to the wooden doors. Satisfied with her work, she tapped Jathan on the shoulder and they began walking back to the Garden. Tonight, she felt like celebrating.

"The guys tell me a mage visited you today," Jathan said.

Hells, not this again. "Yup."

"Who was she, an old contact?"

Rosaline let out an annoyed sigh, but against her better judgement, decided to regale Jathan with her messy relationship with Clarice before the Bloody Brotherhood. "I met Clarice here in Winterhelm. I was young, didn't know anybody, and needed a friend to watch my back. With her magic and my skill with a blade we were unstoppable. Unfortunately, things became rocky when she wanted to 'do good' and 'help people'. The world is an evil and wicked place – nobody looked out for us so why should we look out for anybody else?"

"So, what happened?"

"After countless fights, and countless nights making up for those fights, she conceded we could still be together as long as I didn't involve her, which I was fine with, but that put me into a bit of a bind."

"You didn't have anybody to look out for you."

Rosaline winked. "Exactly. So that led me to Greaver's doorstep. I pledged my fealty to him and served him loyally until the legendary Bloody Brotherhood came to pay their dues. Blacktooth immediately started talking to me, clearly trying to wet his cock for the night, but after he saw what I could do with a blade, he had a different idea."

"What do you mean?"

"He saw potential in me, and skill. He proposed I join the Brotherhood. I agreed, much to the other Brothers' chagrin, but Blacktooth stood by his decision and had my back."

"So why take the gang over, then?"

"You know exactly why, Jathan. Blacktooth's ambitions and plans were focused solely on finding something to fuck, or getting enough gold so he could buy something to fuck. A man that short-sighted should not be leading us."

Jathan went silent for a moment before asking. "What happened with Clarice?"

"When she heard I was joining the Brotherhood, she lost it. I told her I had made up my mind and tried to storm out, but before I could leave, she grabbed my shoulder, so I spun around and sliced her ribs open. Not deep enough to kill, but deeper than I wanted to cut. We stared at each other for several seconds as she clutched her bleeding side, and I left without saying another word."

"That's... cold," Jathan said absently.

"We live in a cold world," Rosaline stated with a matter-of-factness that made it clear she was done with the conversation.

As the two bandits entered the Garden, she could hear the rest of the Brotherhood celebrating inside the tavern. It wasn't until she climbed the inn's steps that she noticed something amiss. There was a small leather pouch sitting by the door of the tavern, barely concealed by a wooden chair. Rosaline waited until Jathan went inside to join his Brothers before walking over to the pouch. She opened it, and her heart sank into her stomach. Inside was a fistful of loose teeth, all dyed black. *Blacktooth.*

CHAPTER THIRTY-THREE
GRIMM

The first few days of hard labour were physically excruciating. Uriel had told him that the community needed some kind of cropland; the only problem was that the settlement was in the middle of dense woodlands. As his punishment, Grimm had to clear a section of land of any brush, roots, and rocks that could interfere with planting the crop. For two whole days he swung his axe relentlessly, chopping down any tree that stood in his way. By the time the sun set on the second day, Grimm was exhausted. He collapsed in his bed and slept a long, dreamless night.

However, after two days of clearing trees, his body seemed to adjust, and he could finish the next day with some amount of energy remaining.

Since the incident with Godfrey's father, people had been avoiding the Islander, even more than usual. He would often catch them casting nasty looks his way or whispering behind his back. Despite the tension, Grimm went about his day contentedly. His body was getting stronger and there were a few people he could turn to when he needed some company. Isobel and Seamus frequently invited him over for dinner, Gareth would sneak away from his duties to help Grimm with the project, much to his wife's chagrin, and Uriel came by from time to time to chat idly late into the evening.

On the seventh day of the week, all the underbrush had been cleared and Grimm began tilling and preparing the soil for planting. It was not a large section of cropland, but it would allow the community to become more self-sufficient and not be so reliant on trade. Grimm had never been a farmer, despite owning a fair parcel of land as Shield of the Isles, but he respected the craft. It was hard, physically demanding work, and required the same type of stubborn endurance that a soldier needed. Unfortunately, farming proved to be very monotonous. He had heard of people spending their entire lives farming the same plot of land over and over and over again. He could not imagine a worse fate. The longer he stayed in the commune, the more he craved for excitement, for adventure... for battle.

"Hard labour suits you!" Uriel joked as he approached, pulling Grimm from his thoughts.

"It's coming along."

The two men stared at one another for some time. Grimm could tell that Uriel had something to say, and judging by his expression it wasn't good news.

Finally, after a long and somewhat painful silence, Uriel cleared his throat. "Your place got ransacked again."

Grimm let out an annoyed breath through his nose. Ever since he punched Godfrey's father, Talsin, he had noticed that someone had been rummaging through his belongings. It started with his bedding being stolen, then it was his clothes from the clothesline, and now things had escalated beyond petty theft, as this was the second time somebody had trashed the inside of his dwelling. There was no doubt in Grimm's mind that Godfrey was behind this. But as much as he wanted to punish the little shit, he knew he was on thin ice. Unless he caught the bastard red-handed, there was nothing he could do.

"I'm so sorry, Grimm," Uriel continued. "I'm doing what I can to find out who did this and hold them responsible, but—"

Grimm waved off his apology. He knew Uriel was just as helpless as he was. Ever since the incident between Talsin and Grimm, the community had divided into two factions. Most people supported Talsin and wanted Grimm exiled, as well as Uriel removed from his post as their leader. Then there were a few that stood beside Uriel and Grimm, although they were vastly outnumbered.

Diplomacy and politics had never interested Grimm, and he was never sure how Uthredd did it. There was always someone unhappy with your decision, regardless of whether it was right or wrong. To make matters worse, you had to cater to and listen to these people, otherwise you could have a revolt on your hands.

"You should've exiled me when you had the chance."

Uriel vehemently shook his head. "No. It's like you told me – no matter how hopeless your dream is, you must have faith. I have faith that you can leave your violent past behind you, where it belongs."

Grimm rolled his eyes. It was moments like this when he regretted encouraging Uriel to pursue his pacifist dream; he knew it was going to bite him in the ass, eventually. "How bad is it?" Grimm asked, hoping to change the subject.

"Bad enough."

Grimm set his mattock down and bid farewell to Uriel as he went to go check on the state of his home. As he approached the settlement, he saw several people turn away from him and pretend to be busy. At one point, he locked eyes with Talsin, before the bruised man sheepishly averted his gaze. A satisfied smile appeared on Grimm's lips before he forced it to disappear, knowing that his pride should not be visible for all to see.

Upon entering the small doorway of his house, he saw the inside was in complete disarray. A small table and the accompanying chair had been smashed to bits, his mattress had been ripped open, hay was strewn about the room, and the small bag containing the belongings of the dead Islanders had gone missing. As frustrating as it was, it was not a huge loss. Several gold coins, some rings, and a pouch of mushrooms.

Grimm spent the rest of the day cleaning up his house. The busted furniture was hauled to the woodpile, the hay was swept out onto the grass, and he tried to patch up the holes in the mattress before ripping it more in his frustration. He had slept underneath the stars for plenty of nights in his life, and he was more than content to do so again.

Just when the house was getting into some semblance of order, there was a soft knock on the door. Grimm opened it and saw a smiling Isobel standing on the other side.

"I heard the little shits broke in again."

"Mhmm."

"Come, I've made dinner, figured you'd need something to cheer you up."

Grimm smiled politely, but there was a reason that Isobel never cooked for the camp – she was awful. She had cooked both lunch and dinner for Grimm multiple times since the fight, and each time it was all Grimm could do to keep it down. It was burnt, undercooked, or somehow both. Unable to think of an excuse, Grimm reluctantly followed her to her house.

"Grimm!" Seamus shouted as he saw the Islander and his mother approach as he prepared the table for the three of them.

Despite all odds, the boy had made a speedy recovery. He had no recollection of what happened in the clearing, but he knew it was likely that Godfrey and the others were beating him. Despite his fast recovery, Isobel kept him locked inside most days, preventing him from running around and possibly hurting himself again.

"Make yourself comfortable and I'll bring the food out," Isobel said as she slipped inside.

Grimm nodded and sat down at the table across from a beaming Seamus. Seamus reminded him of both his son, Einar, and Sara. He felt an aching pain in his chest whenever he looked into Seamus' eyes, as he thought about how he lost both of them. There were several nights when Grimm failed to sleep because of the guilt that constantly gnawed away at him in the back of his mind. Despite Einar being his blood, he thought more often of Sara. He remembered the fearless little slave girl that had followed him into the wilderness, lived amongst an army, and even tried to fight alongside him.

"What's wrong?" Seamus said, his voice interrupting Grimm's thoughts.

The Islander raised a questioning brow, not sure what the boy meant, but then he felt it. He had a single tear rolling down his cheek. "Nothing," Grimm grunted, hoping that would end the questions.

"For fuck's sake!" A shout came from inside the kitchen.

Grimm went to stand up only to see Isobel walk out of the hut with a plate full of what appeared to be coal. If he was being honest, Grimm wasn't sure what kind of food it was supposed to be. It could be bread, meat, potatoes... hell, knowing Isobel's lack of culinary skills, he wouldn't be surprised if she had figured out a way to burn water.

"I'm sorry," Isobel started, "I don't know what happened."

"Too much heat, by the looks of things."

Isobel furrowed her brow, as both Seamus and Grimm laughed. "Looks like we'll be having oatcakes again tonight, I hope that's okay."

Grimm nodded as Isobel hurried back inside with the plate of burnt food in her hands.

"What was it like to be a soldier?" Seamus asked.

Grimm winced at the question. He hated it for two reasons, the first being that it was a reminder that he was *not* a soldier anymore. The second part of why he hated Seamus' question was because it reminded him of Sara. The dwarven girl had a seemingly never-ending supply of questions, and he would have given anything to hear her ask him one just once more.

"It's hard," Grimm stated, not sure how much he should divulge to Seamus.

"Have you ever killed anyone?"

"Mhmm."

"Were they bad guys?"

Grimm opened his mouth and paused. He had never really thought about the morality of killing someone. After some quick reflection, he decided to lie. "All of them."

"Wow! You know, last time Mom went to town she got me a book about the deeds of knights and how they stand up against evil. Were you a knight?"

Grimm shook his head. "The Isles don't have knights, just regular folk who picked up a sword and became good at it."

"Will you teach me to use a sword?"

"Absolutely not!" Isobel shouted as she walked out of the hut carrying a plate of oatcakes.

"I thought you wanted me to teach him? Every man should know how to fight."

"Out of the question."

"But, Mom, if I know how to use a sword, I can finally give Godfrey what he deserves!"

"I said no." Isobel's voice was cold and stern, her narrowed eyes glaring at the two of the them. "That's final, and if you say one more word, Seamus, I'll send you to bed with no supper."

Seamus slammed his hands on the table. "This isn't fair!" He stormed inside the hut and slammed the door behind him.

"The boy's got a point."

"*Enough,*" Isobel snarled. "When I told you I wanted you to teach my son how to defend himself, I did not mean with swords."

Grimm let out a sarcastic laugh. "So, what, when bandits come brandishing swords and spears, you want him to use his fists? Everyone should know how to use a weapon... even you."

Isobel's angry expression quickly shifted to one of disbelief. "Me? But I'm a woman, women don't fight."

"In the Isles they do. I have fought alongside ferocious shield-maidens that can strike fear in the heart of even the hardest of men."

Isobel crossed her arms. "I don't know how it's done back in your savage homeland, but here ladies do not fight."

"Then you die," Grimm replied, although judging from Isobel's angry scowl, it was a mistake. Thankfully, a blood-curdling scream came from the middle of the settlement, sparing Grimm from a verbal lashing. In an instant, he rose to his feet and sprinted towards the camp.

At the centre of the settlement was a large grey wolf that was close to the size of a horse. The beast was tearing through camp and was currently trying to bash down the door to Talsin's house. Grimm's eyes darted around the ground to find a weapon and saw a pitchfork nearby. He picked it up by the haft and shouted at the monstrous beast.

The wolf spun on its heels and snarled as it locked eyes with Grimm. The creature lowered itself and slowly began moving towards the Islander.

Grimm held the pitchfork firmly, and waited patiently for the beast to make the first move. Suddenly, the wolf lunged towards him, moving across the settlement at a blistering pace.

Grimm pirouetted out of the way, missing the beast's maw by a hair's breadth, but was knocked off balance by the creature's powerful tail.

The wolf turned around again, and stared at the prone Islander with predatory eyes full of contempt. The beast snarled once more, as if smiling at the idea of feasting on his flesh. The wolf lunged again, its mouth open, ready to deal the killing blow.

Grimm quickly rolled to the side and pointed the tines of the fork towards the beast. The weight of the wolf crashed into Grimm's side as the creature impaled itself on the tool, letting out a shrill yelp as the metal prongs dug into its flesh.

After a quick twist of the pitchfork to ensure the wolf was dead, Grimm tossed the corpse of the creature aside and rose to his feet, covered in the beast's blood. People began to cautiously exit their huts, and upon seeing the corpse of the wolf, cheered.

Gareth was one of the first people to come up and congratulate Grimm, patting the Islander hard on the shoulder. Others came up and expressed their gratitude to him and how thankful they were that he could singlehandedly kill such a fearsome beast.

As a smile appeared on Grimm's face, there was a shrill scream that broke up the celebrations.

Everyone turned around and saw that the wolf's body was moving. The creature twitched and spasmed uncontrollably as its body changed shape. Several people vomited and gasped in horror once the wolf had finished transforming. Grimm's heart sank into his stomach when he saw that the wolf he had slain had turned back into Godfrey, a bloody pitchfork protruding from his skull.

CHAPTER THIRTY-FOUR

ELBERT

A bell tolled ominously in the distance. A light fog had rolled over the hills and descended upon Oxworth. It was eerily silent in the city, and if the king did not know any better, he would say that it was abandoned. They were about a half a day's ride from the walls and would reach the city just before noon. The demonic mare stamped its hooves impatiently, as if she was just as eager as her master to arrive in Oxworth.

"We're close," Mikkel said, as he emerged from the thicket.

Elbert eyed the monster hunter carefully. During their travels, Mikkel had frequently dismounted and gone into the bush. At first, Elbert thought that perhaps the man needed to relieve himself or stretch his legs from being stuck in a saddle for too long. But either the man had a bladder the size of a thimble, or Mikkel had another trick up his sleeve.

"How can you tell?" the crippled king asked.

Mikkel tapped his chest, where the odd medallion was embedded. 'It's getting warmer."

As soon as he mounted the horse, the mare broke out into a full gallop towards the silent city. The thundering hooves echoed across the plains, and Elbert bounced helplessly on the horse's hindquarters. His midsection slammed repeatedly into the thick muscles of the black mare, to the point that he thought he had begun to bleed internally.

Once the city's walls became a mere stone's throw away, Elbert could see that a long line of people were waiting at the gates to get in. Mikkel quickly veered the horse off the main road and rode it into a small copse nearby. When they were concealed in the trees, Mikkel dismounted and lifted Elbert off the horse. The crippled king massaged his aching ribs, but was too scared to remove his shirt to see how badly they were bruised. The hope that they were not bruised had left the king several hours prior.

"What are we doing?" Elbert asked, as he watched Mikkel pull out a large hunting knife, a piece of cloth, and a small flask of vodka.

"That lineup of people means Oxworth is restricting entry into the city for some reason, which usually means you need a permit to get in. Which we don't have," Mikkel explained as he poured the clear spirit onto the blade of the knife.

"So?"

"So, guards will usually make an exception if you throw enough gold at them, or if you have a medical emergency."

"What are you getting at?"

Without explaining any further, Mikkel drove the large knife deep into the side of Elbert's right leg, just above the kneecap into the meat of his thigh. As the king watched the large steel blade pierce his flesh, he let out a horrified scream, mostly out of shock, as he didn't feel any actual pain.

"You fucking stabbed me!" Elbert screamed.

"Shut up!" Mikkel hissed as he began bandaging the wound. "If this is going to work, the guards need to think this happened elsewhere and not right outside their fucking front gate."

"I can't believe you stabbed me..." Elbert repeated.

"Quit your whinging, A few stitches and you'll be fine. I missed all the major arteries."

"You're a real whoreson, you know that?"

"A whoreson would've left you alone in the woods. So far, you've been very useful." A sly smile appeared on the monster hunter's lips, and a disgusted scowl appeared on Elbert's in turn. Rising to his feet, Mikkel touched the black mare's head and whispered: "*Domini Canis.*"

As soon as the infernal words left the man's lips, the horse let out a sharp whinny and collapsed to the ground. The beast spasmed and writhed violently as it shrank in size. Elbert could hear bones breaking and skin tearing apart. It was so visceral that he closed his eyes and plugged his ears with his fingers, but it was no use – he could still hear the muffled sounds of the violent transformation taking place. After several, long, agonizing seconds, there was silence. Elbert unplugged his ears and opened his eyes and saw that in the place of the black mare stood a large black war hound. He had crimson eyes, pointy, dagger-like ears, and a drooling mouth full of razor-sharp teeth.

"What the hells did you do?" Elbert asked in disbelief as he stared fearfully at the menacing dog in front of him.

"Horses can't go into buildings, and horses have a tendency to go missing in cities. I don't know about you, but I'd rather not kill another imp."

Elbert nodded in agreement. Mikkel then hooked his arms underneath the crippled king's and slung Elbert over both shoulders. He began jogging at a feverish pace towards the gate and whistled for his new hellhound to follow.

Once again bouncing uncontrollably on top of another crea-ture, Elbert stared at the mysterious monster hunter in awe. There was something about Mikkel that went beyond the secretive training and education that happened inside the Order of Swords. There was something that he wasn't sharing, and Elbert was going to find out what.

"Any chance you want to tell me the truth on how you know all of this stuff?"

"When we get to the gate, I need you to wail in pain, as if your leg is actually going to fall off. Think you can manage that?" Mikkel responded, completely ignoring the king's question as he continued to hurry to the city walls.

"And if I don't?"

"Then you'll stop being useful to me and I'll *actually* leave you behind."

Elbert gulped. Judging from the tone of Mikkel's voice, this was not an empty threat. Once they got within earshot of the city, the king cleared his throat and wailed uncontrollably at the top of his lungs. He screamed so hard and so loud that he thought he was going to rip the lining in his throat.

Everyone in the line to gain access to the city turned and looked at the howling man on top of another's shoulders accompanied by the large, black war hound. As Elbert continued to scream, Mikkel quickly ran to the front of the line and towards the guards at the gate.

"What in the *actual* fuck is going on here?" a guard said as they approached.

"Bandits attacked us on the road. Please, my brother needs a healer, or he'll die!" Mikkel lied.

"By the way he's hollering, I'd've thought that leg woulda been chopped off," another guard commented under his breath.

Elbert reached out and grabbed the first guard's gambeson. "Please! You have to let us in! I can't lose my leg. Oh Gods, I can feel the infection spreading. Please, kind sirs! Please! I don't want to be a cripple!"

"Fuck sakes!" the first guard exclaimed as he swatted the king's hands away. "Fine, go on in, if only so I don't have to hear ya scream anymore."

Mikkel nodded his head, and Elbert clasped both of his hands together. "Thank you! Thank you! May the Gods bless you for your kindness!" the king continued the charade until they were well out of earshot of the guards, and then finally gave his voice a rest.

"Well done, that was some performance," Mikkel said. "Very convincing."

Elbert smiled. "I drew on some life experience."

"You should've been a mummer. Although I think I'm bloody deaf in this ear now."

As the two ventured further into the city, Elbert could tell something was amiss. People walked the streets refusing to make eye contact with one another, whispering in hushed voices as other people walked past them, and the air was heavy with suspicion. It wasn't until they reached the town square that it became clear why everyone was on edge. The cobblestone market had been bathed in a deep coat of crimson. Townsfolk were wailing and laying flowers and bouquets at memorials to the victims while a number of men were desperately trying to wash the freshly spilled blood away from the stones.

"What the hells happened here?" Elbert asked as he stared at the scene in front of him.

"Our demon," Mikkel grunted as he set the crippled king down against the foundation of a nearby building. "Stay," he said, before turning and walking into the crowd of mourning townspeople.

"Not sure where I'm going to go," Elbert mumbled under his breath, but it wasn't until he turned his head and saw the large black war hound staring at him that he realized Mikkel was talking to the dog, not him.

Elbert watched the people while he waited for Mikkel to return. They were huddled into small groups, silently offering small wreaths and flowers in memory of the victims. Every once in a while, someone would shriek and wail inconsolably, and had to be helped back to their feet. Watching the people's grief made Elbert's stomach churn. Their pain was palpable, and had he the ability to walk, Elbert would've risen to his feet and fled. But despite how much he then wanted to, his legs refused to move, so he sat there watching the heart-wrenching grief of the citizens of Oxworth.

Finally, after what seemed like an eon, Mikkel returned. The monster hunter patted the dog on the head and effortlessly threw Elbert over his shoulders once again.

"Where are we going?" Elbert asked, thankful to be going anywhere else.

"The morgue."

"Why?"

"Four of the five blacksmiths in the city were brutally murdered last night. I need to make sure that this is because of our demon and not some deranged lunatic."

The two men made their way out of the town square and towards the city morgue. Elbert could tell when they were close, as the putrid aroma of decay became thick in the air. A bit of bile rushed up the crippled king's throat, and he swallowed the acidic liquid back down.

"If you puke on me..." Mikkel growled.

"Ugh..." Elbert moaned. "The smell."

A small laugh escaped the monster hunter's lips. "City boy."

Judging by the strength of the stench in the air, they had now arrived at the morgue. It was a small stone building with a shabby wooden door in the front, bent iron hinges on its side. Mikkel set Elbert down and knocked on the door with his studded gauntlet.

"The fuck d'ya want!?" a muffled, gruff voice called from behind the door.

"Here to inspect the murder victims."

"The guards already been here!" the voice replied. There was the sound of metal scraping against metal as the door's deadbolt unlocked. A small, dirty dwarven man opened up the door and sneered at Mikkel. "We don't need any soddin' corpse-sniffers round here!"

Just as the man was about to shut the door, Mikkel let out a sharp whistle and the black hellhound lunged through the doorway and pinned the mortician to the ground. The beast leered at the dwarf, drool dripping off its razor-sharp teeth, and a low, menacing growl escaping its lips.

Mikkel once again picked up Elbert and stepped over the pinned dwarf. "Stay," he commanded. "We'll only be in there for a few minutes." The dog's gaze did not leave the dwarf's, and the two men made their way into the morgue.

Inside were four cadavers lying on tables. One of them had been cut open, and the acrid scent of sulfur filled the room. Mikkel walked in and set the crippled Elbert down into a wheelbarrow that was clearly used to transport bodies. Elbert winced as he felt the cold, sticky blood of the deceased seep through his clothes and stick to his skin.

"I think I'm going to—" Elbert started before a torrent of vomit spewed from his lips and onto the stone floor.

"Pull yourself together," Mikkel growled as he began examining the body.

"What do you see?" Elbert asked as a way of distracting himself.

"The left hand of each victim has been hacked off, with the wound being cauterized," Mikkel said as he leaned over one of the unexamined corpses. He plunged a knife into the cadaver and began carving the body open. The sulfuric smell intensified, and Elbert was forced to plug his nose as his eyes watered.

"The heart, liver, lungs, and most of the other internal organs have been charred, as if burnt by fire. The blood is dark and flaky, as if it were baked onto the sides of the body."

"Sounds like a demon to me," Elbert said as he squirmed uncomfortably in his blood-soaked clothes.

"Where did you go?" Mikkel mumbled, barely audible under his breath.

Elbert lifted his arm and saw his sleeve drip with blood. He swallowed another rush of bile before speaking. "Can we get out of here? I'm covered in someone else's blood, and I think I can literally smell myself starting to decay."

"City boy."

The bathwater was hot and mountains of bubbles rose from the porcelain tub, along with thick clouds of steam. Elbert allowed himself to relax and for the briefest moment, he felt all the worries in his life disappear. He wasn't sure when the last time he had a bath was, and he had honestly forgotten how good it felt. Removing layers and layers of grime off his skin was almost euphoric. The servant had to keep adding fresh water to the tub as it constantly became dark and cloudy with the filth that had clung to Elbert's body over the last several months.

There was a sudden knock on the door and the servant girl poked her head back into the room. "How are ye farin', master?" she said in a sweet, almost melodic voice.

Elbert looked at his hands and saw the wrinkles starting to form on his fingertips. He then turned his hand over and saw that even the dirt underneath his nails was gone. A smile appeared on his lips. "I think I'm clean."

The servant girl smiled, and with a clap of her hands, she and another, much more burly woman entered the room. The two women lifted Elbert out of the tub and set him gently on the soft furs that were on the floor.

"Thanks Mailie," the first servant said, dismissing the burly woman.

Elbert looked up at the servant and felt his heart begin to race. Not only was he naked, but he was also on his back looking up at her, much like a new babe would look up at its mother. The servant seemed to not notice his anxiety as she pulled a small bundle of fresh clothes from one of the shelves in the room.

"Wait, those aren't my clothes," Elbert said.

The young woman frowned slightly. "I'm sorry, master, but yer old clothes were beyond savin', I'm afraid."

Elbert nodded his head and watched as the woman dressed him. He figured they were around the same age and he found her very attractive, which only added to his embarrassment. She was tall and lanky, but her muscles were honed from years of working in the tavern. She had deep, emerald eyes and long, silvery-blonde hair that was tied up into a messy bun.

As the woman struggled to shimmy his new pants onto his lifeless legs, Elbert could feel his cheeks turn red. Unable to bear the embarrassment anymore, he felt the need to say something to break the silence.

"Sorry, the legs don't work like they used to." He winced as the words left his mouth. *Of course they don't work like they used to!* he scolded himself. *Any idiot can see that.*

The woman grinned, showing off a single crooked tooth in an otherwise perfect smile. "It's alright. Sometimes me own legs don't work when I crawl outta bed in the mornin'."

"I wish it was just in the mornings," Elbert said under his breath. "Sorry I'm being such a hassle."

With one last heave, the woman was able to lift the crippled king's trousers up to his waist. Letting out a satisfied grunt, she smiled and patted his chest. "Yer not a hassle, I'm just glad ye didn't take a swipe at me."

Elbert's heart sank. "I'm sorry—" he began.

The woman instantly grabbed his shoulder and gave it a firm squeeze. Her green eyes stared deep into Elbert's as if she was looking into his very soul. "Ye apologize too much – stop. Ye've been nothin' but proper with me."

Elbert smiled, feeling more relaxed, and nodded his head. It was rare to meet someone who didn't laugh at him. Ever since he lost his legs to that demon, it seemed everyone found amusement in his misfortune. Whenever he passed by, people snickered, whispered, and pointed at the king who couldn't walk on his own two feet. Although the irony was not lost on Elbert, he was tired of being the subject of their amusement.

The woman returned the king's smile with one of her own and pulled him into a sitting position. "Arms in the air now!"

Elbert did as he was told. As the woman slid the cloth shirt over his head, he spoke again. "I'm Elbert."

Once the collar of the shirt was past his eyes he saw the woman staring at him, a playful smile stuck on her lips. "Kaliope."

"Pretty name."

"Pfft!" the woman scoffed. "Me dad thought if he named me somethin' pretty that I'd actually leave this dump."

"You've never left Oxworth?"

Kaliope shook her head. "Nah, I've been stuck in this shithole me whole life."

"Where would you want to go?"

Kaliope beamed at Elbert's question. "I'd love to go to Winterhelm and see the castle! See all them fancy lords and ladies in their fancy clothes dancin' around like chickens at a feast." She paused, the excitement slowly dying in her voice. "Sad I'll never see 'em."

Elbert opened his mouth to tell her the truth about who he was and how he would take her away from this place, but he stopped himself. Revealing his true identity would surely only put her into harm's way. And although he couldn't reveal who he was, he refused to sit and watch her descend into a pit of doubt and disappointment. He placed a hand softly on hers. "Your story doesn't end here," he said reassuringly. "I'm sure once you set foot in that castle, the king himself will see you and invite you to dance like a chicken yourself."

Kaliope's smile returned as she grabbed Elbert's hand and gave it a small squeeze. "That'd be a dream come true! I hear the new king is quite handsome."

Elbert raised a brow as his cheeks flushed with colour. "Oh?"

"Oh, yes!" Kaliope exclaimed. "Both of King David's sons are said to be very handsome." She paused, the twinkle in her eye fading as she came back to reality. "I bet yer hungry. Yer friend bought a whole feast for the two of ye!"

Before Elbert could ask a follow-up question, Kaliope expertly wrapped one of the king's arms around her shoulder and lifted him to his feet.

"Have you done this before?" Elbert asked.

Kaliope nodded. "Yer no different than takin' care of a drunkard. Except the company is much more pleasant." A coy smile appeared on her lips as she locked eyes with Elbert before leaving the room.

She dragged him down the long wooden hallway of the upper floor of the tavern until they came to a pair of large oaken doors. Kaliope pushed them open to reveal a luscious dining area. The room was dimly lit by several sconces on the wall with a gently crackling fireplace in the corner, where the hellhound was curled up in a ball, sleeping peacefully. She gently set Elbert down in a soft, padded chair in front of a large table filled with mouthwatering food.

After catching her breath for several minutes, Kaliope placed a small bell on the table. "If ye need anythin' else, please ring." The servant gave a flawless curtsy and exited the room, closing the door behind her.

Elbert breathed in the intoxicating aroma of the food and greedily devoured it. It had been ages since he had a proper meal and he would not squander the chance to savour it. Mikkel sat on the other side of the table, picking bits of food from his teeth with a small knife. The king paid him little mind – when he wasn't staring at the exquisite food in front of him, he was eying the bell from the corner of his eye. He couldn't get Kaliope out of his head, and he wanted to ring for her so he could keep talking to her, but couldn't think of a reasonable excuse to bother her. She was more intoxicating than the finest vintage.

"Having fun?" Mikkel asked suddenly, breaking the silence.

Elbert nodded. "New clothes, a bath, a literal feast fit for a king, and a private dining room. Feeling generous?"

"It's because you aren't going to like what happens next."

Elbert paused and slowly swallowed the clump of potatoes that filled his mouth. "What do you mean?"

Mikkel pulled the knife from his teeth, stared at the hunk of food that was stuck on the tip, and flung it across the room before answering. "I'm sure you've probably guessed, but our demon is no longer in Oxworth." Elbert nodded. "Which means there is no reason for us to stay here and that we have to move on and follow the trail."

The king let out a sigh. "Any chance that trail leads back to Winterhelm?"

The monster hunter shook his head. "That's just it, I don't know where to go next."

"Doesn't that medallion in your chest tell you where he is?"

"It doesn't work like that; it just burns hotter when I'm in the presence of something that has come in contact with him. Either corpses, or people who agreed to deals with him."

"So now what?"

Mikkel squeezed his hands into fists and let out a long breath. Before answering, he swallowed and looked Elbert in the eye. "I need help."

The crippled king raised a brow. "From who?"

"Someone who doesn't offer help for free."

"I don't understand, what are you—" Elbert paused as he followed Mikkel's eyes to the small bell on the table. The king's stomach sank. "You can't be serious!"

"There is no other way," Mikkel replied. "Plus, why do you care? She's just some serving girl."

"She's not just some girl!" Elbert exclaimed. "She's a person who has hopes and dreams and—"

Mikkel instantly erupted into laughter. "Holy hells, Elbert," he said, wiping a tear from his eyes. "You just met her! Plus, what makes you think a girl like that would even be interested in you?"

Elbert's face contorted into a nasty frown. "I'm a king."

"A king that doesn't have a working cock," Mikkel replied through several chuckles.

"Why does it have to be her? There are hundreds of people in this town, pick one of them!"

Mikkel's laughter died down. "The person I need help from has a type."

"Blonde? Young?"

"Innocent," Mikkel said gravely. The monster hunter's face hardened as he rose to his feet. "I'm sorry, Elbert, I'd love nothing more than to see her reject you at the end of the night, but there is no other way."

"No!" Elbert shouted, lunging at Mikkel to stop him as he walked by.

The monster hunter quickly sidestepped out of the way, and the last thing Elbert felt before passing out was the knuckle of Mikkel's studded gauntlet hitting his head.

The cool evening breeze stung as it blew across the king's bruised face. Elbert tried to open his eyes, but only the left one did; he touched his right eye and felt that it was swollen shut. He winced as he felt the skin around the eye. He looked around and, although his vision was blurry, he could tell that he was no longer in the tavern, but out in the wilderness once again. With a throbbing head, Elbert tried to piece together what had happened. He remembered arguing with Mikkel about something, but could not quite remember what. It wasn't until the foul aroma hit his nose that it all came back to him. An aroma that he hadn't smelt since Tjørholm – the putrid scent of burnt flesh. The king quickly rubbed his good eye to get a clear view and saw the charred corpse of a young woman lying in front of him. There was no mistaking it. Mikkel had done it, he had sacrificed Kaliope.

"If it's any consolation, I made it quick," Mikkel said abruptly. "She didn't feel a thing."

Elbert craned his head so he could scowl at the monster hunter. Mikkel sat on a nearby fallen tree, sharpening his knife on a small whetstone. Elbert wasn't sure what disgusted him more, the fact that Mikkel had just murdered an innocent person, or the fact he seemed so undisturbed by it.

"You're a fucking monster..." Elbert growled, spitting in the man's direction before lying back down.

"What's one life against the lives of hundreds, if not thousands of people?" Mikkel paused, looking at the blade of his knife. "It had to be done," he added, although Elbert wasn't sure if it was directed at him or not.

"I hope you got what you wanted. I hope it was enough to justify taking her life."

"I don't know."

Elbert craned his head once more. "What do you mean, you don't know?"

"My patron hasn't arrived yet."

"Maybe he's disgusted by you," Elbert snapped.

"Doubt it."

The two men sat in a tense silence for some time until the air suddenly became still. Elbert looked up at the trees and noticed that the leaves didn't move in the slightest. He looked back down and saw the burnt remains of Kaliope begin to glow a soft orange. His body tensed as he watched the glow grow brighter and brighter with each passing second. Mikkel slowly rose to his feet with a pained grunt, his knees popping as they straightened.

It wasn't until Kaliope's burnt husk was so bright that it illuminated the entire clearing that it started to writhe and spasm uncontrollably. For a moment, Elbert thought she was still alive, that she had somehow survived. But it quickly became apparent that she was dead as her body contorted in unnatural ways. Elbows popped away from the body, fingers snapped backwards towards the wrist, and her head turned so violently that it cracked free from her spine. Kaliope's chest began heaving as if she was taking large breaths, her ribs snapping until they finally broke free of her chest cavity with a sickening crunch.

Rising from her charred corpse was a large creature that stood nearly nine feet tall. It had crimson skin, large black horns that extended towards the sky, and a pair of bat-like wings protruding from its back. The creature had a barbed, red tail and eyes that looked as if the pupils were made of hellfire itself. Once free of Kaliope's body, it stretched its back and wings and let out a guttural roar that seemed to let out a shockwave of terror across the woods.

"Greetings, Abaddon," Mikkel said nonchalantly, as he stepped between the creature and Elbert.

For several seconds, the monstrous creature eyed both Mikkel and Elbert with a hungry curiosity. Then, a wicked smile appeared on its lips, showcasing the creature's black, obsidian-like fangs.

"You have a friend," Abaddon said with a gravelly, low voice, as if it came from the depths of the hells themselves. "He stinks of Mammon."

"A victim," Mikkel answered curtly. "He's helped me track the demon so far, but the trail's gone cold."

"So, that's why you called me?" Abaddon snarled, turning his head to face Mikkel.

"I—"

Abaddon raised a silencing hand. "Let me take a look at this friend," he hissed as he pushed Mikkel to the side.

"The cripple means nothing. I—"

Abaddon shot a menacing glare towards the monster hunter, which, surprisingly, was enough for Mikkel to back away and retake his seat upon the fallen tree. The demon then bent down and studied Elbert from head to toe with an unnerving scrutiny. Elbert's jaw tightened, and he crawled backwards away from the beast as quickly as he could. His hands trembled as he reached for the next handful of grass.

"Does the friend have a name?"

"El... El... Elbert."

Abaddon's smile grew. "Allow me to introduce myself, I am Abaddon, Lord of the Seven Hells, and Mikkel's patron." The amusement suddenly vanished from the creature's face as he narrowed his eyes and leaned down so that his nose was mere inches away from Elbert's. The crippled king could feel the demon's hot, sulfuric breath on his skin. "What did Mammon promise you?"

"He promised to make me the greatest king Artanzia had ever known."

"King?" the creature said in disbelief. "Where is your castle? Where is your crown?"

Elbert swallowed what little spit he had in his mouth and tried to find the words. "My throne has been... temporarily... seized."

A chilling laugh escaped the demon's mouth as he rose back to his full height. "How rich! The greatest king has lost his kingdom! It takes a very *great* man to lose a throne."

"And I'll be a greater man once I've taken it back. Especially without the help of a demon like you."

Abaddon's smile quickly vanished and his brow furrowed. The hair on the back of Elbert's neck stood up on end as the creature lowered himself once again to the king's eye level.

"I like you. You have spirit. But if you ever compare me to filth like Mammon again, I'll rip out your tongue and feast on your innards."

"You're not a demon?" Elbert asked.

"I am not a mere demon like Mammon, I'm a devil. A minor distinction in the eyes of mortals, but an important distinction nonetheless."

"What's the difference?"

A sly smile appeared on Abaddon's lips as he looked at Elbert before answering. "As a king, I'm sure you can appreciate the need for subjects. Without people to rule over, what's the point of having a crown? Demons like Mammon are my subjects,

subjects that I want to stay *within* my domain." Abaddon paced back and forth as he continued. "But every once in a while, a pesky demon wants their freedom and escapes the hells to live amongst you mortals. That is when I find someone like Mikkel. I give them all the tools they need to succeed. That medallion in his chest, the knowledge and ability to summon infernal beasts, and that chilling black sword, are all because of *me*."

"What happens when the demon is returned to you?"

"They learn a very important lesson," Abaddon replied, malice colouring his voice.

"Enough!" Mikkel yelled suddenly. "I didn't summon you to make a new friend. I already gave you a toy. Are you going to help me or not?"

The creature's grin took on an even more sinister quality as he eyed Kaliope's charred corpse before turning his attention back towards the monster hunter. "I already have. Mammon will sense my presence on this plane and, like a rat sensing a cat, he will run. He and his disciples are a day and half's ride from here to the north. You should be able to pick up their trail at the village they're resting at."

"Thank you," Mikkel said as he readied his bags.

Abaddon walked over to the corpse of Kaliope and placed both of his cloven hooves into the hole that he had originally burst out of. "And don't worry about the girl, Mikkel, I'll be sure to show her all the hospitality the hells have to offer."

Before anyone could respond, Kaliope's husk illuminated in a bright orange glow once again and the devil sank back into the ground. The blinding light slowly faded until it completely died out, leaving nothing but a corpse in the woods illuminated by the stars.

Elbert focused on the charred remains of Kaliope and all of his anger came back, the rage rising from his stomach like an inferno.

"You whoreson," Elbert growled, his voice trembling over every syllable.

"I told you," Mikkel replied, "it had to be done, there was no other way."

"As long as you get your demon at the end of the day, you're happy, right? I can't believe I used to look up to you people. When I was little, my brother would tell stories about members of the Order of the Swords. I used to grab sticks and fight imaginary monsters throughout the palace. You're no better than the monsters you kill."

Mikkel threw one of the saddlebags forcefully against the ground. "You want to know something about those stories? They're all lies! Propaganda to get idiots like you to join the Order. Most members die within a week of their first contract. It's tough to get recruits when your life expectancy after graduating is seven days or less. I convocated with thirty other members – do you know how many of us are still alive? One. I survived because I saw an opportunity to stack the deck in my favour. You can't ask people to fight werewolves, vampires, leshens, necrophages, and any other horror that lurks in the dark, and not expect them to take every advantage they can get. So, if you're disgusted by me, fine! I'll leave you here and you can find more *esteemed* company to take you back to Winterhelm."

A long silence fell over the clearing as Elbert chose his next words carefully. Every fiber of his heart screamed at him to take this opportunity to leave Mikkel's side. He was a murderer and a monster, but his words had some truth to them. You did have to do what it took to survive, and right now, Elbert needed to stay with Mikkel if he ever hoped to sit upon his throne again.

"You know I can't do that," the crippled king said, finally breaking the silence.

An amused snort escaped Mikkel's lips as he tossed a bag at Elbert's feet. "Then grab your shit. We're leaving."

CHAPTER THIRTY-FIVE
ANNA

It had been three days since Mason's deal with Master Mammon, and Anna had refused to speak to either the demon or any of his disciples. It was bad enough that Mammon had swindled and preyed on Mason's desperation, but it was even worse when she found out what had happened to the city's other blacksmiths. A series of gruesome murders in the city allowed Mason to corner the market and save his father's forge, just like Mammon had promised him. Anna figured that the realization that Mason's deal had cost people their lives made the young man sick to his stomach, and she couldn't care less. The boy had been stupid enough to make a deal with a demon, even after Anna revealed Mammon's true nature to him. He deserved every ounce of heartbreak.

A little more than a day's ride outside of Oxworth, Mammon declared that they stop at a nearby village. He was feeling invigorated, and wanted to "celebrate". The village, which Anna didn't catch the name of, was rather small and seemed to be a farming community. Open fields surrounded the settlement and pens of pigs, chickens, and sheep were outside almost every building, including the tavern. Mammon immediately purchased a room in the tavern for several nights for himself and his disciples, but not Anna. Which truth be told, she didn't mind. She was angry and disgusted that Matthew, Desmond, and Evelynn allowed the deal to happen. Outside the inn there was a small lean-to that housed the hay for the animals which Anna claimed as her bed, choosing to socialize more with the animals rather than people.

On the second day of their stay, around midday, Anna debated whether to leave Mammon and his disciples. She wasn't sure if the demon could force her to stay, but she didn't want to witness any more people trading their lives away just for the demon to exploit them. But every time the thought of running away crossed her mind, there was a slight stabbing pain in her heart. It didn't feel right to just let Mammon swindle the people of this world and do nothing about it. Sure, Mason didn't listen to Anna, but perhaps the next person would. If she sat around and did nothing, she would be no better than Mammon. That's not who she was, that's not who her father raised her to be. It was like Matthew had told her; she was the only one who could stop Mammon.

Trying to decide the right thing to do, Anna fed some of the animals and watched them. She had tossed a small bag of oats into the pen and watched as two pigs approached the pile. The first, much larger pig, began greedily devouring the grain while the second grunted and oinked, seemingly asking for a share of the oats. The first pig let out a shrill squeal at the second pig before turning its attention back towards the food. Defeated, the smaller pig retreated to a corner, snorting quietly to itself. Anna was leaning against the wooden fence, arms folded, watching their interaction when she heard footsteps coming from behind her. She had been travelling with Mammon and his disciples for so long that she knew it was Desmond, most likely looking to make amends for what happened in Oxworth.

"Figure you could use some more," Desmond said, setting down another small bag of oats. "It seems that one pig is being a bit of a... *hog.*"

A snorty laugh escaped Anna's lips before she could stifle it at the corny joke. She remembered how her dad always told jokes like that, and it seemed that the worse they were, the funnier they'd be. Anna curved her lips into a frown and clenched her jaw, hoping that Desmond would get the message that she was in no mood for company. The disciple either didn't pick up on Anna's hint, or ignored it, as he stayed there for some time. The two of them watched the enormous pig devour the bag of oats entirely while the smaller pig stood in the corner, seemingly shaking its head as it watched the fat pig eat its fill.

"Those pigs are just like us, you know," Desmond said, breaking the silence.

Anna rolled her eyes.

"We're both just doing what we need to survive," he continued, unbothered by the lack of a response. "When someone comes along and offers you everything you wanted, who can say no? Mammon offered us a pile of oats, and, like that pig, we ate it up without a second thought. We all just want our oats, but we don't think about the consequences until after."

"This doesn't make me hate him any less," Anna muttered petulantly.

"I don't want you to hate him, I want you to hate us." Anna looked up at Desmond, and was surprised to see that the disciple was not looking at her. He was just staring at the pigs, tears welling in the corner of his eyes. "Mammon is just doing what he needs to survive," Desmond continued. "He is no different from anything else. If you want to hate something, hate humanity. We are the ones who allow him to stay here, and we are the ones who devour each pile of oats he offers, not knowing that it brings us closer to the butcher's block."

"How did you become a disciple?"

Desmond closed his eyes and let out a long breath. "My wife and I were farmers, who lived north of Eastwindale, along the western borders of Keten. We lived in a small village, not unlike this one. We had a daughter, named Aila. Life was good until a sickness rolled through town. My wife and I were lucky, but our daughter..." Desmond paused, the column of his throat moving as he swallowed. "We tried everything to save her. Herbs, mages, healers, elixirs, everything. We spent all we had trying to save her, but it was no use; she died from a fever a few weeks later."

"Desmond, I'm—" Anna started.

The disciple shook his head and continued. "A couple days after burying Aila, I went to the inn to drown my sorrows. That's where I met a decrepit old man who could barely walk on his own. After sharing a couple of ales, he told me he was a travelling magus and that he knew of a way to bring my daughter back. I mentioned I had no coin, but he said he had no need for coin. 'Raising the dead is no easy feat,' he told me, 'I need someone to help me with my business.' I didn't know what that meant, but I didn't ask. He could've told me we would be killing a king and I still would have agreed. I just wanted my daughter back."

"What happened next?" Anna asked, not sure she really wanted to hear the answer.

"I brought Mammon home to meet my wife. She was vehemently against the idea. She said, 'No matter how painful, the dead should stay dead.' But, being a complete ass, I went behind her back and agreed to be Mammon's disciple. I thought all would be forgiven between me and my wife when we had our sweet Aila in our arms once again." Desmond paused for a moment, before continuing, "Mammon did as he said and brought her back. Not how she was, but as a walking corpse. He said that I should've asked to have her back the way she was. I raged, I tried to hit him, to strangle him, but I couldn't. This mark," Desmond said, pointing to the small scar behind his ear, "prevents me from ever laying a hand on him."

"What did your wife say?"

"Nothing," Desmond replied. "She saw what I did to our daughter and refused to talk to me. I could see in her eyes how it broke her heart, and she locked herself in our room. That was the last time I ever saw her, nearly a century ago. I was bound to follow Mammon for eternity; I couldn't even say goodbye."

"And your daughter?"

Desmond paused, his lips quivering as he tried to find the words. "I killed her," he finally said, breaking into sobs. "She didn't deserve to live like that, she deserved peace."

"How can you not hate him, then?" Anna asked. "He took everything from you, he—"

"No," Desmond interrupted. "For years I hated him, tried to find ways to kill him, to break his hold on me, until I eventually realized that I'm the one to blame. He didn't take my family, I gave it to him." He stopped to wipe the tears from his eyes and turned to face Anna for the first time since the conversation started. "Don't hate Mammon, Anna, hate people like Mason and myself. Idiots who don't know when to walk away."

Without waiting for a response, Desmond left, quietly sniffling to himself as he did so. Anna watched him walk away with a lump in her chest. Desmond had lost everything, and instead of fighting for it back, he had just resigned himself to defeat. She spent some time thinking about how Desmond found himself in Mammon's company, and whether the demon always capitalized on people's desperation to get what he wanted, or if he had other methods of enticing hosts.

Anna tossed some more oats into the pigpen before finally walking back to the lean-to and collapsing on a small pile of hay. Her conversation with Desmond left her more uncertain than before. She still was not sure which was the right path to take: to leave Mammon and the others, refusing to endanger any more innocent people, or to stay with them and try to undermine Mammon and potentially save his future victims. Each choice seemed to be the wrong one. She pinched her brow in frustration and noticed her fingers were hot to touch. She quickly pulled her hand away from her face and noticed that the tips of her fingers were glowing red, like coals in a fire.

A frustrated sigh escaped her lips. She had almost forgotten about her magical powers, and she was still no closer to mastering them than when she started. She shook her hand, trying to cool off her fingertips, but they only burned brighter. Soon, small columns of flames flashed from under the fingernails. In a panic, she ran out of the lean-to and plunged her hand into a trough of water by the nearby pigpen. The water hissed and bubbled and Anna let out a sigh of relief as she watched the glow in her fingers fade.

"Neat trick," Evelynn said with a hint of venom in her voice. "What's got Desmond all worked up? Looks like he's been cutting onions."

Anna shrugged her shoulders, her hand still plunged in the cold water of the trough.

"Let me guess," Evelynn continued, "he told you that sob story about his wife and daughter and how it's all his fault."

"He'd still have his family if Mammon hadn't come along," Anna growled.

Evelynn's eyes narrowed. "Gods, you are as thickheaded as Matthew. Mammon is not some evil being that is filled with malice – he's a tool like an axe or a sword. Tell me, if someone cuts themselves with a knife, is the knife to blame?" Evelynn paused smugly, allowing her rhetorical question to sink in. "Mammon helps just as much as he hurts, you just have to know how to use him."

"Are you going to finally tell me how you became a disciple then, if you're so smart?"

"My heart was broken," Evelynn replied bluntly. "I was in love with a girl, Maylene. She was the most breathtaking woman you'd ever seen. She wouldn't go anywhere until she looked absolutely picturesque. Men and women, both lowborn and high, proposed to her daily, and she loved every second of it. As did I – it was like having a shiny, brand new toy that only I could play with."

"Let me guess, she moved on?" Anna chimed in, interrupting the story.

"Yes," Evelynn scowled. "She stopped receiving me, avoided me, and acted as if I didn't exist! She had caught the eye of some lordling who showered her with the most expensive gifts gold could buy. I was furious. We were in love and this was the thanks I got? To be treated as a ghost, as a nobody? That's when I met Mammon. He told me he needed a helper, someone to help him find gullible, ambitious people to con. Immediately, I thought of Maylene, and my heart sank. Desperate for any kind of solace, I agreed to help him on one condition, that he made the pain in my heart disappear."

"What happened next?"

Evelynn smiled like a viper, eyes gleaming with satisfaction. "Unburdened by love, I organized for Maylene and Mammon to meet. She had a very predictable schedule – every morning she would go to the seamstress and see if any new fabrics had come in. The girl's only real aspiration was to be the prettiest woman to ever live, to receive constant gratification and reassurance. Mammon met her in that seamstress shop and the plan went off without a hitch. She took his deal, and when I saw her next, she had transformed into a living goddess."

"Sounds like Mammon screwed you."

Evelynn tapped her nose. "That's what I thought, at first. He had given Maylene everything she ever wanted. He told me to 'give it time', so I did. After a few days, I saw her around the city and I noticed it. The light in her eyes had vanished. Whenever people complimented or swooned over her, she didn't blush, but instead frowned in disgust. Next thing I knew, she broke off her betrothal with the lordling and became a hermit, sealing herself away from the outside world. I was free of pain and guilt, and that little harlot got what was coming to her." A giddy, childlike laugh escaped Evelynn's lips as she recounted the story.

"So Mammon used your need for revenge to get a host."

The elf's mirth vanished. "I used *him* to ruin the life of the woman who broke my heart without a second thought. Looking back, I wouldn't change a fucking thing."

Just as Anna was about to give a fiery retort, Mammon burst through the tavern door, frantically donning a shirt. "Get your things! Get your things, we have to get out of here!" he shouted.

"What's going on?" Desmond said, approaching from behind Anna and Evelynn.

"He's here! We have to go before he finds us!" Mammon replied.

"Who are you talking about?" Desmond continued, arms outstretched, trying to calm Mammon down.

The demon shoved Desmond aside forcefully and towered over him. "We need to leave!" A small crowd of bystanders emerged from the tavern and the homes in the village to see what all the commotion was about. The demon turned his head and locked eyes with Anna. "Why are you just standing there? Go get the horses ready!"

Anna's eyes darted between Mammon and a sprawled-out Desmond on the ground, and in that moment, she knew what she needed to do. "No."

The demon's brow furrowed. "No? What do you mean, 'No'?" he growled as he stormed over to her. Evelynn quickly backed away, giving the two of them as much distance as possible. "I brought you back from the dead, you ungrateful little shit. My blood courses through your veins; you belong to me!"

He grabbed Anna's wrist so hard that she winced in pain. "No!" Anna shouted as she closed her eyes and pushed Mammon away while pulling her arm free from his grasp. There was a deafening boom and a shockwave rippled through the air, rattling windows and scattering loose debris. The smell of sulfur mixed with the sharp sting of ozone hung in the air, and Anna felt her heartbeat in her ears as silence settled over the stunned crowd. When she opened her eyes again, Mammon was a good twenty feet away from her, his eyes as wide as saucers. She looked around and noticed that both the townsfolk and Mammon's disciples were averting their gaze.

"Fuck it," Mammon spat as he dusted himself off, rising to his feet. "She wants to become his plaything, be my guest. Evelynn, make yourself useful and ready the horses. We need to leave."

Dutifully, Evelynn sprang into action. As the crowd dispersed, Matthew sheepishly shuffled up to Anna. "Why aren't you coming with us? You promised you would find a way to get rid of Mammon."

"Look at him," Anna replied, gesturing towards Mammon screaming orders at Desmond. "He's scared. I need to find whoever he is talking about – they might be the key to getting rid of Mammon once and for all." She paused and placed a hand on Matthew's shoulder, giving it a reassuring squeeze. "I promise I'll be back."

The disciple's lips curved into a smile as he pulled her into a long embrace. "Hurry," he whispered as he let go of her.

Anna watched as Mammon and his disciples rode hastily out of town, a bittersweet feeling in her heart. Once again, she was on her own. Even though she hated being in Mammon's company, the idea of continuing on alone frightened her. She had never truly been alone. She had lived her whole life with her father in the woods, then she travelled with Solin and Muril until she reached Winterhelm, and then she was adopted by Randall into the Maggots. As the fear and sadness swelled, she quickly swallowed the pain and steeled herself. She had a job to do – fear and sadness could wait. She had to learn to control her demonic powers, and, more importantly, she needed to find who Mammon was terrified of, and end this. Once and for all.

CHAPTER THIRTY-SIX

RANDALL

"**W**hat do you mean they are leaving!?" Randall shouted as he slammed his fist into the table in the war room.

"You can hardly blame them, Your Majesty," Madame Dupont answered. "With the naval blockade gone, there is a way out of this city. Nobody wants to stay in a place under siege with an army gnashing its teeth against the gates."

"An army without a king," Randall retorted. "Any day now, A'Chula will return with Elbert in chains and this whole thing will be behind us."

"I'm not sure about that," Corbin Strongarm replied. "Slavers don't become slavers by being honest, trustworthy people."

"I paid them a fortune for Elbert."

"Even if the crippled king makes his way back to us, there is still the possibility of one of his commanders rising up and taking control of the army," Virgil Walker interjected. "Gods know they want things to stay the same."

"And with the legitimate king killed with no apparent heirs," Cassius added, "they might view you as an easy conquest in order for them to seize absolute power."

"The nobles have always underestimated us. That was their downfall the first time, and that will be their downfall this time."

"The people are scared, Your Majesty," Madame Dupont said, a tinge of exasperation colouring her voice. "My girls are telling me that the clients feel trapped, and are trying to find a way out while they can."

"Exactly," Virgil Walker added. "When you took the throne, they felt safe and hopeful, but when Elbert returned, that hope turned into fear, and this city into a cage. Now that a bar from the cage is broken, of course the animals are going to escape."

"But we took this city! All of us; it's as much their city as it is mine."

"It seems that the people don't see it that way."

"Or if they do," Cassius chimed in, "then they do not share your willingness to die for it."

"I need to think," Randall said abruptly, rising to his feet to leave.

"Your Majesty," Cassius replied, rising to his feet as well. "We must discuss this further."

"I *said* I need to think!" Randall snapped. Without giving his councillors another word, he exited the war room and wandered the castle hallways, brooding on his betrayal.

How could they do this to me? Randall's thoughts churned as he walked through the empty corridors, his footsteps echoing off the cobblestone walls. *We risked everything together. All I wanted was a better life – for all of us.* He stopped mid-step, the bitter irony of his own words cutting through his thoughts. There was no "us" anymore.

Maeve, Chuckles, Anna – they were dead. Tig had abandoned him, and who knew when, or if, A'Chula would return. The Maggots were gone. His closest friends, the people he had hoped to help the most, were nothing but memories now.

The weight of it all crushed him, as if his heart had been torn from his chest. He was alone, and the realization left him feeling hollow and empty, like the hallways that surrounded him.

The king walked absently for some time, dwelling in the bottomless pit that was his thoughts, before finding himself in front of the large oaken doors of the infirmary. He thought about going inside and visiting Grandmaster Velus, but he didn't know if his heart could take any more disappointment. On the off-chance that Velus' mind had returned to him, Randall wanted to be there to see it. Swallowing his fear, he pushed open the wooden doors to the infirmary and walked up to Velus' bed. The halfling was asleep in his bed, his chest almost imperceptibly rising and falling with each shallow breath.

"Velus?" Randall whispered as he knelt by the bedside. "It's me, Randall."

The halfling's eyes shot open, and immediately locked onto Randall's. Despite looking directly into Randall's eyes, there was no recognition in Velus' gaze. He stared, not at the king, but more through him.

"Velus?" Randall asked in a hushed, shaking voice.

"Tie the knot," the halfling replied in a barely audible whisper. "Flee the flames."

Randall shook his head. "What?"

Suddenly, Velus' eyes shifted and were instantly filled with hatred and rage. "You killed us all!" the mage screamed, as he thrashed against the restraints in his bed. "Swallowed by sword and flame! You did this!"

Velus continued to writhe and spasm, his body contorting as if it was being ripped apart by invisible hands.

"Damn it all!" the physician cursed, running from across the room to his desk, where he grabbed a small syringe full of a clear liquid. "Hold him still!" he instructed as he plunged the needle into the halfling's arm, pushing the mysterious liquid into Velus' veins.

"It burns! It burns!" Velus screamed. "Make it stop! Why did you do this to me? Why... why... why... wh—" The halfling's voice faded to a soft whisper as his body went deathly still.

"Will he ever recover?" Randall asked, backing away from the mage's bed.

The physician shook his head.

"He finally reached his breaking point, I presume," a familiar voice replied from behind them. Randall turned around and saw Cassius approach, with a solemn look on his face. "Magic is like a blade without a hilt – the longer you wield it, the more it cuts you. I'm sorry, Your Majesty, that must have been hard to watch."

"Why are you here?" Randall asked, rising to his feet and backing far away from Velus' bedside.

"You were upset," Cassius replied bluntly. "I wanted to check on you."

Randall's lips quivered, but only for a second, before he swallowed his emotions.

"Come, Your Majesty. I want to show you something."

As the two men exited the room, the physician called out, "What do you want me to do with him?"

Randall paused and turned around. "Keep him asleep until we can find a way to fix him."

After leading Randall down a spiral staircase, deep in the bowels of the castle, Cassius paused at a large stone door. The door had a small iron handle and an iron lock that was covered in a thin layer of dust. Cassius pulled a key from his pocket and inserted it into the lock. With a loud thud, he then pushed the door open, revealing a dark corridor filled with a stale air that stunk of decay.

"What is this place?" Randall asked as he entered the eerily silent room.

"This is the royal crypt," Cassius answered before lighting a torch on the wall. The former sommelier picked up the torch and led the king around the crypt, the small orange glow of the light briefly illuminating each of the sarcophagi as they passed. "All of Artanzia's greatest rulers are within these walls, each of them cementing both their names and legacies into the annals of time."

Cassius led him to a sarcophagus, its stone surface weathered but still remarkable. The lid bore the carved effigy of a man with long, flowing hair, a neatly trimmed moustache, and prominent muttonchops. A handsome face with high cheekbones was clouded with a stern, imposing expression. "Here lies King Eldric the Just. A man of unwavering conviction, whose word was his bond. When reports were received that one of his settlements had an outbreak of the plague, King Eldric ordered for the town to be surrounded and quarantined. No matter how much the sick, dying people begged, he would not waver. Although the entire town perished, it was Eldric's foresight that prevented the plague from spreading, sparing the countryside and saving the kingdom from devastation."

Before Randall could reply, Cassius led him to another sarcophagus. This one depicted a woman. She had short hair and a crooked smile, but despite this, Randall could tell the sculptor still depicted her with an almost divine beauty. "Here is Queen

Elara the Bloody, the only woman to hold Artanzia's crown without a husband."

"The bloody? Sounds charming."

"Two houses warred with one another under her rule," Cassius continued, ignoring Randall's comment. "Hundreds of innocents perished in a needless blood feud. Unable to stop them via royal decree, Queen Elara revoked the two houses of all titles and lands they possessed. And although the two houses had no formal titles, they still had considerable sway in the region and were able to command considerable forces. After exhausting all peaceful resolutions she could think of, Queen Elara ordered the army to seize every member of both houses for execution. Men and women, young and old, all were sent to the chopping block. An extreme decision to some, but after the executions, the kingdom entered a time of peaceful prosperity."

Shuffling further down the crypt, they stopped at one final sarcophagus. Carved into the lid was a man with a weathered, scarred face, with only one hand. "Who's this?" Randall asked, looking at the carving with unease. Unlike the other carvings he had seen, which depicted the rulers with an ethereal beauty, this one was made to strike fear into anyone's heart. This king was a warrior, first and foremost, and he had the scars to prove it.

"Here is King Daelor the Iron Will. He was known for his extreme pragmatism, to the point of being cold. He valued logic over emotion and always considered the needs of the kingdom over the individual needs of his subjects. He is also known as the 'The King Who Burned the Fields'. When the Valerian Empire invaded, looking to expand northward, Daelor ordered his armies to set fire to all the lands and settlements as they retreated. Artanzia dealt with famine after famine, but thanks to Daelor's decision, they remained a free, independent kingdom."

"Why are you showing me this?"

"What do all three kings have in common?"

"They were entitled nobles who didn't care about the people."

"They all made the hard decisions. Decisions that needed to be made for the betterment of the kingdom. That's what makes a good ruler, doing what has to be done. No matter how unpleasant it is."

Randall shook his head. "No, you're wrong. The people—"

"The people's allegiances are as fleeting as the wind," Cassius replied, a tinge of frustration colouring his voice. "They are abandoning you, and do not deserve any reprieve for it. It's about time that you realize that those people are your lessers. You are their king, and sometimes that requires bringing down the hard hand of the law."

Randall clenched his fists. There was a sudden pain in his chest and he clenched his jaw. The people of Artanzia were not his "lessers", they were his people. People who believed in his dream. A dream that they fought, bled, and died for.

Cassius took a step closer, his voice becoming coloured with disgust and cynicism. "You're too soft on them, Your Majesty. Your compassion for these people will be your downfall. They are scarcely better than mindless beasts. When the opportunity presents itself, they will turn on you as quickly as they turned on the nobles. The fact that they openly flee the city is blatant disrespect. They might as well spit in your face. It is time that you show them that their defiance has consequences. With me at your side, we can teach them to fear the crown once again."

There it was. A slight slip of the tongue betrayed Cassius' true nature. He didn't believe in Randall's dream; the eunuch was just using him to reestablish the old order, an order where this time, he was at the top.

"Rosaline told me about Catalonia," Randall replied. A deathly silence filled the crypt as the two men stared at one another. Despite his best attempt to hide it, Randall could see the rage bubbling underneath Cassius' skin.

"That woman is a snake who only values her own skin, I would take everything she says—"

"Funny," Randall interrupted, "she said the same thing about you. She told me everything, and I finally understand now. I hate that it's taken this long, but I get it. You used me, just like you used Catalonia. A means to an end."

"Your Majesty," Cassius said through gritted teeth, "you must listen to me—"

"I am done listening to you!" Randall shouted, his voice reverberating off the empty walls of the crypt. "Ever since I gave you my ear, you've poisoned it. You made me turn against the man who helped raise me, drove a wedge between me and my friends, and made me kill the girl I love." Randall paused, as he tried to steady his voice. "You're right in that a king has to make hard decisions, and this will be my first. Cassius, you are hereby relieved of your post, and I sentence you into exile. If I ever see you again, I will do what Greaver should've done all those years ago. I will take your head." Cassius' complexion paled as the king's words faded into the stone walls of the crypt. With a satisfied smile, Randall turned on his heels and walked back towards the door.

"You can't do this!" Cassius called out. "I made you! You are nothing without me! I'm the reason you have that crown on your head, you little shit. Come back here!"

No matter how much the eunuch raged, Randall refused to turn around. Cassius had outlived his usefulness, and it was time for Randall to start a new chapter of his reign, one where he was clear of mind and free from toxic influence.

CHAPTER THIRTY-SEVEN
GRIMM

After everyone saw that the monstrous wolf was actually Godfrey, the settlement erupted into chaos. Accusations were thrown, threats were made, and the air in the camp became so tense that a person could cut it with a knife. Uriel had calmed tempers and focused on giving Godfrey a suitable burial and funeral. For the next day and a half, the community worked as one in preparing a beautiful ceremony. The men built a pyre, the children gathered flowers, and the women crafted wreaths and bouquets to burn alongside Godfrey's body. Everyone was grieving together as they prepared to say their final goodbyes to Godfrey, all except Grimm. Talsin and his wife, Liza, forbade the Islander from contributing in any way.

Grimm spent his time alone in the forest, trying to stay out of everybody's way. First, he spent a large part of the day finding his stolen belongings. After that, he occupied his mind by chopping trees and tilling the future cropland so it was ready for seeding once it got warm enough. When his day was done, he returned to his hut and sharpened his axe, waiting to see the light from the funeral pyre. Once the sky was pitch black and full of stars, he saw the faint orange glow of the flames illuminate the far side of the camp. He heard the sobbing wails of the mourning party and the crackling of the flames from the pyre.

Grimm stopped what he was doing and offered Godfrey a moment of silent condolence. Once several seconds had passed, Grimm resumed sharpening his axe. Although he had been on countless raids, he had never killed a child. It was a line that he did not think he could cross. But now that he had, it unnerved him just how unbothered by it he was. Perhaps it was because he didn't know it was a child – he told himself he would've acted differently had he known that Godfrey had taken the Beastfolk berserker's mushrooms. But he wasn't sure it would've made a difference. Although he'd never admit it aloud, Grimm had loved the fight with Godfrey. The intoxicating feeling of adrenaline coursing through his body as he faced the monstrous wolf felt like pure ecstasy. Knowing that at any second the breath he just took could be his last... there was no greater feeling in the world. Not only that, but he felt better than he had in months. His body had regained all of its former strength, but this time he was leaner, and while fighting Godfrey, he discovered he was faster on his feet than before.

Eventually the sobbing from across the camp faded, as did the orange glow from the fire. There was a stillness to the evening air as people retired to their homes. Tomorrow was a big day – it was the day that they would decide Grimm's fate. Just as he was about to turn in for the night himself, he heard footsteps approaching. He turned his head and saw the shadow of a woman emerge.

"How was the funeral?" Grimm asked, setting his freshly sharpened axe down.

Isobel smiled before sitting down on the rickety chair beside the Islander. She looked up to the stars silently for some time. Grimm was about to ask again when she finally spoke. "It was sad. No parent should ever have to bury their child. I can't imagine what Liza and Talsin are going through."

"I can," Grimm replied bluntly. "My son, Einar was killed, along with my wife. I had to put both of them to rest before I left the Isles."

Isobel's eyes softened, and she immediately grabbed Grimm's arm and pulled it tight against her chest. She rested her head on his shoulders as they stared into the night. "I'm so sorry, Grimm, I had no idea. What happened?"

"I did. I was the Shield of the Isles, High King Uthredd's right-hand man, and I thought I was untouchable. That I could get away with anything." Grimm paused as the words left his mouth, not sure where they came from. "Heimer has a funny way of teaching us lessons that we need to learn."

Isobel let out a small laugh. "The gods usually do. I also find that they tend to be a bit heavy-handed." She paused for several seconds, turning her head to look at Grimm. "Are you nervous for tomorrow?"

Grimm shrugged. "Whatever happens, happens." He didn't know how to word it, but he wasn't worried in the slightest. He had been dragged behind an army, thrown into kennels, and sentenced to starve while chained to the mast of a ship. Any sentence that these people gave him would pale in comparison to the justice of the Islanders.

Isobel squeezed his muscled arm. "Try not to worry. No matter what happens tomorrow... I know you're a good person. You saved not only Seamus and me, but all of us. You're a hero, Grimm."

Grimm's heart pounded in his chest. Her words, like a physical blow, left him breathless. A muscle in his jaw twitched as he forced a smile, gently pulling his arm free from her grasp. "It's late. I should get some rest."

Isobel nodded before leaning over and giving Grimm a peck on the cheek. "Goodnight, Grimm. Try to get some sleep."

He watched as she walked into the night, back towards the settlement, before going inside his hut, closing the door, and climbing into bed. He stared up at the ceiling and let out a long breath as he thought about what tomorrow would bring. The people would have their trial and their so-called justice. But could you even call it that? Hard labour, exile, servitude? That was not justice, justice was something cold and unforgiving, like the steel of an axe. Grimm doubted he would face any real justice in the morning. He stretched out on his bed, the creaking wood beneath him a familiar comfort. Whatever tomorrow held, it wouldn't keep him awake tonight. With a slow exhale, he closed his eyes, letting the darkness take him without a second thought.

A sudden knock on the door jarred Grimm from his peaceful sleep. Rubbing his eyes, he crawled out of bed and opened the door, seeing a sombre Uriel standing before him with two plates of bread in hand.

"Did you get much sleep last night?" Uriel asked as he gently pushed his way into Grimm's lodgings.

"No," Grimm lied, although he wasn't sure why. He closed the door and joined Uriel at the table in the center of the small hut.

"The tribunal has been formed. Talsin, Gareth, Dominica, and myself will serve as your adjudicators."

Grimm tore off a piece of bread and popped it into his mouth, chewing slowly. "Alright." He gave Uriel a long look, noting the tension in his shoulders. "What else?"

"It's Liza. She's been talking to the others... She wants your blood."

"I thought you hated violence?"

"We do," Uriel said in a grave voice. "But I'm afraid that the tragedy of Godfrey's death has darkened the rays of the Golden Sun. It's... clouding our community's judgement. Many share Liza's sentiment."

A small smile spread across Grimm's lips. Perhaps he would face some *actual* justice today.

"We have had these conversations a lot since Gareth found you half-dead on the shoreline, but it's important that you answer me honestly. Can you live a peaceful life, can you become a civilized member in a society of decent people, or are you too corrupted by the savagery of the Isles?"

Grimm let out an amused snort. "Civility and decency? They're just masks, Uriel. They slip off the moment trouble rears its head. When the world crumbles, it's violence that holds the pieces together."

Uriel shook his head. "And you truly believe that? If that's the case, I don't know what I can say to convince the others not to ask for your head."

"Tell them that if they want my head," Grimm said as he leaned over and grabbed the axe from beside the door and tossed it on the other side of the table, the weapon landing with a heavy *thunk*, inches from Uriel's plate, "they can come take it."

With wide eyes, Uriel stared at the axe before him with an unblinking fear. After several seconds, he curled his nose in disgust, forcefully rose from his chair and made to leave the hut. He paused in the doorway, head hung low. "Someone will come and get you when it's time for the trial. I'll see you there." Without waiting for a response, Uriel closed the door and left.

Shrugging his shoulders, Grimm pulled Uriel's plate next to him and began leisurely popping bits of bread in his mouth with one hand, his finger rhythmically tapping the haft of the axe with the other.

It wasn't long before there was another knock on the door. Grimm rose to his feet with a grunt and opened it. On the other side was Gareth and a few others all holding sticks, pitchforks, or whatever weapons they could get their hands on. The Islander looked at them curiously, raising a brow as he waited for one of them to speak.

"Morning, Grimm..." Gareth said, the shakiness of his voice betraying his nervousness. "It's time."

Voicing no protest, Grimm exited his hut and followed everyone back to the settlement. He looked around at the people surrounding him and tried hard not to laugh at their pathetic display of strength. Had he wanted to, he could've cut through them like a scythe through a field of wheat. It also gave him peace of mind that if the trial ended with the tribunal calling for his head, he would have no problem fighting his way to freedom.

In the middle of the settlement was a large wooden table where Uriel, Talsin, and Dominica were already sitting. The rest of the settlement sat in a large semicircle, eager to see the outcome of the trial. It was eerily quiet as Gareth and Grimm approached the table. Gareth took his seat, and Grimm stood several paces away, staring at his judges with an apathetic expression.

Uriel rose to his feet. "We are gathered here today because tragedy has found its way into our humble community. Blood has been spilt, and not only that, but the blood of a child. The man before you is the one responsible for spilling that child's blood," he paused, surveying the crowd, "but that is not what this trial is about. This trial is going to find out the truth surrounding the claims that Grimm killed the wolf, knowing full well that it was Godfrey, and not some mindless beast terrorizing the settlement." Uriel paused as he looked along the table of judges before giving a solemn nod. "As many of you know, the accused and I have spent considerable time together. Unsurprisingly, because of this, many of you doubt my ability to give a fair and just verdict. That is why I am recusing myself as an adjudicator. Talsin, Gareth, and Dominica will hear Grimm's defense and render the verdict that they see fit."

There were several murmurs in response to Uriel's proclamation, and although he hated to admit it, Grimm's confidence faded slightly. Talsin would undoubtedly sentence Grimm to death, Gareth would vote in favour to spare him, but Dominica could go either way. He had spent hardly any time talking to her, aside from occasionally exchanging pleasantries in passing. He knew nothing about her, aside from the fact she had three little ones, and a head of orange hair that glowed like fire.

Uriel left the table and found a seat beside Isobel and Seamus. Talsin grabbed the small iron hammer and banged it on a small, circular block of wood. "Let's get this over with," he said, his eyes still purple and his nose crooked from where Grimm had punched him. "Grimm White-Eyes, did you kill the wolf knowing full well that it was my son?"

"No."

"Are we truly going to sit here and listen to this farce!?" Liza stood up and shouted. "This man is a murderer, and deserves to be put down like the rabid dog he is!" Suddenly, the commune erupted into a heated debate. Some agreed with Liza and hurled insults at Grimm, while others defended Grimm's actions and argued that killing the Islander was not only wrong, but unwarranted.

Talsin hit the hammer on the circle of wood several times before the crowd calmed down. "Liza," he said, in a surprisingly authoritative voice, "if you cannot keep comments to yourself, this tribunal will ask you to leave." His wife crossed her arms petulantly but voiced no objection.

"Grimm," Gareth said in a sympathetic voice, "what can you tell us about the mushrooms?"

"I took them off one of the dead Islanders who brought me here. He was a member of the Beastfolk clan. I—"

"And how did these Islanders die?" Talsin interrupted. "Did sickness consume them? Was it wild animals?"

"I killed them," Grimm said bluntly, causing several gasps of shock from the crowd.

"And how did you kill them?" Dominica asked in a husky voice.

"I tricked one into giving me a dagger, and the others I killed in their sleep."

"Doesn't sound like it was self-defence," Gareth muttered with a half breath.

"It seems as if we have a habitual murderer on our hands," Talsin added smugly.

Before Grimm could reply, Dominica spoke up. "Let's circle back to these mushrooms. When we asked Godfrey's friends what happened, they said that they found a bag of mushrooms in your lodgings. They then told us that Godfrey ate those mushrooms and transformed into the wolf that you killed. My question is, did it not occur to you that the wolf was one of the boys who had broken into your house? Surely, you had to know that the mushrooms were missing?"

"I knew that the little shits stole from me, but I didn't realize what the mushrooms did."

"You seriously expect us to believe that you had a bag of mushrooms that came from your homeland, and that you had no idea what their effects were?"

"If you would've let me finish before," Grimm growled, "I took those mushrooms off a Beastfolk berserker. The clan is very secretive about their mushrooms and berries, and although there were tales of the warriors transforming into their spirit animals during battle, I never truly believed it. Just tales you tell the kiddies before you put them to sleep, nothing more."

"Grimm, you have had multiple incidents of violence since arriving at the commune," Gareth replied. "Not only have you punched a member of this tribunal, but you have also picked up a child that was not yours by the collar of their shirt and shook them in an altercation that did not involve you. Considering your past indiscretions, do you think you can live peacefully amongst us?"A hush fell upon the settlement, and Grimm glared at the tribunal. He knew that question was not Gareth's but Uriel's. The words were practically the same that Uriel had asked him this morning. The Islander gritted his teeth and stared at Uriel out of the corner of his eye. If the priest expected a different answer, he was sorely mistaken. It was time Grimm was honest with everyone about his true nature, including himself.

"No." Another round of shocked gasps escaped from the crowd, and Talsin once again had to quiet them down with the iron hammer. "I made a promise to someone that I loved – a promise that I would bury the man I once was and try to live a peaceful life. But during my time here, I have learned that I am not a peaceful man." There was a pause, as Grimm felt his frustration start to bubble over. "I was born bloody. When my parents left me alone in the woods, thinking me blind, they found me the next morning on their step covered in blood. Violence is all I have ever known, and all I ever will know. So go ahead – banish me, or if you have the stones, come try to take my head."

The commune erupted into absolute chaos. Talsin hammered the small circle of wood, but he could not restore order. Uriel buried his face in his hands, Isobel had a look of shocked horror on her face, while Liza had a satisfied grin on hers. Grimm stood tall in the eye of the storm, unshaken by the swirling chaos around him, a wolf among sheep.

After several smacks of the hammer, and with Uriel's help, the tribunal finally regained control of the situation. "Grimm," Uriel started, "return to your house. We will summon you once the tribunal has reached a decision."

Shrugging his shoulders, Grimm did as he was told. He walked back to his hut and waited to be summoned. He prepared his things, as he was confident that the tribunal would, at the very least, sentence him to exile. If by some miracle, they sentenced him to something else, he wasn't sure he even wanted to stay. He missed the intoxicating rush of adrenaline, and the pride that came from knowing he'd bested another man in battle. He wanted it, more than he wanted anything else. But he also wanted to keep his promise to Freja. He meant it when he said he wanted to be the man that she always wanted him to be. Unsure of which path he should take, Grimm slowly dropped to his knees, clasped his hands together and prayed.

"Heimer," he whispered, "if you can hear me, I need your steady hand to give me guidance. Show me which path I am meant to take." He allowed his words to fade as he opened his eyes, hoping for an answer. After several seconds with still no response, Grimm readied his things in case the tribunal sent him into exile. He put what few belongings he had in a small, burlap rucksack. Seeing the small axe that he had dropped in front of Uriel earlier that morning, he decided to tuck it discreetly in his belt under his cloak. Once prepared, he sat at the small table, staring at the door, waiting for someone to summon him.

Several hours passed before there was a knock on the door. Grimm opened it up and saw Uriel standing on the other side. "It's time." Nodding in understanding, Grimm closed the door and followed the priest into the settlement, back towards the tribunal table.

"Grimm," Dominica spoke once there was total silence, "where we last left off, your words had sparked much controversy. After a lengthy discussion, the tribunal has come to a verdict." She paused, allowing suspense to build in the air. Just as her lips parted, the jingling of tack and the whinny of horses could be heard clear across the camp. Everyone's head shifted to see several armed, dark-skinned men approach on horses. The caravan of Kovari men also had a wagon equipped with a cage. A cage filled with young boys.

After stopping his horse several feet from the tribunal table, one of the men dismounted, prominently displaying the curved sabre that rested at his hip. He was quite large and wore colourful robes. His head was shaved to the scalp, with the only hair on his head being a well-trimmed beard.

"Well, well, well," the man laughed as he grabbed the hilt of his sabre with one hand. "What do we have 'ere?"

Instantly, Uriel rose to his feet and spoke to him in a throaty language that Grimm had never heard before. Uriel seemed to plead with the bald stranger. The strange man smiled venomously as Uriel continued to beseech him. Grimm looked around and saw the rest of the strange men's hands move towards their weapons. The Islander quietly reached for the axe tucked into his belt and slowly approached the tribunal table while everyone was distracted by the unexpected guests.

Uriel reached out and grabbed the man's silk robes, which instantly evaporated the stranger's smile. The man swatted Uriel's hands away with one hand and pulled out his sabre with the other, slicing Uriel's throat in one fluid motion. Several people screamed in terror as Uriel fell to the ground, clutching his neck as a torrent of blood spurted through his fingers. He writhed on the ground, his wide, pleading eyes locked on to Grimm, desperate and unblinking. As the light within Uriel's eyes faded and the torrent of blood spurting from his neck slowed to a barely perceptible leak, Grimm tore his eyes from Uriel's and glared at the slaver's smug grin. His jaw clenched and his breath slowed, every inhale feeding the storm of rage building within him. His hands trembled with anticipation.

The crowd erupted into chaos, shrieks of terror piercing the air as Uriel's lifeless body lay motionless on the ground. Men scrambled to shield their families, while others shouted for someone to do something. But no one moved – no one except Grimm.

Grimm's hand closed around the iron hammer on the tribunal table, his grip tightening as he slipped it into the folds of his cloak. His eyes burned with cold fury as he stalked toward the stranger, each step measured and deliberate.

The bald man, seemingly unaffected by Grimm's approach, smiled and let out an amused laugh. "My, you are a big one! A bit old for Kovar, but don't worry, my friend, Xerxes will fetch a good price for you!"

It wasn't until Grimm was three feet away that the Kovari man's smile faltered. He shifted his weight, his hands tightening around the sabre's hilt, but his movements were too slow. Grimm quickly threw the concealed hammer, the tool flying through the air until it smashed into the slaver's face. The wet crunch of bone filled the air. The slaver reeled back, blood pouring from his shattered nose, but Grimm gave him no time to recover. With practiced ease, he tore the axe from his belt and swung it in a savage arc. The blade sank deep into the man's neck, biting through flesh and bone with a sickening crunch.

There was the thrum of a bow, and Grimm quickly ducked behind the body of the dying slaver. The barbed head of the arrow burst through Xerxes' chest, mere inches from Grimm's face. The Islander grabbed a fistful of the man's silk robes, heaving Xerxes' dying body up with a laboured grunt. His muscles strained under the weight, but he pushed forward, his rage and bloodlust fuelling him as he used the limp body to shield himself from the arrows that flew toward him.

Two more arrows pierced the slaver's body, one of the arrowheads grazing the top of Grimm's forearm. As he heard the archer reach for another arrow, Grimm tossed Xerxes' corpse aside with one hand and threw his axe with the other. The axe spun end over end in the air until it embedded itself in the archer's chest, causing him to fall lifelessly from his horse.

Two slavers charged, their sabres held high in the air. Now without a weapon, Grimm removed his cloak and held it in his hands. As the slavers closed in, Grimm whipped his cloak at their faces, forcing them to falter. He stepped in fast, seizing the wrist of the nearest attacker and twisting it sharply. The man let out a pained cry as his sabre clattered to the ground. Grimm then kicked out the man's legs from under him. The slaver landed against the ground with a hard thud, wheezing as the air was forcefully expelled from his lungs.

The second man rushed Grimm again, his sword slashing in desperate arcs, each swing more reckless than the last. Grimm quickly back-pedalled, missing the blade's edge by a hair's breadth each time. His eyes watched the man's movements. They were sloppy. It was clear these men were used to attacking innocents who couldn't protect themselves. The slaver thrust his sword forward, and Grimm spun on his toes out of the way until he was behind the attacker. Quickly, Grimm grabbed the man's throat with his calloused hands, and with one fluid motion, snapped his neck.

Behind him, he could hear the gasps for air as the first crawled towards his discarded sabre. Casually, the Islander sauntered over and stepped on the man's back, pinning him to the ground. Grimm picked up the discarded sabre, the weight of the weapon unfamiliar but welcome in his hands. He spun it once, testing its balance, before bringing it down with brutal precision. The blade cleaved through the slaver's skull, splitting bone and flesh in a spray of red. The man's body twitched violently before going still beneath Grimm's foot.

The settlement was completely silent, aside from Grimm's deep breaths. He looked across the field of carnage and saw the shocked and horrified faces of Uriel's colony staring back at him. Several people had passed out, while Talsin and Gareth puked profusely on the ground. He turned around and saw the boys in the cage staring at him with an equal expression of horror and awe.

Stumbling out of the crowd, Isobel approached Uriel's body and knelt down beside it. Grimm had taken a step towards them when Isobel shot up to her feet and quickly backed away.

"Get out of here..." she said in a voice barely audible. Raising a brow, he took another step. "Get out of here!" she screamed. "Get out of here, you monster!"

Grimm stopped in his tracks and looked once again at the crowd of settlers. He saw women comforting sobbing children, and men timidly standing in front of their families. The sight caused a slight pain in Grimm's chest, and his throat tightened. Stomaching his discomfort, Grimm walked over to Xerxes' corpse, took his sabre and began rummaging through the silk pockets. He found a small iron key and a bag full of gold. Tossing the pouch of gold into his burlap sack, he approached the caged boys, who backed away against the iron bars in fear.

One boy was older than the rest and was the only one with dark skin like Uriel and the slavers. Grimm tossed the boy the key and nodded his head. The boy returned the gesture but said nothing.

As Grimm walked away from the camp, he turned around to get one final look at the peaceful chapter of his life. He had prayed for a sign, and Heimer had answered. He sent these slavers here with a clear message. Grimm was supposed to die with a sword in his hand, not old and alone on a comfy bed.

INTERLUDE PART 1
LORD GRELIN

The canvas of the tent billowed slightly in the evening breeze. The audible and rhythmic thumping of the thick fabric hitting the wooden posts nearly drove him mad. Lord Grelin massaged his temples, trying to ease some of the stress, but it was to no avail. It felt like his head was going to burst at any second, which at this point would be a blessing. He eyed the nearly empty case of stolen Islander mead in the corner of his tent. When they left Tjørholm, he had planned on saving it for a special occasion, but now it was the only thing that allowed him to keep a semblance of sanity. The flap of the tent opened, and Lord Penerack, acting commander of the army in King Elbert's absence, poked his head in.

"What now?" Lord Grelin growled as he rose from his chair and pulled out the second-to-last bottle of mead from the case.

"The situation is turning dire, Franklin," Lord Penerack explained, joining Lord Grelin at his desk.

Using my first name? We must be in trouble, Grelin thought as he poured both of them a cup of the mead. "Every day more men are deserting, we are stone broke, and our king is missing, most likely dead. *Dire* is an understatement," Grelin replied, taking a sip from his cup.

"Our scouts have now reported that a large mass of soldiers are approaching from the east," Penerack added gravely, swirling the mead around his cup.

"It's not wine, Gus, you can just drink the swill."

Penerack's face contorted into a frown. "I miss wine." The lord paused for a minute before taking a sip, immediately recoiling at the taste. "Reports indicate the army is coming from Keten."

"Ketenish bastards," Grelin growled. "They'll make quick work of us. We've lost nearly a quarter of our forces to desertion, and the men that *are* here are blatantly insubordinate. The boy king has a better chance at fighting Keten with his mob of peasants than we do."

"Still no word from the search party?"

"You know as well as I do that they haven't found anything, Gus. They found a company of royal guardsmen ambushed and slaughtered, but no sign of Elbert. He's probably halfway to the Forsaken Lands by now."

Penerack smiled. "Not a bad life, being a pleasure slave to those dark-skinned goddesses."

"He's a cripple, Gus. Won't be doing much pleasuring when his cock doesn't work."

"There are more ways to please a woman than just by using your cock, Franklin."

"Please. Every woman wants to be fucked. Everything else pales in comparison."

"Your poor wife, I feel sorry for her."

"Don't," Grelin replied, "it won't be long until she hears of my demise at the hands of some lowly Ketenish foot soldier. Then she'll be free to discover all those other ways to be pleased that I never bothered to learn." The two men chuckled slightly before an unnerving silence fell over the tent. The only sound, besides the occasional sip of mead, was the rhythmic thumping of the tent's canvas against the support posts. After enduring the silence for long enough, Grelin set his drink down. "What are we going to do, Gus?"

Lord Penerack also set his drink down and leaned back in his chair. "I'm not sure. We don't have a lot of options."

Suddenly, a page burst through the flap of the tent, gasping for air. "Your lords!" the page wheezed. "We... we... we..."

"Out with it, boy!" Lord Grelin shouted.

"We captured a man trying to enter our camp. He is asking to speak to King Elbert. He is wearing Ketenish colours."

"Bring him to us at once," Lord Penerack ordered gravely.

The three men sat silently in the tent, staring at one another, while a group of soldiers rummaged through the envoy's bag. Despite being in an enemy camp, the Ketenish man showed no fear or worry on his face. He was young, well below twenty years of age, and had a small clump of peach fuzz at the bottom of his chin. After a long and thorough investigation, the soldiers returned the man's bag to him.

"All clear, Your Lords. No weapons," one of the men grunted bluntly. Lord Penerack nodded his head in thanks and dismissed the guards, leaving him and Grelin alone with the envoy."What brings you to our camp?" Lord Penerack began.

"I was instructed to deliver my message to King Elbert, and only King Elbert."

"King Elbert is indisposed," Grelin retorted. "If you haven't noticed, he is busy planning a siege. Now speak, while you still have a tongue."

Lord Penerack glared at Grelin out of the corner of his eye, but he didn't care. People from Keten were tricksy people, who almost always lied. Grelin didn't trust this boy as far as he could throw him.

The boy pointed to his bag. "May I?"

The two lords gave each other confused looks, but eventually conceded and nodded in permission. The boy then began rummaging around the bag and pulling out long pieces of brass, assembling them until they formed a large, pedestal-like structure. He then pulled a small crystal from his pocket, placed it at the top of the pedestal, and secured it into place.

With his hands around the crystal, the envoy whispered something before the crystal pulsated with a pale blue light. Three orbs floated around the pedestal, connected by a thin beam of light.

Out of the corner of his eye, he saw Lord Penerack reach for the knife tucked into his belt. And although Grelin didn't trust anyone from Keten, he knew that whatever the envoy was building was not a weapon. Had the mage wanted to kill them, he would have done so already. Just as Penerack's blade was sliding out of its scabbard, Grelin reached out and grabbed the younger lord's wrist firmly. "Patience," he whispered. "If he meant us harm, we would've been dead already."

Lord Penerack gave Grelin a wary glance, but ultimately relented and tucked his knife back into the sheath.

The envoy adjusted the crystal, and the blue light shifted to a blinding orange. The air began to hum and vibrate with magic. Grabbing a small piece of parchment from his coat, the envoy tossed it into an orb, the piece of paper vanishing in a puff of smoke.

Moments later, the orbs went still and turned green. They collided and a window of light opened. On the other side was a middle-aged man wearing elegant clothes and an ostentatious crown. He had a smug smile on his face, but upon seeing Lord Grelin and Lord Penerack, the smile quickly faltered.

"Who are you? I instructed my envoy to bring my message to King Elbert directly!"

The envoy parted his lips to speak, but Lord Penerack quickly rose to his feet before words could escape the boy's mouth. "As we explained to your man, King Elbert is currently indisposed. We are his top advisors, and he trusts us to act as an extension of himself during meetings and assemblies he cannot attend."

"Hmm," King Kalvin laughed, "if King Elbert is too busy to correspond with me, perhaps I need to rethink my plan of offering him aid."

"Aid?" Lord Grelin snarled. "Who says we need your help?"

A sly smile appeared on the foreign king's face as he locked eyes with Grelin through the portal of light. "From what I can gather, you are in quite the predicament," King Kalvin said in a slow, deliberate meter. "King Elbert's throne has been usurped, by a filthy commoner, no less. And your army is in disarray. My men have observed desertion, and it wasn't until recently that your scouts discovered our presence, which leads me to believe that your men are no longer taking their posts seriously. My army has been within a day's ride from your camp for weeks now, and yet, there seems to be no acknowledgement of our presence."

"Perhaps that's because we aren't scared of an army made up of Ketenish cowards."

King Kalvin's smile curled into a frown. "Gentlemen, please, let's cut the horseshit. Let's not pretend like everything I just said isn't true and that King Elbert's siege to reclaim his city and crown isn't a total disaster. I am here to offer help."

"How did you even find out about the boy king?" Lord Penerack asked.

Grelin thought it was a fair question, but Kalvin only chuckled. "Because news of this debacle is everywhere. A commoner took the crown. It spread like wildfire. I'd be surprised if the savages in the Forsaken Lands haven't heard by now."

He leaned forward, his tone sharpening. "And then I got a letter from someone in Randall's court, confirming the rumors and proposing an alliance – marriage, even. A peasant king, asking to wed into a royal line." He scoffed. "At first, I played along. I was curious. Any man who rises that far from the gutter deserves a second look."

Kalvin paused, the smile draining from his face. "But curiosity faded. Because Randall isn't just a bold upstart – he's dangerous. If my people see him wearing a crown, they'll start thinking *anyone* can rule. That the gods no longer choose kings, that blood doesn't matter. And that kind of thinking?" He tapped the table. "It spreads. Like rot."

"So you came here to stop it," Lord Grelin said.

"I came here to cut it out," Kalvin replied. "Before it festers."

"Aid rarely comes for free. What are you asking in return?" Lord Penerack asked.

"Randall has made me an offer, a percentage of Artanzia's lumber yield for coming to his aid. I only ask that King Elbert matches this percentage and honours it in full, indefinitely. I also ask that my men, should you accept our aid, have their own autonomy. They will fight, bleed, and die beside your men, but I cannot have Artanzians ordering my people around."

"That's it?" Lord Grelin asked.

"That is it. I expect to hear a decision by dusk tomorrow. Give King Elbert my best – perhaps we can speak face to face next time, as allies."

Suddenly, the portal of light disappeared, and the air became still. The envoy quickly and adeptly began dismantling the device. "When you reach a decision with the king," the mage said as he began returning pieces of brass back into his bag, "please send a rider to our camp, and I will return to reassemble the megascope." Once the device had been completely dismantled, the envoy gave a deep bow and left the two lords alone in the tent.

"Fuck sakes," said Lord Grelin as he walked over to his desk and poured himself another glass of mead."What choice do we have, Franklin?" Lord Penerack said in a hushed voice.

"We have the choice to not work with those Ketenish bastards!" Grelin snarled before slamming back the cup of mead in one gulp. "My father lost a leg fighting those pricks, I'll be damned if I have to fight beside them to retake our – *our* – city!"

"You said it yourself – we don't stand a chance against them. We need to be practical. This is the only way we get King Elbert back onto the throne. His demands are excessive, but still reasonable given our situation."

"What about his men operating independently of ours? What happens when the Ketenish soldiers don't want to breach the walls? How do we explain to our men that they must die when our so-called allies won't do the same?"

"Franklin..." Penerack began.

"You are inviting a succubus into bed, Gus," Grelin said in a defeated voice. "This is a bad idea."

Lord Penerack cleared his throat and straightened his back. "Your counsel is much appreciated, Lord Grelin, but as acting commander of this army, this is my decision to make, and I say we accept King Kalvin's offer."

Grelin bit his tongue in frustration, but bowed his head in understanding. Without another word, Lord Penerack exited the tent. Lord Grelin collapsed into his chair and stared at the canvas roof as it rippled and thumped against the wooden support beam. "We might regain our city, but we are going to lose our men."

INTERLUDE PART 11
CASSIUS

Hidden above the attic of Madame Dupont's den of sin was a small room covered with exotic tapestries, lavish furniture, and masterful artwork. In the center of the room was a large bed with silk sheets. A luxurious leather couch and a cloth armchair sat along the opposite wall, facing the bed. In between the bed and the far wall was a circular table adorned with a carafe of wine and a burning stick of incense. The room was strictly reserved for distinguished guests who demanded privacy above all else. Cassius sat down at the table and wiggled his nose, desperately trying to stave off a sneeze as the smoke from the incense drifted up his nostrils. Soft moans of ecstasy could be heard through the wooden floorboards, the perfect mask for the conversation at hand.

"Are you going to tell me why we are here?" Cassius asked impatiently, as he fanned his hand in front of his face.

Sensing Cassius' discomfort, Madame Dupont extinguished the stick of incense and moved it off the table, placing it on the bedside end table. She then took her place back at the table across from Cassius. "We are still waiting for Virgil and Corbin," the madam said calmly as she poured herself a glass of wine. "It must be frustrating being in a whorehouse and not being able to... *indulge* yourself."

A forced smile appeared on Cassius' lips. "I assure you, Amelia, that there is no frustration at all."

An expression of smug amusement appeared on Madame Dupont's face, but before she could give a likely snarky reply, the door to the room opened. Virgil Walker and Corbin Strongarm walked in and took seats at the table.

"Now that everyone is here," Cassius began, "care to tell me what this is all about?"

Madame Dupont folded her hands together and cleared her throat. "Let's be blunt. Your experiment has failed, Cassius. Randall is not under your thumb like you said he would be, and I hear rumours he cast you into exile."

Cassius curled his lips into a sneer. He did not need a reminder of his humiliation in the crypt.

"If Randall will not be our puppet, then we have no use for him," Virgil Walker interjected.

"Let's not be hasty," Corbin Strongarm replied. "Although Cassius failed in getting Randall's ear, he did a good job in driving a wedge between the king and his closest friends. Randall's isolated. Perhaps one of us could sway him, succeed where Cassius couldn't?"

"No." Cassius' voice was firm as he rose to his feet, pacing the room like a caged predator. "Randall's no fool. He knows I hand-selected each of you, and because of that, he will trust none of you. To make matters worse, it seems that Rosaline has poisoned him against me, which in turn, poisons him against you." Cassius paused as he looked at his three conspirators with a heavy stare. "Virgil is right. We must kill Randall before he ruins everything."

"How do you propose we do that?" Madame Dupont asked. "You are supposed to be in exile, and if he doesn't trust us, we will never get close enough. What about that boy in the cellar?"

Cassius' mind turned to Tig, who was currently bound and gagged in the brothel's basement. After his fight with Randall, Cassius had snuck into Tig's room and laced his wine with a sleeping elixir. Once the boy was under the effects of the potion, Cassius and Corbin Strongarm snuck him out of the castle and into the basement of the brothel. "No," he said after pulling himself from his fantasy. "Tig is loyal, and would never turn on Randall. He is the king's oldest friend."

"I have ways of making people co-operate," Virgil Walker growled maliciously. "Give me a night with him, and he'll do exactly what we tell him."

Cassius shook his head. "No, I have someone else in mind, someone perfect for the job. And I know exactly where to find him."

The decayed building rested, half collapsed, against Winterhelm's sturdy stone walls. Charred pieces of wood showed that the building had recently been set aflame, but the bones of the former alehouse remained, as if defiant to the fickle passing of time. Ensuring his hood was pulled discreetly over his head, Cassius approached the building and peered inside the empty doorway. Filly's Flophouse was once an iconic tavern in Winterhelm, not because of its distinguished guests or refined decor, but because the swill was the cheapest in the city. If you only had three coins to your name, you could get always get at least three drinks at Filly's. Cassius had only visited the establishment once before, and that was enough. He remembered that there was a thick film of something on all the surfaces. It appeared to be dust until he touched it and realized it was damp. It was as if the entire tavern was sweating. He also remembered the smell. He could never place his finger on what exactly it was, but calling it putrid would be an understatement. In truth, he did not miss Filly's Flophouse one bit, and was glad to see it gone. However, some people had sentimental attachments to the fetid bar, like the man he was meeting.

A sudden creak alerted the eunuch that he was not alone. Underneath his cloak, he slowly grasped the handle of his knife.

"Who goes there?" a slurred voice called out from behind the damaged bar, which, by some miracle, was still standing.

"A friend. I've come to offer you a job."

A growl emerged from behind the bar. "I don't have any friends."

"I remember you used to come here often, when you used to live in the city," Cassius continued, ignoring the man's disbelief. "I remember how people said that, even though it was Filly's name outside, it was actually your bar." Cassius paused as he found a scorched chair in the middle of the room. He dusted off the seat and sat down. The old chair creaked under the eunuch's weight. "You have fallen quite far since those days."

The man stood up from behind the counter, a shattered wine bottle held tightly in his hands. His face was cut and bruised, and his skin was covered in dried blood. "Who are you?" the man said, taking a step out from behind the bar.

Swiftly, Cassius tossed a small leather bag at the bar. The pouch landed with a loud clink, and several gold coins spilled out of the top and across the counter. The man's eyes stared at the bag, his eyes glittering like stars as he stared at the coins.

"Like I said," Cassius replied, "I want to hire you. I believe we can help each other."

After several seconds, the man tore his eyes away from the sack of gold and back towards the eunuch. "What do you need me to do?"

"I need you to take care of someone for me. Some—"

"You mean killin'?" the man replied.

Cassius pinched the bridge of his nose. *Simpleton.* "If you must word it so crudely."

"Who?"

"Randall, the king."

The man's eyes went wide, and he took a step back before pausing as he looked at the gold once again. Cassius could see the man's lip quiver as he eyed the coin, his hands trembling with anticipation.

"That's only half. The other half is when the job is complete."

"How am I supposed to touch him? He's a king."

Cassius threw back his hood, revealing his face. "My contacts will get you inside. They are aware of the king's comings and goings. We'll give you the opportunity. We just need you to do what you do best."

The man smiled upon seeing the eunuch's face, his teeth rotten and black with decay. "It's been a while, Cassius. I'll do it on one condition – you help me kill that cunt Rosaline."

"When I heard you were in the city, I figured it had something to do with her."

"That bitch took everything from me... so, you'll help me?"

The eunuch smiled and stood up, donning his hood back over his head. "Of course, Blacktooth, that's what friends are for."

ACT III

CHAPTER THIRTY-EIGHT
ROSALINE

There was going to be hell to pay. It wasn't surprising that Blacktooth had followed them into Winterhelm before Elbert's army had encircled the city. The man was never one to forgive a grudge. However, the fact that Blacktooth knew where they were staying only meant one thing. There was a rat. Someone had betrayed her, and that person had thrown their entire operation in jeopardy. Not only had they told Blacktooth, but they could go to Randall or Cassius at any time and turn over the Brotherhood. This had to be resolved quickly. Rosaline sent the Brothers to Blacktooth's usual hiding places, knowing full well they wouldn't find him. She just needed time alone to think, free from the traitors surrounding her. The only problem was that she didn't know who had stabbed her in the back.

The most likely person was Malek – he was Blacktooth's oldest friend and had been his right-hand man during the old regime. The two of them had practically founded the Bloody Brotherhood together. However, Malek supported Rosaline's takeover of the Brotherhood, and had never given her a reason to doubt his loyalty prior to now. Then there was Phillip, a kindred spirit with Blacktooth. Both men's ambitions were solely based on finding something to fuck. That shared desire often led the men into conflict during the old days, though, as Phillip often got the scraps of their spoils, only after Blacktooth got to taste them first, which undoubtedly created a seed of resentment in Phillip. Jathan was unlikely to be behind the betrayal. After how much Blacktooth had tormented and abused him in the past, she thought it was almost impossible that he would ally himself with his former boss. However, Jathan was at the bottom of the pecking order, and if he helped Blacktooth become leader of the Bloody Brotherhood again, his voice just might carry more weight. The last Brother was the least likely, Duncan. Blacktooth had made it known how much he despised nonhumans, and during his time as the Brotherhood's leader, Duncan was often the scapegoat for when a job went wrong, even when in reality it was most likely Blacktooth's fault. However, Duncan was smart. That royal education taught the half-elf to play all angles. If allying with Blacktooth would somehow benefit him, Rosaline wouldn't put it past Duncan.

Of course, there was the small possibility that the traitor was not actually a Brother at all. Stitch, Fletcher, and Clarice all had history with the bandit leader. Stitch and Fletcher obviously knew Blacktooth from working in the Garden; all three of them had a long relationship with one another and old allegiances could spark given the opportunity. Next was Clarice, and although the mage hated Blacktooth, Rosaline was sure that she hated her more. Clarice was vindictive, and if she knew helping Blacktooth would bite Rosaline in the ass, Clarice wouldn't hesitate.

Finding Blacktooth was a moot point, though, as Duncan had previously reported that slavers had captured King Elbert and now there were mutterings of a foreign army approaching. Their window was closing fast, and she needed to either find Blacktooth right away, or cut her losses and leave the city with her fortune.

Twirling Boris around in her fingertips, she let out an exasperated breath. She stared at the doorway of the tavern and waited for someone, anyone, to return from their search. She grabbed the bottle of red wine in front of her and took a sip. She looked at Fletcher out of the corner of her eye, trying to see any sense of nervousness about him. But the man was stoic as ever, just standing behind a bar and polishing a glass. Churning her brain, she tried to remember anything that might point to him as the person behind Blacktooth's freedom. But there was nothing. Every time the man spoke it was only a syllable long, save for three occasions, and he was never greedy. He seemed content getting paid to serve drinks. Was there more to the stoic barkeep, or was Rosaline being paranoid? Suddenly, the door to the tavern swung open and Jathan, Duncan, and Phillip walked in, heads held low.

"Give me a drink, Fletch, I'm parched!" Phillip bellowed as he plopped down in a chair across from Rosaline. Duncan and Jathan stood at the bar, noticeably keeping their distance from Rosaline.

"Did you find him?"

Phillip shook his head. "He's not at any of the brothels on the Corridor of Pleasure."

"Nobody's seen him at the docks," Jathan added.

"I checked all the old hideouts and no sign of him," Duncan said, grabbing a freshly poured whiskey.

Rosaline shook her head. "That prick is still in this city, somewhere. Where's Malek?"

"Dunno," Phillip shrugged. "Perhaps I should check the brothels again."

Rosaline pushed her chair back forcefully and kicked the edge of the table, sending the wood right into Phillip's gut. In a flash, she was beside Phillip, grabbing him by the hair on the back of his head and slamming his head repeatedly into the table. Blood spattered against the wood and the floor as Phillip's nose crunched against the tabletop. Jathan and Duncan took a step forward, but Rosaline glared daggers in their direction. Sensing it was enough, she tossed Phillip's head back, sending the man sprawling to the floor. She bent down on one knee and lifted the man's battered face with the tip of her blade. "That's all you fucking think about, is it?" she seethed, breath hot with hate. "If I have to hear about your cock one more time, I will cut it off myself and shove it down your throat. Then, I'll carve out your eyes and shove your balls into the sockets. Do I make myself clear?"

Phillip nodded his head and spat a mouthful of blood onto the floor.

"Then make yourself useful and go fucking find him!"

With a grunt, Phillip picked himself off the floor and stumbled out of the tavern, Jathan closely following him. Duncan was the only one who stayed, a look of disappointment colouring his eyes. He took a step towards Rosaline before she shook her head. "Don't." Duncan clenched his fists, but did as he was told. He turned on his heels and left the tavern.

Rosaline stared at the scene before her. Blood and red wine mixed together on the tabletop and the floor, where there were also now two turned-over chairs. There was an uncomfortable silence. She knew that if Blacktooth was going to be found, it had to be her. Tucking Boris back into his sheath, she exited the tavern at a frantic pace.

Walking through the city, she kept her eyes focused, scanning the streets for any sign of Blacktooth. Winterhelm was the largest city in Artanzia and with no direction, finding Blacktooth, and more importantly, the person who betrayed her, could prove to be an impossible task. Wandering around aimlessly wasn't the answer, but she couldn't rely on anyone else. Right now, Rosaline could only trust herself. Her walking took her to the Corridor of Pleasure, then to Merchants' Square, then the Upper City. There was no sign of Blacktooth, or really anyone for that matter. Winterhelm's streets were always packed with people, but now they seemed empty. There was actually room to breathe. It wasn't until she reached the docks that it all made sense. Ships lined the harbour and crowds of people were clamouring to get aboard. There was screaming, shouting, shoving, and occasionally fistfights broke out. The city had descended into chaos; everyone was clamouring to get out of the cage. She had heard people were fleeing the city, and it seemed that the rumours of a foreign army approaching had spurred the people into a frenzy. Another reason to get out of the city while they could.

Watching the spectacle from a distance, Rosaline noticed a woman in a hooded cloak weaving her way through the crowds of people. Despite not being able to see her face, Rosaline recognized the woman as the one that she had caught Cassius with on the night she burnt down the sailor's ship. Intrigued by Cassius' lackey, Rosaline followed from a distance. The woman stopped away from the crowd and met with the dwarven dockmaster. Then a gruff-looking man with a city guard uniform on joined the two. The man whistled and a handful of city guards charged towards the docks and dispersed the crowds. Rosaline watched the unlikely trio slink away into a nearby warehouse before hearing one of the guardsmen shout at the crowd of people.

"Hold! His Majesty, King Randall, implores you all to reconsider!" His voice was rigid and monotone. "He calls for every citizen to make their way to the palace; he wishes to hold an audience. Do not throw away all that we have gained together! Listen to your king speak; he has fought alongside you, bled for this city as we all have. Let us stand by his side once more!"

Rosaline wasn't sure which was more comical, the stiff and nearly lifeless way the guardsman recited the king's words, or that Randall was naïve enough to believe that he could still rule over these people as an equal.

The crowd slowly dispersed, their faces filled with worry and desperation as they made their way back into the city. Whether it was the king's stirring words, or the line of armed guards blocking the docks, she couldn't say which was the stronger motivator.

Slipping through the thinning masses, she made her way to the warehouse that she had seen the unlikely trio enter. The building was old and weathered, but besides the rust coating the steel doors, seemed to be in decent condition. A crate of boxes lined the far side of the building, and at the top was a cracked, dirty window. Moving with a practised ease, Rosaline climbed the crates and perched outside, straining to hear the ongoing conversation inside.

"Are we sure about this?" the dwarven man asked, wringing his hands together. "Can we trust someone like him?"

"We made an agreement with Cassius," the woman said bluntly. "He's always delivered on his promises." A laugh began to creep out of Rosaline's lips, but she quickly stomached it back down.

"I'm not talking about Cassius," the dwarf replied. "Can we really trust someone like him to get the job done?"

"Corbin's right, Amelia," the gruff-looking man with the permanent scowl on his face interjected. "He has a certain reputation surrounding him."

"What else are we supposed to do?" Amelia snapped. "Not only did Randall banish Cassius, now he won't even listen to us. We *told* him not to hold this audience, but here you are, Virgil – sending your guards to drag people back to the palace, anyway."

"Maybe we'll get lucky," Corbin suggested. "Maybe one of the commoners will take matters into their own hands."

Virgil shook his head. "We need the boy gone. The sooner, the better."

Rosaline had heard enough. Carefully, she climbed down off the crates and quickly hurried back towards the Garden. This city was about to burn, and she needed to make sure she wasn't caught in the fire.

The sound of muffled voices from inside the tavern told Rosaline that everyone had returned. However, what she didn't expect was Malek sitting on the steps to the inn waiting for her outside. Alone. The two locked eyes as she approached, but said nothing. Knowing that he had something to say, she stopped a few feet away and stared at him with a growing impatience.

"Did you find him?"

"The Brothers told me what happened to Phillip," Malek replied, clearly ignoring Rosaline's question.

"Are you going to lecture me, Mal? That it?"

"Roz—"

"Don't fucking start," Rosaline growled. "Now tell me, did you find Blacktooth?"

A sour sneer appeared on Malek's lips, and after several seconds he shook his head. "No. I checked Filly's Flophouse, and the place is nothing more than a pile of ash. Someone was staying there, but can't be sure it was him. Either way, they're not there anymore."

Rosaline swallowed her disappointment. "Get inside. We need to talk."

Once back inside the tavern, Rosaline whistled for the rest of the Brotherhood to gather. She ordered Fletcher to pour a round of drinks, and served each of the Brothers a pint, deliberately giving Phillip his drink last. Then she sat down at the table and took a sip. She could feel the anxious tension building in the room. After a refreshing drink, she set her mug down with a loud thud. "We have come to a crossroads," she began. Her eyes scanned each of her Brothers, looking for any sign of guilt or anxiety on their faces. "While I was out, trying to do your job, I came across an interesting conversation. It seems Randall has banished Cassius from court and now the rest of his advisors are turning on him as well. From what I heard, I assume they plan to kill him."

"Shit," Duncan and Malek said in unison.

"So?" Phillip grunted through a broken nose. "What's this gotta do with us?"

"It means our goose is almost cooked," Malek explained. "We need to get out of the city while we still can. Fuck Blacktooth, let's take our gold and piss off. No need to make a bad situation worse."

"So just let that fucker walk free so he can bite us in the ass later?" Jathan snarled. "No, I want to see that bastard flayed. We should've killed him the first time."

Duncan let out a sigh. "As much as I want to see Blacktooth dead, Malek's right. If we stay trying to tie up loose ends, we may miss our chance to leave. We've been lucky so far that Elbert's men haven't tried to breach the walls yet. The last thing we need is a new king who will only complicate things further."

"How much gold we got, Fletch?" Phillip asked, leaning back.

"Lots," Fletcher said, in his familiar monotone.

"Let's put it to a vote," Rosaline said after an uncomfortable silence. "Do we take our loot and run? Or do we fix this Blacktooth problem once and for all?"

"Even if we do run," Jathan interjected, "how are we going to get out of here? The city is surrounded by Elbert's army, and do we really want to chance it with the ships? Lots of the people we robbed will be on those ships – what if we are recognized?"

There was some murmuring and muttering at the table at the young Brother's remarks.

"What about the slave tunnels?" Duncan said. "That fellow who claimed to have King Elbert had to sneak into the city some way."

"Won't work," Malek replied plainly. "Only slavers know those tunnels, and they are a maze to get through. They are designed for people to get lost in if you don't already know the route."

Suddenly, the low, hearty chuckle of Phillip filled the room. The man winced with every throaty chortle, his belly rising and falling with each laugh. "Well, well, well," he said, a sly grin appearing on his face. "Looks like ol' Phillip is going to save everyone's asses, again."

"What the fuck are you talking about, Phil?" Rosaline asked, pinching her brow in frustration.

The smug smile on Phillip's face quickly turned venomous as he locked eyes with his leader. "You know those brothels I spend all my time at? The very reason you cheap-shotted me earlier today? Well, just so happens, those brothels occasionally get slaves. And when I was in one today, looking for Blacktooth, I noticed a man with dark skin and a gold tooth drinking in the lounge."

"Get to the point," Jathan sighed.

"The man's a slaver, I'd bet my entire share on it. If I can lay on the ol' Phillip charm, I'm sure he can lead us through the tunnels."

"Your charm?" Duncan asked in disbelief. "We're fucked."

Phillip glared at the half-elf, but Rosaline quickly intervened. "What brothel was this?"

"The Harpy's Nest."

"Go," Rosaline ordered. "Set a meeting up. We need to leave tonight. Tell him to name his price."

"Seriously?" Malek asked.

Rosaline shrugged. "If he asks for too much, we'll just slit his throat and take our gold back." This received a few laughs and smiles at the table. As Phillip rose to his feet, Rosaline turned her thoughts to the one problem that they couldn't outrun – who had betrayed her?

CHAPTER THIRTY-NINE
RANDALL

Dark clouds loomed overhead, painting the sky a miserable grey. Flags and banners billowed atop the ramparts against the howling wind, their poles bending against the strong gale. Randall's fingers curled against the rough and porous limestone of the crenellations. Despite the cooling breeze, a fiery rage burned inside his chest as he looked at the army that had been outside his gates for the last month. He had looked at Elbert's army countless times in the past, but this time was different. Now he saw the banners of both Artanzian and Ketenish nobility. King Kalvin had betrayed him. Not only did the man lie to his face, but he had joined the enemy. Randall knew it was a mistake trying to negotiate with nobles. Why did he think they would ever listen to him? He was a threat to their rule, a threat to the status quo. Cassius had made a fool of him. The king's tense hands turned into fists as he thought about his former advisor. He tried to steel the anger in his heart, reassuring himself that with Cassius banished, he would be free of toxic influence, but he knew this was not true. Cassius was not a man to fade into obscurity. There was no doubt in the king's mind that the eunuch was still in the city, and still pulling the strings of the remaining councillors.

The loud, metallic clanks of armoured footsteps ascending the battlement stairs stirred the king from his thoughts. He turned around and saw a guardsman, red in the face, standing at a crisp salute. "They are ready for you," he said, in an airy, exhausted voice.

"Are we ready at the barracks?" the king asked, casting Elbert and Kalvin's armies one last look over his shoulder.

The guard nodded. "The men have received your instructions and are prepared to carry out your orders. Captain Walker instructed us to—"

"Captain Walker does not have the people's best interest at heart. I do." Randall turned and placed a hand on the wheezing guard's shoulder. "Do exactly as I instructed, and I promise everything will be fine. I will deal with Captain Walker myself."

Nodding his head, the guard took a sharp intake of breath and descended the spiral staircase back towards the throne room. Randall waited several seconds before following. The only thing stronger than his anger was his anxiety. The beginning of his rule had not gone as he had planned. He had lost friends, the people's support in him had wavered, and now he was surrounded by Cassius' vipers. He was totally and utterly alone. What he wouldn't give to have Tig or A'Chula by his side once more. Truth be told, there was really only one person who he wished he had right now: Anna. It wasn't until he was free of Cassius' venom that he realized how much he valued her presence during the uprising. Randall knew that he would have blood on his hands when he stole the crown, he just didn't think so much of it would be his friends'.

A hushed murmur of voices echoed throughout the marbled throne room until the doors opened. Everyone turned in unison and watched as Randall walked through the middle of the crowd and up the dais to his throne. He slowly took his seat and said nothing. He looked out at the crowd of people and saw their faces. They were coloured with fear, hunger, worry, anger. Clearing his throat, Randall let out a sigh and took the crown off his head.

"I've failed you." His voice echoed through the hall, cutting through the murmurs. "I thought we could build a future where no one would go hungry, where power belonged to all of us and not just a select few. I believed we could forge a kingdom where the strong helped the weak, instead of preying upon them. A kingdom where a man would rise in status by merit, and not the status of his birth. I was a fool. I thought taking this city would be the end; I see now that it is the beginning."

His words hung in the air, his fingers tightening around his crown.

"I don't blame you for wanting to run. All your lives, you've been caught in someone else's war, used as pawns, as bodies to be thrown into the mud. But hear me now – this is not someone else's war. This is *our* war. This is the moment we decide if we are truly free, or if we are still the worthless maggots they believe us to be."

Randall stepped forward, pointing towards the doors that led back into the city. "Look at the banners beyond these walls! Those armies do not come to liberate you. They come to put the chains back around your necks. They come to punish you for daring to take what you were owed. They do not seek justice, they seek vengeance."

The king's voice grew sharper and louder.

"You think they will spare your families if you flee? You think they will let you live in peace? No! They will hang you in the streets as a warning to the next man who dares to dream of a life beyond the gutter. They will burn this city to the ground, and laugh as the flames melt our bones."

Randall held the crown high in the air. "I will not let that happen. I will fight. Not for this throne, not for some noble's game, but for every man, woman, and child who dares to want the life that they are owed! If you must go, go. I will not stop you. I will not be a tyrant. But, if you have ever held a sword in your hand, if you have ever burned with the rage of injustice, if you have ever dreamed of a life where your fate is your *own* – then stand with me now. Not as subjects, but once again as brothers and sisters in arms. Fight with me, and we will show the world that people of Winterhelm. Do. Not. Kneel!"

The crowd of people in the throne room cheered and raised their fists high in the air. Randall stood before them, his chest heaving. He placed the crown once more upon his head and raised a silencing hand. "Report to the barracks," he instructed. "Each neighbourhood will be its own battalion, with a rotation of responsibilities among all of the neighbourhoods. The guards will arm you, train you, and prepare you once again." The people cheered once more. A smile appeared on the king's face as he descended the dais and walked through the sea of people, their hands reaching out and touching him as he walked past.

The crowd of people followed their king into the courtyard, shouting praise, until the city guards stepped in and redirected the people to the barracks. Walking up the palace steps, Virgil Walker, Amelia Dupont, and Corbin Strongarm approached.

"Your Majesty," Madame Dupont greeted with a flawless curtsy. "I see the audience went better than we had initially expected."

Randall straightened his back and lifted his chin slightly as he eyed each of Cassius' minions with extreme scrutiny. "Yes, the people have rallied behind me once more. They will not give up their freedom without a fight."

"Your Majesty," Virgil Walker began, "my men told me you instructed them to—"

Randall raised a hand. "That brings us to my next order of business." There was a long pause as the courtyard emptied save for Randall, his councillors, and a handful of guardsmen.

"Each of you are hereby relieved of your duties as councillors."

Corbin's eyes widened. "Your Majesty, surely—"

Randall ignored the protest. "Corbin, Amelia, you may return to your previous lives. You should count yourselves lucky." He then turned to Virgil. "As for you, Captain Walker, you are stripped of your rank."

Virgil's jaw tightened, and his face darkened into a menacing scowl. "You've gone mad! You need me, you need all of us!"

"I need people I can trust."

"You can't cast us aside like this!" Madame Dupont snarled. "Without us, the wolves will be at your door. You need people who know how to govern, how to lead, how to—"

"You said it yourself – the audience went better than you expected. I think it's clear that I know how to lead and govern, and the people of this city will never be free unless they are rid of your influence. Winterhelm and Artanzia deserve to have leaders who serve the people, not themselves."

"Without me, you don't have the guards. My men will never follow you," Virgil responded, a smug smile appearing on his face.

"Is that so?" Randall asked, tilting his head. He waved over a pair of guards who stood dutifully at the palace entrance. Quickly they stood on either side of the king, their hands on their sword hilts. Virgil's smile instantly disappeared. "Please return your sword, armour, and cloak to the armoury," Randall said. His tone was calm, but his eyes were narrow with contempt.

Virgil hesitated, his hand slowly inching towards his blade. "If you prefer, I can have these men take them from you."

The former captain scowled and unbuckled his belt, tossing his blade at the king's feet. "I've been a guardsman my entire life," Virgil muttered through clenched teeth. "What am I supposed to do now?"

Randall gave him a cool smile. "I hear the Valerian Empire is lovely this time of year. Perhaps you should retire there." With a sharp nod to the guards, Amelia, Corbin, and Virgil were forcefully escorted off the castle grounds.

Twisting in their grip, Corbin turned back and shouted, "You're condemning this city to death!"

"You need us!" Amelia added.

Virgil threw one last violent glare over his shoulder. "These people will burn, and it will be by your hands!"

"Then they shall burn as free men and women of Artanzia," Randall said quietly under his breath as he walked back into the palace.

Inside, the king's chambers were cool and dark. Randall poured himself a glass of wine and walked over to his balcony. A satisfied smile appeared over his face as he overlooked his city. Now that he was free of Cassius' influence, he could finally become the king that he was meant to be. The king that his people deserved.

"Pouring a glass for only yourself and not your guests is quite rude," a voice spoke suddenly from the darkness.

Randall quickly spun on his heels and saw a man emerge from the shadows of his chamber. He was dirty and disheveled, and his teeth were as black as coal. The man twirled a small blade in his hands with a practised ease, approaching menacingly, each step deliberate and calculated.

"Who are you?" Randall asked, his eyes frantically darting around, desperately trying to find something to defend himself with.

The man with the black teeth laughed. "A businessman," he replied, before stopping three feet away from the king.

Randall backed up to the edge of the balcony. He looked over his shoulder, wondering if he would survive the fall.

"You see, a mutual acquaintance of ours has paid me to take care of you. I imagine he wants to wear the crown himself."

"Cassius," Randall growled.

The man touched the tip of his nose with the dagger. "For a man without balls, he certainly has some guts." The man snickered at his own joke. "Truth be told, I couldn't care less who wears the crown. But he promised to help me take care of a problem of my own. You see, I had something of a kingdom once, and then some bitch came and stole it from me. I want it back."

Randall swallowed what little spit remained in his mouth. "Why are you telling me this?"

"I have a man close to her. He told me where she is going to be, and where to set the trap. Figure royal guards are better than whatever rogues Cassius can scrounge up." The man's brow furrowed and his eyes became as cold as steel. "The choice is yours, boy. Lend me a few of your men to fix my problem, and you'll never see me again. Or—" the man paused as he looked at the tip of the dagger "—we end your story, here and now."

Randall's eyes ran over the man from head to toe, making sure to drink in every detail and scrutinize him thoroughly. It was then that he recognized him as the man that Rosaline and the Bloody Brotherhood had chained up outside of Fletcher's tavern. "You want me to help you kill Rosaline?"

"All I want is a little help taking care of a rat problem," the man replied.

Randall's mind turned as he mulled over his choices. He did not want to hand Rosaline over to this man, but on the other, he had given her a chance at redemption, and she was undoubtedly exploiting that trust in some way. He also didn't fancy his chances in a fight with this man. Although Randall was younger, faster, and healthier, this man was clearly more experienced in fighting than Randall was. Swallowing his pride, Randall nodded his head. "Fine, I'll write a note and you can take that to the quartermaster at the barracks. He'll give you all the men you need."

The man's smile widened, his obsidian-like teeth gleaming. "Glad to see that you're a king of the people." He bowed in false deference.

CHAPTER FORTY
ELBERT

The journey to the village was filled with an agonizing silence. The air between the monster hunter and the crippled king was tense. Elbert did not want to be in Mikkel's company any longer than necessary – he was a means to an end, nothing more. As soon as another option presented itself, Elbert swore that he'd take it. Mikkel was a liar, a murderer, and a coward. A man who sold himself into the servitude of a devil. Elbert's stomach churned with disgust whenever he caught a glimpse of the monster hunter out of the corner of his eye.

There was one thing that eluded the king, however – why didn't Mikkel just leave him? As far as he could tell, Elbert didn't bring any *real* value to Mikkel's hunt, and that he couldn't walk only made him more of a burden. And yet, despite all of this, Mikkel kept the crippled king at his side. Elbert tried to rationalize the monster hunter's reasoning in his head, but unfortunately he couldn't think of any sound reason other than Mikkel was not completely heartless, that the man did not relish and invite needless death.

Elbert shook the idea out of his head. *No,* he told himself. *He's a monster. Any man with a soul would not butcher an innocent girl like Kaliope. There had to be another way to find Mammon, he just took the easy way.*

The sudden stop of the horse jolted Elbert from his thoughts. Ever since their meeting with Abaddon, the horse had hardly slowed from a gallop, so the abrupt halt of their progress was unexpected. On the side of the road was an abandoned wagon. The side of the wagon was covered in blood, headless bodies littered the ground, and the eviscerated corpse of a draft horse lay in front of the wagon. Mikkel dismounted from his saddle and approached the caravan, pulling his black sword from its sheath.

"What are you doing?" Elbert asked, realizing that was the first thing he had said in well over a day.

The monster hunter didn't answer. He continued stalking towards the wreckage, his stance low and each step careful and deliberate. He knelt down beside one of the headless bodies and investigated, touching the severed stump of the neck and dipping his fingers in the blood. Mikkel then sheathed his blade and rose to his feet.

"What is it? Is it Mammon?" Elbert asked.

Mikkel shook his head. "Necrophages," he answered dryly as he climbed into the back of the wagon.

That was when Elbert saw something glitter underneath one of the corpse's cloaks. He strained his eyes, not able to make out what it was exactly, but he knew that it was metallic if it gleamed in the sunlight like that. *Gold?* Perhaps it was a brooch or insignia that he could sell at the village. He knew that, if he was ever going to leave Mikkel's side, he was going to need gold and lots of it to convince someone to take him back to Winterhelm. The crippled king then began to wriggle and squirm until he fell off of the horse's back end, landing on the ground with a hard thump.

Mikkel stuck his head out of the wagon and saw a wheezing Elbert lying on the ground. "What are you doing?"

"Needed... needed to take a piss," Elbert gasped, as he tried to get air back into his lungs. Either believing the king's lie, or simply not caring enough to find out what the truth was, Mikkel resumed looting the back of the wagon.

Sensing his window closing, Elbert rolled onto his stomach and began crawling through the dirt and dried blood towards the corpse. Each handful of earth carried him closer, his eyes never leaving the piece of glittering metal. After an arduous crawl, he pulled back the corpse's cloak and, instead of finding a brooch or a badge, he saw a small hand crossbow concealed against the man's body. The weapon was about twelve inches long and rested in a leather holster. He wasn't sure what he was going to do with a crossbow – truth be told, he had never even fired one before. But it couldn't be that hard, just point and shoot, right? Elbert quickly fumbled with the buckle of the holster and tore it free from the corpse. He turned his head to make sure Mikkel hadn't noticed, and, seeing the coast was clear, quickly strapped the crossbow and holster to his chest, concealing it under his cloak.

"Ahem," Mikkel cleared his throat suddenly.

Elbert spun his head around and stared at the monster hunter with wide eyes.

"How was the piss?" he asked sarcastically. Elbert stammered, trying to think of an excuse, but when no words left his mouth, Mikkel waved his hand. "You don't need to lie about looting the dead. They're not using it anymore – why let something go to waste?"

Elbert breathed a sigh of relief and nodded his head.

"Find anything good?"

"Nothing but dried blood."

Mikkel held his gaze for a moment longer than was comfortable before shrugging. "Shame."

Elbert began crawling back towards the horse, and upon reaching it, Mikkel lifted him up and placed him over the back of the beast once more before he himself hopped into the saddle. Elbert tried to get a look at the monster hunter's face to see if he had noticed the small weapon beneath his cloak, but if he did, Mikkel showed no sign of it on his face. With a swift kick of his feet, the horse sprung into a gallop once more, feverishly heading towards the direction Abaddon had pointed them in.

As they got closer to the town, Elbert could hear something odd, a faint sound that was masked by the horse's heavy breaths and thundering hooves. He thought he heard sizzling meat, but he didn't smell any, so he convinced himself that he was hearing things. The king's hand rubbed and caressed the smooth wooden handle of the crossbow under his cloak. This weapon would be his ticket to freedom. He only had to wait for the right moment to reveal it.

"Err," Mikkel grunted suddenly.

Elbert raised his head, and out of the corner of his eye saw the monster hunter grimacing in pain. He heard the sizzling sound once more and, this time, a familiar stench assaulted the king's nose. Burnt flesh.

"What's wrong?" he asked, pinching his nose.

Mikkel winced again; a barely audible hiss escaped his lips. "We're... we're close." He kicked the horse once again, and the great beast complied with another unbelievable burst of speed. Chunks of mud and grass flew through the air as the horse's hooves smacked against the soft earth.

Just as the sun had started to make its descent, it happened. Letting out a whispered curse of pain, Mikkel let go of the reins and lifelessly fell from the saddle, causing the horse to come to a sudden, lurching stop. Elbert had to grab part of the saddle to stop himself from being tossed off the back as well. Once he regained his balance, he looked back and saw Mikkel lying on the ground, clutching his chest in agony. The king knew that the medallion in the man's chest burned as they got closer to Mammon, but he never expected it to be this painful.

"Mikkel?" Elbert asked, casting a wary glance at his companion on the ground. When he didn't answer, Elbert glanced at the horse, which seemed indifferent to the whole ordeal. He thought about taking the horse for himself and leaving Mikkel behind, but there were two problems with that thought. First, this was a beast that was conjured from the hells by Mikkel's hand, he doubted the horse would even listen to him. Second, he didn't think he even *could* ride the horse. Without the ability to kick the beast or sit up straight in the saddle, his chances of getting far without Mikkel were still slim. For right now, he still needed him.

"Mikkel?" Elbert asked again. "Are you okay?"

"Ugh..." Mikkel groaned as he rolled over onto his side, his hand still clutching his chest.

The king looked at the ground with a sense of dread. He had flopped off the horse several hours ago and did not wish to do it again, but he was left with no choice. Taking a deep inhale, he flopped off the horse one more time like a dead fish and smacked against the ground with a solid thump. The fresh air that he had just breathed in was forced out of his lungs by the hard earth, and his stomach twisted as a wheezing gasp escaped his lips.

There they were, two men lying in the middle of the road, writhing in pain, while their horse stood dutifully watchful over them. Later, Elbert was sure he would find the humour in that, but for now he was focused on getting his breath back. It took several minutes, but finally he felt like he had enough air to breathe once again. He crawled towards Mikkel on his stomach, his useless legs dragging behind him in the dirt.

"Mikkel," Elbert wheezed, "hold on."

"I don't understand," Mikkel responded in a whisper. "Why does it hurt? It never hurts this much..."

Elbert wasn't sure if Mikkel's words were meant for his ears, but that was of little consequence; he needed to get him back on his feet. Just as the crippled king got to the agonized monster hunter, he heard a soft, feminine voice from behind him.

"Hello?"

The voice sounded familiar, and when the king saw Mikkel's eyes shoot wide open, his heart leapt in his chest. *Could it be? Kaliope?*

Mikkel forcefully shoved Elbert aside and sat upright, grimacing in pain as he did so. Once he was on his back, disappointment quickly spread over Elbert's body as he saw that the woman behind them was in fact, not Kaliope. She was probably halfway through adolescence and had hair as white as snow. She looked road-worn, and her clothes were covered in filth. She stood several feet away, her body tense and ready to spring into action at a moment's notice. That was when Elbert noticed her eyes. They were as red as blood. Suddenly, the air got cool and the shrill hissing of a blade leaving its scabbard sung through the air. Elbert turned his head and saw Mikkel pull his blade free and point it at the girl.

"What are you doing?" Elbert shouted.

"You," Mikkel growled as he approached the girl. "What are you?" Elbert could tell by the sound of Mikkel's voice that he was still very much in pain, and each step the monster hunter took was with shaky, uneven legs.

"Mikkel, stop!" Elbert shouted once more. "She's just a girl!"

"She stinks of Mammon!"

"Mammon?" the girl replied. "You know Mammon?"

"Don't play dumb with me," Mikkel snarled. "I've never met a disciple like you before, but it doesn't matter – tell me where your master is and I'll make your death quick."

"He is not my master."

Elbert watched in horror as Mikkel took another laboured step towards the girl. Despite the menacing monster hunter approaching her, the girl's stance did not waver. Elbert felt sick to his stomach as the inevitable, bloody conflict neared. He felt something poke in his side and suddenly remembered the crossbow. He reached under his cloak and grabbed it by the handle, pointing it at Mikkel's back. "Stop!" he shouted. "Last warning, or I'll shoot."

Surprisingly, Mikkel stopped in his tracks. The man looked at Elbert over his shoulder and sneered in disgust at the sight of the crippled king pointing a crossbow at him. "You wouldn't dare."

"Drop the sword and step away from the girl," Elbert ordered, surprised by the conviction and authority his voice had.

"She's not a girl, she's one of Mammon's lapdogs."

"I am not one of his disciples." The girl glowered as her eyes darted between the two men.

"Liar!" Mikkel shouted. "Then why do you reek of the same infernal magic as Mammon? Why does my medallion burn like hellfire all of a sudden? If you're not a disciple, you're a demon, same as him."

"Don't make me do this," the girl pleaded, her voice tinged with frustration and fear.

"Mikkel, I'm warning you," Elbert repeated. "Not. Another. Step."

"She's lying through her teeth, and if you're too dumb to realize it then you deserved to have Mammon steal your legs."

"I can explain, please," the girl said, her tone suddenly shifting. Raising two outstretched hands, she relaxed her body. "Please, let me explain."

Elbert's finger touched the cool brass trigger of the crossbow. He could feel the tension on the string and he was shocked by how enticing it felt to pull the trigger. Part of him dared him, begged him to launch the bolt at Mikkel's back. But he stopped himself. He would not become a murderer, not if there was still a chance to solve this without bloodshed.

Mikkel paused, and after several seconds, relented with a heavy breath, lowering his blade, but still gripping the hilt tightly in his hand. "Talk."

"My name is Anna, and I travelled with Mammon and his disciples until recently." Mikkel's sword raised slightly before the girl hastily continued. "It wasn't my choice! They told me I had to, that since Mammon resurrected me, that I had no choice."

Mikkel lowered his sword once again. "What do you mean, resurrected?"

Anna's eyes slowly left Mikkel's and met Elbert's. For the briefest of seconds, they flashed with recognition. Like she had seen him before. Like she knew who he was. Elbert raised a brow and opened his lips to speak but the girl's gaze quickly shifted back to Mikkel. "It's a long story."

CHAPTER FORTY-ONE
ANNA

The gentle crackling of the fire filled the otherwise silent air. The firelight cast flickering shadows over the scowling monster hunter and the crippled king. Anna stared at the two men with bated breath. She had told them everything; well, almost everything. She told them how Mammon resurrected her, how he intended for her to be another loyal disciple for the demon to control, only to become something else. She told them about her new powers, and how she and the other disciples found hosts for Mammon. First was the bard in Eldersburg, then there was Mason, who made the deal with Mammon even after learning of the demon's true nature. The story was long, and the more she told, the more insane it sounded, even to her. It was clear, though, that this monster hunter had experience with demons, and Anna hoped that experience would validate some of her story.

The only parts of the story she left out were how she died and that she was responsible for erasing Eldersburg off the map. She recognized the crippled king from when she first arrived in Winterhelm. He was in the city square, and executing a nobleman, from what she remembered. This was the king that she and Randall had rebelled against. This was the man whose throne was taken by Randall. When the question about her death came up, she said that she died during the revolt. While not exactly untrue, she worded it in a way that portrayed her as a victim, and not one of the main perpetrators. As for Eldersburg, she figured it would be wise not to admit to mass-murdering a town with her new, uncontrollable powers.

The monster hunter stroked his chin, his eyes intensely scrutinising her. After some thought, the man rose to his feet. "Where did Mammon go?"

"I don't know," Anna responded. "Like I said, he came out of the tavern in a panic, demanding for all of us to gather our things."

"What about you?" the man asked. "What do we do about you?"

Anna raised a brow. "What do you mean? I told you, Mammon must be stopped. Let me come with you, I can help!"

"Absolutely not."

"Why not?" the crippled king cut in. "Her powers would be useful in the fight to come."

The man shot a glare at the former king and then turned his eyes back towards Anna. "Powers she can't control."

"Mikkel…"

"If you open your mouth again, Elbert, you're going to wish that you shot me with that crossbow when you had the chance."

Suddenly a spark of recognition flashed in Anna's mind. She remembered her conversation with Professor Moretz. "Wait, do you know a Professor Moretz?"

Mikkel turned his head, eyes wide with surprise, before his lips curled into an amused smile. "That nutcase? Unfortunately, I've had the displeasure of meeting him."

Anna crossed her arms. "He's not a nutcase. He's a brilliant mind in the world of demons."

"Ha!" Mikkel exclaimed. "That man knows as much about demons as a horse knows about the stars – fuck all."

"He told me about you," Anna growled. "He said that if anyone could help me get rid of Mammon, it'd be you. That you know things, like how to write Mammon's name in infernal script."

Mikkel's smile widened. "You're spending too much time in that old man's books. It's easier to kill them than to trap them."

"How do you kill them?"

"With this," Mikkel said, pointing to the large black sword on his back.

"Where did you get it?"

"He sold himself to a devil for it," Elbert interrupted with a mocking tone. At first Anna thought he was joking, but upon seeing the scowl on Mikkel's face, she knew the former king was telling the truth.

"Wait, you made a deal?" Anna asked in disbelief.

"I don't have to justify myself to you." Mikkel's voice was like ice. "You're a monster – just like him."

"Well, if I'm a monster," Anna responded snidely, "then so are you."

Mikkel's eyes narrowed and he took a measured step towards her. "I did what I had to do to protect the people from abominations like you. How much blood is on your hands, girl?"

"Your hands aren't clean either, Mikkel," Elbert snarled. This time the hand crossbow was held tightly in his hands and pointing at Mikkel's chest. "You butchered Kaliope."

A sigh escaped the monster hunter's lips. "I told you it was the only way. Her death served the greater good. What is one life measured against thousands?"

"Unless that life is yours," Anna added.

Mikkel's eyes darted between the two of them, before he threw his hands up in the air. "Fuck it! I'll kill Mammon myself. You two are each other's problem now."

Anna watched as the monster hunter stormed off towards the horse. Elbert called after him, but his cries fell on deaf ears. In an instant, Mikkel had mounted the horse and galloped off into the evening horizon.

The fire had burned low, its embers pulsing like a dying heartbeat in the quiet night. Stars had taken shape in the black sky, and the gentle night breeze rustled the dry grass. Anna sat across from Elbert, the silence between them stretching longer than she would have liked. He watched her expectantly, like a dog waiting for a command, his expression unreadable in the dim firelight. She shifted, rubbing the back of her neck, hoping that he did not recognize her. Although it was unlikely, the thought of Elbert discovering that she had a hand in deposing him unsettled her. The silence gnawed away at her nerves, each lengthy second sharpening her unease. Unable to bear the weight of her anxiety any longer, she spoke.

"Why were you travelling with Mikkel?"

The crippled king let out an amused chuckle before relaxing his body and setting down the crossbow beside him. "I've asked myself that same question several times. He freed me from a group of slavers that captured me. At first, he just wanted more information about Mammon, but he kept me by his side. I used to think that he couldn't live with himself and let an innocent person die, but I know now that's a lie. That man's just as evil as this Master Mammon."

"Hmph," Anna scoffed, "I doubt that."

The king tilted his head to the side and raised a brow at her snort. Anna watched as the cripple's eyes examined her, as if he was peering inside her mind. Her skin turned to gooseflesh and a shiver ran up her spine. "I don't know as much as you or Mikkel about demons," Elbert began. "But I'd guess that they can't help themselves. That it's in their nature to prey upon people."

Anna opened her mouth to snap back a fiery retort when she caught herself. He was right, in a sense. Demons needed to have hosts in order to stay on this plane of existence. However, she was convinced that even Mikkel's most heinous crimes paled compared to the lives that Mammon had destroyed. She closed her mouth and stared at the fire some more, not wanting to get into an argument over who had the more evil companion.

"Any chance you can get us to Winterhelm?" Elbert asked after a brief pause.

"Why?" Anna asked, her throat tensing as she locked eyes with Elbert.

"My kingdom needs me, my people need me. They need someone who is fit to rule, not some petulant, childish commoner pretending to be king."

"Randall?" Anna asked, a bead of sweat dripping down the base of her neck.

"Mhmm," Elbert replied. "A terrible name for a king. I met him once, after he took my city. Can you actually believe that he thinks he would be a better leader than me? Ruling is in my blood – hells, it's my birthright! I have stopped a coup, I negotiated a peace with the bloodthirsty Islanders after I decimated their army... what has that little shit done, beside steal what isn't his?"

Anna nodded her head as Elbert continued his tirade, his voice becoming louder and more animated with each passing second. Now that she was face to face with one of the so called "tyrannical nobles" that Randall had preached about, she completely understood why he wanted to take the throne for the people. A man like Elbert was not fit to rule.

After what seemed like a small eternity, Elbert stopped and caught his breath. The king adjusted his hair and took a few deep breaths. "Sorry, even just thinking about that thief taking what is mine, is enough to boil the blood." The king paused and stared at Anna earnestly. "I imagine you want to go home too... you said you died in the uprising, I'm sure you'd like to see your family again."

A sudden pain gripped Anna's heart. Her family was gone. Chuckles and Maeve were dead, Randall murdered her, and who knew if Tig or A'Chula had even survived the revolt? No, there was nobody left for her. She was alone. Gaining some composure over her emotions, she shook her head. "No, there's nothing left for me there."

"Not even revenge?" This caught Anna's attention. She locked eyes with the crippled king and saw the bubbling hatred behind his eyes. "You died during Randall's uprising, an innocent person caught up in the deluded dream of a fool. Surely you'd like to make him pay for that?"

A small smile crept onto Anna's lips. She had tried to push Randall from her thoughts, but the idea of seeing his face twist in shock – just before she slit his throat – warmed her heart.

Elbert's mouth curved into a knowing grin, and the king pointed a finger at her. "See? There is still something left for you there." He took a deep breath in and grabbed a handful of grass before letting each individual blade slip from his fingers.

"Spring is the best season for vengeance." There was a long pause, before Elbert continued. "Now we just have to figure out how we are going to get there."

Anna shook her head. "No, we need to stop Mammon first. Before he destroys any more lives."

Elbert rolled his eyes. "I tried to explain this before, but my people *need* me, and I—"

"The people Mammon is preying upon *are* your people," Anna interrupted. "They might not live behind the fancy walls of Winterhelm, but they farm your fields and pay their taxes to you just like anyone else. They need you now more than anyone else."

Elbert paused, and an expression of deep reflection appeared on his face. After a lengthy deliberation, the king turned to Anna once more. "How am I supposed to stop a demon? I can't even walk."

"Could use your new toy," a familiar voice called out from the dark.

Both Anna and Elbert turned their heads and stared at the brooding Mikkel, standing in the shadows. Anna's body tensed expectantly; the surprise of his return unsettled her and the fact that she didn't hear him approach unnerved her more.

"What are you doing here?" Elbert said, asking the obvious question.

Mikkel approached the dying fire and took a seat, looking at Anna. "She's right. Mammon is the greatest threat to your kingdom right now, and we need to stop him." Mikkel paused, the column of his throat shifted as he swallowed. "I need your help," he said, his eyes staring directly at Anna.

"You're going to trust me? Just like that?"

Mikkel shook his head. "I don't trust you, but from what I've heard, you really do hate Mammon, and see him for the threat that he really is. Fighting demons is extremely dangerous, that he has three disciples only complicates things more. If you help, we can minimize the bloodshed."

"Now he cares about bloodshed," Elbert muttered under his breath.

"What happens after we kill Mammon?"

Mikkel leaned back, straightening his spine, his hand shifting towards the pommel of his sword. "That depends entirely on you."

The two stared at each other for several seconds. Anna didn't trust Mikkel. From the little that Elbert had told her, he was a man who was not afraid to cross certain lines. However, he was also her best chance of keeping her promise to Matthew and sending Mammon back to the hells where he belonged. Anna turned her attention to Elbert, and out of the corner of her eye, she could see the growing disappointment in the former king's body.

"I'll help on one condition." Mikkel raised a brow. Anna pointed towards Elbert. "After Mammon is dead, you pay for our passage back to Winterhelm. We have unfinished business there."

A light sparked in Elbert's eyes and Mikkel nodded his head thoughtfully before rising to his feet. "Then we better get moving."

CHAPTER FORTY-TWO
ROSALINE

By some miracle, Phillip had organized a deal with the slaver from the Harpy's Nest. Surprisingly, the man demanded a reasonable price of five hundred crowns, which, given their newfound fortune, Rosaline was more than willing to part with. They were to meet the man at the docks, after sunset when it was dark. It took the Brotherhood little time to prepare to leave Winterhelm. They had bled the city dry, and the sooner they got out of there, the better. A large Ketenish host had been seen joining Elbert's army and a violent siege could happen at any moment. There was also the looming threat of a power vacuum opening up in the city after Randall's assassination. As much as Rosaline would've loved to stay and find Blacktooth, the situation had become too unpredictable. The walls were closing in, and it was time to move.

As the final rays of sunlight faded behind the horizon, Rosaline tossed Fletcher an extra pouch of coin for his hospitality. It would be a long time before the Bloody Brotherhood was ever in Winterhelm again, and she wanted to make sure she had a friendly place to rest her head when she returned. However, upon receiving the coin, Fletcher did not greet her with the curt nod that she had become accustomed to. Instead the man snatched the pouch of coin and tucked it within his apron, giving a grunt in thanks instead.

Weaving through the city underneath the cloak of darkness, the Brothers were on edge. They had enough gold in the small magical pouch to buy a title and the appropriate land. The feeling that they could get ambushed at any moment was palpable. However, the journey to the docks was incredibly uneventful, as most of the streets were abandoned and anyone who was out paid the bandits no mind.

Upon reaching the docks, they noticed the entire district was empty. A chill ran up Rosaline's spine and she was slowly reaching for Boris when she heard the sharp, shrill whistle. Everyone's heads turned and saw a man, almost completely concealed by the shadows, standing by a large grate and flipping a coin. A sigh of relief escaped Rosaline's lips and her hand let go of Boris' handle. As they approached, Rosaline saw the man's mouth curve into a wicked smile, displaying a mouth with a single gold tooth surrounded by yellow, misshapen ones.

"You brought the gold, yes?" the man asked in a thick accent.

Rosaline tossed a small pouch of gold at the slaver. "Five hundred crowns, like you asked. Now, tell us where to find these tunnels."

Despite the annoyance in her voice, the slaver paid her no mind. Instead, he opened the bag of coins and began counting each gold piece individually.

"Are you fucking kidding me?" Duncan whispered.

"A'Dir," Phillip cleared his throat, "we're in a bit of a hurry."

The man lifted his head and raised a brow before going back to counting his coins. "A'Dir has been cheated before. A'Dir will not be cheated again."

"We don't have time for this, just tell us—" Rosaline started before A'Dir raised a silencing hand, which made her blood boil with anger.

"You are the Bloody Brotherhood, yes?" the man asked, tucking the gold into his cloak. "A'Dir has heard of you, this will make it easy for A'Dir to find you if you are light."

"Wonderful. The tunnels, please."

A'Dir looked around to make sure they were alone before pulling out a small skeletal key from beneath his robes. He placed the key in between two stones in the wall and turned it to reveal a hidden doorway. The tunnels beyond reeked of mould and dust, but a line of lit torches adorned the walls, illuminating the path.

"Follow the torches till you reach the moon, then follow the darkness," the slaver said cryptically as he moved out of the way.

Rosaline rolled her eyes and marched into the tunnels, not sure what the man's nonsensical words meant, but was too annoyed to ask for clarification. How hard could navigating tunnels be? As they entered the tunnels, the stone door clicked shut with an ominous thump, leaving the Brotherhood alone in the eerily silent slave tunnels.

"You couldn't have met someone normal at the whorehouse, Phillip?" Jathan asked, a hint of mirth colouring his voice.

"I didn't see you coming up with any better ideas," Phillip snarled in retort.

"That mad bastard was about to count five hundred coins in front of us," Duncan replied.

"Listen—"

"Quiet!" Rosaline hissed. "We aren't out of this yet. Once we are finally outside these walls, then we can tell Phillip how much of an idiot he is. For now, stay alert."

The five bandits carefully made their way deeper into the tunnels. The corridors were tight and winding, making a sharp, ninety-degree turn every twenty paces. Other secondary corridors branched away from the main tunnel every thirty paces, their long narrow corridors shrouded in a suffocating darkness. It was clear that the tunnels were designed to confuse and disorient any who entered. It didn't take long before Rosaline lost her sense of direction, but trusted in their contact's advice of following the torches until they reached the moon. Whatever that meant. Finally, they reached a large semi-circular chamber where the trail of torches ended. The chamber had four branching tunnels from it, all of them dark.

"The fuck do we do now?" Jathan asked.

"Gods dammit, Phil..." Rosaline seethed.

"How is this my fault?"

"Look around, see if there is a clue on which way to go."

The gang of thieves branched out, examining every stone that lined the tunnel walls. Each of the tunnels had a carving of a person on top of the archway, as if symbolizing which path was the correct way. Unfortunately, the carvings meant nothing to Rosaline, and judging by the look on her Brothers' faces, meant nothing to them either.

"I can't see fucking shit in here!" Phillip exclaimed. "Can't you elves see in the dark?"

"I'm a half-elf," Duncan sighed. "Besides, I got my father's vision."

"Does anyone know what any of these mean?"

"I think they're gods," Malek replied, his voice cutting through the darkness.

"I don't recognize any of them," Jathan answered.

"Not that you would recognize them anyway," Malek retorted, "but I don't think they are ours. I think they are from the Forsaken Lands."

Rosaline pinched her brow. "Does anyone here know anything about Kovari gods?"

Duncan stepped forward and began scrutinizing each carving. "Now that you mention it, they do look Kovari. I had a teacher from Kovar – she would teach me about her homeland after our lessons quite often."

"Back when you were a noble?" Phillip chided.

Duncan paid his Brother no mind, and continued examining each carving, before ultimately pointing to a certain tunnel. "This is the way."

"How do you know?" Rosaline asked.

He pointed to a carving of a woman cloaked in a veil, her face hidden. She had two outstretched hands, one holding a dagger and the other holding chains. "I think this is Nyxara, the Veiled Mother," Duncan replied. "Goddess of moon and shadows."

"You think?" Jathan asked.

"What happens if we go down the wrong tunnel?" Malek asked.

"I don't know, but do you have any better ideas?" Rosaline responded. "Lead the way, Duncan."

The half-elf nodded his head and led the group of bandits down the tunnel, with Rosaline bringing up the rear. The audible crunching of the sand beneath their feet echoed through the stone corridors. It wasn't until they reached another small chamber that the scent of fresh air hit their noses. They had made it. They were free. A smile appeared on Rosaline's face, and she took a step forward before hearing the crack of a bowstring and the whizzing of an arrow.

The loud smack of an arrow hitting a chest and a groan of pain filled the small chamber. Rosaline quickly crawled to a stone wall, trying to find whatever cover she could. It was dark, too dark, to make out faces, but she could still see shadows. She saw one of her Brothers writhing in pain on the sand, while the others had seemingly fled to find cover as well. A sickening laugh emerged from the darkness, and the spark of flames illuminated a hidden alcove with a familiar face standing in the shadows.

"What do we have here?" Blacktooth goaded, tossing the torch into the middle of the room, lighting the entire chamber in a soft orange light. "I had a feeling I'd run into you here."

Rosaline could see Jathan on the ground, the shaft of an arrow protruding from his shoulder. "Duncan, you bastard—" Rosaline hissed.

A laugh escaped Blacktooth's lips as he pulled his sword free from his scabbard and stabbed the tip deep into the sand. "Don't cry, Roz, your precious half-breed didn't sell you out. In fact, it was an old friend of mine."

Rosaline's eyes darted towards Philip and Malek, but their expressions showed just as much confusion as hers, staring back at Blacktooth, who was now suddenly surrounded by men wearing city guard uniforms.

"Fletch and I go way back. I actually saved his life once, and now he's saved mine," Blacktooth continued, his voice rich with arrogance. "And now, I have King Randall as a friend – gave me some of his guards for tonight."

Rosaline gritted her teeth. She wasn't sure how Blacktooth had weaselled his way into a deal with the king, but she had a few suspicions. She looked at each of her Brothers, who were steeling themselves for a battle. Rosaline pulled Boris free from his sheath and gripped him tightly in her hands. "Let's get this over with."

"Ha!" Blacktooth laughed. "Save the bitch for me, lads, kill the others."

The city guard sprang into action, unsheathing their blades and charging towards the Bloody Brotherhood. Rosaline grabbed a fistful of sand and sprinted across the chamber towards the wounded Jathan. The clanging of steel filled the small stone room in a cacophony of noise. Quickly, she helped Jathan to his feet, only to turn around and see a guardsman swinging a sword at her head. Ducking out of the way, she tossed the handful of sand at the man's eyes and pounced, plunging Boris deep into his neck.

Another crack of a bowstring, and Rosaline heard the arrow whiz by her head, the fletchings kissing her cheeks as it flew by. She darted to the side, using the fighting bodies as cover. She saw Malek locked in a stalemate with one guard, until he head-butted the man, breaking his nose. She turned her head the other way and saw Phillip pinned to the ground, a guardsman's sword inches from his throat. She moved towards Phillip, but stopped herself as she heard the crack of Blacktooth's bow. The arrow was not meant for her; she heard someone else cry out in pain. This was her chance – she had to stop Blacktooth.

In a flash, she charged Blacktooth. The man smiled, showing his rotten teeth, tossed his bow aside, and grabbed his sword from the sand. As soon as she came within range, Blacktooth swung wildly at her. Rosaline dodged and danced away from the blade's edge, missing death by a hair's breadth each time. Blacktooth's sword was longer, and he could keep her at bay. She kicked up a cloud of sand, but Blacktooth easily sidestepped out of the way. She lunged anyway, hoping to take him by surprise.

The pommel of Blacktooth's blade connected with her cheek with a chilling crunch, and sent her sprawling to the ground. Bloody sand entered her mouth, and she spat out a few pebbles before rolling out of the way, Blacktooth's sword barely missing once again.

Planting her feet, she lunged, hopping on Blacktooth's back. She had hoped to stab Boris deep into the man's neck, but Blacktooth turned as she landed on him, and her dagger sank into the meaty flesh below his collarbone. With a violent elbow to the gut, Blacktooth shook Rosaline free. She fell on her back, gasping for air, staring up at the stone ceiling. The sound of battle became muffled and her vision blurred.

Rolling onto her stomach, she crawled towards a dead guardsman and his nearby bloody sword. She willed her body forward, refusing its desperate plea for air. Suddenly, there was a stomp on her ankle. She looked over her shoulder and saw Blacktooth standing over her. She kicked wildly with her other foot and connected with something hard. Rising to her hands and knees, she prepared to leap for the blade, only to be caught by her hair.

Her head was yanked back, and she could feel several pieces of hair ripped from her scalp. Before she knew it, she was looking at Blacktooth's rotten smile once again, his blade touching her throat.

"You have no idea how long I've waited for this," he said menacingly, pulling Rosaline to her feet.

Desperately, she reached for Blacktooth's blade, but he easily pulled it out of her reach. "Oh, ho ho!" Blacktooth chuckled. "I like it when they fight. Go ahead, love, try it again."

Locking eyes with Blacktooth, Rosaline reached for the blade again. Once again he pulled it out of her reach, but this time, she twisted her body so violently that the hair Blacktooth was holding ripped free from her skull. Free of his grasp, Rosaline kicked as hard as she could in the former bandit leader's groin. Blacktooth instantly dropped to his knees. Rosaline tore Boris free from Blacktooth's shoulder and plunged the weapon into the man's eye, not stopping until the entire blade was deep inside the man's skull.

"You have no idea how long I wanted to do that," Rosaline said as she twisted her dagger and ripped it free from Blacktooth's head. His corpse collapsed to the ground and began spasming wildly, a torrent of blood leaking from the man's eye socket.

The chamber was silent, save for some laboured breathing. Rosaline turned her attention to the others and saw the sand in the chamber had turned black with blood. Blacktooth and his four guardsmen were the only corpses on the ground. Jathan clutched his wounded shoulder, while Malek and Duncan bandaged minor wounds of their own. Phillip leaned against the wall, a steady stream of blood oozing out of his belly. The man wheezed with each breath.

Rosaline slowly walked over to the dying Brother and looked at his wound. She could smell the acrid scent of bile masked by the metallic aroma of fresh blood. She locked eyes with Phillip, and was surprised to see tears in them.

"Fuck me," Phillip gasped, blood escaping from the corner of his lips.

"Not even on your deathbed," Rosaline replied.

A chuckle escaped Phillip's lips before a coughing grip took hold, and speckles of blood escaped his lips. His belly bounced with each cough, and a small fountain of blood erupted from the wound.

"Make it quick," Phillip asked. "I don't want to be in pain for long."

Rosaline placed a comforting hand on Phillip's shoulder, before another hand was gently placed on top of hers. Then another. Then another. Each of the remaining Brothers stood over Phillip and silently gave their condolences. Swallowing what Rosaline was surprised to admit was sorrow, she plunged Boris deep into Phillip's heart.

He gasped as the cold steel sank into his flesh, and let out a relieved breath when the dagger was pulled free. He looked at each of his Brothers with a smile on his face, before the light slowly died behind his eyes.

Returning Boris back to his sheath, Rosaline rose to her feet, wiping the fresh blood on her hands onto Phillip's shirt. "Let's get out of this fucking city, I need a drink."

CHAPTER FORTY-THREE
ELBERT

The way that Mikkel clutched his chest told Elbert that they were getting close to Mammon. They had ridden through the night, but their pace was slowed by Anna not having a horse and having to walk beside them. As much as Elbert hated the idea of venturing far from his home and his army, both of which desperately needed him, he knew that this was the best path forward. Help Mikkel and Anna banish this demon back to the hells, and then he could ride back to his home and finally reclaim what had been stolen from him. Plus, there was the added benefit of preventing this demon from preying on any more of his subjects and ruining their lives with his twisted deals.

As they travelled, it quickly became apparent that Anna had lots of knowledge of not only demons, but other monsters as well. Apparently, her father had raised her to fight and hunt down monsters in a secluded forest. This seemed to cool the tension between Mikkel and her, and at one point the monster hunter even asked some questions, probing her knowledge. As the two continued to converse, it became quickly apparent that Elbert was the odd one out, which filled his stomach with knots. Not only was it painful to be excluded and treated as an afterthought, unable to contribute to a conversation in a meaningful way, but he realized that both Anna and Mikkel were well-prepared for the upcoming fight, whereas he was not.

His mind raced as his hand caressed the handle of his small crossbow – would this be enough to save him from a demon? He would have to rely heavily on the others. Part of him knew he should stay out of the fight, but he wanted to be there for Mammon's downfall. This demon stole his legs, and he wanted to ensure that Mammon felt every second of excruciating embarrassment that Elbert had felt since their deal. In an ideal world, they would defeat Mammon, Elbert would kill Mikkel, and then he and Anna would travel to Winterhelm to get their revenge against Randall.

"Why won't writing Mammon's name in infernal script work?" Anna asked, interrupting the king's thoughts.

"It would," Mikkel replied dryly. "But a trap takes a lot of time and preparation. We would have to draw Mammon out, lure him into standing on a seal that bore his name in infernal script, and keep him there until the ritual is finished. Killing him is the easiest and fastest way to send him back to the hells."

"What about Balazar's Snare?"

Mikkel shook his head. "Only works against fey. Like demons, they're not from this plane, but that's where the similarities end."

Elbert nodded along, as if he understood what was going on. The knots in his stomach curled once again, the uncomfortable feeling spreading to the rest of his body.

"What about the others? The disciples will fight for him, even if they don't want to."

"Then we kill them."

There was a pause in the air. Elbert craned his neck from the back of the horse to see what Anna's expression was, but couldn't. It wasn't until she spoke he realized she cared for her former companions. Despite her obvious disdain for Mammon, she did not share the same animosity for his disciples.

"But maybe..." she started.

"They will die anyway once Mammon is sent back to the hells," Mikkel interrupted bluntly. Again there was a small pause, before Mikkel added, "If it's any consolation, I'll try to make their deaths quick. They don't have powers, so it should be easy."

"Do you know of any other members of the Order of the Sword that can help us?"

"No. I hear there are less than twenty of us left, and only two of them I know personally."

"Are they as big of an asshole as you?" Elbert chimed in, relishing the chance to finally engage in the conversation for once.

Despite the verbal jab, Mikkel let out a small laugh. "Bigger, actually."

"I find that hard to believe," Anna added, although her tone was surprisingly playful.

"One I met on a contract half a decade ago. Colin was his name. He convocated the year after me. I remember seeing him in the guildhall, but since he was a year below me, we didn't talk much."

"What were you hunting?" Elbert asked.

"There were a series of ritualistic killings down by the free city of Damask. To me, it reeked of demon worshipping. People often try to summon demons from the hells and think they can control them into doing their bidding. Colin thought it had to do with a cult of necromancers that he was tracking. Naturally, a wager was made, and we decided to work together until we found out who was right."

"And?" Anna asked. "Who won?"

"Neither of us. Turned out the killings were done by a man who simply hated anyone different from him. He killed people based on their race, their skin colour, who they fucked, and even who they worshipped." There was a slight pause, and Mikkel's earlier mirth faded. "Hatred. That was the real monster."

Neither Elbert nor Anna spoke as they let Mikkel's words hang uncomfortably in the air for several seconds. Curious about the other monster hunter, Elbert broke the silence. "And the second?"

Mikkel sighed. "A man who graduated many decades before me, and despite that, is still the most dangerous man with a blade I've ever met. His name was Andronikus. He came to the guild when I was in my first year, and I saw him train with the masters. He outclassed them all. He attacked with such reckless abandon, unbothered by the master's swords as they cut and carved into his skin. He was going to beat you through sheer willpower alone."

Elbert gulped. The man Mikkel was describing sounded a lot like Grimm, a man with relentless focus and determination. During their time together, the king had witnessed the Islander come close to death several times, and no matter how gravely wounded he was, the man always found his feet. It was as if Grimm willed his heart to keep beating.

The horse came to a sudden stop and Mikkel clutched his chest. A faint sizzling sound came from beneath his clothes. A pained grunt escaped the man's lips as he folded over. Elbert lifted his head and examined their surroundings. They were in the middle of nowhere. It was flat prairie, with the odd copse of trees littering the landscape. The snow had almost completely melted, and the ground was just regaining some of its previous colour.

"What is it?" Anna asked, her voice measured and precise.

"He's... close," Mikkel grunted as he straightened his back, rising above the pain that was burning into his chest. "Keep an eye out."

Elbert nodded his head at the instruction, but thought it was useless. They were out in the open – if Mammon wanted to ambush them, he could've picked a better locale. Suddenly, there was a scream for help from one of the nearby thickets. The three companions looked at each other, and Mikkel kicked his horse into a gallop, riding towards the group of trees with reckless abandon. Elbert bounced along on the horse's hindquarters, his ribs slamming into the creature's muscular frame. He looked back and saw that Anna was chasing after them on foot. The king tried to tell Mikkel to slow down, to let Anna catch up, but it was no use. It was as if he, too, was being spurred towards the trees by an unseen force.

The horse came to a jarring halt at the start of the grove. Mikkel quickly dismounted, unsheathed his blade, and marched in. Elbert let out a pained groan and saw the mist rising from his breath. The air was cold, and his arms were covered in gooseflesh. "Wait!" he called out. "You can't go in alone, what if it's a trap?"

To Elbert's surprise, Mikkel actually paused for several seconds, before turning back towards the horse and grabbing the reins in his hand, leading the beast, and Elbert atop it, inside the trees. "I sure hope you know how to use that thing, and you weren't bluffing before," Mikkel said dryly, as the trees swallowed them.

Elbert gulped nervously as he pulled out the small crossbow from his cloak. When he had told Mikkel not to go in alone, Elbert hoped he would see sense and wait for Anna to rejoin them. Unable to change things now, Elbert placed the small weapon in his hand and readied himself for what they might find. The handle felt comfortable in his grip, at least, and the small brass trigger was pleasantly cool to the touch.

"Oh, thank the Gods! You heard me!" a relieved feminine voice called out. Elbert strained his neck to see, catching a glimpse of a woman kneeling beside an unconscious man. It looked like the man was pinned beneath a large, fallen tree; an axe lay just outside his grip. "Please!" the woman cried out again. "You have to help my husband. When he hadn't returned home for several hours, I came out and found him like this. I think the tree fell on him!"

The creaking sound of leather pricked Elbert's ears as he saw Mikkel's grip tighten around the hilt of his sword. It didn't take a scholar to realize that Mikkel didn't believe the woman, and, taking in to account everything that Anna had told them about Mammon, Elbert didn't believe her either. Clearly this was one of the demon's disciples.

"Please," the woman begged. "There's no need for the sword. I just need to lift the tree off my husband."

Elbert scanned the trees as the stranger pleaded with Mikkel, and saw nothing. If this was a trap, the ambushers were doing a remarkable job at hiding themselves.

Suddenly, he heard rapid footsteps approaching from behind them. Elbert turned his head left and saw Anna burst through the trees and come to a dead stop. Her eyes widened as she locked eyes with the strange woman.

"Anna!?" the woman asked in disbelief.

Before anyone could answer, Mikkel took a step forward. "Where's Mammon?"

There was the sudden snap of a bowstring and a whizzing arrow soared through the air. A sickening thunk came as the arrow sunk into the horse's flesh, mere inches from Elbert's head. The horse reared up and whinnied in pain, sending the crippled king sprawling to the ground.

The world spun as Elbert smacked against the ground. He knew he let go of his crossbow but didn't see where it went. He blinked away the discomfort and tried to get his bearings. He saw Mikkel and Anna fighting the woman and her husband, while a third man also joined the fray, swinging a sword wildly at anyone within reach.

He wasn't sure which one was Mammon, but Elbert knew it had to be one of the two men. This was it. This was his chance to take control of his life. Quickly, Elbert scanned the grove's floor for his crossbow. If he could send a bolt through the bastard's heart, he would have his revenge, and be one step closer to reclaiming his throne.

A small glint from the brass trigger caught Elbert's eye. There it was, at the bottom of a small hill, tucked behind a stump close to the fighting. With a surge of determination, Elbert crawled towards the edge of the hill, his hands dragging his paralyzed body across the dead grass. His eyes locked onto the crossbow, unwilling to take it out of his sights even for a second. He was going to have his revenge. He was going to get his life back.

Suddenly, a loud, thunderous boom filled the air and Elbert flinched at the sound. He tore his gaze away from his crossbow and saw one of Mammon's disciples flying backwards through the air. The sight gave the king sudden pause. He wasn't sure who was responsible for that, Anna or Mikkel. Shaking the thought out of his head, he turned his attention back towards his crossbow. He pulled himself to the edge of the hill, and upon reaching the crest, rolled himself down it.

The world spun by him at a sickening speed. His body bounced and careened as it hit the hard earth. He crashed into stumps, rocks, and branches as he tumbled down the hill. He felt the bottom of his head slam into something hard, and he winced in pain, only to realize that closing his eyes made him feel sick. He came to a stop as he collided with the sturdy trunk of a tree at the bottom of the hill.

Waiting for the dizziness to subside, Elbert looked at the fight once more. Blood had been spilt, but it was unclear whose. Mikkel was on the offensive, hacking and slashing at one disciple, who was backing up with every swing of the black sword. He couldn't see Mammon, Anna, or the other disciple from where he was.

Turning his attention back to the stump where his crossbow lay, Elbert crawled towards it. His heart slammed against his chest. Adrenaline and anticipation coursed heavily through his veins. The intoxicating feeling that he was one step closer to taking control of his life filled his body. He swore he could taste it.

As his fingers curled around the handle of the crossbow, a heavy foot stepped onto his wrist. Elbert yelped in pain as he looked up and saw a familiar, albeit younger, face grinning down at him.

"Been a while, Your Majesty," Mammon said with a venomous smile.

CHAPTER FORTY-FOUR
ANNA

The loud burst of magic that sent Matthew flying through the air left a tingling sensation in Anna's hands. She hoped he would stay down; she didn't want to hurt him. Turning her head, she saw Desmond backing up frantically, desperately swinging his blade, trying to parry Mikkel's attacks. Instinctively, she took a step forward to help Desmond, then, out of the corner of her eye, she saw a figure rise to its feet. Turning her head again, she saw Matthew glaring at her, axe in hand.

The disciple charged at her, swinging the axe with murderous intent. Anna jumped, spun, and dodged out of the way of every swing, trying to disarm Matthew without hurting him. He swung the axe again, aiming for her neck, but she pirouetted out of the way and grabbed the wooden haft firmly in her hands before sweeping out Matthew's legs from under him.

With the axe in her hand, she looked down at Matthew and saw an expression of sadness on his face. "Why are you doing this?" she asked, tossing the axe aside. "Help me stop Mammon!"

Matthew craned his head to the side, as if moving it a single inch caused him great pain. That's when she saw it – the mark that was on the back of his neck, glowing bright red. "Can't... he...controls..." Matthew whispered before rolling back onto his feet.

Anna's heart sank when she realized that none of the disciples were themselves; they were being controlled by Mammon. Puppets forced to fight on behalf of their master. A loud clang of steel made Anna turn her head, and she saw Desmond's sword fly through the air, Mikkel's black blade now pointed at the disciple's chest.

"Mikkel—" she cried out, before she was tackled to the ground, Matthew completely on top of her, his hands tightening around her throat. She looked up at him and saw the tears in his eyes. He was a prisoner in his own body, being forced to commit someone else's crimes. Anna tried to conjure another spell, but nothing happened. The tingling sensation was gone, and she could feel her empty lungs spasm, hungry for just one more breath. She closed her fists and drove them upward into Matthew's ribcage, trying to break his grip around her neck. When that didn't work, she attacked his elbows, hoping to buckle his arms and give her more time. But it was no use, Matthew's hands were like a vice, and soon the edges of her vision blurred. The frozen look of horror on the disciple's face was the last clear thing she could see.

Suddenly, a spray of warm, sticky liquid coated her face, and Matthew's grip loosened. She gasped for air, and her vision slowly returned. Rolling onto her knees, she coughed and wheezed, her diaphragm straining with every breath. A strong hand grabbed her by the collar of her shirt and lifted her to her feet. Wiping the blood off her face, she turned and saw a smiling Mikkel.

"Looked like you needed help," he said bluntly before walking by her to pull his sword free from Matthew's head.

Anna's stomach twisted. She knew that Matthew had died once the blood hit her face, but she never expected it to be so gruesome. Mikkel's black sword had cleaved the disciple's head clean in two. Brains and bits of skull littered the ground as his body lay there, still twitching uncontrollably.

Turning her head around, she saw that both Desmond and Evelynn had suffered the same fate. A large hole had been carved into Desmond's chest and Evelynn's head had been completely severed. Anna's knees buckled slightly and she let out a small breath, steadying herself. This was not what she wanted; this was not the fate they deserved. They deserved better.

"Mammon!" Mikkel called out, wiping the fresh coat of blood off his blade and onto his sleeve. "It's time for you to go home."

"I don't think so," Mammon's voice said, then the demon emerged, holding Elbert at knifepoint. "Let me go, or the king gets it."

Anna looked at Elbert and saw the fear in his eyes. She didn't understand why until she turned towards Mikkel and saw the unbothered expression on his face.

A small laugh escaped the monster hunter's lips as he slowly approached Mammon and the crippled king. "Not another step!" Mammon yelled. "I'm warning you!"

"I don't care about him," Mikkel replied plainly. "Kill him, let him go, it makes no difference. All that matters is that you go back to where you belong."

"Let's make a deal – I know where you got that sword. Whatever Abaddon is offering you, I can offer you more."

Anna watched as Mikkel approached the two, twirling his sword casually with every step. Mammon's face betrayed the increasing terror that was filling his body, and Elbert's showed that the king was slowly resigning himself to death. Her eyes frantically searched for something, anything she could use to help, but there was nothing. Mikkel was mere paces away from them, and she could see Mammon's grip on the dagger tighten, his muscles coiling with anticipation, ready to end Elbert's life when all was lost. Mammon would take Elbert down to the hells with him.

Locking eyes with Elbert, she reached out, not with her hands, but something else. She had no plan, no course of action, just a raw need for *something* to happen. Suddenly, there was a tingling sensation, starting at her feet, before it surged up her legs, rushing through her body like a tidal wave. A beam of bright energy erupted from her, streaming through the air and striking Elbert in the chest with such force that it sent both the crippled king and the demon sprawling to the ground.

Sensing the opportunity, Mikkel quickly closed the distance, his black blade singing through the air. The sword came down like a guillotine, cleaving Mammon's skull with a sickening crunch. The demon's body convulsed in a final jerk – then stillness, paired with an uncomfortable silence filling the grove.

Anna fell to her knees, taking long, laboured breaths. Her whole body tingled and vibrated, as if someone had hit it with a tuning fork. On wobbly legs, she rose to her feet and walked over to Elbert, who lay motionless on the ground. Mikkel stood over Mammon's body and was whispering something, and although she could not make out what he was saying, she knew it was not in the common tongue. Collapsing to Elbert's side, she placed a hand on the king's chest to feel for a pulse, but when a pained groan escaped his lips, Anna let out a sigh of relief.

"Are you okay?" she asked.

"I feel like someone hit me in the chest with a hammer," Elbert said, wincing as he talked. "My body feels... different. Like it's shaking."

Anna looked down at Elbert's body and noticed nothing different. "I think it's—"

"You were going to let me die!" Elbert shouted, turning his head and glaring at Mikkel. "You fucking whoreson!"

The monster hunter finished whatever he was whispering, and let out an annoyed sigh. "What's one life against—"

"But it's my life!" Elbert interrupted. "Mine! And you were just going to let him kill me!"

Mikkel rose to his feet and turned towards the crippled king and Anna, and instead of seeing the usual cold indifference on the monster hunter's face, Anna saw the faintest hint of fear. Mikkel's hand tightened around his sword. "What are you?"

Anna was taken aback by the question. "What do you mean?"

There was a grimace on the monster hunter's face, before he took a step forward. "Nobody should be able to cast magic like that." Anna slowly backpedalled away from Elbert's body, her knees bent in anticipation. "I'll ask again, what are you?"

"She's a bloody hero! Unlike you," Elbert chimed in.

"Shut up," Mikkel growled before turning his eyes towards Anna once again.

"I told you, when Mammon resurrected me, I could do things..."

"Things like that?" Mikkel questioned, his voice tense with anger. "Wizards can't cast spells like that without going insane, and demons aren't able to channel that much energy through their bodies while staying on this plane." The monster hunter's brow furrowed. "Tell me what happened in Eldersburg, because when I got there a few days after Mammon had been there, the entire town had been turned to ash." Mikkel stepped over Elbert's body and strode menacingly towards Anna. Impulsively, she backed away, putting as much distance between them as possible.

"You killed those people, didn't you?!" Mikkel shouted, the veins protruding from his neck. "I knew you were a monster the moment I saw you."

"No, it's not like that! I didn't mean to—"

"Lies! You are just like them. You can give them my regards when you see them in the hells," Mikkel growled, raising the sword above his head.

"Stop!" Elbert shouted, and Anna's eyes went wide. Behind the monster hunter was Elbert, near the brush where he and Mammon had emerged, with his crossbow in hand. "Take one more step and I'll shoot."

"Elbert, I know you don't understand but—"

"Last warning. Back away now."

Mikkel stood still for several seconds, his eyes darting between Elbert and Anna. After a moment of thought, the monster hunter took another menacing step forward. Anna lowered her body, ready to dodge the swing of the sword, when she heard the thwack of the crossbow. There was an audible *thud*, and Mikkel's eyes went wide as he looked down and saw the head of the bolt protruding from his stomach. The black blade fell to the ground seconds before Mikkel did, clutching his stomach as torrents of blood oozed out of the wound.

"Fuck..." Mikkel coughed, blood spurting out of his mouth.

Anna quickly ran over to Elbert, giving the wounded monster hunter a wide berth. The king sat there, frozen, the crossbow still aimed at where Mikkel had been standing.

"Elbert! Elbert!" Anna said, trying to shake some sense into him.

"I... I shot him," the king replied absently.

"Yes, you did. But we have to go," Anna answered, casting Mikkel a worried look over her shoulder. Back when she was living in the woods with her father, she had seen more than her fair share of gut-shot deer. It was a slow death, and one where the animal could still run for days after the fact. She knew that the bolt in Mikkel's stomach would not keep him down for long. They needed to get out of there. Now. "Come on," she said, looping the king's arms around her shoulders and beginning to drag him out of the grove. "Let's get back to the horse."

It was a long and arduous task dragging Elbert's body out of the thicket of trees, and Anna's body was thick with sweat by the time they reached the tree line. She fell onto her back and wheezed, greedily taking in the fresh air as she looked skyward. It felt like a lifetime ago since she was dragging dead stags out of the woods, but the act of pulling the crippled king's body out of the trees filled her with an exhausting nostalgia. She closed her eyes, taking another deep breath, savouring the few seconds of rest she was afforded. Suddenly, there was a snort. Anna turned her head and saw the black mare that Mikkel rode staring at her. The horse stomped its hoof against the ground several times before letting out an annoyed nicker.

Swallowing what little spit she had in her mouth, Anna nodded her head and got to her feet once again. She grabbed one of Elbert's arms and pulled it over her shoulder before dipping into a deep squat and hooking his far leg. She took a moment to brace herself, before driving her feet against the ground, forcing her legs to stand up straight. There was a slight wobble, before she regained her balance. Slowly and carefully, she backed up to the horse. Elbert reached out with his arms and pulled himself onto the hindquarters of the animal. Once the weight of the king was off her shoulders, Anna let out a relieved sigh before walking to the other side and climbing on top of the horse herself.

Anna kicked the horse into a walk before looking over her shoulder at the trees one last time. Elbert lay across the back of the horse, his head also turned back towards the copse.

"Do you think he'll live?" Elbert asked with a slight shake in his voice.

"No," she lied.

CHAPTER FORTY-FIVE
RANDALL

The rhythmic tapping of the hammer was music to the king's ears. Since he had rid himself of Cassius and his vipers' influence, he was free to be the king he wanted to be. The king he was meant to be. He had spent most of his time outside the castle and among his people, working with them side by side, creating barricades and maintaining a sense of order. As a result of this, the city had regained an air of calmness that hadn't been seen since the siege started. People no longer fled for ships, but instead worked beside the young man they chose as their king, helping him protect their city against the armies that sat outside their walls. The city guard armed and trained the citizens, while working with each individual neighbourhood to divvy up the duties fairly amongst the populace.

With one last swing of the hammer, Randall wiped the sweat that dripped down his brow and admired their handiwork. This was the last spiked barricade that lined the main road into the city, each of them standing six feet tall, preventing any of the former king's cavalrymen from leaping over them. A couple of people patted the king on the back, and Randall replied with a nod and a smile. For the first time since taking the crown, he was happy. Or as happy as he could be. He still wished that some of his friends were alive to see that he had returned to his old self. He thought about his last conversation with Tig. He regretted every word he had said in that argument. He regretted striking the only person left who had the courage to tell him the truth. Now he was gone, and Randall would pay any price to have him back.

Suddenly, an audible splat came from down the street. Everyone lifted their heads, not sure if they heard something, or if their minds were playing tricks on them. Then there was another. And another. Soon, a storm of human carcasses fell from the sky, exploding against the ground, painting the city in a fresh coat of rot and viscera. The stench of decay filled the city streets as people panicked to get inside their homes.

"Your Majesty!" one of the guardsmen called, raising a shield high above Randall's head. "Back to the castle."

Following his entourage of guardsmen, Randall weaved through the city streets as bloated corpse after bloated corpse fell from the sky, colliding against the cobblestones in violent explosions. The guards continued escorting Randall up towards the castle, but came to a sudden stop as a wave of putrid blood splashed over them. Randall heaved at the stench, his knees shaking with disgust. It wasn't until he opened his eyes again that he could clearly see what the former king's army was raining down on them. It was people, but not just any people. He recognized them. He had seen their faces in the streets during the uprising, during his time as king. It was then that a sinking feeling gripped Randall's stomach and twisted it like a dagger sinking into flesh. This was the fate of the people who fled the city. They were butchered and had now returned to the city as corpses.

CHAPTER FORTY-SIX
ROSALINE

The Temple of Old Man was many things, but a temple wasn't one of them. What was once sacred ground now reeked of ale, sweat, and blood. An inn, a gambling house, a brothel, and a fighting pit all under one roof, it had become a shrine to sin itself. The former holy site had been abandoned decades ago, and under the careful hands of three men, Ryne, Tylen, and Braydo, the temple had become a haven for thieves, bandits, and cutthroats.

The scent of fresh food and stale ale wafted up through the floorboards and stirred Rosaline from her sleep. Her head throbbed violently as she opened her eyes and found herself at the bottom of a mountain of whores. Naked bodies littered the rooms, and the bedding was soaked with every fluid imaginable. A small smile crept along Rosaline's lips. *Phillip would've been proud.*

She kicked one of the whores off the bed and he landed with a loud thunk against the floor. Rolling out from the pile of bodies, Rosaline stood and stretched her back. The food down below smelt divine, and although she could painfully feel every heartbeat in her skull, she was going to go enjoy herself. She had earned it. Hells, they all had.

Rosaline quickly put on her clothes and tightened her belt against her waist, making sure Boris was secure before taking the stone stairs down to the tavern. At the bottom of the steps she smiled as she saw her Brothers terrorizing the other patrons and enjoying themselves. She slowly walked to a table and ordered a drink. Malek drunkenly stumbled over and fell onto a chair with a loud thud, nearly tipping it over.

"Finally, you joined us!" the bandit slurred, slamming his almost empty mug onto the table. "Had your fill of flesh?"

Rosaline laughed as the barmaid brought a frothy pint glass over to the table. Taking a sip from the mug, Rosaline couldn't hide the coy smile spreading on her lips. "I had to honour Phillip's sacrifice somehow."

A small chuckle escaped Malek's lips. "Look at them, Roz," he said, pointing to Duncan and Jathan, who were tossing knives into a wall on the far side of the tavern. "They're in heaven." A small hiccup escaped Malek's lips as he took another drink from his mug. "And so am I. We have more gold than we know what to do with!"

Rosaline's smile widened. "We only get to celebrate killing Blacktooth once, we might as well enjoy it."

Malek's smile faded slightly, and he leaned close over the table. "What about Fletcher?"

Rosaline shrugged. She was too happy to worry about that mute of an innkeep. "He'll get what's coming to him. For now, let's enjoy ourselves. Courtesy of the good people of Winterhelm."

The two bandits clinked their glasses together before finishing their drinks. There was a call from across the bar and Rosaline lifted her head to see Jathan standing beside a large, cloaked man.

"Hey, look at this!" Jathan called out. "We got a blind man at the bar!" He laughed as he waved his hand in front of the man's face.

Rosaline quickly studied the man, how he reached for his glass, how his eyes darted from side to side in a slow, calculated matter. Although his eyes were milky white, he definitely was not blind. He was a killer. Just as Rosaline was about to bark at Jathan to leave the man alone, the boy clumsily tried to reach into the man's pockets.

In an instant the stranger jumped to his feet, grabbing Jathan's wrist with one hand and snapping it with ease. Jathan let out a scream of pain as he stared at his exposed wrist bone, blood spurting out of the wound. Malek and Duncan, despite being drunk, sprang into action. Duncan tossed several knives at the large man, who lifted Jathan in his hands, using the bandit's body as a shield from the blades. Each knife sank into Jathan's back and soon a steady stream of blood leaked from his mouth.

Malek smashed a bottle on the bar and leapt at the man's back. The stranger tossed Jathan's body to the side with ease and spun out of the way of Malek's clumsy strike. Malek swiped at the stranger's midsection, but he backed up nimbly before grabbing the Brother's head with his meaty palm and repeatedly slamming it into the corner of the wooden bar. There was a sickening crunch and a spurt of blood before Malek's body slumped to the ground, leaving behind a steady streak of crimson on the bar.

Rosaline watched in horror as she saw her Brothers get picked off one by one, each of them falling with sickening ease. Whoever this stranger was, he was skilled. He had been in fights before, and not just against thieves and cutthroats. This man was a professional.

Duncan charged at the man, knife raised, but the man danced around him with ease. Rosaline's heart pounded in her chest and her gaze darted between the chaos and the corpses of her Brothers. She wanted to fight, to help, but she was frozen. Her limbs felt impossibly heavy.

Then, the unmistakable gurgling sound of someone being stabbed in the throat echoed through the room. Rosaline's eyes widened with terror as she saw Duncan's confused face looking down at the smashed bottle protruding from his neck. The half-elf watched as torrent after torrent of blood spurted out of his neck and through the bottle with every heartbeat.

The rage in Rosaline's heart finally spurred her into action. She pulled Boris from his sheath and charged at the stranger. Nobody did this to the Bloody Brotherhood. Absolutely nobody. She tossed a mug of beer at the man before changing direction, hoping the drink would distract him. However, the stranger saw through her trick, and followed her with his eyes as the mug of beer smashed against his body. As she stabbed Boris at the man's throat, he expertly caught her wrist and swept her legs, sending her crashing to the ground.

The air left Rosaline's lungs as she stared up at the stranger, now on top of her, wrestling Boris free from her grasp. She tightened her grip on Boris' handle but it was no use; the man was much stronger than her. He tore Boris from her hand, spun him around, and leaned against the blade as he drove it towards Rosaline's skull.

"No... no!" Rosaline screamed as she tried to push up against the man's burly arms. The tip of Boris' blade glinted in the light as it slowly approached her eye.

"Argh!" Rosaline screamed as the tip of the blade punctured her eye. Blood poured from the socket and streamed down her face, mixing with her tears. She could feel the blade sink deeper and deeper into her eye, painfully slicing every tendon and nerve.

"AHHHH!" Rosaline screamed once again, as she felt the sharp edges of Boris' blade carve into the bone of her skull. She looked up at the stranger with her good eye, and saw that her vision blurred, clouds of darkness closing in. *No. No! Not like this. Not like this.* As the blade of her dagger pierced her brain, the last thing she saw was the smiling face of the white-eyed stranger, staring back down at her.

EPILOGUE
MIKKEL

Blood stained his fingertips as he drew intricate lines of crimson in the grass. His heart thumped slowly; the bolt embedded in his belly twitched with every beat. He felt his eyes start to grow heavy. He blinked away the abyss, forcing himself to focus on the runes. It had to be right. Spelling out a name in infernal script took an agonizingly long time, a luxury that he was running out of. He had almost bled out during the time it took to write his lord's name in his blood. He wasn't even sure if Abaddon would come when called like this, but he was desperate. Plus, he figured that he had an ace up his sleeve.

A sudden lurch of the stomach gave him pause, and he started coughing wildly. Blood spurted from his lips and he felt the world begin to spin. He steadied himself and tried to clear his vision, but the world was still blurred. He looked down on the sigil he had painted on the ground in his blood, and hoped it was close enough.

"Abaddon..." he whispered, placing one hand on the rune and another on the medallion embedded in his chest. "Help me." The hair on his arms and on the back of his neck stood up on end as a demonic vibration tore through the air. He could feel the heat of the hellfire on his face as his patron emerged from the bloody sigil, arms crossed and a look of contempt on his face.

"This is what you summoned me for—" Abaddon started, but stopped to take a deep inhale through his nose. His one brow lifted and a shiver ran through the devil's body. The Lord of the Seven Hells' lips curled into a sinister, snakelike smile as he bent low, locking eyes with Mikkel. "What is that delectable smell?"

A knowing smile appeared on Mikkel's lips. "A girl..." he winced through gritted teeth. "She helped me send Mammon back to you. Thought you might be interested in her... Help me... and she's yours."

Abaddon's smile widened. "Good dog," the devil chuckled as he rose to his full, towering height. "I'll help you on one condition – you bring her to me... alive."

"And the cripple?"

"Do as you see fit."

AFTERWORD

If you've made it this far, I want to personally thank you for seeing this book through. This was a fun story for me to write, and I hope you enjoyed the continuation of the story from *Season of Kings.* If you enjoyed it, please consider leaving a review on Amazon or Goodreads, it truly means the world to us self-published authors. Once again, thank you for giving my book a chance, and I sincerely hope that you were able to lose yourself in my world.

ABOUT THE AUTHOR

A.J. Rettger is a grimdark fantasy author from Saskatoon, Saskatchewan, Canada. His debut novel, *Oathbreaker*, quickly became a bestseller and stayed on the FriesenPress Bestseller's list for two weeks. His Second book, *Season of Kings* - the first installment of *The Raven's War Trilogy* - was critically acclaimed and was named a semi-finalist in the 2024 Self-Published Fantasy Blog Off (SPFBO). When he is not hard at work on his next book, A.J. can be found playing Dungeons and Dragons, exploring the corners of the world, or unwinding with his friends and family.

ALSO BY A.J. RETTGER

The Raven's War Trilogy
Season of Kings
Season of Vengeance

The Oathbreaker Series
Oathbreaker